P9-CQJ-908

JULIA LONDON

THE SCOUNDREL AND THE DEBUTANTE

HQN™

HQN™

ISBN-13: 978-0-373-77951-2

The Scoundrel and the Debutante

Recycling programs for this product may not exist in your area.

www.HQNBooks.com

Printed in U.S.A.

This book is about Prudence, the third Cabot Sister. I am also a third sister and I sort of want to dedicate the book to me, because, like Prudence, I have been heavily influenced, unfairly put upon, greatly appreciated and dearly loved by my older sisters, one gone too soon, one still here and my best friend. So I think I will dedicate this book to them instead. To my two much adored sisters, Karen and Nancy.

CHAPTER ONE

Blackwood Hall, 1816

IT WAS AN UNSPOKEN truth that when a woman reached her twenty-second year without a single gentleman even pondering the *possibility* of marriage to her, she was destined for spinsterhood. Spinsterhood, in turn, essentially sentenced her to the tedium of acting as companion to doddering dowagers as they dawdled about the countryside.

A woman without prospects in her twenty-second year was viewed suspiciously by the *haut ton.* There must be something quite off about her. It was impossible to think otherwise, for why would a woman, properly presented at court and to society, with means of dowry, with acceptably acknowledged connections, have failed to attract a suitor? There were only three possible explanations.

She was unforgivably plain.

She was horribly diseased.

Or, her older sisters' scandalous antics four years past had ruined her. Utterly, completely, *ruined* her.

The third hypothesis was presented by Miss Prudence Cabot days after her twenty-second birthday. Her hypothesis was roundly rejected by her scandalous older sisters, Mrs. Honor Easton and Grace, Lady Merryton.

In fact, when her older sisters were not rolling their eyes or refusing to engage at all, they argued quite vociferously against her theory, their duet of voices rising up so sharply that Mercy, the youngest of the four Cabot sisters, whistled at them as if they were the rowdy puppies that fought over Lord Merryton's boot.

Her sisters' protests to the contrary notwithstanding, Prudence was convinced she was right. Since her stepfather had died four years ago, her sisters had engaged in wretched behavior. Honor had *publicly* proposed marriage to a known rake and bastard son of a duke *in a gaming hell.* While Prudence adored George, it did not alter the scandal that had followed or the taint it had put on the Cabots.

Not to be outdone, Grace had endeavored to entrap a rich man into marriage in order to save them all from ruin, and somehow managed to trap the *wrong man.* It was the talk in London for months, and while Grace's husband, Lord Merryton, was not as aloof as Prudence had always heard, his entry into the family had not improved Prudence's prospects in the least.

Nor did it help in any way that her younger sister, Mercy, had a countenance so feisty and irreverent that serious thought had been given to packing her off to a young ladies' school to tame the beast in her.

That left Prudence in the middle, sandwiched tightly between scandals and improper behavior. She was squarely in the tedious, underappreciated, put-upon, practically invisible middle where she'd lived all her life.

This, Prudence told herself, was what good manners had gotten her. She had endeavored to be the practical one in an impractical gaggle of sisters. The responsible one who had taken her music lessons just as faithfully as she'd taken care of her mother and stepfather while her sisters cavorted through society. She'd done all the things debutantes were to do, she'd caused not a *whit* of trouble, and her thanks for that was now to be considered the unweddable one!

Well, Mercy likely was unweddable, too, but Mercy didn't seem to care very much.

"*Unweddable* is not even a proper word," Mercy pointed out, adjusting her spectacles so that she might peer critically at Prudence.

"It's also utter nonsense," Grace said tetchily. "Why on earth would you say such a thing, Pru? Are you truly so unhappy here at Blackwood Hall? Did you not enjoy the festival we hosted for the tenants?"

A festival! As if her wretched state of being could be appeased with a festival! Prudence responded with a dramatic bang of the keys of the pianoforte that caused the three-legged dog Grace had rescued to jump with fright and topple onto his side. Prudence launched into a piece that she played very loudly and very skillfully, so that everything Grace or Mercy said was drowned out by the music.

There was nothing any of them could say to change her opinion.

Later that week, Prudence's oldest sister, Honor, had come down from London to Blackwood Hall with her three children in tow as well as her dapper husband, George. When Honor heard of the contretemps between sisters, she'd tried to convince Prudence that a lack of a viable offer of marriage did not mean all was lost. Honor had insisted, with vigor and enthusiasm, that her sisters' behavior had *no* influence on Prudence's lack of an offer. Honor now reminded her that Mercy, against all odds, had been accepted into the prestigious Lisson Grove School of Art to study the masters.

"Well, naturally I was. I am *quite* talented," Mercy unabashedly observed.

"Lord Merryton had to pay a pretty sum to sway them, didn't he?" Prudence sniffed.

"Yes," Grace agreed. "But if she were as plagued with scandal as you suggest, they would have refused her yet."

"Refused Merryton's purse?" Prudence laughed. "It's not as if they had to *marry* her, for God's sake."

"I beg your pardon! What of my talent?" Mercy demanded.

"Hush," Grace and Prudence said in unison. That spurred Mercy to push her spectacles up her nose and march from the room in her paint-stained smock.

Grace and Honor paid her no mind.

The debate continued on for days, much to Prudence's dismay. "You must trust that an offer will come, dearest, and then you will be astonished that you put so much stock into such impossible feelings," Honor said a bit condescendingly as the sisters dined at breakfast one morning.

"Honor?" Prudence said politely. "I kindly request—no, pardon—I *implore* you to cease talking."

Honor gasped. And then she stood abruptly and flounced past Prudence with such haste that her hand connected a little roughly with Prudence's shoulder.

"Ouch," Prudence said.

"Honor means only to help, Pru," Grace chastised her. "Honor means only to help."

"I mean more than *that*," Honor said sternly, charging back around again, as she really was not the sort to flee in tears when there was a good fight to be had. "I insist that you snap out of your doldrums, Pru! It's unbecoming and bothersome!"

"I'm not in doldrums," Prudence said.

"You are! You're *forever* cross," said Mercy.

"And moody," Grace hastened to agree.

"I will tell you only what a loving sister will tell you truly, darling." Honor leaned over the dining table so that she was eye level with Prudence. "You're a bloody chore." But she smiled when she said it and quickly straightened. "Mrs. Bulworth has written and asked you to come and see her new baby. Do go and see her. She will be beside herself with joy, and I think that the country air will do you good."

Prudence snorted at that ridiculous notion. "How can I possibly be improved by country air when I am already in the country?"

"Northern country air is vastly different," Honor amended. Grace and Mercy nodded adamantly that Honor was right.

Prudence would like nothing better than to explain to them all that calling on their friend Cassandra Bulworth, who had just been delivered of her first child, was the *last* thing she wanted to do. To see her friend so deliriously happy made Prudence feel that much more wretched about her own circumstance. "Send Mercy!"

"Me?" Mercy cried. "I couldn't possibly! I've very little time to prepare for school. I must complete my still life painting, you know. Every student must have a complete portfolio and I haven't finished my still life."

"What about Mamma?" Prudence demanded, ignoring Mercy. They could not deny their mother's madness necessitated constant supervision from them.

"We have her maid Hannah, and Mrs. Pettigrew from the village," Grace said. "And we have Mercy, as well."

"Me!" Mercy cried. "I *just* said—"

"Yes, yes, we are all intimately acquainted with all you must do for school, Mercy. On my word, one would think you were the only person to have ever been accepted into a school. But you aren't leaving us for another month, so why should you not have the least responsibility?" Grace asked. Then she turned to Prudence and smiled sweetly. "Pru, we're only thinking of you. You see that, don't you?"

"I don't believe you," Prudence said. "But it so happens that *I* find *you* all quite tedious."

Honor gasped with delight and clasped her hands to her breast. "Does that mean you'll go?"

"Perhaps I shall," Prudence sniffed. "I'll be as mad as Mamma if I stay any longer at Blackwood Hall."

"Oh, that's wonderful news," Grace said happily.

"Well, you needn't rejoice in it," Prudence said missishly.

"But we're so happy!" Honor squealed. "I mean, happy for you," she quickly corrected, and hurried around the table to hug Prudence tightly to her. "I think your mien will be *vastly* improved if you just step out into the world, dearest."

Prudence scarcely thought so. *Out into the world* was where she lost all heart. Happy people, happy friends, all of them embarking on a life that Prudence had always hoped would be hers, made her terribly unhappy. Prudence was filled with envy, and she could not beat

it down, no matter how much she would have liked,
no matter how much she had tried. Even mortifyingly
worse, Prudence's envy of the happiness surrounding
her was apparent. Lately, it felt as if even sunshine was
a cruel reminder of her situation.

But as Mercy launched into her complaints that so
much attention was being paid to Prudence when *she*
needed it, Prudence decided she would go. Anything
to be free of the happy chatter she was forced to endure
day in and day out.

GRACE ARRANGED IT ALL, announcing grandly one afternoon that Prudence would accompany Dr. Linford and
his wife north, as they would be traveling that way to
visit Mr. Linford's mother. The Linfords would deposit
Prudence in the village of Himple where Mr. Bulworth
would send his man to come and fetch her and bring
her to their newly completed mansion. Cassandra, who
had come out with Prudence and had received several
offers of marriage in her debut Season compared to
Prudence's astounding lack of them, would be waiting with her baby.

"But the Linford coach is quite small," Mercy said,
frowning so that it caused her spectacles to slide down
her nose. She was seated at her new easel, drawing a
bowl of fruit for her painting. That's what the masters
did, she'd informed them earlier. They sketched first,
then painted. "Prudence will be forced to carry on a
conversation for *hours*," she added absently as she studied her sketch.

"What's wrong with conversation?" Honor demanded as she braided the hair of her daughter, Edith.

"Nothing at all if you care so much for the weather.

Dr. Linford speaks of nothing else. *It's a fine day*, and what not. Pru doesn't care so much for weather, do you, Pru?"

Prudence shrugged. She didn't care much for anything.

On the day of her departure, Prudence's trunk and valise were carried downstairs to a waiting carriage that would ferry her to Ashton Down, where Prudence was to meet the Linfords at one o'clock. In her valise, she included her necessities—some ribbons for her hair, a silk chemise Honor had brought for her from the new London modiste she raved about, some lovely slippers, and a change of clothing. She said goodbye to her overly cheerful sisters and started off at a quarter to twelve.

The ever-efficient Blackwood Hall coach reached Ashton Down at ten past twelve.

"You needn't wait with me, James," Prudence said, already weary. "The Linfords will be along shortly."

James, the driver, seemed uncertain. "Lord Merryton does not like the ladies to wait unattended, miss."

For some reason, that rankled Prudence. "You may tell him that I insisted," she said. "If you will deposit my things just there," she said, waving absently at the sidewalk along High Street. She smiled at James, adjusted her bonnet, and took herself up the street to the dry goods and sundries shop, where she purchased some sweetmeats for the journey. When she made her purchase, she walked outside. She saw her things on the sidewalk as she'd asked, and the Blackwood Hall carriage was gone. *Finally.*

Prudence lifted her face to the late-summer sun. It was a warm, glorious day, and she decided to wait on the village green just across from her luggage. She ar-

ranged herself on a bench, folded her gloved hands over
her package of sweetmeats and idly examined some
flowers in a planter beside her. The blooms were fading…just like her.

Prudence sighed loudly.

The sound of an approaching coach brought her to
her feet. She stood up, dusted off her lap, tucked her
package in the crook of her arm and looked up the road,
expecting to see the Linford coach roll down the street.

But it wasn't the Linford coach—it was one of two
private stagecoaches that came through Ashton Down
every day, one midday, one later in the afternoon.

Prudence sat down heavily on the bench once more.

The coach pulled to a halt on the road before her.
Two men jumped off the back runner; one of them
opened the door. A young couple stepped out, the
woman carrying an infant. Behind them emerged a man
so broad in the shoulder he had to turn to fit through
the opening. He fairly leaped out of the coach, landing sure-footedly, and adjusted the hat on his head. He
looked as if he'd just returned from an architectural dig,
dressed in buckskins, a lawn shirt and a dark coat that
reached his knees. His hat looked as if it was quality,
although it showed signs of wear. And his boots looked
as if they'd not been shined in an age. He had a dusty
shadow of a beard on his square jaw.

The man turned a slow circle in the middle of the
street, oblivious to the young men who rushed to change
the horses and deposit luggage onto the curb. Whatever the passenger saw caused him to suddenly stride
to the front of the coach and begin to argue vociferously with the driver.

Prudence blinked with surprise. How *interesting*.

She straightened her back and looked around, wondering what the gentleman had seen to anger him so. But observing nothing out of the ordinary on the village green or on the high street, she stood up, and as casually and inconspicuously as she might, she moved closer, pretending to examine some rose blooms so that she might hear his complaint.

"As I said, sir, Wesleigh is just up the road there. A half-hour walk, no more."

"But you don't seem to understand my point, my good man," the gentleman said in an accent that was quite flat. "Wesleigh is a *house*. Not a *settlement*. I understood I'd be delivered to an estate. An estate! A very large house with outbuildings and various people roaming about to do God knows what it is you do in England," he exclaimed, his hands busily sketching the estate in the air.

The driver shrugged. "I drive where I'm paid to drive, and I ain't paid to drive to Wesleigh. Ain't a grand house there by no means."

"This is preposterous!" the man bellowed. "I've paid good money to be delivered to the proper place!"

The driver ignored him.

The gentleman swept his hat off a head full of thick brown hair and threw it with great force to the ground. It scudded along and landed very close to Prudence. He looked about for his hat and, spotting Prudence at the edge of the green, he suddenly strode forward, the paper held out before him.

Prudence panicked. She looked about for a place to escape, but he guessed her intention. "No, no, stay right there, I beg you," he said sternly. "I must have someone speak to that man and explain to him that I am to be delivered to Wesleigh!"

"Wesleigh?" Prudence asked. "Or Weslay?"

That drew the man up, midstride. He stared at her with eyes the rich color of golden topaz, which slowly began to narrow on her, as if he thought she meant to trick him. He hesitantly moved forward, the paper still held out before him. "If you would be so kind?" he asked through clenched teeth, practically shoving the paper at her.

Prudence took it between forefinger and thumb and gingerly extracted it from his grip. Someone had written—scrawled, really, in long bold strokes—"West Lee, Penfors."

"Hmm," she said, squinting at the scrawl. "I suppose you mean Viscount Penfors." She peeked up at the stranger, who was staring darkly at her. She could feel the potency of his gaze trickling into her veins. "Lord Penfors resides at Howston Hall, just outside of Weslay."

"Yes, exactly as I wrote," he said, pointing to the paper.

"But this says 'West Lee.'"

"Just as you said."

"No, sir, I said 'Weslay.' I've never heard of West Lee," she said, trying to enunciate the subtle difference in the sound of the names. "And unfortunately, it appears you've mistakenly arrived in Wesleigh."

The stranger's face darkened, and Prudence had an image of him exploding, little bits of him raining down on the street. "I beg your pardon, miss, but you are not making any sense," he said tightly. He reached for the edge of the paper with his forefinger and thumb as she'd done and yanked it free. "You have said West Lee three times now, and I don't know if you mean to tease me or if there is something else at work here."

"I am not *teasing* you," she objected, horrified by the suggestion.

"Then it must be something else!"

"Something else?" What could he possibly mean? Prudence couldn't help but smile. "I assure you, I am not privy to any scheme or conspiracy to keep you from Weslay, sir."

His frown deepened. "I am happy to amuse you, miss. But if you would kindly point me in the direction of at least *one* of these West Lees, and preferably the one where I may find this Penfors fellow, I would be most grateful."

"Oh." She winced lightly.

"Oh?" he repeated, leaning forward. "What does 'oh' mean? Why are you looking at me as if you've lost my dog?"

"You've gone the wrong direction."

"So I gathered," he drawled.

"*Wesleigh* is just down the road here, a small village with perhaps five cottages. *Weslay* is north." She pointed in the direction the stage had just come.

He looked in the direction she pointed. His face began to mottle. "How far?" he managed, his voice dangerously low.

"I can't be entirely certain, but I'd say...two days?"

The gentleman stranger clenched his jaw. He was big and powerful, and Prudence imagined his fury shaking the ground beneath his feet. "But that is indeed where you will find this Penfors fellow," she hastened to add, and once again tried not to smile. It was absurd to refer to a viscount as a fellow!

"North?" he bellowed, throwing his arms wide.

Prudence took one cautious step backward and nodded.

The man put his hands on his waist, staring at her. And then he turned slowly from her. She thought he meant to walk away, but he kept turning, until he'd gone full circle, and when he faced her again, his jaw was clenched even more tightly. "If I may," he asked, his voice strained, "have you a suggestion for how I might *reach* this West Lee that is two days away?"

"It's not West—" She shook her head. "You might take the northbound stagecoach. It comes through Ashton Down twice a day. The first one should be along at any moment."

"I see," he said, but it was quite apparent he didn't see at all.

"You might also buy passage on the Royal Post coach, but it's a bit more costly than the passenger stages. And it comes through only once a day."

He eyed her distrustfully. "Two days either way?"

She nodded. She smiled sympathetically. She would not like to be sausaged into a stagecoach for two days. "I fear it is so."

He shoved his fingers roughly through his dark brown hair and muttered something under his breath that she couldn't quite make out but sounded as if she ought not to hear.

"Where might I purchase passage?" he asked briskly.

She looked around him—that is, she leaned to her right to see around his broad chest—to the stagecoach inn. "I'll show you if you like."

"That," he said firmly, "would be most helpful." He bent down, scooped up his hat, dusted it off by knocking it against his knee, then put it back on his head. His gaze traversed the length of her before he stepped back and swept his arm before him, indicating she should lead him.

Prudence walked across the street, pausing as the gentleman instructed the coachman to leave his trunk and bag on the sidewalk with the other luggage pieces to be loaded on the northbound coach. He stared wistfully at the coach as it pulled away, headed south, before turning back to Prudence and following her into the inn's courtyard. She walked through a pair of doors that went past the public room and into a small office. It was close, and she had to dip her head to step inside. The ceiling was uncomfortably low, and the smell of horse manure permeated the air, as the office was situated between the stables and the public rooms.

The gentleman passenger was well over six feet and had to stoop to enter. Once inside, his head brushed the rafters. He batted at a cobweb and grunted his displeasure.

"Aye, sir?" said a clerk, appearing behind the low counter.

The gentleman stepped forward. "I should like to buy passage to West Lee," he said.

"Weslay," Prudence murmured.

The gentleman sighed loudly. "What she said."

"Three quid," the clerk said.

The gentleman removed his purse from his pocket and opened it. He fussed through the coins there, examining each one as he withdrew them. Prudence stepped forward, leaned around him, and pointed at three of the coins.

"Ah," he said, and handed them to the clerk, who in turn handed the gentleman a ticket.

"The driver requires a crown, and the guard a half," the clerk said.

"What?" the gentleman said. "But I just gave you three pounds."

The clerk tucked the coins into a pocket on his apron. "That's for the passage. The driver and the guard, they get their pay from the passengers."

"Seems like a dodge."

The clerk shrugged. "If you want passage to Weslay—"

"All right, all right," the gentleman said. He peered at his ticket and sighed again. He gestured for Prudence to go out ahead of him, then fit himself through the door into the inn's main hall and followed her into the courtyard.

They paused there. He smiled for the first time since Prudence had seen him, and she felt a little twinkle of desire when he did. He looked remarkably less perturbed, and in all honestly, he looked astoundingly pleasing to the eye when he smiled. It was a rugged, well-earned smiled. There was nothing thin about it. It was an honest, glowing sort of smile—

"I am grateful for your assistance, Miss…?"

"Cabot," she said. "Miss Prudence Cabot."

"Miss Cabot," he said, and bowed his head slightly. "Mr. Roan Matheson," he added, and stuck his hand out.

Prudence glanced uncertainly at his hand.

So did he. "What is it? Is my glove soiled? So it is. I

beg your pardon, but I've come a very long way without benefit of anyone to do the washing."

"No, it's not that," she said with a shake of her head, although her thoughts were spinning with the how and why and from where he'd come such a long way.

"Oh. I see." He removed his glove and extended his hand once more. She noticed how big it was, how strong. How long and thick his fingers were and the slight nicks on his knuckles. A hand that was not afraid of work. "My hand is clean," he said impatiently.

"Pardon? Oh! No, it's just that it's rather unusual."

"My hand?" he asked curiously, holding it up to have a look.

"No, no." She was being rude. She looked up at his startling topaz eyes. And at his hair, too, dark brown with streaks of lighter brown, and longer than the current fashion, which he had carelessly brushed back behind his ears. It was charmingly foreign. *He* was charmingly foreign and...*virile*. Yes, that was it. He looked as if he could move mountains about for his amusement if he liked. Her pulse, Prudence realized, was doing a tiny bit of fluttering. "It's unusual that you are offering your hand to be—" she paused uncertainly "—shaken?"

"Of course I offered it to be shaken," he said, as if it were ridiculous she would ask. "Why else would one offer a hand, Miss Cabot? To shake. To acknowledge a kindness or a greeting—"

She abruptly put her hand in his, noting how small it seemed in his palm.

He cocked his head. "Are you afraid of me?"

"What? No!" she said, flustered. Maybe she was a tiny bit afraid of him. Or rather, the little shocks of light that seemed to flash through her when he looked at her like that. She curled her fingers around his. He curled tighter. *"Oh,"* she said.

"Too firm?" he asked.

"No, not at all," she said quickly. She liked the feel of his grip on her hand and had the fleeting thought of his grip somewhere else on her altogether. "I beg your pardon, but I am unaccustomed to this. Here, men offer their hands to other men. Not to ladies."

"Oh." He hesitantly withdrew his hand. But he looked at her with confusion. "Then…what am I to do when I meet a woman?"

"You bow," she said, demonstrating for him. "And a lady curtsies." She curtsied, as well.

He groaned as he pulled his glove back on. "May I be brutally honest, Miss Cabot?"

"Please," she said.

"I have come to England from America on a matter of some urgency—I must fetch my sister who is enjoying the fine hospitality and see her home. But I find this country confounding. I sincerely—" He suddenly turned his head, distracted by the sound of a coach rumbling into town. It was the northbound stage, and it pulled to a halt on the street just outside the courtyard. Two men sitting atop the coach jumped down; two young men climbed down from the outboard. Another man was waiting on the sidewalk to catch the bags that one of the coachmen began to toss to him.

The coach looked rather full, and Prudence felt a moment of pity for Mr. Matheson. She couldn't possibly imagine how he would maneuver his large body into that crowded interior.

"Well, then, there we are," he said, and began to

stride toward the coach. He paused after a few steps and glanced over his shoulder at Prudence. "Aren't you coming?"

Prudence was momentarily startled. She suddenly realized he believed she was waiting for the coach, too. She opened her mouth to correct him, to inform him she'd be traveling by private coach, but before the words could fall from her tongue, something warm and shivery sluiced through her. Something silky and dark and dangerous and exciting and *compelling*...so very compelling.

She wouldn't.

But why wouldn't she? She thought of riding in a coach with the Linfords, and the talk of weather. She thought of riding on a stagecoach—something she had never done—and riding with Mr. Matheson. There was something about that idea that thrilled her in a way nothing had in a very long time. He was so masculine, and her pulse fluttered at the idea of passing a few hours with him. "Ah..." She glanced back at the inn, debating. She'd be mad to do such a thing, to put herself on that stagecoach with him! But wasn't this *far* more interesting than traveling with the Linfords? She had money, she had her things. She knew how to reach Cassandra Bulworth. What was stopping her? Propriety, for heaven's sake? The same propriety that had been her constant companion all these years and had doomed her to spinsterhood?

She glanced again at Mr. Matheson. Oh yes, he was *very* appealing in a wild, American sort of way. She'd never met an actual American, either, but she imagined them all precisely like this, always rebelling, strong enough to forge ahead without regard for society's rules.

This man was so different, so fresh, so incurably hand-some and so blessedly *lost*! She might even convince herself she was doing him a proper kindness by see-ing him on his way.

Mr. Matheson misunderstood her look, however, because he flushed a bit and said, "I beg your pardon. I didn't mean to rush you."

Prudence smiled broadly—he thought she wanted the privy.

Her smile seemed to fluster him more. He cleared his throat and looked to the coach. "I'll…I'll see you on the coach."

"Yes," she said, with far more confidence than she had a right to. "Yes, you will!"

He looked at her strangely, but then gave her a curt nod and began striding for the coach, pausing to dip down and pick up one of the bags with one hand, then toss it up to a boy who was lashing the luggage on the boot.

There was no time to debate it; Prudence whirled about and hurried back to the office, her heart pound-ing with excitement and fear. A little bell tingled as she walked in.

The clerk turned round and squinted at her. "Miss?"

"A ticket to Himple, please," she said, and opened her reticule.

"To Himple?" he repeated dubiously, and peered cu-riously at her.

"Please. And if you have some paper? I must dash off a note."

"Two quid," he said, and rummaged around until he found a bit of vellum she might use.

He handed her a pencil, and Prudence dashed off a

hasty note to Dr. Linford that she would ask the coach boys to deliver to him. She jotted down the usual salutations, her wishes that the Linfords were well and his mother on the mend. And then she wrote an explanation for her change of plans.

I beg your pardon for any inconvenience, but as it happens, I have taken a seat in a friend's coach. She is likewise bound for Himple and it was no trouble for her to include me in her party. Do please forgive the short notice, but the opportunity has only just come about. Thank you kindly for your offer to see me safely to my friends', but I assure you I am in good hands.

She shivered at the sudden image of the gentleman's hands.

My best wishes for your journey and your mother's health. P.C.

She folded the note, smiled at the scowling clerk, and picked up her ticket. "Thank you," she said, and fairly skipped out of the office.

Her heart was racing—she couldn't believe she was doing something so daring and bold! So fraught with risk! So very unlike her! But for the first time in months, perhaps even years, Prudence felt as if something astonishing was about to happen to her. Good or bad, it didn't matter—the only thing that mattered was that *something* different this way came, and she was giddy with excitement.

CHAPTER TWO

THE INTERIOR OF the coach was suited for four people, but as the extra seating on top of the coach was filled, Roan had to fit himself inside, wedging into the corner of an impossibly hard bench, his knees knocking against the bonier ones of the old man who sat across from him and unabashedly studied him. Next to the old gent was a boy who looked thirteen or fourteen years old. He sat with a hat pulled so far down his head that Roan couldn't see anything but his long, angular nose and his small chin. He held a small battered valise on his lap, his arms wrapped securely around it.

Beside him was one of two robust women, whose lace caps looked too small for their heads, and whose thick tight curls hung like mistletoe over their ears. Roan didn't think they were twins, exactly, but he supposed they were sisters. They wore identical gray muslin gowns and so much frilly lace across their expansive bosoms that at first glance, Roan thought they were wearing doilies.

However, the most notable feature of the two women was their astounding capacity to talk. They sat across from each other and they hadn't as much as taken a breath—talking over and under and around each other—since he'd fitted himself inside the coach. Moreover, they spoke so quickly, with an accent so thick, that Roan couldn't begin to make out what they were saying.

He could feel the pitch and pull of the coach as the fresh horses were put into their traces. He managed to withdraw his pocket watch from his waistcoat without elbowing anyone in the eye and checked the time. It was just a little more than half-past twelve. They'd be departing soon, and there was no sign of the beautiful woman with the shining hazel eyes who had helped him.

She was an angel in an otherwise horrendous day, the one thing that had made his entire ordeal seem less tedious. Miss Cabot was, at least to him, surprisingly beautiful, far comelier than anyone he'd seen before departing New York, and most assuredly the comeliest thing he'd seen since arriving in England. Granted, he'd first set foot in Liverpool, in the shipyards, which was not the most attractive place on God's blessed earth, but still. She had a mouthwatering figure, a wide mouth with pink, full lips, and dark lashes that framed her lovely almond-shaped eyes. They were more green than brown, he thought, more summer than winter. He'd felt the male in him snapping to attention when he'd reached her in the middle of the village.

The older woman next to him settled in, removing herself from the wall of the coach and taking up what was left of the bench. There were only a few precious inches between them, not enough space for even a slender thing. Had Miss Cabot gone on top?

As if to answer his question, in the next moment, the door swung open and Miss Cabot's bonneted head appeared. "Oh dear," she said, peering into the interior. "There doesn't seem to be room, does there?"

"Nonsense, of course there is," said one of the women. "If the gentleman will kindly move aside, we'll make space for you here. It will be a bit tight, but we'll manage."

Roan realized the woman beneath the tiny lace cap was referring to him. He looked at the coach wall against which he was smashed, and at the woman, who had taken up more than her share of the bench. "I beg your pardon, but I am as *moved aside* as I can possibly be."

"Just a smidge," the woman said, fluttering her fingers at him and making no effort to add any room to the bench from her end.

"Thank you," Miss Cabot said, and hesitantly stepped inside, pushing past the knees of Roan and the old man. "Pardon me," she said as she navigated her way into the middle of the coach, leaving a wisp of her perfumed scent as she did.

She balked when she saw the sliver of bench that was to be allotted to her.

"Isn't much of a seat, is it?" one of the women asked. "But you're a small thing. You'll be quite all right."

"Umm…" Miss Cabot smiled uncertainly at Roan and by some miracle of physical science, she managed to gracefully turn about in that small space without touching anyone except with the sweep of her hem. She settled delicately on the very edge of the bench, her slender back straight. Her knees, Roan noticed, touched the boy's knees, and he could see the stain of acute awareness of that touch in the boy's cheeks. Roan had been just like him at that age—as desperately fearful of females as he was desperate to be near them.

"You cannot remain perched like a bird for any

length of time. You'll exhaust yourself," Roan said. "Please, do sit back."

Miss Cabot turned her head slightly, and while all Roan could see beneath the brim of her bonnet was her chin and her wide, expressive mouth, he could sense her skepticism. She wiggled her bottom and slid back an inch or two. The woman shifted slightly. Miss Cabot wiggled her bottom again, and Roan could feel every inch of him tense as she continued to wiggle her bottom into the narrow spot between them. By the time she was done—every delicate bit of her pressed against every hard bit of him—he was, imprudently, thinking of creamy bare bottoms. Hers in particular. He imagined it to be smooth and heart-shaped. He imagined playfully biting the firm flesh—

Stop that. The last thing he needed was to be thinking salacious thoughts about a woman no older than his sister.

Roan clenched his jaw, adjusted his arm, and still he could not escape the heightened sensation of the slender lines of her body against the hard planes of his. He argued with himself that he was imagining her body indelicately next to his, not because he was a scoundrel and a rogue, but because he'd sailed across the Atlantic with a crew of men, had bounced about this part of England in coaches much like this and had not touched a woman in weeks.

Well. Perhaps he was a bit of a scoundrel. But it was true that he'd not had the pleasure of a woman's lusty company since Miss Susannah Pratt had arrived in New York.

"Well!" Miss Cabot said gamely, squirming once more. She folded her hands onto her lap over the small package she carried. "If we're plagued with bad roads, I might pop right out, mightn't I?"

No one answered that; no doubt because they all feared it was true. The boy slid down in his seat, disappearing into his coat. The old man had yet to remove his two black pea eyes from Roan, his study so acute that Roan began to wonder if his private erotic thoughts were somehow apparent in his expression.

"On the whole, it looks to be a good day for travel, does it not?" Miss Cabot said cheerfully.

Roan sincerely hoped she was not the sort to find good fortune at every turn and announce it to one and all. He preferred his traveling companions to be as out of sorts and cross as he was when traveling in this manner.

"Quite nice," one of the women said, and launched into something so quickly and with such verve that Roan could not begin to follow.

He took the opportunity to surreptitiously look at Miss Cabot. Her clothing was expensive. This, he knew, after having paid the clothing bills for his sister, Aurora; he'd become intimately acquainted with the cost of silk and muslin and brocade and fine wool. Miss Cabot had delicate hands, the sort that he guessed excelled at fine needlework. He could see a strand of hair on her shoulder—it was the color of wheat.

Was it disloyal to think that Miss Cabot was what he'd envisioned Susannah Pratt to be before he'd actually met her? Golden-haired and elegant, her countenance and appearance to spark the deepest male desires? But Susannah had turned out to be dark, wide and shapeless. Roan liked to think he was not so shallow as to form his opinion of the woman based on looks alone, but it didn't help that Miss Pratt had nothing to *say*. When she'd arrived from Philadelphia and had come to his family's home on the arm of Mr. Pratt, all Roan could think was that he couldn't believe he'd actually agreed with Mr. Pratt and his own father that a marriage of the two families was something that ought to occur.

The coach suddenly lurched forward, and Miss Cabot was tossed against him. She turned her head slightly toward him and smiled apologetically. "I do so beg your pardon," she said. "It's awfully close, isn't it?" She resituated herself, her back perfectly straight once more, her hands on her lap.

But it was hopeless. Every rut in the road, every bounce, pressed her body against his—once, causing her to brace herself with her small hand to his thigh—and Roan was reminded with each passing mile how softly pliant she felt against him, how insubstantial she seemed, and yet strangely sturdy at the same time. He looked out the window and tried not to think of her lying naked on soft white linens, her golden hair spilling around her shoulders, her breasts pert. He managed it by looking at the old man every time his thoughts drifted in that direction.

They'd been gone only one excruciating hour when one of the women took a deep breath in her endless conversation and announced loudly, "I know who you are! You're Lady Merryton!"

All eyes riveted on Miss Cabot, including Roan's.

"Not at all!" she exclaimed.

"No?" The woman seemed dubious.

"*No!* I assure you, if I were Lady Merryton, I'd travel by private coach." Miss Cabot smiled.

"Yes, I suppose," the woman said, looking disappointed.

What, did the old crow really believe royalty would be carted about the countryside in a public coach? Even Roan knew better than that. He didn't keep up with the princes and queens and whatnot of England, but he assumed a "lady" was some sort of royalty. When his aunt and uncle had returned from London this summer—without Aurora, whose person had been placed with all due confidence by Roan's family in their care—they'd talked quite a lot about an earl here, a viscount there. Aurora dined with Lady This, danced with Lord That. Roan had paid little heed, and because he had not, he was at a disadvantage—he had no idea what the significance of any of it was, only that royalty seemed to abound in England.

"But I am acquainted with Lady Merryton," Miss Cabot added casually.

Roan cocked his head to one side, trying to see her face. She was *acquainted* with Lady Merryton? What was she, a countess or some such thing? Didn't that make her the daughter of a queen and king? And did that therefore mean that Miss Cabot kept company with kings and queens?

"Just as well you're not her, I think, what with all the folderol around *that* marriage, eh?" The larger woman snorted and shook her head.

"Simply shocking," the smaller agreed.

Roan could see the blush creep into Miss Cabot's neck. He didn't know what *folderol* meant, but as both sisters were practically congratulating each other on their opinions, it made him very curious.

The women looked as if they were poised to ask

more questions, but the coach began to slow. Roan leaned forward a bit, could see a row of whitewashed cottages with red and purple flowers spilling out of the window boxes. They'd arrived in a village he'd seen earlier today, and if he were not mistaken, there was nothing here but a change of horses. Yet he, for one, could not wait to be disgorged from this coach.

They rolled into the village, and the coach swayed to one side as the coachman hopped down from the seats atop to open the door and release the step. Roan was always a gentleman, but today, he could not help himself from launching out of the interior of the crowded coach and taking several steps away to drag some much needed air into his lungs, and hopefully, erase the feel of Miss Cabot against him from his flesh. By the time he turned about, the coachman had helped all the passengers from the interior, and the boy was assisting the old man onto a bench. The two ladies, likewise regurgitated from the coach, stood in identical fashion, their hands on the small of their backs, bending backward... and still talking.

Miss Cabot was standing apart from the others, holding a small wrapped package. She looked remarkably fresh, cheerful as a bluebell in her blue traveling gown.

The driver strolled into their midst with the posture of a mayor in spite of his dirty breeches, worn shoes and a waistcoat that seemed two sizes too small. "Beggin' yer pardon, ladies and gents!" he announced grandly. "The coach will depart at a quarter past two."

Roan glanced around him. There was a small public inn and a smithy, but very little else. He would very much like to drown the morning with a pint or two, but instead began striding down the road, needing to stretch his legs and shake off the exquisitely torturous feeling of having a lovely young woman pressed practically into his lap for the past hour and a half. It wouldn't hurt him to find the last tattered remnants of his patience, either. He paused, searching for it. It was not available.

Roan was not generally an impatient man. On the contrary—he thought most would say he could be depended upon to be the center of calm in the midst of a storm. But he was devilishly out of sorts—he'd been in England for all of two days and could still feel the sea swells beneath his legs after a month at sea. He'd been turned completely around by the fellows in Liverpool, who, he'd realized after some minutes of trying to understand them, were actually speaking English to him. Those lads had sent him on this fool's errand, sent him south when he should have gone north.

Moreover, Roan was a man accustomed to fine carriages and better steeds. Not stagecoaches on rutted roads, squashed in between a dirty squab and a woman with skin that felt as smooth as butter.

He came to a full stop in the road and breathed deeply of the warm air. The short walk had not improved his mood as much as he would have liked. He turned his face up to a bright blue sky and roared his frustration with his missteps, with his sister, with everything in general.

Now he felt better.

Roan pivoted about and strode back to the little hamlet.

He spied Miss Cabot perched on top of a fence post. She had opened the package she'd held protectively in her lap and appeared to be eating something. Next to the fence, the sisters were seated side by side on a trunk, each with a pail in their lap. They, too, appeared to be eating.

Roan strolled to Miss Cabot's side. He tried not to ogle what was in her lap, but he couldn't resist it, particularly as a quick review of the past twenty-four hours reminded him that he'd not eaten.

Miss Cabot glanced up, turning her head so that he could see her hazel eyes from beneath the deep brim of her bonnet. "Oh. Mr. Matheson."

"Miss Cabot."

She held up the brown cheesecloth so that a variety of small bites were displayed just below his nose. "May I offer you a sweetmeat?"

He peered more closely at the contents. They looked like the fried cakes that Nella, his family's longtime cook, often made. "No, thank you." He wasn't so out of sorts as to take her food.

"No?" She took one and popped it into her mouth. *"Mmm,"* she said, and closed her eyes a moment. "Delicious."

Much to his consternation, Roan's stomach grumbled.

Miss Cabot smiled and held up the cheesecloth a little closer to him. "You must at least try *one*."

"You don't mind?" he asked, but he was already reaching for one.

She watched him closely as he put the morsel in his mouth. Good God, she was right—it was delicious.

"Have another. Have as many as you like."

"Perhaps one more," Roan said gratefully, reaching. When he opened his palm, he found three instead of the one he'd intended.

Miss Cabot laughed, the sound of it crystal and light.

"One might think you've not eaten today, Mr. Matheson."

"I've not eaten since yesterday morning."

"What! Why ever not?"

He shrugged. "I've been traveling and it's not always convenient. Frankly, I thought I would have reached my destination by now."

Miss Cabot hopped down from the fence and squatted down beside a small bag by her feet, which she opened and rummaged in before removing another cheesecloth. She handed that one to him.

Roan unwrapped it. It was bread.

"I've cheese, too."

"No, I—"

"I must insist, Mr. Matheson! My youngest sister put it in my bag." She smiled up at him, her eyes sparkling like diamonds in the sunlight. "She wanted me to be properly provisioned. She has high hopes that we will be set upon by highwaymen and forced to live in the woods."

"She has *hope* of that?"

"She has a keen sense of drama. Please, help yourself. There is more."

"I'm grateful," he said, and went down on one haunch and tore off a chunk of the bread. He ate it much more savagely than he intended as Miss Cabot climbed back onto the fence railing. He helped himself to the cheese, too, surprised by how ravenous he suddenly realized he was.

"Yoo-hoo!"

The two sisters wiggled their fingers at Miss Cabot, even though they sat only a few feet away. "We've solved the mystery!" one of them trilled loudly.

"We have indeed! It was *quite* a puzzle—"

"Quite," said the more robust of the two.

"What mystery?" Miss Cabot asked.

"Well, *you*, my dear. But we have deduced it. You are Lady Altringham!" she said proudly.

"Oh dear me, no," Miss Cabot said laughingly. "She's twenty years my senior."

"Oh," said the woman, clearly disappointed once more.

"But I am acquainted with her," Miss Cabot said. "Her daughter and I were presented together."

"Ooh," said the smaller one, her eyes lighting with delight.

"Presented?" Roan said uncertainly.

"To the *king*, sir!" one of the women said crossly, as if he should have known it.

Roan looked up at Miss Cabot curiously. "Why? Did you do something of note?"

Miss Cabot burst into a delightful laughter. "Not at all! It was all I could manage to curtsy properly."

"I should like to know from where *you* hail, sir, for you seem *quite* ignorant," said one of the women.

"Doesn't he, though?" agreed the other. "Everyone knows that presentation in court is the rite of passage for a young lady of pedigree," said the other in a bit of a huff.

Roan didn't understand. "For what purpose?"

"The purpose!" the woman scoffed, clearly annoyed. "Wouldn't you like to be presented to the king?"

Roan had to think about that. If it prolonged his time in England, he would say no.

"Where are you from?" the woman demanded.

"America," Roan said. "New York, to be precise."

"And why have you come all this way?"

He didn't think it was any business of hers, but he said, "To collect my sister who has been visiting your fair country for several months. Does that meet with your approval?"

The woman didn't answer. She had turned her attention to Miss Cabot again, eyeing her suspiciously. "And if you're not Lady Altringham, then who *are* you? What young lady travels without escort, I ask you?"

Roan wondered that, too, and his curiosity was the only thing that kept him from stuffing the woman's cloth from her pail into her mouth. He glanced at Miss Cabot. Her cheeks had flushed in a way that made her look a bit guilty. Good God, she wasn't another Aurora, was she?

"Oh, ah…please, allow me to introduce myself. I am Miss Prudence Cabot. And who might I have the pleasure of addressing?"

"Mrs. Tricklebank," said the smaller. "And my sister, Mrs. Scales."

Miss Cabot peeked up at Roan. "May I introduce you to Mr. Matheson?"

Before Roan could say a word, he was spared by the driver's announcement that the coach would depart in fifteen minutes.

"Oh!" Mrs. Tricklebank cried. "Come, come, Ruth! We don't want to miss the coach," she said frantically, as if they were miles from the coach instead of the few feet that they were. Both women gathered their things and hurried back to the coach, clutching one another's arms, their pails bumping against their hips.

Roan wrapped what was left of the bread and cheese once more, a bit embarrassed by how much of it he'd eaten. "Thank you for your kindness, Miss Cabot. I'll see to it your supplies are replenished."

Her smile was so sunny, Roan felt it slip right through him. "Please, don't trouble yourself. I shall reach my destination by the end of the day."

"Are you certain? Those two might convince the driver to stop and hold an inquisition."

She laughed. "They're harmless, really. I think they are much in love with the sound of their own voices." She gave him a saucy smile and hopped off the fence railing. She stooped to pick up her valise. Roan unthinkingly took it from her hand and politely offered his arm to her.

She kept that pert little smile as she laid her hand on his arm so carefully that he could scarcely feel it. He looked at her. He didn't want to see a young woman of obvious privilege with the same misguided sensibilities as his sister. "Pardon, but how is it that you are traveling without escort?" he asked. "Not a maid? Not a groom?"

Miss Cabot smiled as if his was a trifling question and averted her gaze. "Don't you think it is interesting how people are so keen to fret over such small details?"

Small detail, indeed. That was precisely the sort of answer his incorrigible sister would give—an answer that answered nothing at all. "I'm not fretting," he said. "Merely curious."

"Thank you, Mr. Matheson, for not fretting." She flashed another smile at him, but this one was a bit more cautious.

Yes, there was definitely something amiss with this beauty, he would stake his fortune on it. But he had enough trouble brewing in England to delve too deeply.

When they reboarded, Roan noticed the boy had

moved to the seats on top of the coach, still holding tight to the battered valise. Roan helped Miss Cabot into the coach, his fingers closing around the small bones of her elbow, his hand on the small of her back to guide her. He waited until she was seated, then put himself on the step, and looked inside, determining how he would fit himself onto the bench beside her and directly across from the old man once more.

"Wouldn't you be more comfortable there?" Mrs. Scales asked him, pointing to the tiny bit of bench between her sister and the old man. "There's more room, isn't there?" And to Miss Cabot, she said, "The gentleman takes up *quite* a lot of space."

He couldn't believe this woman would impugn his size again. She was fortunate that he had been raised properly and did not voice aloud his opinion of *her* girth.

"Oh, I think one spot is as good as the other," Miss Cabot said smoothly. She scooted over. Roan eyed the bench warily. Miss Cabot scooted more. He glanced at her, silently pleading for more space. With a slight roll of her eyes, Miss Cabot scooted all the way into the doughy side of Mrs. Scales.

He stepped inside—hunched over in that confined space—and somehow managed to settle himself on the bench beside her. Miss Cabot shifted to free her arm from behind him, but when she settled once more, her elbow settled firmly in his ribs and would no doubt poke him with every bounce the coach made.

As the coach began to move, Mrs. Scales fixed a slightly suspicious gaze on Miss Cabot. "May I inquire, to where are you traveling today, Miss Cabot?"

Roan could feel Miss Cabot shift about, uncomfortable with the busybody's scrutiny of her. "Actually, I am on my way to see a dear friend. She's just been delivered of her first child."

"Oh, a *baby*!" Mrs. Tricklebank said.

"Yes, a baby!" Miss Cabot agreed enthusiastically. "Poor thing sent a messenger and begged me to come straightaway. It's her first child and she's feeling a bit at sixes and sevens."

"She didn't send someone for you?" Mrs. Scales asked. "One would think you might have had *some* escort," she added curiously.

Miss Cabot's elegant neck began to turn pink. "There was no time. My friend hasn't any help with the baby, and I think she can't do without her husband."

"Hmm," Mrs. Scales said gravely.

She rankled Roan. Who was she to pass judgment on Miss Cabot? He didn't believe her, either, and thought she was up to mischief because he was well versed in the way young women dissembled. But he wouldn't prosecute her for it as Mrs. Scales seemed determined to do. "An interesting custom," he said, fixing a cold gaze on Mrs. Scales. "Is it common to interrogate fellow passengers on every stagecoach, or just this one?"

Mrs. Scales blinked. She drew her mouth into a bitter pucker. Miss Cabot graciously looked away from the old crone and pretended to gaze out the window. But he could see her smile.

The coach swayed down the road at a fine clip, and the eyelids of the coach inhabitants eventually began to grow heavy. Before long, Miss Cabot began to sag. Roan tried to ease her toward Mrs. Scales for the sake of propriety, but Mrs. Scales had also nodded off and Roan couldn't manage it. Miss Cabot's head—or more accurately, her bonnet—settled adamantly onto his shoulder, and the ghastly feather that protruded from the crown bounced in his eye. Roan tried to turn his head to avoid it, but it was impossible, especially given his desire not to jostle and wake her. Or more important, his desire not to wake Mrs. Roly or Mrs. Poly.

He himself felt his lids sliding shut when a sudden bump in the road startled Miss Cabot, and her elbow protruded so deeply into his side that he feared she might have punctured his liver. But the coach was quickly swaying again, and the passengers settled once more. Save the old man, whose gaze was still fixed on Roan.

But then the coach suddenly dipped sharply to the right, tossing them all about, and over an expletive loudly shouted from the driver, it shuddered to a definite halt.

CHAPTER THREE

PRUDENCE'S CHIN BOUNCED off something very hard, and her hand sank into something soft. Her first groggy thought was that it was a lumpy pillow. But when her eyes flew open, she saw that her chin had connected with Mr. Matheson's shoulder…and her hand with his *lap*.

He stared wryly at her as awareness dawned on her. She gasped; he very deliberately reached up to remove the tip of her bonnet's feather that was poking him in the eye.

Prudence could feel the heat flood her cheeks and quickly sat up. She straightened her bonnet, which had somehow been pushed to one side. "What has happened?" she exclaimed, shuffling out from the wedge between Mrs. Scales and Mr. Matheson to the edge of the bench, desperate that no part of her was touching any part of that *very* virile man. But her hip was still pressed so tightly against his thigh that she could feel the slightest shift of muscle beneath his buckskins.

It was alarmingly provocative. Prudence didn't move an inch for several seconds, allowing that feeling to imprint itself in her skin.

"I assume we've broken a wheel," Mr. Matheson said. The coach dipped to the right and swayed unsteadily. The driver cursed again, loudly enough that the round cheeks of the two sisters turned florid.

Mr. Matheson reached for the door and launched himself from the interior like a phoenix, startling them all. Prudence leaned forward and looked through the open door. The coach was leaning precariously to that side. She looked back at her fellow travelers and had the thought that if the two ladies tried to exit the coach at the same time, it might topple over. She fairly leaped from the coach, too, landing awkwardly against a coachman who had just appeared to help them down.

"What has happened?" Prudence asked.

"The wheel has broken, miss."

Mr. Matheson, she noticed, was among the men who had gathered around the offending wheel. He'd squatted to study it, and Prudence wondered if he was acquainted with wheels in general, or merely curious.

There ensued quite a lot of discussion among the men as Mr. Matheson dipped down and reached deep under the coach with one arm, bracing himself against the vehicle with his other hand. Was it natural to be a bit titillated by a man's immodest address of a mechanical issue? Certainly she had never seen a gentleman involve himself in that way.

When Mr. Matheson rose again, he wiped his hand on his trousers, leaving a smear of axle grease. That did not repulse Prudence. She found it strangely alluring.

"The axle is fine," he announced.

There was more discussion among the men, their voices louder this time. It seemed to Prudence that they were all disagreeing with each other. At last the driver instructed the women and the old gentleman away from the coach while the men attempted to repair the wheel. Mr. Matheson was included in the group that was shooed away.

The team was unhitched, and some of the men began to stack whatever they could find beneath the coach to keep it level when the wheel was removed.

"My valise!" Prudence cried, and darted into the men to retrieve it, pulling it away before it could be used as a prop.

Then Mrs. Tricklebank and Mrs. Scales made seats on some rocks beneath the boughs of a tree, taking the old man and the boy under their wings and fussing around them. There was no seat left for Prudence, so she sat on a trunk.

They watched the men prop the carriage up with rocks and luggage and some apparatus from the coach itself, then remove the wheel. Mr. Matheson had returned to the problem and was in the thick of it, lending his considerable strength to the work. Prudence wondered if he had some sort of occupation that required knowledge of wheels. She couldn't see why else he might be involved. It wasn't as if there weren't enough men to do the work. The only other slightly plausible explanation was that he somehow *enjoyed* such things.

The elderly gentleman grunted a bit and moved around in an effort to find some comfort, forcing the sisters to the edges of the rocks.

"He may be an American and a bit crude, but one cannot argue that he cuts a fine figure of a man," Mrs. Scales said wistfully.

Prudence blinked. She looked at Mrs. Scales and realized that both sisters were admiring Mr. Matheson's figure.

"Mrs. Scales, how vulgar!" Mrs. Tricklebank protested. But she did not look away from Mr. Matheson's strong back.

The ladies cocked their heads to one side and silently considered his muscular figure. Frankly, his size and bearing made the Englishmen around him look a bit underfed.

He'd removed his coat, and Prudence could see the ripple of his muscles across his back, the outline of his powerful legs and hips straining against his trousers as he dipped down. Prudence could feel a bit of sparkly warmth snaking up her spine and unbuttoned the top two buttons of her spencer. "It's rather too warm this afternoon, isn't it?" she asked no one in particular. No one in particular responded.

As they continued to privately admire Mr. Matheson, another heated discussion broke out among the men. This time, a coachman was dispatched under the coach, crawling in so far that only his boots were visible. The other men hovered about, making sure the coach stayed put on its temporary perch. The coachman at last wiggled out from beneath the coach and in a low voice delivered a piece of news that was apparently so calamitous that it caused the men to burst into even louder argument all over again.

The driver ended it all with a shout of "Enough!"

At that point, Mr. Matheson whirled away from the gathered men, his hands on his waist. He took a very deep breath.

"What do you suppose is his occupation?" Mrs. Scales mused, clearly unruffled by the shouting and arguing. "He seems so...*strong*."

"*Quite* strong," said Mrs. Tricklebank. "Perhaps a smithy?"

"His clothes are too fine for a blacksmith," Prudence offered.

Mrs. Tricklebank produced a fan, and with a sharp flick of her wrist, she began to fan herself. "Yes, I think you're right. I think he comes from means."

Mr. Matheson suddenly whirled back to face the men and roughly loosened his neckcloth. He began to speak sternly, rolling up his sleeves as he did, revealing forearms as thick as fence posts. He reached for the wheel and picked it up.

The sisters gasped in unison with Prudence; such a display of brawn was unexpected and stirring. She very much would have liked to see what he meant to do with that wheel, but the driver, clearly unhappy with Mr. Matheson's efforts, wrested the wheel from his grip. Mr. Matheson reluctantly let it go, grabbed up his coat and stalked away from the men as the driver carefully leaned the wheel against the coach.

He kept stalking, striding past the ladies, his expression dark.

"What has happened?" Mrs. Tricklebank cried.

"What has happened?" Mr. Matheson repeated sharply, and whirled around to face the ladies and the old man. "I'll tell you what has happened. That fool driver," he said, pointing in the direction of the men, "insists that we wait for another coach instead of repairing the wheel and being on our way." He jerked his shirtsleeves down as he cast another glare over his shoulder for the driver. "One would think a man who drives a team and a coach for his living might carry a tool or two with him." He shoved into his coat, then dragged his hand through his hair. He muttered something under his breath and turned away from the coach, taking several steps toward an overgrown meadow, and then standing with his back to them, his legs braced apart, his arms akimbo.

For a moment, Prudence thought he meant to stomp away. She could imagine him striding across the fields all the way to the seashore, his jaw clenched, boarding the first ship he found and sailing to America.

"Why should that make him so desperately unhappy?" Mrs. Scales asked loudly.

"Because the good Lord knows when another coach might happen along!" he shouted over his shoulder.

The women exchanged a look. They all knew that two stagecoaches traveled this route every day, as did the Royal Post. A conveyance of some sort would be along shortly. But no one dared say it to Mr. Matheson, as he seemed very perturbed as it was. He was so perturbed in fact, muttering something under his breath, that it struck Prudence as oddly amusing. Try as she might to keep the smile from her face, she could not.

Unfortunately, Mr. Matheson chose that moment to turn back to the group. His gaze landed on her and his brow creased into a frown at the sight of her smile. "What is it?" he demanded irritably. "Have I said something to amuse you?"

All heads swiveled toward Prudence, which only made her amusement more irrepressible. She had to dip her head, cover her mouth with her hand. Her shoulders were shaking with her effort to keep from laughing out loud.

"Splendid," Mr. Matheson said, nodding as if he was neither surprised nor unsettled by her laugh.

"I beg your pardon," Prudence said, and stood up,

the smile still on her face. "I do sincerely beg your pardon. But you're very...distraught."

He looked her up and down as if she puzzled him, as if he couldn't understand what she was saying. His study of her made Prudence suddenly aware of herself—of her arms and limbs, and her bosom, where his gaze seemed to linger a moment too long. "Of course I'm *distraught*," he said, in a manner that had her curious if he merely disliked the word, or if he disliked that she was not equally distraught. "I have important business here and the delays I've already suffered could make this entire venture disastrous!"

Prudence paused. "Ah. The delay you brought on by going in the wrong direction, of course, and then this one on top of that."

He glared at her.

"Oh. Pardon," she said, and glanced at the others. "Was it a secret? But another coach will be along shortly," she cheerfully added. "You may depend that there are at least *two* more coaches that travel this route each day."

"That's wonderful news, Miss Cabot," he said, moving toward her. "And what are we to do while we wait? Nothing? Should we not try and solve our problem?" he asked, gesturing to the coach.

"Well, I certainly don't intend to *stand* and wait," Mrs. Scales announced grandly.

As no one seemed inclined to stand and wait, or solve their problem, the waiting commenced.

The men settled on the side of the road on upturned trunks, the ladies and the old man on their rocks. Mr. Matheson made several sounds of impatience as he wandered a tight little circle just beyond them. Occasionally, he would walk up to the road and squint in the direction they'd come, trying to see round the bend in the road and through the stand of oak trees that impeded the view of the road. And then he'd swirl back again, stalking past the men sitting around the broken wheel, and to the meadow, only to repeat his path a few moments later.

Mrs. Scales, Prudence realized, was studying her as Prudence studied Mr. Matheson. "Did you say there was *no one* who might have seen you safely to your friend, my dear?" she asked slyly.

The woman was impossible. But Prudence had grown up with three sisters—she was well versed in the tactics of busybodies and smiled sweetly. "I didn't say that at all, Mrs. Scales. What do you think? Perhaps the time might pass more quickly if we think of something to do," she suggested, hopping up from her seat.

"What might we possibly do?" Mrs. Scales scoffed.

"A contest," Prudence said, her mind whirling.

"God help me," Mr. Matheson muttered.

"Yes, a contest!" Prudence said, stubbornly standing behind her impetuous idea.

"Such as?" Mrs. Scales inquired. "We've no cards, no games."

"I know! A footrace," Mrs. Tricklebank suggested brightly, which earned her a look of bafflement from her sister and the old man.

"And who do you suggest engage in a footrace, Nina?"

"Perhaps something a bit less athletic," Prudence intervened. "Something—"

"Marksmanship."

This, the first word uttered by the elderly gentleman, was so surprising that they all paused a moment to look at him.

"I had in mind a word game or something a bit tamer, but very well," Prudence said. "Marksmanship it is."

"That's absurd!" Mrs. Scales exclaimed. "Again, who shall participate?"

"Well, the gentlemen, certainly," Prudence said. "I've yet to meet a proper gentleman who wasn't eager for sport."

"I'm not sure you want to put firearms in the hands of some of our fellow travelers," Mr. Matheson said.

Prudence looked at the men lounging about. He had a point. But Mrs. Scales was watching her so intently that Prudence didn't dare sit back down. "Then *I'll* participate," she said, turning about.

Her pronouncement was met with a lot of snorting.

But Mr. Matheson laughed…with great amusement. "That's preposterous."

Prudence's mouth dropped open. "How can you say so?" she objected. "I've been taught to shoot!"

"Why ever for?" Mrs. Scales cried. "On my word, Mrs. Tricklebank, the state of society is exactly as I feared—ladies are not ladies at all!"

Now Prudence was doubly offended. "I beg your pardon, I was taught to shoot for sport, obviously!"

"I think there is nothing obvious about it," Mrs. Scales said, and snapped open her fan and began to wave it in time with her sister's.

"I like this idea," Mr. Matheson said, nodding. He folded his arms and studied Prudence intently, a droll smile on his face that transformed him. His eyes were suddenly shining. "I like it very much, in fact. What do you say we limit the contest to just the two of us to begin," he said, gesturing between them. "Anyone here may challenge the victor."

Prudence looked back at the others. She expected some gentleman to stand up and express a desire to shoot. But no one did.

"Well, then, Miss Cabot?" Mr. Matheson said. "Wasn't it your idea to pass the time?"

It was. And in hindsight, it appeared to be a very bad idea. It was very unlike her to speak so boldly and impetuously, and now Prudence knew why her sisters were accustomed to talking out of turn and saying outrageous things. How did they do it? How did they say impetuous things and then *do* impetuous things?

Mr. Matheson was watching her with far too much anticipation. As if he couldn't wait to put a firearm in her hand. His smile had broadened. "Perhaps these good people might like to wager on our contest," he said smoothly, gesturing grandly to the ladies.

"Wager," said the old man, nodding.

"Ooh," said Mrs. Scales. "I certainly have been known to enjoy a wager or two." She tittered as she opened her reticule. Prudence gaped at the woman in surprise. Mrs. Scales glanced at her expectantly. "Well? As the gentleman said, it was *your* idea."

"Yes, all right," Prudence said crossly. What a fool she was! She *had* been taught to shoot. The earl, as they had always referred to her stepfather, had insisted his stepdaughters be properly instructed in riding, shooting, gaming and archery. He said that they should be prepared to meet their match in a man. Unfortunately, Prudence had not met her match in a man in such a long time that she was quite unpracticed at shooting now.

"We will need a target," Matheson said with all the

confidence of a man who knew he would win and win handily. That trait, Prudence discovered, was just as maddening whether a gentleman was British or American.

"I've one," said the old man. He reached into his pocket and withdrew a flask. He tipped it up at his lips and drained what was left, then handed it to Mr. Matheson.

"A perfect target. Thank you, sir," Matheson said. He was enjoying this now, winking slyly at Prudence as he passed her, carrying the flask.

That flask looked awfully small to Prudence. "I don't have a firearm," she quickly pointed out, hoping that would be the end of it.

"Then you may use mine," Mr. Matheson said, and smiled as he reached deep into his coat and withdrew it. "I suggest you remove your gloves, Miss Cabot."

The sisters fluttered and cooed at that, and then unabashedly admired Mr. Matheson as he strolled away to set the flask on another rock.

There was no escape. Prudence yanked her gloves from her hands, muttering under her breath about fools and angels.

Mr. Matheson walked back to where she stood and, with the heel of his boot, he scraped a line in the dirt. "Give me your hand," he said.

"My hand?"

He impatiently took her hand, his palm warm and firm beneath hers. He pressed the gun into her palm and wrapped her fingers around the butt of it. He squeezed lightly and smiled down at her, his gold-brown eyes twinkling with what Prudence read as sheer delight. "Ladies first," he said, and let go of her, stepping back.

Prudence looked down at the gun. It had a pearled handle and silver barrel, not unlike the pistol her step-brother, Augustine, liked to show his friends. But Augustine kept his pistol in a case at Beckington House in London. He did not wear it on his person. Moreover, Mr. Matheson's gun was smaller than the gun she'd been taught to fire.

"You know how to fire it, don't you?" he asked as she studied the gun.

"Yes!" She lifted the gun to have a look. "That is, I assume that the trigger—"

"I suspected as much," Mr. Matheson said. He stepped forward, took her by the wrist and swung her about so that her back was against his chest. "I would feel more comfortable," he said, a bit breathlessly, "if you do not point it at me."

"Oh, I beg your pardon."

He leaned over her shoulder and extended her arm with the gun, helping her to sight the target. He showed her how to cock it. "Would you like a practice round?"

A practice round? No, she wanted this over as quickly as possible. "Not necessary," she said pertly.

One corner of his mouth tipped up. Prudence had to force herself to look away from that mouth. Those lips, full and moist, made her a little unsteady and she needed all her wits about her.

"Let the contest begin," Mr. Matheson said, and stepped back once more to take his place among the few gentlemen passengers who had wandered over to have a look.

As Prudence studied her target, there seemed to be a lot of chatter at her back as well as the sound of coins clinking when they were tossed into the hat the old man had taken off the young man's head as people made their bets. There was laughter, too, and Prudence wondered if it was directed at her.

"Go on, Miss Cabot. We don't want night to fall before you've had your chance," Mr. Matheson said, and someone snickered.

Prudence glanced coolly at him over her shoulder. She lifted her arm. The pistol was heavy in her hand as she tried to sight the flask. Mr. Matheson had put it at what seemed like a great distance. Her arm began to quiver—she was mortified by that. She aimed as best she could, closed one eye...and then the other... and fired.

The sound of breaking glass startled her almost as much as the kick from the gun that sent her stumbling backward. She'd not expected to hit the target at all, much less head-on as she seemed to have done in a moment of sheer dumb luck. Prudence gasped with delight and relief and whirled about. "Did you *see*?" she demanded of all of them.

"Of course we saw!" Mrs. Scales said. "We're sitting right here."

Prudence squealed with jubilant triumph, as if she'd known all along she could do it. "Your turn, Mr. Matheson," she said cheerfully as two men hurried by her to examine the flask. "But it appears we'll need another target." She curtsied low and held out the gun to him.

The slightest hint of a smile turned up the corner of his mouth. "It certainly does," he said, and looked at her warily, as if he expected her of some sleight of hand. He took the gun Prudence very gingerly held out to him.

"I've a target!" Mrs. Scales called out. She held up a small handheld mirror.

"Ruth, Mr. Scales gave that to you!"

"Hush, now. He can give me another one, can't he? Make your wager."

A man took the mirror and walked across the meadow to prop it where the flask had been.

"Watch now, Miss Cabot, and I will demonstrate how to shoot a pistol," he said. He stepped to the line he'd drawn in the dirt. He put one hand at his back, held the gun out and fired. He clearly hit something; the mirror toppled off the back of the rock. Two gentlemen moved forward to have a look; Prudence scampered to catch up with them and see for herself. One of them leaned over the rock, picked up the mirror and held it aloft. The mirror was, remarkably, intact for the most part, but a corner piece had either broken off or been shot off.

"I *win*!" Prudence cried with gleeful surprise. "You missed!"

"I most certainly did not miss," Mr. Matheson said gruffly, gesturing to the broken mirror. "Do you not see that a piece is missing?"

"Must have grazed it," one of the men offered. "You hit the rock, here, see? And the bullet—"

"Yes, yes, I see," Mr. Matheson said, waving his hand over the rock. "Nevertheless, the object has been hit. We have a tie."

"Then who is to receive the winnings?" Mrs. Scales complained as the sound of an approaching coach reached them.

Prudence didn't hear the answer to that question— her heart skipped several beats when she saw the coach that appeared on the road. It was not the second stagecoach as they all expected—it was Dr. Linford. Prudence's heart leaped with painful panic. One look at her and Dr. Linford would not only know that she'd lied, but he would also demand she come with him at once. He would tell her brother-in-law Lord Merryton, who would be quite undone by her lack of propriety. That was the one thing Merryton insisted upon, that their reputations and family honor be kept upmost in their minds at all times. As Merryton generously provided for Prudence and Mercy and her mother, and had indeed paid dearly to ensure that the patrons of the Lisson Grove School of Art overlooked Mercy's family and placed her in that school, Prudence couldn't even begin to fathom all the consequences of her being discovered like this. Moreover, she had no time to try—she looked wildly about for a place to hide as the Linford coach rolled to a halt. But the meadow was woefully bare, and there was nothing but Mr. Matheson's large frame to shield her, so she darted behind him, grabbing onto his coat.

"What the devil?"

He tried to turn but she pushed against his shoulder. *"Please,"* she begged him. "Please, sir, not a word!"

"Are you *hiding*?" he asked incredulously.

"Yes, obviously!"

"Good God," he muttered. His body tensed. "Miss Cabot," he said softly, and she thought he'd say he would not help her, that she must step out from behind him. "Your feather is showing."

"Please indulge me in this. I shall pay you—"

"Pay! Damn it, your *feather* is showing!"

The feather in her bonnet! Prudence gasped and quickly yanked the feather from her bonnet and dropped it. She stepped closer to his back, practically melding herself onto him. She could smell the scent of horse-flesh, of leather and brawn, and she closed her eyes and pressed her cheek to the warmth of his back. The superfine felt soft against her skin, and she closed her eyes, feeling entirely safe in that sliver of a moment.

"What are you doing?" he demanded softly.

"Hiding," she whispered. "I told you."

"I understand you are hiding, but you're *touching* me."

"Yes, I am," she said with exasperation. Was he unfamiliar with the concept of hiding? "I would crawl under your coat if I could. That's what hiding *is*."

"Good afternoon!" she heard Dr. Linford call out to all. "May we help?"

Prudence was doomed. She would be humiliated before Mr. Matheson and exposed to scandal—all of which seemed far worse than Mr. Matheson's displeasure that she was touching him.

"Turn about," Mr. Matheson said.

"No," Prudence squeaked, her voice sounding desperately close to a whimper. "Please don't—"

"Turn about and walk to the stand of trees just beyond the rocks. No one will see you there, and if they do, you'll be at too great a distance for anyone to determine who, exactly, you are."

"I *can't*—"

"You can't stand here hiding behind me, Miss Cabot. It's entirely suspicious. Go, and I'll walk behind you and block any view."

Prudence lifted her cheek from the warmth and safety of his back. He was right, of course; she couldn't hide like a dumb cow in the middle of a meadow. She glanced at the trees Mr. Matheson had suggested.

"Miss Cabot?"

"Yes," she said quickly, earnestly.

"Let go of my coat and turn about."

"Oh. Yes." She reluctantly released his coat and tried to smooth out the wrinkle she'd put in the fabric with her grip.

Mr. Matheson hitched his shoulders as if she'd tugged him backward, and straightened his cuffs. "Have you turned about?"

"Ah…" She turned around. "Yes."

"Then for God's sake walk on before the passengers begin to wonder why I stand like a damn tree in this field."

Prudence did as he instructed her, her hands clasping and unclasping, her step light and very quick, trying not to run. She didn't dare look back for fear of Dr. Linford seeing her. When she reached the safety of the trees, she whirled about and collided with Mr. Matheson's chest.

He caught her elbow, his grip firm, and dipped down to see her beneath the brim of her bonnet. His gaze was intent. Piercing. It felt almost as if he could see through her. "I'm going to ask you a question and I need you to be completely honest with me. Are you in trouble?"

"No!" she said, aghast. Not as *yet*, that was. "No, no, nothing like that."

"Do you swear it?"

Good Lord, he acted as if he knew what she'd done. Prudence looked away, but he quickly put his hand on her cheek and forced her head around to look at him. She opened her mouth to respond, then thought the better of it and closed it. She nodded adamantly.

He unabashedly continued to study her face a moment, looking, Prudence presumed, for any sign of dishonesty, which made her feel oddly vulnerable. She looked down from his soft golden-brown eyes and dark lashes, from the shadow of his beard, and his lips. His *lips*. She was certain she'd never seen lips like that on a man and, even now, as terrified as she was of being discovered, they made her feel a little fluttery inside.

"Stay here," he said. He strode away from her, toward the carriage.

When he reached the small crowd, there was a lively discussion, the center at which seemed to be Mrs. Scales. Mr. Matheson gestured toward Linford's carriage. Mrs. Scales bent over and grabbed up her pail and a bag, and hurried toward the Linford coach. Her sister was quickly behind her, dropping her pail once and quickly retrieving it. But at the coach door, there was another discussion.

There was a shuffling around of the luggage, and then Mrs. Scales, Mrs. Tricklebank and the elderly gentleman all joined Dr. Linford and his wife in their coach. Dr. Linford climbed up to sit beside his driver. After what seemed an eternity, Dr. Linford's coach drove on, sliding around the stagecoach, and then moving briskly down the road.

Prudence sagged with relief. A smile spread her face as she realized she had managed to dodge Dr. Linford completely. How clever she was! Prudence had never thought herself capable of subterfuge, but she appeared to be quite good at it. She felt oddly exhilarated. At last, something exciting was happening in her life! It was only a single day, but she was completely enlivened by the events thus far.

Now that the Linford coach had gone, Prudence noticed Mr. Matheson began striding toward her, his gait long and quick, his tails billowing out behind him.

She couldn't see the harm in this, really. She'd had her lark with a handsome pair of eyes and stirring lips, and no one would be the wiser for it. She would arrive at Cassandra's house as intended, and none would be the wiser of her flirt with adventure, would they?

Prudence might have strained her arm reaching about to give her back a hearty, triumphant pat, but she had a sudden thought—Mrs. Scales or Mrs. Tricklebank could very well say her name to Mrs. Linford, who would know instantly what she'd done, and worse, that she'd purposely eluded Dr. Linford in this meadow as if she had something very dire to hide.

Prudence went from near euphoria for having arranged an escapade she would long remember to terror at having done something quite awful. *Now* what was she to do?

CHAPTER FOUR

MISS CABOT APPEARED to shrink slightly as Roan strode back to the stand of trees, which he took as another sign that she was hiding something. The woman reminded him very much of Aurora. Roan loved his sister, adored her—but she was the most impetuous female he'd ever known. Without a care, heedless of the consequences of her actions, and therefore at risk of being irrevocably compromised. Of course he grudgingly admired Aurora's independent spirit—he had a bit of that himself—but he wouldn't trust his sister for even a moment.

Looking at Miss Cabot glance around as if planning her escape, he had the same feeling of utter distrust for her.

Miss Cabot apparently thought the better of running and engaging him in a true footrace, but she took a tentative step back.

Roan stopped himself from grabbing her by the arms and giving her a good shake. He put his hands on his waist and stared at her. "All right, then, the sisters have gone. You may safely confess what you've done."

"Whatever do you mean? I've done nothing," she insisted unconvincingly.

"Thievery?" he asked flatly.

She gasped.

"Murder?"

"Mr. Matheson!"

"Don't look so aghast, Miss Cabot, for I can't think of a single reason why you would hide herself from a doctor with a superior coach."

Miss Cabot paled. She had nothing to say for herself and bit her bottom lip in a manner that Roan believed was a universal sign of guilt on a woman. He honestly didn't know if he should deliver a lecture of conduct or bite that lip, too, as he desperately wanted to do. He thought of a man with Aurora under similar circumstances—another lip biter—and inwardly shuddered.

"Admit it—you were to be in that coach."

She lifted her chin, clasped her hands together tightly at her waist. "Yes."

Any number of scenarios began to race through Roan's mind, none of them good. "Is he...are you involved in an affair with him?"

"What? *No!*" she exclaimed, her cheeks flooding with color.

"Are you affianced to him?" he asked, wondering if perhaps she was avoiding her engagement. Again, the similarity to Aurora was uncanny and strangely maddening.

"Did you not see his wife? He's married!"

"Then what is it, Miss Cabot? What has you hiding in these trees like a common criminal?" he demanded, his anger—admittedly, with Aurora—ratcheting.

"I am *not* a criminal," she said hotly.

"Mmm," he said dubiously.

"I was..." She swallowed. She rubbed her nape. "It is true," she said, putting up her hand, "that Dr. Linford was to escort me to Himple, where I am to be met by Mr. Bulworth, who will see me the rest of the way to my friend Cassandra's side. But this coach will also stop in Himple."

Roan waited for her to say more. At the very least he expected her to say why she was on the stagecoach at all. But Miss Cabot merely shrugged as if that was sufficient explanation.

It was not.

"Why didn't you go with him? Why would you put yourself in an overcrowded stagecoach with any number of potential scoundrels instead of in a coach with *springs*?" he asked, incredulous.

Miss Cabot rubbed her nape once more. She sniffed. "It's rather difficult to explain, really."

"Difficult? The only difficulty here is your reluctance to admit whatever it is you've done. I can't begin to imagine what you're doing." A thought suddenly occurred to Roan, and anger surged in him. He abruptly grabbed her elbow and pulled her forward. "Has he attempted... Has he taken *liberty* with you?" he softly demanded and glanced over his shoulder at the others. He would get on the back of one of the horses from the coach and catch up with the bastard if that was the case. He'd break his damn neck—

"No! No, not at all! Dr. Linford is a good man, a decent man—"

"Then what in blazes is the matter?"

Miss Cabot drew herself up to her middling height, removed her arm from his grip with a yank. "I beg your pardon, but I owe you no explanation, Mr. Matheson."

"No, you don't," he agreed. "And neither do I owe you my help. So I will explain to the driver that you must be met by a responsible party at the very first opportunity—"

"All right! I thought traveling with the Linfords would be tedious. I thought the stagecoach would be more…" She made a whirling motion with her hand, as if he should understand her and reach the conclusion quickly.

But he had no idea what she was talking about. He leaned forward, peering at her. "More what?"

"More—" her gaze flicked over him, top to bottom, and her cheeks bloomed "—exciting," she murmured.

That made absolutely no sense. This cake-brained young woman thought a stagecoach would be more exciting than the doctor's comfortable coach? That a stagecoach with its close quarters and ripe strangers was more exciting than a padded bench? Roan couldn't help himself—he laughed. Roundly.

Miss Cabot glared at him. "So happy to amuse you."

"Amused? I'm not amused, I'm astounded by your foolishness."

She gave a small cry of indignation and whirled about, looking as if she intended to march into the woods, but Roan caught her arm before she could flee, pulling her back. She fell into his chest, landing like a pillow against him.

"All right, then, unlace your corset a bit," he said. "But a *stagecoach*? It's the worst sort of travel, second only to the sea if you ask me. Whatever would make you think it would be exciting? A walk over hot coals would be more pleasurable."

Miss Cabot shrugged free of him and folded her arms across her body. She glanced at him from the corner of her eye. Her flush had gone deeper. "I'm sorry you found it so reprehensible, Mr. Matheson."

Roan blinked. Understanding slowly dawned, and

frankly, he could not have been more delighted. Or flattered. But delighted, utterly delighted. "I *see*," he said jovially, aware of the wide grin on his face.

"You don't."

"Oh, I think I do. You wanted to travel with me," he said, and poked her playfully on the arm.

"You flatter yourself," she said imperiously.

"There is no need for me to flatter myself, because you have flattered me beyond compare," he said with a theatrical bow. "I'll admit it, I'm surprised. Granted, I am highly sought after in New York, what with my handsome looks and fat purse…" He was teasing her, but that really wasn't far from the truth. Just ask Mr. Pratt if it wasn't true. "But to be admired so by a fair English flower makes my heart pitter-patter."

"God in heaven, I could *die*," Miss Cabot said, and turned her head.

Roan laughed. "Please don't." He put his hand on her shoulder and coaxed her around. "You're far too comely to die, and after all, you've gone to so much trouble now." He squeezed her shoulder. He meant to let it go, but his hand slid down her arm, to her wrist.

She clucked her tongue and turned her head away from him.

"I am teasing you, Miss Cabot. A rooster can't help but crow, can he? I am truly flattered." He moved his hand from her arm to her waist and pulled her closer. "If I'm to be admired, I am very pleased to be admired by someone as beautiful as you."

"Oh Lord," she muttered, blushing furiously. "Don't trifle with me. I'm mortified as it is." And yet she made no move to step out of his loose embrace.

"I am very sincere. Nevertheless, as pleasant as this

has been for me, you know very well that you shouldn't be gallivanting across the countryside with strangers. You could very well fall victim to some rogue on the road. At the next stop, I intend to put you in a private conveyance to Hipple myself."

"It's *Himple*," she corrected him, and regrettably, stepped away from him. "And I will see myself there, you need not concern yourself."

Just like Aurora. *It's my life to ruin, Roan. You needn't concern yourself with it.*

"Seeing yourself there is not inconsequential, Miss Cabot. You don't want to have your reputation marked by an impetuous moment, do you?"

"No, it's not inconsequential, Mr. Matheson," she said pertly. "But the ruin has already been done. I highly doubt that I could make it worse."

And what did *that* mean? Roan wondered. In what way had she been ruined? Or was she prone to overly dramatic interpretations of the events of her life as was Aurora?

"Ho! The coach!" someone shouted. A cry of relief went up from the other passengers, and there was a sudden flurry of activity, of gathering luggage. As the second stagecoach pulled in behind the first, Roan watched the men over his shoulder a moment, then glanced at Miss Cabot. He looked her over, the purse of her lips, the color in her cheeks. Why were the most alluring women the most trouble? He couldn't imagine Pratt would never dream of doing what Miss Cabot had done today. Which he supposed was what made her the perfect wife. Didn't it? At present, Roan would keep telling himself that. He hadn't actually offered to make Susannah his wife, but it was expected that he would. *He* expected he would, for all the reasons Susannah was not standing here under this tree with him.

Yes, he would keep telling himself that.

Roan looked away from Miss Cabot's hazel eyes. "I should make myself useful in the repair of the wheel."

"Yes, of course." She held his gaze, watching him closely. A smile slowly appeared. "Thank you for not revealing me to Dr. Linford."

He sighed. "I am unduly swayed by the smile of a beautiful woman. It is my cross to bear."

Her smile deepened. "I'll wait on the rocks." She walked past him—gliding, really, with an elegance that was not learned, he knew from experience. She took a seat where they'd gathered previously, picked up her valise and balanced it on her lap, her hands folded primly on top. She looked straight ahead, as if she were at a garden party.

Roan couldn't help his smile as he walked past her and touched her shoulder. "I didn't thank *you*."

"Thank me?" she asked, looking up at him.

"For your great esteem," he said, and winked.

Miss Cabot muttered something under her breath that sounded very much like *rooster* and more, then turned her head, fidgeting with a curl at her nape.

Roan joined the men, discarding his coat. The driver of the second coach had the tools necessary to repair the broken wheel. Roan would have had the wheel repaired more quickly had he been allowed to conduct the work himself. He was familiar with broken wheels; he and his family were in the lumber trade, their teams bringing loads into New York City from as far north as Canada. It was arduous work, cutting and hauling lumber, and Roan had been pressed on more than one occasion to lend a hand to help with the work and the transport. He didn't mind it—he liked the way physical labor made him feel alive and strong. As a result, he had repaired more wheels and axles and that sort of thing than perhaps even these men had seen.

But the driver was adamant that the work be done his way.

The wheel was fixed and attached to the axle, and the men began to load the luggage onto the coach once more. As the team of horses was harnessed, the driver asked the passengers to board.

Roan donned his coat, then collected his smaller bag from the pile of luggage that would be reloaded. He turned and looked back to the rocks, intending to rally Miss Cabot.

She was not sitting on the rocks.

Roan walked into the meadow, scanning the tree line and the road. The woman was nowhere to be seen. Had she boarded the second coach? He looked back to that coach. The passengers were gathering their things and boarding.

Roan strode back to the second coach. "Excuse me," he said, and stepped through the passengers to look into the interior. Only a woman and a small girl sat inside.

Roan turned back to the others. "Have any of you seen a woman? About yay tall," he said, holding his hand out to indicate her height. "With a bonnet?" he asked, gesturing to his head.

No one had seen her.

Roan was baffled. Where could she be? He hurried back to the first coach, where the luggage was now secured. One of the men reached for Roan's bag, but he held tight. "Have you seen Miss Cabot?" he asked the man. "She got on in Ashton Down."

"No, sir," the man said. "Shall I put your bag up top?"

"I'll hold on to it, thank you," Roan said. He stepped around the coachman and peered into the interior of the first coach. Two gentlemen who had ridden on top put themselves inside next to the young man who was scrunched down on the bench, swallowed in his coat, still holding the battered valise.

No Miss Cabot.

A sliver of panic raced up Roan's spine. He turned to the driver, who was overseeing the last adjustments to the team's harnesses. "Have you seen Miss Cabot?"

"The comely one?" the driver asked, squinting up at him.

Roan didn't have time to think why it annoyed him the driver would refer to her in that way and said, "Yes, that one."

The driver shook his head. "Heeding the call of nature, I'd say."

Yes, of course. Roan looked back to the trees across the meadow.

"Come, then, climb up," the driver said. "We're late as it is."

"But we're missing one," Roan said.

The driver glanced back at the trees. "I'm not in the business of chasing strays," he said, and hauled himself up to his seat. "It's been plain enough we're on our way. Are you boarding?"

Roan glared at him. "You would leave a young woman unattended in the middle of the countryside?"

he snapped as the second coach pulled around them and began to move down the road.

"How long do you suggest I wait, Yankee? I've a schedule to keep and passengers to deliver. They've not had any food. I'll be lucky to reach Stroud by nightfall."

Roan whirled around. "Miss Cabot!" he bellowed. "Miss Cabot, come at once!"

There was nothing, no answer. They waited, Roan pacing alongside the coach.

"Come on, then, move on!" shouted one of the men.

"Last chance, Yankee," the driver said.

"What of the luggage?" he demanded, gesturing at the bags and things strapped to the coach. He had helped load her trunk and there it was, strapped onto the coach beneath all the rest, including his trunk.

"All unclaimed luggage will be left at the next station," the driver said, and picked up the reins. "Will you board?" he asked once more.

Roan glanced over his shoulder at the empty meadow.

"*Ack*, I'll not wait," the driver said, and slapped the reins against his team. He whistled sharply and the stagecoach lurched away, the wheels creaking, the dust rising to envelop Roan as he stood on the side of the road with his bag.

Where the hell was she? Roan turned a full circle, his gaze scanning the quiet countryside, seeing nothing but a pair of cows grazing across the way.

And why the hell did he care, precisely? Wasn't it enough that he had to leave his thriving business in New York to come after Aurora? It was just his luck—Roan's father was too old to chase after his wayward daughter, and Roan's brother, Beck, was even younger than Aurora. There had been no one but him, no one who could be depended upon to fetch his sister and bring her home to marry Mr. Gunderson as she had promised she would do.

He supposed that perhaps contrary to what Aurora had claimed, she didn't love Mr. Gunderson after all. It had seemed highly improbable to him that she did, really, seeing as how her engagement had been carefully constructed by Roan's father.

Rodin Matheson was a visionary, and he'd devised a way to increase the family's wealth in a manner that would provide generously for generations of Mathesons—aunts, uncles, cousins, grandchildren. All of them. By marrying his daughter to the son of the building empire that was Gunderson Properties, he made certain that Matheson Lumber would be used to build New York City for years to come.

Roan thought it was brilliant, really, and Aurora had easily agreed to it after a few meetings with Sam Gunderson. "I adore Mr. Gunderson," she'd said dreamily.

Perhaps she did…in that moment. That was the problem with Aurora—she flitted from one moment to the next, her mind changing as often as the hands on the clock.

It was Mr. Pratt who had suggested to his friend Rodin Matheson that perhaps Roan would be a good match for his daughter Susannah. Mr. Pratt was the owner of Pratt Foundries, and Rodin began to see a bigger, more successful triumvirate of construction. He explained to Roan that between Pratt Foundries, Gunderson Properties and Matheson Lumber, their business and income would soar as they became *the* construction industry of a growing city.

It was a heady proposition. Roan had never met Susannah, learning that she summered in Philadelphia. But Mr. Pratt had insisted that his daughter was a delight, a comely, agreeable young woman who would make him a perfect wife. Roan hadn't thought much about the qualities of a perfect wife—he wasn't a sentimental man, and when it came to marriage, he accepted it as something that had to be done. Neither had he given much thought as to who he would marry; that had been the furthest thing from his mind as they'd worked to expand Matheson Lumber. He'd supposed that whoever it was, familiarity would eventually breed affection. Affection was all that was necessary, wasn't it? His parents had found affection somewhere along the way and seemed happy. Roan imagined the same would be true for him. As for siring children, he hardly gave that a thought—he could not imagine any circumstance in which he'd be anything less than willing and eager to do his part.

And then he'd met Susannah Pratt.

She'd come to New York just before Roan's aunt and uncle had returned from England. She was nothing as Mr. Pratt had described, and worse, Roan could not find anything the least bit attractive about her. It was impossible for him to accept that *she* was the one he was to acquaint himself with and then propose marriage. Privately, he'd chided himself for that—a woman's value was not in her face, for God's sake, it was in her soul. So he'd valiantly tried to see beyond her appearance. Unfortunately, she was not the least bit engaging. He could find no common ground, and even if he had, the woman was painfully shy and afraid to look him in the eye.

Just before his aunt and uncle had come home, he had decided he would speak to Susannah about her true desires. Perhaps she found him as odious as he found her. Perhaps she was desperate for escape from this loose arrangement.

But the news his aunt and uncle had brought home trumped everything else. They were all desperate to find Aurora before she was lost to them, and Roan had put aside his own troubles to chase after her. What could he do?

He could curse Aurora for the weeks it had taken him to cross the Atlantic, that's what. The longer Susannah Pratt thought he would be her husband, the harder it would be to disengage from her. Roan was even angrier with Aurora for not being in West Lee, or whatever the hamlet he'd been directed to, but in the other West Lee, north. That alone was enough to concern him. Did he really need to fret about *another* incorrigible, intractable, disobedient young woman?

No. No, he did not. He didn't care that Miss Cabot's eyes were the color of the vines that grew on his family's house. Or that she had boarded this coach because she'd been attracted to him. Or that he'd teased her and embarrassed her and thereby was probably the cause of her running off.

She was *not* his concern, damn it. And yet, she was.

For the second time that day, Roan swept his hat off his head and threw it down onto the ground in an uncharacteristic fit of frustration. Damn England! Damn women!

He kicked the hat for good measure and watched it scud across the road.

And then, with a sigh of concession, he walked across the road to fetch it. But he discovered he'd kicked his hat into a ditch filled with muddy water. Roan muttered some fiery expletives under his breath. He'd find another hat in the next village. He picked up his bag and hoisted it onto his shoulder and walked on.

Now, to figure out where that foolish little hellion had gone.

CHAPTER FIVE

PRUDENCE HADN'T ACTUALLY intended to flee. She'd been as anxious as anyone to board the coach and be on her way. But as the repair work had dragged on, she began to imagine any number of scenarios awaiting her at the next village. Dr. Linford and his wife, first and foremost, their displeasure and disgust evident. Worse, Dr. Linford and his wife in the company of someone in a position of authority, who would escort Prudence back to Blackwood Hall in shame. She could just see it— made to ride on the back of a wagon like a convicted criminal. As they moved slowly through villages, children and old women would come out to taunt her and hurl rotten vegetables at her. *Shameless woman!*

That public humiliation would be followed by Lord Merryton's look of abject disappointment. Merryton was a strange man. He was intensely private, which Grace insisted was merely his nature but, nevertheless, everyone in London thought him aloof and unfeeling. Now that Prudence had lived at his house and dined at his table these past two years, she knew him to be extraordinarily kind and even quite fond of her. But he did seem almost unnaturally concerned with propriety and if there was one thing he could not abide, would not tolerate, it was scandal and talk of his family.

As he had been her unwavering benefactor and her

friend, Prudence could not bear to disappoint him so. She held him in very high regard and, shamefully, she'd not thought of him in those few moments in Ashton Down when she'd impetuously decided to seek her adventure.

She'd begun to wonder, as she sat on the rock, watching the men repair the wheel, if she ought not to find her own way back to Blackwood Hall and throw herself on Merryton's mercy. To be ferried back to him by Dr. Linford, who would be made to alter his plans to accommodate her foolishness, would only make Merryton that much more cross. She decided it was far better if she arrived on her own, admitted her mistake and begged his forgiveness.

That's why, with one last look and longing sigh at Mr. Matheson's strong back and hips, Prudence had picked up her valise and had begun to walk. She wanted to thank Mr. Matheson for his help, but thought it was probably not a very good idea to draw attention to the fact she was leaving.

She had in mind to find a cottage. She would offer to pay someone to take her back to Ashton Down. And, if she reached the next village before finding a cottage, she could keep herself out of sight until Dr. Linford had gone on. He'd be looking for her coach.

She walked along smartly, trying to be confident in her new plan. All was *not* lost, she told herself. She was at least as clever as Honor and Grace. She *would* see her way out of this debacle.

She hadn't walked very far when she heard the approaching coach, and her confidence swiftly flagged. It was surely the stagecoach, and the driver would stop, insist she board the coach. She hadn't thought of that wrinkle. But Prudence was determined not to be delivered into the hands of Linford. "You will *not* falter," she murmured under her breath. "You have as much right to walk along this road as anyone."

Prudence lifted her chin as the coach rapidly approached. It wasn't until the last possible moment that she understood the coach did not intend to stop and inquire about her at all, and with a cry of alarm, Prudence leaped off the road just as the team thundered by, cloaking her in a cloud of dust.

When the coach had passed, Prudence coughed and picked herself up with a pounding heart, dusting off her day gown as best she could. "He might at least have slowed to see if I'd been harmed," she muttered, and climbed back on the road, squared her shoulders, and began to walk again.

She had no sooner taken a few steps than she heard the sound of the second coach. Now an old hand at navigating passing coaches, Prudence hopped off the road and stood a few feet back.

But *this* coach slowed. The team was reined down to a walk, then rolled to a stop alongside where she stood.

The driver, *her* driver, peered down at her a moment, then turned his head and spit into the dirt. "Aye, miss, wheel's fixed. Climb aboard."

"Thank you, but I prefer to walk," she said lightly.

"Walk! To where? There's naught a village or a person for miles."

"Miles?" she repeated, trying to sound unimpressed. "How many miles would you say?"

"Five."

"Well! Then it's a good thing that I wore my sturdy shoes," she lied. "A fine day for walking, too. Thank you, but I shall walk, sir." She wondered if Matheson was sitting in the interior of the coach overhearing her, laughing at her foolishness. Was that why he hadn't shown himself? Perhaps he didn't want anyone to think he was in any way familiar with a featherheaded debutante who was walking down the road in slippers more fitting for a dance?

"Suit yourself," the driver said, and lifted the reins, prepared to send the team on.

"Sir!" Prudence shouted before he could dispatch the team. "Will you see that my trunk is delivered to Himple?" She opened her reticule to retrieve a few coins and began to make her way across the ditch to the road. "Please. If you will leave it at the post station, someone will be along for it." She climbed onto the road—slipping once and catching herself, then climbing up on the driver's step. She held up a few shillings to him.

"You're alone, miss?" one of the gentlemen riding behind the driver called down to her.

She ignored him. Her heart was racing now, not only with fear, but also with anger that was very irrational. She could imagine Mr. Matheson sitting in the coach, rolling his eyes or perhaps even sharing a chuckle with the boy. One could certainly argue that she deserved his derision given what she'd done today, but she didn't like it one bit.

"You're certain, are you?" the driver said, taking the coins from her palm and pocketing them.

"Quite. Thank you." Prudence stepped down.

The driver put the reins to the team. Once again, Prudence was almost knocked from the road. As it was, she stumbled backward into the ditch, catching herself on a tree limb to keep from falling.

She watched the coach move down the road and disappear under the shadows of trees.

Five miles from a village.

She looked around. There was no one, and no sound but the breeze in the treetops and the fading jangle of the coach. Prudence had never been alone like this. But, as her poor, mad mother used to say before she'd lost the better part of her mind, no one could correct one's missteps but oneself. The sooner one set upon the right course, the sooner one would reach the right destination.

Prudence would argue the point about the right destination, but there was nothing to be done for it now. And for God's sake, she would not shed a single tear. There was nothing she detested more than women who resorted to tears at the first sign of adversity. Yes, walk she would, in shoes that were meant to wander about a manicured garden…just as soon as she gave her aching feet a rest.

Prudence dropped her valise and sat down on top of it, her knees together, her legs splayed at odd angles to keep her balance on the small bag. She folded her arms on top of her knees, pressed her forehead against her arms and squeezed her eyes shut. *How could you be so stupid?*

Reality began to seep into her thoughts.

Whatever made her believe she could be like her sisters? She'd never been like the rest of them, had never taken such daring chances, disregarding all propriety on a whim. What made her believe that she could step out of bounds of propriety *now*? Yes, she'd been at sixes and sevens of late, unsatisfied with her lot in life, but still! She was alone on a road, perfect prey for highwaymen, thieves or other horrible things she couldn't even bring herself to think of. *Gypsies!* Prudence gasped and her heart fluttered, recalling the frightening tales Mercy had insisted on telling.

"Well."

The sound of a man's voice startled her so badly that Prudence tried to leap up and scream at the same time and managed to knock herself off her imperfect perch and onto her bottom.

Mr. Matheson instantly reached for her, and Prudence, in a moment of sheer relief, grabbed him with both hands, hauled herself up with such vigor that she launched herself into his person and threw her arms around his neck.

Perhaps he was as stunned as she—he caught her, but neither of them moved for one long moment. Then Mr. Matheson put his hands firmly on her waist and carefully set her back, staring down at her as if she'd lost her mind.

"I beg your pardon," she said apologetically. "I was momentarily overcome with relief! What are you doing on foot?"

"Isn't it obvious? Rescuing you."

Prudence could feel the color rising in her cheeks, the *thump, thump, thump* of her shame and delight in her chest. "You gave me such a fright," she said, pressing her hand to breast. "I thought I would perish with it."

"Well, I think we've sufficiently delayed your ultimate demise for at least an hour or so," he said. "What the devil are you doing here? Why did you leave the coach? Where in hell do you think you're *walking*?"

"To the next village or cottage," she said, gesturing

lamely in that direction. "I mean to pay someone to return me to Ashton Down."

He squinted down the road in the direction she gestured. "What a perfectly ridiculous thing to do," he said gruffly. "*Why* would you? You had a seat on a coach!"

"Because I feared Mrs. Scales would not be able to restrain herself from reporting all that had happened since leaving Ashton Down, and she…might possibly utter my name."

"I think the odds of that are excellent," he said, nodding, as if it were a foregone conclusion. "And your solution to this was to, what, run away?"

"No," she said, as if it were absurd to suggest she'd run, even though she obviously had. "My *solution* was to go at once and find someone who would return me to Blackwood Hall. I should rather my family learn of this…turn of events…from me."

"Mmm." He folded his arms and stared down at her with such scrutiny that her skin began to tingle. "So you thought you might march up to anyone with a conveyance and ask that they see you to this hall where you might report your folly?"

When he put it like that, it sounded ridiculous. Prudence sniffed. She scratched her cheek and gazed down the road, then looked at him sidelong. "Well, you needn't look so smug, Mr. Matheson. You've made your point. I've been foolish."

"I haven't even begun to make *that* point, Miss Cabot, but I'll happily do so as we trek into the next village and find that conveyance. At the moment, however, I'd very much like to turn you over my knee like a child, for God knows how childish you've been."

"Yes, so it would seem!" she said, miffed. "You're not my father, Mr. Matheson."

"Your father!" he sputtered. "I'm scarcely thirty years old. And yet I have *twice* as much sense as you."

"If you had *twice* as much sense, you might have made your way to Weslay instead of Wesleigh!"

He was momentarily disabled by the truth in that statement. "I will allow that," he said, holding up a finger, "at least until I see you to some means for a safe return home." He bent down, reaching for her bag.

But Prudence was faster and snatched it up before he could take it. "I will carry my own bag, thank you."

"For the love of— It's a long way to the next village."

"I am aware of how far it is to the next village. It's five miles. And I am perfectly capable of carrying my own bag!"

He muttered under his breath and hoisted his own bag onto his shoulder. "Shall we?"

"Do I have any other choice?" Prudence began to walk, her bag banging uncomfortably against her knee. "Where is your hat?" she demanded, wishing he'd stop looking at her so intently.

He frowned. "Lost," he said curtly. "Why is it that you misses are all alike?" he added irritably, as if he was constantly running into unmarried women in the countryside.

"We *misses*? Have you some vast experience with *misses*, Mr. Matheson?"

"I have enough. Why do you think I am here in this godforsaken—"

Prudence looked at him sharply.

"Pardon. In this foreign land," he amended.

"I don't know," she said insouciantly. "Presumably to instruct all of the young misses in proper behavior."

"If only I had the time that would require. But no, I am here to instruct one miss. Imagine, it's not even you! I am in pursuit of my incorrigible, equally head-strong and impulsive sister."

Prudence tossed her head. "I wouldn't be the least bit surprised if she was trying to keep her distance from you and your opinions."

"She won't escape them," he said flatly.

"I can't imagine anyone could," Prudence retorted pertly.

They walked in silence for a few moments while Prudence wondered what the sister had done, what had caused him to come in "pursuit" of her. "Where is she?" she asked.

"Yes indeed, where *is* Miss Aurora Priscilla Matheson?" he asked. "I very much hope she is at West Lee," he said, gesturing impatiently with his hand at his failure to grasp the subtle differences between the names of the villages. "Shall I tell you the tale of this young woman? My aunt and uncle brought her to London last spring. It was a wedding gift of sorts, an opportunity to see a bit of the world before she marries Mr. Gunderson. But Aurora is quite impetuous, and she made many friends in London, some of whom, apparently, convinced her to stay another month or so more than was intended. When it came time to leave, she refused to return home with my aunt and uncle. She wrote my father and said she'd be along in a month or so."

"She's alone?" Prudence said, awed by the cheek of that.

"I assume so," Mr. Matheson said. "That's Aurora

for you—she wouldn't listen to reason, which surprises no one, and it has caused quite an uproar. Her marriage to Gunderson is very advantageous for my family. Almost as advantageous as—" Mr. Matheson suddenly stopped talking and looked away. "Never mind. Just believe me when I say that Mr. Gunderson was not pleased. And I was dispatched to fetch her before she does irreparable harm to her reputation, her engagement and to our family."

"But how do you know where she is?" Prudence asked.

"I don't, really. The last letter we had from her before I set sail said that she was traveling about, staying here and there—but that she'd been invited to visit the home of this Penfors fellow. Given the details of her letter and the date it was marked, we believe she ought to be there now."

Prudence almost laughed out loud. It was impossible to believe, and in some respects a delight to know, that there was a young woman out there who was more incorrigible than any of *her* sisters. Abandoning her family for a foreign land, with no apparent regard for her virtue? Prudence would very much like to meet Miss Aurora Priscilla Matheson. She would like to lay eyes on the unmarried woman brave enough to do *that*—

Wait—was she truly feeling a bit of admiration for a woman like Aurora Matheson?

Mr. Matheson noticed it, too. "What's that smile? Do my sister's antics amuse you? Then she may count one person who she has made smile, because my family is not amused. Much is riding on her marriage. Not to mention, she is a fool."

"One can hardly fault her for wanting a taste of

adventure. Being an unmarried woman can be quite tedious you know. Always sitting about in parlors, speaking of the weather." Prudence shifted her bag to her other hand.

Mr. Matheson snorted. "Aurora has *never* sat around a parlor," he said. "She's had as privileged a life as any young woman could expect in New York. She has squads of friends, attends all the social events—I would wager her derriere has not touched a parlor seat in months."

Startled, Prudence looked at him.

"What?" he said. "Ah. I forgot. I'm not to say such things to the fragile English flower."

"I am not a fragile English flower! Who has said so?"

"My aunt. She informs me you all have tender feelings and to be careful of them. She said the English debutantes are not as sturdy as American women. Fragile, she said."

Prudence gasped with great indignation. "That is not true! We are quite sturdy!" she cried. "Look at me now, walking along, carrying my own bag."

"Gracious, you *are* carrying your own bag," he said with mock wonder, and then laughed as he easily wrested it from her hand and held it in the same hand as his bag now. "Don't look so shocked. You are obviously very sturdy, Miss Cabot," he said, and his gaze slid down the length of her. "And perhaps not as impetuous as Aurora."

He smiled, and Prudence felt the smile trickle through her. She blushed and glanced away, absurdly proud that he thought her sturdy.

He sighed. "Ah, but I can never stay cross with Aurora for long. And my father has coddled her all her life, so I suppose it's not entirely her fault. She's the only girl, between me and my younger brother, Beck, and my father has doted on her."

"And is Mr. Beck Matheson as impetuous as his sister?" she asked.

"Beck is not at all impetuous. He's much like me—responsible, careful and, above all, industrious," Mr. Matheson said proudly.

Prudence gave him a pert smile, amused by his pride. "Your industrious nature is quite American, I suppose."

"Of course," he said instantly, then shot her a look. "America *is* industrious."

"Fond of hard work there, I've heard."

A crooked smile of delight turned up the corner of his mouth. "Should one be disdainful of hard work?" he asked, as if it were preposterous to be anything but fond of it, and gave her a playful nudge with his shoulder.

"What sort of hard work does your family engage in?"

"We are in lumber."

Prudence had supposed he was in trade—wasn't everyone in American involved in one trade or another? But *lumber*? It sounded so…common. But then, without titles and no *haut ton* to speak of, she supposed everyone must work for what they had. "Do you mean you cut down trees?" she asked, surreptitiously examining his hands.

Mr. Matheson laughed. "I've cut one or two, but no. My family owns one of the largest lumber suppliers in America. We buy lumber from Canada, employ men to transport the lumber from Canada to New York, and then we sell it to builders. We sell it to Gunderson Properties, one of the largest builders in the city. A marriage between Aurora and Sam Gunderson will guarantee our supply has a demand, you see? We've also recently partnered with Pratt Foundries."

"Oh," Prudence said.

"Lumber and iron, that's what construction requires. Our partnership with Gunderson and Pratt will be very lucrative for all of us. We'll see our family through for generations to come."

That did sound industrious, and it also sounded interesting to Prudence. No one ever spoke to her of such things. "It seems ambitious," she said.

"Very ambitious," he agreed. "My father has forged these relationships, but they depend on…" His voice trailed off for a moment. "On understandings. On marriages. That sort of thing."

He didn't have to explain that to Prudence. She understood very well how "understandings" and "marriages" created wealth.

"But enough of me," he said. "How many siblings do you have, and are they all as impetuous as you?"

Prudence laughed outright. "I have three sisters, Mr. Matheson."

"Roan, please," he said, his eyes shining with his smile.

Roan. His name swirled around inside her. It sounded American. It sounded industrious, as if it chopped down trees and forged iron and erected great buildings. Prudence let it roll around her thoughts. "My sisters are more impetuous than me, do you believe it? I am the one who is considered the most responsible."

"No," he said with a disbelieving laugh.

"At least until today," she amended, and he laughed again. "There is Honor, Mrs. Easton, and Grace, Lady Merryton—she's a countess. They are both older than me. And then there is the youngest, Miss Mercy Cabot, who is two years my junior, and who vows to never marry but become a famous artist."

"Four sisters, one of them a royal countess. That must delight the English princes."

"Royal! Whatever gave you that idea?"

He arched a brow. "Isn't a countess royal in some way?"

Prudence burst into laughter, bending backward a little with her gaiety at that preposterous remark, catching herself with a hand to his arm. "Grace is a countess, but not a *royal* one. And really, how many princes do you think there are in England?"

He puffed out his cheeks as he thought about that. "A dozen?" he guessed hopefully. When Prudence giggled, he said, "All right, I'm woefully ignorant of monarchies in general. It seems unnecessarily complicated to outsiders."

"But I thought Americans understood the monarchy perfectly."

"I am sure most do, but as we've cleanly emancipated ourselves from it, I don't give it much thought. If you come to America someday, you'll see what I mean."

For a moment, Prudence tried to imagine herself in America. She imagined a throng of people with scythes and pitchforks, emancipating themselves from what they perceived to be tyranny. "I've never been beyond England's shores," she said thoughtfully. "But Sir Luckenbill. He's traveled to New York."

"And who is this Luckenbill fellow?"

"He is a friend of my sister's husband and has come to dine on occasion. He's a distinguished scholar," Prudence said. At least Sir Luckenbill claimed to be one—a scholar of science, although the exact nature of his scientific knowledge seemed rather vague to her and her sisters.

"Well? How did he find it?"

She smiled up at him. "Should I tell you the truth?"

"Yes."

"He found it rather primitive in comparison to London. And the people…" She paused. "Well, he said they were rather boorish, really."

Mr. Matheson laughed. "That's because in America, men are men. We don't wear our kerchiefs in our cuffs and sniff smelling salts."

"English gentlemen do not sniff smelling salts," Prudence said, but did not deny that many of them did indeed carry handkerchiefs in their cuff. She couldn't imagine this man ever carrying a handkerchief in his cuff.

"If you had brothers, you might understand a bit of what I mean," Mr. Matheson said. He suddenly caught her elbow and pulled her into his side to keep her from stumbling over a rabbit hole.

"I have a brother," Prudence said, hopping around the hole. "The Earl of Beckington is my most beloved stepbrother."

"An earl you say," he said, sounding impressed. "*He* must be royalty, then."

Prudence laughed again. "No!"

He still had hold of her elbow as he groaned skyward. "What is the damn point of all these titles if they aren't meant to be royal?"

"Would you like me to explain it?" she asked as he let go of her arm.

"No," he said. "I never cared much for history and all that looking backward. I much preferred the here and now in my instruction. Arithmetic and science. The science of democracy. But never mind that, you have me curious—why isn't your brother escorting you? He shouldn't allow you to roam around the country-side alone."

"There you are again with this notion that someone else may *allow* me, a grown woman, to do as I please. Augustine is not my king, sir, and besides, I find it highly ironic that you are asking these questions of me, given that you don't really even know where your sister is."

"Touché, Miss Cabot. Had I known she would be left unattended, I would never have *allowed* it," he said, and winked at her. "What is your earl's excuse?"

"Augustine has not the slightest notion of where I am and nor should he. He is well occupied by his life in London, and I am well occupied by mine. And *you* are very opinionated, Mr. Matheson."

"Am I?" he said, sounding surprised, and halted his step as if to contemplate it. He dropped the two bags and nodded. "Perhaps I am. I won't apologize for it." He smiled, and brushed a bit of hair from her cheek. "You're easily riled, Miss Cabot."

"I am *not* easily riled," she said with a roll of her eyes. "That's what men say to women when they've been put back on their heels."

He laughed. He brushed her cheek again, then pushed the brim of her bonnet back. "Will you remove it?" he asked. "I would very much like to see all of your face."

Prudence felt something swirl between them, a palpable energy curling around her, tugging her closer to him. She held his gaze and loosened the tie of her bonnet, then pushed it off and let it fall down her back and hang around her neck.

His gaze took her in, unhurried, from her hair, which Prudence was certain was a mess, to her face—smiling a little as he did—and down, skimming over her bodice before lifting up again. He met her gaze and smiled. He touched her face with his knuckle. "Thank you. I am always invigorated by the sight of a beautiful woman."

Beautiful. Prudence had been called beautiful all her life, but when Mr. Roan Matheson said it, she believed it. She could feel the warmth of his admiration slipping down her spine and glittering in her groin. She began to walk again with the impression of his finger blistering on her cheek and the look in his eyes burning in her thoughts.

Silence fell over them again. Prudence was acutely aware of the rooster beside her, his body as big as a mountain and apparently twice as strong. He didn't seem the least bit bothered by the weight of the bags he carried, while she tried not to limp in her horrible shoes.

She really had to think of something else, because she had become rather fixated on the way he gazed at her. His gaze was pleasantly piercing, as if he was trying very hard to see past the facade of her skin. "How is it your sister has become acquainted with Lord Penfors?" she asked curiously.

"I suppose in the way Aurora has of meeting anyone—

by inserting herself into situations she has no call to be in. Do you know him?"

"Only by vague reputation. I know that he remains mostly in the country, has a wife, but no children of whom I am aware. You mean to find her and then what?" she asked.

"Escort her home, obviously. And then I will present her to her fiancé and wish him the best of luck."

Prudence couldn't help but giggle. "But if your sister hasn't heeded your advice yet, what makes you think she will now?"

"An excellent question. I may be forced to shackle and bag her. Now I must ask, what will you do once you are put on a coach home?"

The reminder of Blackwood Hall sobered her. Prudence grimaced at the thought of the long winter stretching before her, and fidgeted with the strings of her bonnet, hesitating.

"Ah," he said.

"Ah? Ah, what?"

"Just that I see."

"What do you see?"

"It's obvious," he said, his eyes twinkling with his smile.

Her pervasive ennui was obvious?

"In fact it all makes sense now. Your trip to see a *friend*," he said as if he didn't believe there was a friend. "Taking a coach to gaze at me—"

"Not gaze at you," she sputtered.

"Then quickly deciding you best run home. There must be a gentleman waiting in the wings. If I had to guess, I'd say it's someone you can't decide if you want to encourage, or someone you wish was more encouraging of you."

His reasoning was so ridiculous that Prudence laughed.

Mr. Matheson stopped in the middle of the road once more and dropped the bags again, his hands finding his waist as he turned to face her. "Now what have I said?"

"You couldn't be more wrong!" she cried gleefully. "Perhaps it is different in America, but when one's family is embroiled in scandal, no one is rushing to the door to court the daughters. There is no gentleman. In fact, one might say there is a definite lack of one!"

The moment the words came tumbling through her lips, Prudence clamped a hand over her mouth. If there was one thing a debutante did *not* do, it was to announce, to perfect strangers, that there was no interest in her whatsoever.

Worse, Matheson was staring at her as if she were speaking a foreign language.

"All right, go ahead, laugh if you must," she said, waving her hand to hurry him along. "I've said it. It's the truth."

"I'm sorry," he said with a shake of his head, "but I am astounded."

Prudence groaned. "Go on, make light of it."

"I'm not making light of it. I will say this. In America, when a woman as...as *beautiful* as you, Miss Cabot—and make no mistake, you are very beautiful—has no understanding with a gentleman of means, there would be a line around the city blocks for her. Without any concern for scandal."

Prudence blinked. She felt that slide of warmth down her spine, the internal glittering again.

"Your attentions would be in very high demand," he said again, and his gaze moved over her, the intensity of it seeping in through her pores. A smile of atrociously showy proportions spread across her face.

"That is precisely why women like you should not be walking about roads like this alone," he continued, his voice turning gruff. "Men are beasts and scoundrels and utterly incapable of not following after a woman like you."

Impossibly, her grin spread wider. "I walk everywhere at Blackwood Hall—"

"Ack," he said with a flick of his wrist. "It's not the same. Out here, without protection or any sense at all, you're prey for men like me."

She laughed. "Men like you!"

"Yes. *Me*. Scoundrels, as I said."

"You're not a scoundrel!" she scoffed.

"Oh, but I am every inch a scoundrel, Miss Cabot," he said with a devilish smile. "Don't be fooled. Hasn't anyone ever warned you about the appetites of men?"

A swirl of concern began to nudge in beside her glee at having been called beautiful by such a handsome man. Lord Merryton had indeed warned her of scoundrels and rogues. *Never trust a gentleman, no matter what he says to you, Prudence. There is one thing in his mind that controls him, and it is not a virtue.*

"Well, good heavens, don't look frightened of me now," he said impatiently. He dipped down and retrieved the bags, then casually put his arm around her waist, urging her to walk. A flash of incongruence swept through her—she liked the way this self-named scoundrel felt beside her.

"You remind me too much of my sister. I could no more tarnish your reputation than I could hers."

Prudence did not care to remind him of his sister in that moment, not at all—the comparison sat sourly in her belly.

"What sort of scandal?" he asked as they walked along, like brother and sister.

"Pardon?"

"You said there is no gentlemen at your door because of scandal. What sort of scandal?"

She really didn't care to reveal her family's sordid shenanigans. "My sisters were married in an unconventional manner," she said carefully.

"Forced to marry?"

"Forced?" she repeated, wondering how best to phrase it.

"I mean, were they pregnant?"

Prudence gasped, both with indignation at such a horrible accusation and with shock—no one *ever* said that word aloud. If there was one word in the English language that was carefully concealed with euphemisms, it was that one. "Absolutely not!"

"No?" He shrugged. "What other unconventional manners of marriage are there?"

"More than that," Prudence said.

Mr. Matheson chuckled and gave her a soft squeeze. "You amuse me, Miss Cabot. You're a bit prudish, aren't you? And yet forthcoming in a strange way, especially for a woman walking along a deserted road with a complete stranger."

"I don't feel as if you're a complete stranger any longer," she said.

"Well, I am. You really know nothing about me. You

remind me of a man I ran into the time my horse went lame upstate," he said, and began to relate the tale of what sounded to Prudence like a very long and dangerous walk through the American countryside. This was where, apparently, Mr. Matheson had come up with the idea that there ought to be better modes of transportation between the cities and the north country, and he had very firm opinions about it. Prudence was able to observe this at length, for on this topic, her participation in the conversation was completely unnecessary.

The talk of transportation and the need for a canal had utterly fatigued her by the time they reached the village. Moreover, her feet were killing her.

There was hardly anything to the village. A pair of cottages, a smithy, and a tiny inn and post house. Almost all of the village appeared deserted, save the woman wandering about her garden. Up the road were a few more buildings, perhaps a dry-goods store. The stagecoaches had come and gone, but more important, there was no sign of Dr. Linford.

With a sigh of relief, Prudence sat down on a fence railing across from the inn. She desired nothing more than to remove her shoes and rub her feet, but would settle for at least taking her weight off them.

Mr. Matheson, on the other hand, put down the two bags and glanced around as if it had been nothing to carry them these five miles. "Are you hungry? I'm hungry," he said.

"No, thank you." She glanced up at him. She couldn't deny that their little adventure had come to an end. She had done enough for one day, and no matter what, she couldn't impose on him any longer. For heaven's sake, the man had only just arrived from America. "Thank you for walking with me, Mr. Matheson. I know you're eager to find your sister. I'll be quite all right until a coach comes along."

He looked surprised. "My name is Roan. And I prefer to put you on a coach myself."

"You're not worried for me, surely. There is no one here but an old woman," she said, gesturing toward the white-haired woman bent over a stick and busy with something in her garden. "And besides, a coach will be along shortly. I'll be all right." It took some effort, but Prudence smiled.

Mr. Matheson did not smile. He frowned and seemed to be silently debating what to do with her. "You're certain," he said, sounding uncertain.

"Very."

"Well…then I suppose when the next northbound coach comes, I'll be on it."

Prudence felt foolishly disappointed. She had just told him he shouldn't feel compelled to stay with her. He'd been kind enough to her, for all her folly. So she made herself smile again and said cheerfully, "Good luck to you, sir! I pray you find your sister."

He nodded. He shifted his weight. "Good luck to you, Miss Cabot." He sounded reluctant. He frowned, and he didn't move. He stared at her a moment, his gaze intent, then spread his fingers wide and studied his palm. "So…you'll return to Blackwood Hall, is that it?"

She looked around. Maybe, she thought, she could make it to Himple on her own and spare herself the humiliation of returning to Blackwood Hall. "Perhaps I should carry on to Himple to meet my friend. It's not very far from here at all."

She shielded her face and looked down the road.

But the road bent at an odd angle. She stood up—wobbling a bit, given that her feet had turned to pulp. And it didn't help her see Himple, the distance to which, truth be told, Prudence had no idea.

"I think that's not a good idea," Mr. Matheson said, moving to stand beside her and look down the road, too.

"I don't know," she said thoughtfully. "I think they will never let me out of Blackwood again once they hear of this." She glanced at him from the corner of her eye. "Would you?"

"No. Not a chance of it." He looked over his shoulder.

"Then you see my—"

Mr. Matheson suddenly caught her elbow and whirled her around so that her back was to the road and she was facing him. "What—"

"Step back, beneath that tree."

"The tree! I don't—"

"Step back, step back," he said, pushing her a little, moving with her, pushing her until she had stepped back beneath the low boughs of a sycamore tree and into its shadows. "Make yourself small," he muttered.

"Make myself *small*? How does one make themselves small?" Prudence tried to turn, to see behind the tree at whatever it was that had caught his attention, but his grip of her elbow tightened. "Don't—"

It was too late—she'd already seen what Matheson had seen. Dr. Linford had strolled out of one of the buildings up the street and was walking down the road.

With a gasp Prudence whirled around and pressed her back against the tree. "Oh no, oh *no*," she whispered frantically, her mind racing. She could picture Dr. Linford forcing her into his coach and turning about to take her home. "Where is his carriage?"

"Down at the bottom of the hill," Mr. Matheson said. "Don't panic." He moved closer, so that he was practically touching her.

"How can I not panic? He'll see me!" She grabbed the lapel of his coat and tried to make herself small.

"Be still, or you'll draw attention to—"

"I am *finished*!" she said, jerking his lapel in frustration.

"Miss Cabot," he said sternly.

Prudence would never know how it happened. She knew only that before she realized it was happening, his mouth was on hers. His lips, those gorgeous lips, soft, warm and pliant, were pressed against hers. His tongue was at the seam of her lips. His body was pressed against hers.

And it was *exquisite*.

Her knees began to buckle; his arm went around her waist as if he knew it. He pulled her into his body and angled his head, slipped his tongue into her mouth. His hand was warm against her neck, resting there as he kissed her, his thumb stroking her jaw. Her breasts pressed against his body, and she wondered, insanely, if he could feel her heart slamming fitfully against his chest. His lips moved lightly across hers, softly shaping them, tasting them as if they were some delicacy, and Prudence heard herself moan softly. When she did, the pressure of his mouth on hers intensified, his tongue moving deeper, sweeping against her teeth, her tongue, her cheeks. His hand cupped her face, his thumb gently stroking her cheek.

It was not Prudence's first kiss, but it may as well have been. She was sparkling. She actually felt as if she were sparkling. The air in her was being pushed out by her pounding heart, and she thought she might explode from the delectable torture of his kiss. He shifted against her, pressing her against the tree, and she was aware how intuitively and eagerly her body responded, curving into his, melting against him. He was hard and erect, strength and desire pressed against her and soaking into her. It was the most sensual thing that had ever happened to Prudence. It was the most exciting, provocative and arousing thing that she could possibly imagine. She didn't want it to end, to never end—

But then, suddenly, it was over.

Matheson lifted his head. His eyes swept her face as he ran the pad of his thumb over her bottom lip. "This is *precisely* the reason you should not be left alone on this road, Miss Cabot," he said hotly. "Scoundrels roam every corner of this earth. I don't like to say I told you so, but I told you so."

"Oh," she said.

"I didn't mean that to be a compliment to my sex," he snapped, and leaned to one side to peer around the tree. "I don't see him."

"Ah," she said, smiling up at him.

His gaze slid to her. He frowned. "Lord," he muttered, and stepped back, took her hand and pulled her away from the tree. "I think we best see about a horse or two."

"Pardon?"

He looked at her and squeezed her hand in his. "I can't very well leave you alone now, can I?"

"But I thought I reminded you of your sister," she said.

He frowned. "You don't remind me of anything but a temptress at the moment," he said brusquely.

Prudence's smile widened.

He shook his head. "You can ride, can't you? We best ride to…where is it you're going?"

"Himple," she said, unable to suppress her smile.

"Himple," he echoed, and with a roll of his eyes, he sighed as if that perturbed him, too.

CHAPTER SIX

THE PURCHASE OF horseflesh in this country was not inexpensive. Nor was it easy, especially when one had uninvited help.

Roan had specifically instructed Miss Cabot to remain outside while he went into the post house to inquire about horses. Naturally, she objected, citing his "foreign accent" as a possible deterrent to information. He cited her "unchaperoned and unmarried" situation as a possible deterrent to information, as well. Miss Cabot didn't like the reminder—no surprise in that—and it certainly didn't astonish him when she didn't obey him.

The women in his life never obeyed him—the women consisting primarily of his mother and his sister, and his romantic interests. None of them ever followed his sound advice, but none of them had ever perturbed him quite like Miss Cabot. Perhaps in part because she had a disconcerting habit of speaking when he really preferred she not speak.

Roan held out hope that Susannah Pratt would obey him, but he didn't know enough about her to say. She was pleasant and agreeable, and...and he kept searching for things to admire about her. Today, a little more earnestly than before.

He stepped into the post house, and was instantly

assailed by a number of mail sacks hanging from the ceiling. He batted them aside, stooped beneath them and walked across the creaking plank floors to the counter.

Two elderly gentlemen were sitting behind the counter. Neither of them moved as Roan approached, giving the impression that they'd been sitting there since the beginning of time and were one with their stools. It was a wonder they were not covered in cobwebs. One of them sported a snowy-white beard beneath a flat nose. The other had lost most of his hair, but his body had seen fit to allow him to retain a pair of woolly caterpillars for eyebrows.

"Good afternoon, gentlemen," he said.

The caterpillars nodded at him. The beard didn't seem to have heard.

"I was wondering if there might be any horseflesh in the area for purchase?"

"What you mean?" the beard asked. "You mean to buy a horse?"

Roan couldn't begin to guess what other meaning horseflesh might have here, but he said, "Yes. Two horses."

"Two," the beard said, in a tone that suggested he thought that was excessive.

"Yes. I need two," Roan said. "My ah…" He winced and nodded vaguely at the door. "My wife and I," he choked out. What else could he say? He couldn't very well suggest to these men he was traveling alone with an unmarried woman. Not that he cared a whit what they would think of him, but he could only imagine what they would think—and say—of Miss Cabot.

"Wife," said the caterpillars. He and the beard exchanged a look. Roan swallowed down a small swell of discomfort. Was it possible someone from the stage-coach had mentioned them? Perhaps suggested they keep an eye out for Miss Cabot?

"Two," the beard repeated to the caterpillars.

"Is there a problem?" Roan asked.

"Post coach will be through within the hour," the caterpillars said. "Wife can buy passage on the coach."

"Right," Roan said. "That would be a fine solution if she were not made ill by the movement of the coach."

Neither of the men spoke.

"She's delicate," he said, almost sputtering the word. Miss Cabot did not strike him as the least bit delicate.

"O'Grady. Lives down the road," the beard said. "He take them on that the post be done with."

As Roan was working out what those words put to-gether in that sequence were supposed to mean, the door opened behind him. The old men's eyes slid to the door.

"The missus," the caterpillars announced.

"Pardon?" Miss Cabot asked. "Good afternoon, sirs." She stepped up beside Roan and smiled at him. "Any luck?"

"Yes." He glanced sidelong at the two gentlemen and slipped his arm around her waist. Her gaze dropped to his hand. "I think you'd be more comfortable out-side—"

"Oh, I'm quite all right," she said brightly, and pushed his arm from her waist. "So you found us a horse!"

"It would seem Mr. O'Grady down the road might have a horse or two to spare."

"Wife ought to wait here. It's a ways," said the cat-erpillars.

"The *wife*—" Miss Cabot started, but Roan quickly interjected.

"Thank you!" he said loudly, and this time, he grabbed her and held firmly. "North, you said?" he asked even louder as he pulled Miss Cabot closer to him, into his side, and twisted her shoulders about so that her face was pushed into his chest as he turned her toward the door.

"Aye, north," one of the men said.

Roan opened the door and pushed Miss Cabot out before him.

Outside the post house, she whirled around. Her hands went to her waist, and she glared at Roan. "You told them I was your *wife*?"

"I told *you* to wait outside."

"I did wait outside! But then I wondered why I ought! How long does it take to ask after a horse, I ask you? Why did you tell them such a thing?" she asked, and batted at his arm like a kitten. "As if my situation isn't desperate enough, you would say that?"

"I didn't think it would do to announce that I was traveling with a young woman who was not my wife or my sister and, furthermore, someone I scarcely know."

"Oh," she said, the fire leaking out of her.

"Shall we go and find this O'Grady fellow, then?" he asked curtly, and dipped down to gather their bags. He walked on with them, not looking back.

A moment later, Miss Cabot appeared at his side, shuffling along in her unsuitable shoes.

"Where is this Mr. O'Grady?" she asked crossly after a half hour of walking north on the road.

"I'm not entirely certain."

They walked in silence. Every so often, Miss Cabot

would sigh. She pulled her bonnet up on her head once more, which Roan didn't care for—he liked looking at her.

After some time, she whimpered a little. "I can't… that is, I don't know if I—"

"There," Roan said, pointing. He could see a meadow ahead, and in it five horses grazed. "That must be it."

That news prompted her to quicken her pace, and she hobbled along at an impressive clip.

The meadow had been fenced with rocks, where Miss Cabot promptly sat, removed her shoes and sighed.

"Now the challenge will be to locate the man who has pastured these horses," Roan said. "He can't be far." He glanced down at his charge. "Can I trust you to remain here, on this fence, while I have a look about?"

"Yes," she said, her gaze on her feet.

Roan looked at her feet, too. Her stockings were damp with the fluid of her blisters. He squatted down beside her and took one foot in his hand.

"No!" she gasped. "What are you doing?"

He began to massage the bottom of her foot, and Miss Cabot's entire body sagged with relief.

"You really shouldn't," she said weakly as she inched her other foot next to the one he massaged. "It's inappropriate," she added, her eyes closed.

He smiled, enjoying her expression of bliss as he continued to massage her feet. "What is inappropriate is that you are trying to walk across England in these awful shoes."

"They are from France, Mr. Matheson," she said staunchly.

"What has that to do with anything? They are useless."

"Well, of course! They aren't meant for walking about," she said with breathless indignation, her eyes flying open.

Roan paused in his ministrations to her feet to argue, but Miss Cabot nudged him with her other foot to continue his work. "I never intended to walk across England in them," she said as he began to massage the second foot.

"You've no other shoes in your bag?"

"Yes," she said. "Silk ones. I suppose in America you all strap bits of cowhide to your feet to match the cowhide of your pants and strut about as if *that* were the fashionable thing."

Roan couldn't help himself—he laughed. "Pardon me," he said through a chuckle. "I never meant to impugn your fine French shoes."

"Hmm," she said, and closed her eyes again.

When he had massaged her second foot as thoroughly as the first, he let it go and stood up. Miss Cabot stretched her legs long and began to point and flex her feet.

"Now, then. Can I trust you?" he asked.

"Yes. I'm going with you," she said, her head tilted to one side as she examined her feet.

"What? No! You're not listening." He leaned over her, grasped her chin in his hand and forced her head up.

Miss Cabot smiled.

"No. You will stay here, on this fence, exactly where you are sitting, while I have a look about."

She calmly wrapped her fingers around his wrist and gave his hand a strong yank, removing it from her chin. She sat straighter, bringing her head so close to his that Roan could see the flecks of brown in her very fine hazel eyes. "I'm going. You're foreign and you don't know how to do things." And then she swayed back and turned her attention to her feet.

But Roan was confused. "I don't know how to do what, exactly?"

"Speak to crofters." She winced as she slid her feet into her shoes, ignoring his stare of disbelief.

"Stay," he said.

"No." She began to roll her ankles about, her small stocking feet pointing toward the road. Then she placed her hands delicately in her lap and looked up at him. "Do you intend to stand there and stare at me all day, or shall we find a horse?"

Roan sighed. He knew the look of a stubborn woman and held out his hand to her.

They walked across the pasture and studied the horses as they grazed the grass. They were not young horses, and one of them had a peculiar bump over his right hindquarter.

"Oh dear," Miss Cabot said.

But Roan thought they looked affable and strong enough. "They'll do."

At the other end of the pasture in a meadow just below, Roan spied a few cottages with smoke curling out of the chimneys and some barnlike structures. He paused.

"It's lovely," Miss Cabot said wistfully.

Roan shifted his gaze to her, uncertain what she thought was lovely. With the sun's angle just so, he could see the sprinkling of freckles across her nose. She looked remarkably fresh, considering all that had happened today.

"Don't you agree?"

Roan reluctantly turned his attention back to the scene before them. A pig rooted about one barnyard among a few hens. He could see a dog lying in the shade of a tree near one cottage, his head up, his snout lifted in Roan's direction. "*Lovely* is not the word I would use," he muttered as he watched the dog, sizing him up. "Wait here," he said, and carefully moved forward. The dog began to swat his tail as Roan moved closer, then leaped to all fours and sounded his alarm.

One of the cottage doors opened and a man walked out. He moved toward Roan like a well-fed cow lumbering toward the barn. As he neared, Roan could see that he was missing a tooth and an eye on the same side of his face, as if he'd been struck by something spectacular. Roan was curious to know what, but given that he had some important bartering to do; he thought the better of risking any sort of displeasure.

"Aye?" said the man with his one-eyed curiosity, looking past Roan to where Miss Cabot stood, her hands clasped behind her back, nudging a chicken that was pecking around her foot.

"Good day," Roan said. "Would you perhaps be willing to part with a pair of horses?"

The man looked to the pasture, where his five horses grazed. "Aye?" he said again, and Roan was momentarily confused—did the man misunderstand him, or did he mean for him to continue?

Roan opted for the latter. "And a pair of saddles if you can spare them. I'm to West Lee."

"Wesleigh? Put yourself on the southbound coach," the man said, waving in the direction of the village from where they'd just come, and turned as if that settled that.

"Not that West Lee. The north one."

"What, you mean Weslay?" the man asked, squinting at him. "Then why'd you say Wesleigh?"

Roan took a deep breath. For the life of him, he heard no difference. "I am in need of two horses to carry me north, and you, sir, have seven in your pasture. Are any of them for sale?"

The man said nothing for a long moment as he considered Roan. "Fifteen pound."

Roan blanched at that outrageous sum. "Fifteen pounds for two old horses?"

"No' for two, no, sir," the old man said patiently. "For one."

"One! That horseflesh," Roan said, gesturing blindly behind him, "is not worth a farthing!"

"Oh dear. They are certainly worth a *farthing*. Perhaps you mean a pound?"

It took a feat of monumental control that Roan could turn calmly toward Miss Cabot's voice, take in the nettles that clung to the bottom of her gown and say, calmly and quietly, "I *meant* a *farthing*." He turned back to the old man. "Will you excuse us for a moment?" And with that, he turned back to Miss Cabot, put his hands on her shoulders, twirled her about and marched her out of the old man's hearing.

"What in blazes are you doing? At least allow me to negotiate with that old goat."

"All right," she said easily. "But a farthing is not very much at all. Even a very old horse would be worth more than that. Shall I show you?" she asked, reaching for her reticule.

He put his hand on hers to stop her. "I *know* how much a farthing is worth. Do you think I alighted on English soil and set off merrily on my way without thought to the currency or the customs?"

"Well…" She shrugged and averted her gaze as if she thought exactly that. "You *did* offer a farthing," she murmured.

"I don't have time to explain the nuances of negotiation to you now," he said low. "I am going to step away and bargain for a horse. Not a word from you."

He turned back and strode to the old man, who had settled against a fence railing, the dog at his feet. "I'll give you ten pounds for two," Roan said, and reached into his pocket to withdraw his purse.

"Fifteen pound for one," the old man countered.

"That is preposterous," Roan said. "Do you think I mean to breed them? Produce a herd of swaybacked, used-up post horses?"

The old man shrugged.

"Perhaps twenty pounds is more to his liking?"

God help him but Miss Cabot had appeared again, standing at his elbow, smiling prettily at the old man. "It seems rather fair to me," she said. "Twenty pounds is really quite a lot of money. Our game warden, Mr. Cuniff, sold his cart for twenty pounds and do you know, he sent his youngest off to school? It's a small fortune, isn't it?"

Roan was set to send her back to her spot, perhaps even with a swift kick to her very shapely derriere, but the old man surprised him. He gave Miss Cabot a look that Roan was fairly certain was a smile. "Aye, quite a lot," he agreed.

"It would be very kind of you to accept twenty

pounds. My cousin," she said, gesturing to Roan, "hasn't a lot of money, really, and I, in particular, would be most grateful if you could see your way to agreeing to that price?" She smiled sweetly and looked remarkably angelic.

"Aye, for *you*, lass, I will agree to that price," the old man said.

Roan gaped at Miss Cabot. Had she really agreed to twenty pounds, ten pounds more than he had intended to pay? For two horses? At least Roan hoped it was two—as the old man had been speaking of only one, he wasn't certain. "For that price, we ought to have saddles, too," he said. "I can ride without, but one cannot expect my *cousin*," he said, looking askance at her, "to do the same."

"For that price, you have one horse, no saddle," the old man said.

"What?" Miss Cabot cried. "We agreed to two!"

"We agreed only to price, miss. Not the number of beasts. I said fifteen for one. You countered at twenty. That's twenty pounds for one horse."

She gasped and turned a wide-eyed gaze to Roan. "That's not at *all* what I meant!" She suddenly swung back around to the old man. "See here, sir," she said, pointing at him.

Roan managed to intercept her before she cost him any more money. "That's not fair—"

"No, no, no, no," he said quickly. "Don't speak. Don't say another word."

"But he—"

"He has the horses," Roan said, staring hard at her, hoping that she would read in his eyes how important it was that she not say anything else.

"But you can't agree," she whispered hotly.

"*You* already did," he whispered, just as hotly. He glanced over his shoulder at O'Grady, who was watching with some amusement. Roan pushed her a few steps back. He stood so close to her now that he couldn't help noticing how smooth her skin was, or how fair the hair at her temple, or the tiny lines of laughter around her eyes. And that mouth that he had so impetuously kissed looked fuller, more lush than it had under the sycamore tree.

Her dark golden brows suddenly snapped into a frown. "You're cross and so am I," she said, startling him back to the moment. "But I can't allow you to purchase a horse for that," she said, and lifted the reticule that dangled from her wrist.

"Put that away or I will take it. I do have my pride, Miss Cabot."

"And I have mine!"

"Trust me, *my* pride is greater and stronger than yours ever dreamed of being. If you don't put that silly bag away at once, I will not only sell you to Mr. O'Grady for a wife, I will also take a pig in exchange."

She gasped with shock. And then her lovely face melted into a glare of vexation so intent, he could almost feel the heat of it. She whirled away from him and marched off in the direction of the pasture.

One horse, one bridle, one rope and no saddle later—eighteen pounds all told, as the man had agreed to negotiate the price a bit—Roan lashed their bags on the back of a worn-out horse. He cupped his hands for Miss Cabot, who stomped her foot, heel down, into his linked palms.

He launched her up.

She landed on the horse's back with both legs on one side.

"Hike your hem," he said, gesturing to her gown. "Swing a leg over."

"I will do no such thing!"

"You can't ride in that fashion," he said impatiently. "There are *two* of us who must fit on this horse."

She refused to look at him as she situated herself on the horse, clinging to its mane.

Roan groaned. What was it about young women that made them so damned recalcitrant? It was as if the entire feminine race was out to prove they were capable of all the things men did. He put his hand on her thigh to gain her attention, noticing how small it was, how firm. "The day is wasting," he said.

"Then mount the horse, Mr. Matheson, and let us be on our way."

"Fine," he snapped. "But I will not tolerate your tears if you fall!" He threw himself up on his horse in one leap. The old beast stepped twice to the side, clearly unused to the weight on her back. Roan had to drape Miss Cabot's legs over his right thigh and put his arms around her to reach the reins. The horse gave a flick of its neck, and Miss Cabot slid into him, her shoulder just beneath his chin.

"Of all the…" She suddenly began to squirm, somehow managing to hike her leg up onto the horse's neck. She took several moments to situate herself, tugging at her hem, straightening her bonnet.

It was all too much, the feel of her body rubbing against him.

"You realize, don't you, that if we meet anyone, I will throw myself off this horse?" she said tetchily.

"If you keep up this squirming, I may toss you off myself," he bit out as he set the horse to a trot.

With a squeal of surprise, Miss Cabot bounced back, her bottom fitting far too snugly in between his legs.

This, Roan thought, had all the potential of being the most excruciatingly painful ride of his life. He had never in his life been turned so completely upside down by a woman. He never imagined that he could be compelled in any way to buy an old horse and ride with a beautiful woman in his lap. Frankly, it made Roan fear what else those pretty hazel eyes could compel him to do.

CHAPTER SEVEN

IT SEEMED AS if they rode hours down that narrow country lane without seeing anyone. Occasionally, across a meadow, Prudence would catch sight of a curl of smoke rising from some distant chimney or see a flock of sheep dotting a hillside. But it seemed as if the west country had been abandoned.

The horse—an old draft mare, Mr. Matheson said—plodded along. Nothing Mr. Matheson tried would encourage the beast to go faster. "I can hardly bear to think what I paid for this…nag," he said, the last word uttered with some difficulty as he tried his best to spur the horse on.

They stopped periodically to rest the horse. The late afternoon had turned quite warm; Prudence removed her bonnet and her spencer and tucked them into her valise along with her reticule.

Without her spencer, Prudence was even more keenly aware of Mr. Matheson at her back as they rode. Her skin grew damp from the heat between them. She could feel all the contours of his body, all the man bits, pressed against her hips. It was equally provocative and alarming. She knew it was wildly inappropriate to be seated against him as she was…but she liked it.

Prudence's mind wandered to salacious vignettes, her imagination stretching to see him without his clothing. The thoughts made her moist in a way that felt a little dangerous given the circumstances, but again, Prudence wasn't sure she cared. She'd never been so intimately close to a man and it seemed ridiculous to be concerned about propriety now, not after that kiss, not after sitting so close to him.

Not that Prudence was quite ready to toss aside all of her virtue.

Or so she told herself.

As her awareness of him only intensified, she became increasingly determined to draw attention to something else. Anything else.

She tried talking to him at first—*How do you like New York? Is it very big? Was the voyage very rough? How many sailors do you suppose it takes to man one of those ships?* But Mr. Matheson did not seem in a mood to talk, and soon he was responding to her many questions with monosyllabic grunts.

Prudence therefore resorted to humming. She was regarded as highly accomplished on the pianoforte, to which Prudence would modestly agree. Her singing, however, was not as pleasant. She began to hum to cover up the sound of her growling stomach and to chase away the shivers that ran up and down her spine every time a bobble in the horse's step pressed her more firmly into Mr. Matheson. She began to sing when she noticed how her legs ached from sitting so awkwardly for so long a period of time, but to move them would push her body deeper into his.

She had just burst into a near operatic voice when Mr. Matheson suddenly put his arm around her middle and squeezed it. "Please, I am begging you...*stop.*"

"My singing?"

"Your singing, your talking," he said pleadingly.

"I'm only trying to pass the time," she said, a bit wounded he did not appreciate her efforts. "I should like to halt," she said, feeling suddenly queasy.

"That's what *I* said."

"I mean the horse. I should like to get off."

"Soon," he assured her. "We can't be far."

"Now, Mr. Matheson!" she exclaimed, suddenly *quite* nauseated.

He reined the horse to a halt and lifted himself off its back. Prudence leaped before he could help her, but she hadn't counted on her legs being as useless as they were. They collapsed beneath her and she stumbled onto all fours.

"Miss Cabot!" Mr. Matheson hauled her up to her feet. He pushed her hair and bonnet away from her face. "Are you all right?"

"Yes, I'm fine, I'm *fine*," she said, batting his hands away. She put her hand to her belly.

"What is it?" he asked, his expression full of alarm. "Are you ill?"

"No!" She winced. "A bit."

He cupped her face with his palm. "You don't feel warm. Is it your head? Your belly?"

"I don't know," she said, pressing her hands to her abdomen.

"You need to eat something," he said firmly. "Where is the food you had earlier?"

"In my bag."

He left her and moved to the horse, unstrapping her bag. He unbuckled her valise and held it open to her; Prudence removed the cheesecloth from it and unwrapped it. They bent their heads over the cheesecloth at the same time and peered down at the meager portions that were left. There was a bit of cheese, two sweetmeats and the end of a stale loaf of bread. Prudence glanced up at him.

"Well," Mr. Matheson said sheepishly. "It seems I ate more than I thought I had. Eat what is here. We'll find a village soon and I'll see to it you are well fed."

"There is no next village," she said morosely as she nibbled a sweetmeat. "We've ridden all day and we've seen nothing. We must be near Brasenton Park."

"Near…?"

"The Earl of Cargyle's estate," she clarified. "It's situated between Ashton Down and Himple. Mrs. Bulworth told me it is a vast and untamed estate and this looks vast and untamed to me."

Mr. Matheson helped himself to a piece of cheese. "I came this way, remember? I would say we're a half hour from the next settlement at most."

"A half hour!" she exclaimed, wincing painfully. The thought of getting on that horse again was almost more than she could bear.

"Come," he said, and put his arm around her shoulders. "Think of the bath you can order the innkeeper to draw for you."

"A *bath*," she said dreamily.

Mr. Matheson helped her up to the back of the horse, then walked beside the lumbering beast, his hand on the bridle to lead them down the road.

It turned out that he was almost right—within a quarter of an hour, as the sun began to slide from the sky, they came upon a tavern. "Aha, food ahoy," he said, and gave Prudence a pat on her leg.

The tavern sat by itself on the road with no other

structures around it. Prudence couldn't imagine what sort of food it might have—the building looked rather dilapidated, what with its chipped masonry and sagging roof on the right side. There was a single window, which was cranked open.

As they neared the tavern, a man stumbled out of the small door and around the side of the building, disappearing up a well-worn path that led into the woods.

Prudence eyed the structure warily. She'd never thought of herself as particular, but the thought of eating anything that had been cooked in that tavern turned her stomach a bit. "I'm not hungry," she said anxiously. "There's no need to go in."

"Don't speak to anyone, do you hear?" Mr. Matheson asked, ignoring her. "If someone approaches you, take this horse and ride. You can ride, can't you?"

"Yes, of course I can. But, really it's not necessary—"

"No buts, Prudence. Just wait."

He strode off. Prudence might have argued more firmly for him to continue on, but she'd been momentarily distracted by the way he'd said her given name. As if they were friends. And it sounded so *pretty* when he said it. Not stiff, as she'd always thought her name to sound on the tongues of Englishmen, as if the *pru* stuck in their throats. When Mr. Matheson said it, her name sounded sweet. Easy. Happy.

He disappeared inside, and she slid off the horse, taking care to land properly this time, and stood beside the old girl, stroking her neck and watching the door of the tavern. She could hear laughter within, the low voices of men, the shrill voice of a woman. Prudence stepped back into the shadows, her pulse quickening. She had a bad feeling about this place. What was taking him?

The door burst open and Mr. Matheson came striding outside, his pockets bulging, his expression dark.

"What's the matter?" she cried.

He didn't answer; he grabbed her by the waist without warning and practically tossed her onto the horse's back, and in what seemed like almost the same movement, acrobatically put himself behind her. Wrapping one arm tightly around her waist and taking the reins in the other, he whipped the horse about and yelled, "Ha!" at it, sending it into a jarring gallop. Prudence shrieked with surprise and fright as the horse began to move much faster than it had previously allowed was even capable. He drew her hard against him as the horse ran with an uneven gate, bouncing them about like small children on its back.

The horse quickly slowed to ambling however, apparently preferring the slower pace, no matter how much Mr. Matheson begged and cajoled.

Prudence turned and glanced over his shoulder, expecting to see riders close on their heels. But there was no one. "What happened?" she asked. "Why are we fleeing?"

"I didn't receive a very warm welcome," he said. "I thought it best not to linger." He reined the horse off the road, turning her down a path that ran alongside a flowing brook.

"Where are we going?" she asked, peering into the waning light of the day.

"We are stopping for the night," he said firmly. "The horse is spent."

"But...but there is no inn! No shelter!" Prudence

cried, alarmed. She hadn't even considered the possibility of it—he'd said a village was close at hand.

"What is it, Prudence? Have you never slept beneath the stars?" he asked, sounding a bit jovial.

"No!" she replied, aghast. She could feel his chuckle reverberate against her back as he reined the old horse to a stop and hopped off her back.

"Come down," he said, and without waiting for her reply, he lifted her off. When he had her on the ground, he put his hands in his pockets and removed a cheesecloth from one, and an old, oil-stained flagon from the other. Prudence stared at the offerings. "Meat and bread," he said, handing her the cheesecloth. "And ale."

"You *bought* it?"

"Not exactly," he said with a crooked smile. "I'll say only that a barmaid offered to help me." He had a gleam in his eye. "Help me gather wood for a fire."

She gathered wood, her thoughts filling with explicit images of just how he might have convinced a barmaid to give him these things.

Mr. Matheson proved himself very efficient in the making of a camp. He rubbed sticks together to spark kindling as she'd once seen a gamekeeper do, and in moments, they had a roaring little campfire. He removed their bags from the horse and slapped her rump, sending her downstream to graze and drink. He laid his coat on the ground for Prudence to sit. She rummaged in her bag and found her spencer, and donned that, then drew her knees up to her chest and sat before his fire. She watched him remove his gun from his boot and stuff it into the back of his trousers.

He speared the meat on a stick and held it over the

fire to warm it. Grease dripped and sputtered in the fire. He handed Prudence the stick. "Eat it," he said.

Prudence did as he bade her. The gristly, greasy meat was perhaps the best she'd ever tasted—she hadn't realized how ravenous she was.

He offered her the flagon of ale. She eyed that with a bit more trepidation.

"You do drink ale, don't you?" he asked.

She'd drunk ale perhaps twice in her life. "Yes," she said, and took the flagon from him.

The ale was much better than the meat. It sluiced warm through her, fortifying her against the chill that was beginning to settle around them.

When they'd devoured the food he'd managed to get them, Prudence indelicately wiped the back of her hand across her mouth. "I'll just wash my hands," she said, and moved to the brook. She squatted beside it to clean her hands, and in doing so, looked down at the pale blue gown she was wearing. Lord, it looked as if she'd found it in the woods. Patches of dirt and horse hair were smeared across the muslin, and nettles clung to her hem. She adored this travel gown, but doubted that even Hannah, her mother's longtime maid and caregiver, could remove the stains from it.

She washed her face as best she could, pushing errant strands of her hair away. It felt as if she had a bird's nest in her hair, and she thought she would at least find the ivory combs in her bag and repair it as best she could.

When she came back to the fire, Mr. Matheson was lying on his side, his legs stretched long. He'd been watching her, she realized, and his eyes had taken on a different sheen. They seemed darker to her now.

Stormier, perhaps. Whatever was different, it made Prudence shiver. She lowered herself to his coat, sitting on her knees. Mr. Matheson didn't speak; he rose up and touched the corner of her mouth. It was a small touch, hardly a touch at all, but his finger lingered there, and his gaze didn't leave hers, and the touch, that look, were all a shock of light through Prudence. She felt a bit outside of herself. She was driven by something she couldn't even name, but it had to do with that kiss under the tree in the village, it had to do with the way he was looking at her now. It had to do with a yearning so deep and vast that she felt adrift in it.

She wrapped her fingers around his wrist as far as they would go and pulled his hand from her mouth. And then Prudence shocked herself by taking his forefinger in between her lips. She touched the tip of her tongue to it like a candy and sucked lightly.

Mr. Matheson drew a long breath. His gaze fell to her mouth and lingered there, his expression changing. He looked hungry, as if he could devour her as easily as he'd devoured the bread. Prudence's heart began to flitter in her chest. As astounding a thought as it was, she thought she would like that.

Mr. Matheson slowly pulled his finger from her mouth. He gripped her fingers, squeezing them, as if warning her. "Sit back now."

But Prudence didn't move. She was mesmerized by the look in his eye, by the set of his mouth.

His eyes dropped to her lips. "Unless you are prepared to face the consequences, *sit back now*."

Prudence knew what consequences he meant, and it frightened her. Not because she feared them, but because she didn't fear them at all. What she feared was her willingness to ignore propriety and virtue. Hadn't she caused enough trouble for one day? But what was the point in limiting herself now? Perhaps more important, the idea that she would never have this chance again began to snake its way through her thoughts.

Mr. Matheson sensed her hesitation to move back as he'd commanded her, and shook his head. "You're careless, aren't you, just like my sister."

"I am not your sister," she said to his mouth.

A lopsided smile of appreciation appeared on his lips. "No, you're not." His gaze wandered down, to her spencer. "Have a care, Prudence. There will be a young man who comes along—"

Mr. Matheson suddenly scrambled to his feet, squinting into the shadows that had moved in around them.

"What is it?" Prudence asked, jumping to her feet, too.

He put a finger to his lips, indicating she should be silent and stepped forward, scanning the trees around them. She saw him tense just as three men emerged from the woods, spread out a bit, so that there was no possibility of running past them. Prudence's heart began to pound.

"Wha' have we here?" The one who spoke was tall as a tree and was missing some teeth. "A lovers' tryst?" The other two men, who were just as bedraggled as the tall one, laughed.

Prudence felt ill. The horrible tales that Mercy used to tell her were rearing up in her memory.

"Good evening, sirs," Mr. Matheson said, bracing his legs apart, his hands fisted at his sides. "I'd ask you to dine, but as you can see, we've nothing to share."

The tall man's gaze slid to Prudence. "Don't ye, indeed?" he drawled as his gaze moved over her.

Prudence thought she might vomit. She must have made a sound of distress, because Mr. Matheson gripped her arm and pulled her to stand behind him. "As I said, we've nothing to share," he reiterated, his voice deep and angry.

The tall man moved closer, and his two cohorts circled around them. One of them stooped to pick up Prudence's valise.

"No!" she gasped, then heard the sickening thud of fist on bone. Mr. Matheson had apparently hit the tall man squarely in the face when she'd cried out, knocking him to the ground. He leaped on him before he could gain his feet.

Prudence shrieked as the two men began to roll about on the ground trading punches, rendered almost immobile with her fear for Mr. Matheson's safety. Especially when the tall man's two companions pulled Mr. Matheson off him.

But Mr. Matheson was not ready to end his fighting. He took a swing at one of the two men, connecting with his jaw with such a crack of bone on bone that Prudence thought she might be sick. That man tumbled to the ground, his hands covering his face. Mr. Matherson continued to fight all three of those men, managing to strike them all and to dance just out of their reach. In the melee, his pistol fell and scudded across the grass. Prudence dived for it, picking it up before any of the other men had noticed.

But tackling three grown men at once was all too much for Mr. Matheson—and with some difficulty, the two men finally caught hold of Mr. Matheson's arms and held him while the tall man hit him in the stomach.

Prudence panicked then, fearing Mr. Matheson would be killed, and without thinking, she screamed.

That scream brought all four heads around as if they thought someone else had joined them.

"Are you mad!" Prudence shouted at them. "Do you think his lordship will waste a single moment finding who has done this to his guest?"

The tall man's fist froze midswing. He slowly turned toward her.

"That's right," she said heatedly, nodding with great enthusiasm as she hid the gun in the folds of her gown. "This man is the guest of Lord Cargyle!"

"Prudence, don't—" Mr. Matheson tried, but one of the men ended whatever he might have said with a punch to the ribs.

The tall man laughed. "Cargyle, you say, pretty? He be *miles* from here," he said, slowly advancing on her. "No one to hear yer screams."

Prudence couldn't catch her breath. She suddenly brought the gun up, pointing it at the tall man before he took another step. "Or yours," she croaked.

The gun served its purpose—he hesitated and lifted his hands. "Put the gun down, pretty," he said. "Ye don't know how to use it—"

"But I do," she said. Her voice was hoarse with fear. "My father, the Earl of Beckington, made sure of it."

With a hoot of delight, the man looked back at his companions. "Beckington, is it?" he repeated, and bowed grandly...but his gaze was on her gun.

Prudence cocked it as Mr. Matheson had shown her how to do.

"Prudence, *don't*—"

"Shoot him?" she finished quickly. Her heart was pounding so hard now that she was shaking. "Let him go," she said to the tall man. "Let him go now, or I will shoot you square between the ears!"

"Will you now," the tall man said, and grinned in a lascivious and disgusting manner. She knew instinctively that he sensed her fear. He began to move toward her again. "I like a lass with a bit o' fire in her."

"Prudence!" Mr. Matheson shouted at her, which was followed by another sickening thud of fist on bone.

Prudence was frightened, but she was also very angry. She was suddenly reminded of the lesson Lady Chatham, a grand dame of Mayfair society, had told Prudence and the other debutantes who would be presented at court. "It will not do to look as if you might faint," Lady Chatham had said. "Clasp your hands at your back and squeeze them tight to keep from shaking."

Prudence did that now, clasping her hands so tightly around that gun that it felt as if the metal was cutting into her skin. She lifted her chin, looked the man in the eye, just as she'd met the king's eye. "Take one more step, and I will shoot you, sir. That is your only warning." She sighted him with the gun pointed directly at his head.

The tall man's gaze narrowed. He studied her, clearly debating. "Give me the gun." He lunged for it at the same moment Prudence fired. She couldn't say what part of him she hit, only that she'd hit him— he screamed and fell to the ground. His companions dropped Mr. Matheson and ran for him. In the chaos,

Mr. Matheson managed to get to his feet. He struck out at one of the men with a knife, slashing across his arm.

"Get him up, get him up!" one of the men shouted, and they helped the tall one to his feet. He was clutching his arm as they half dragged, half pushed him back into the woods.

Prudence stood there, the gun pointed ahead of her, trembling badly.

"Prudence? Put the gun down," Mr. Matheson said hoarsely.

Her gaze moved from the trees to him. He was on two feet, weaving. The knife he'd pulled from the air clattered to the dirt. And then he collapsed down to his knees. "Oh! *Oh!*" she cried and scrambled for him, catching him before he toppled over, sinking to her knees with her arms around his shoulders.

"That's right," Mr. Matheson sputtered, wincing with pain, his arm across his abdomen. "Run, cowards."

She couldn't make out all of Mr. Matheson's injuries in the low light of the fire, but one eye was swelling and his nose was bloodied.

He wrapped his fingers around her arm, and she noticed the state of his knuckles. "Help me up. I don't want to die sprawled here like a drunk," he said, wincing as if the words caused him pain.

"You can't die," she said frantically, and with both hands, grabbed his arm, pulling him up. "I won't allow it! Please, Mr. Matheson, please!"

He managed to keep himself upright and grinned at her as she helped him stagger to his feet. "See? Right as rain," he said breathlessly, and threw a heavy arm around her shoulders. "Where's the gun? We should keep it close, I think. And the knife, if you can find it."

She dipped down and picked up the gun. Mr. Matheson swayed unsteadily as he made sure it wouldn't fire. "Well done, Prudence Cabot," he said. "I think you saved our hides. Speaking of which, where is the nag?"

Prudence looked frantically about. "She's here, still eating."

"Smart thieves—they knew better than to take her." He stumbled; Prudence caught him with an arm around his waist. She managed to drape his arm over her shoulder. She struggled under his weight but was able to direct him to a tree and help him down. He settled with his back against it. His breathing was shallow as he attempted a smile for her. "I didn't leave an arm or a leg behind, did I?"

She shook her head. "It's my fault," she said, swallowing back tears. "It's my fault we ever came upon that tavern."

"I won't argue that," he said, and stroked her cheek. "But fortunately for you, I don't hold a grudge."

"I'm so sorry, Mr. Matheson," she said, her voice full of the despair she felt.

He groaned and closed his eyes. He must hate her now for having stolen onto the stagecoach. If she hadn't, he would be safely on his way to Weslay, and she would be waiting for Mr. Bulworth to send his man for her. Prudence felt awfully stupid—what had seemed like such an amusing and harmless stand against propriety this morning now seemed the most frightening and foolhardy thing she'd ever done. She was very fortunate they'd not killed Mr. Matheson. *Stupid, stupid girl!*

"Give me some whiskey, will you?" he asked. "I have some in my bag."

Prudence scrambled up and hurried to the place she'd

last seen the man with her bag. But there were no bags. She whirled around, trying to see past the light of the fire. "They're gone!" she cried. "They took our bags!"

"Goddamn it," he uttered.

She picked up the knife and returned to his side, knelt beside him and put her hands in the pockets of his coat, which was still lying on the ground. She found a handkerchief and used it to dab at the blood around his nose. "You need a doctor."

"I'm sure I look much worse than I truly am. Horrible, is it? Terrifying?"

"Terrifying," she agreed, and tried again to wipe the blood from his nose, but he caught her wrist and pulled her hand away, laced his fingers with hers as he rested his head back against the tree.

"I'm so very sorry, Mr. Matheson," she whispered again.

"Yes, well," he said, wincing deeply as he moved to one side, his hand going to his ribs. "I don't know if I'll die tonight, but if I do, I would like to leave this earth hearing my given name on your lips."

"You won't die."

"That's certainly my sincerest hope, but one can never know when hospitality is extended so violently. I once heard of a fellow who dropped dead two days after a fight."

"Two days!"

"You see? My demise could come at any moment. So give this dying man his wish and say it, Prudence," he said, taking her hand in his. "Say my name."

"Roan," she said. "But you won't die, Roan. You *won't*."

"Ah, at last," he said, and smiled as he closed his

eyes. He rested their hands on her knee. "You astonished me tonight. Very brave and clever on your feet."

Prudence smiled sheepishly. She hadn't been brave, she'd been rash. She looked at his hand atop hers, battered and bloodied. "But…but what am I to do now?" she whispered as she tried to clean the blood from his knuckles.

"Do?" He opened one eye, put his hand on her shoulder, gripping it, pulled her forward, then drew her near enough that he could put his arm around her. He tugged her into his body and held her there, his weight sagging against hers. He set the gun and handed it to her. "You fire if they come back, and this time, hit him square between the eyes, will you?" He sighed and closed his eyes. "In the meantime, I'll think on it."

"They'll kill us if they come back."

He said nothing.

Prudence sat up to look at him. "Mr. Matheson? Roan?" She jostled his shoulder. It was no use—his eyes were closed. The man had fainted. Or had he died?

CHAPTER EIGHT

ROAN WAS BENT over the neck of his favorite horse, Baron, flying as fast as the stallion could run across the fields at his family's home in New York. He was certain he would be too late to warn the lumber train that the wheel would come off the wagon as they headed down into the Hudson Valley. But he and Baron were presented with obstacle after obstacle—fallen trees, swollen rivers, a fence too high for Baron to vault. As he neared the road, Roan saw that the wagons had already started down the hill. He opened his mouth to bellow at them at the same time the strong odor of manure enveloped him—

Roan awoke with a grunt.

He blinked against the dark light, his gaze finding the embers of what was left of the fire. He wrinkled his nose at the offensive smell, courtesy of the nag, who stood only a few feet away. Roan grimaced at the stiffness in his body; the shooting pain in his side. That damn Goliath might have broken his rib. But Roan's heart and his lungs appeared to be working. Nothing more than a few painful bruises.

He'd live, then, which was more than he could say for that tree of a man. He wasn't sure where the bullet had struck him, but there had been enough blood for Roan to know he wouldn't come back for more.

He glanced to his left, and his gaze landed on Prudence curled onto her side, her back to him, the gun still in her hand. Her golden hair spilled around her. He leaned closer, squinting—she had leaves in her hair. He wondered idly what had become of the bonnet with the bothersome feather.

Roan watched her sleeping, the slow rise of her chest, the gentle fall.

Now he felt something else, too. Desire—pure, hot and urgent. He put his hand on her hip.

Prudence came up with a gasp, rolling onto her back, waving the gun about. Roan caught it. "It's all right," he said.

When she saw that it was he who had disturbed her sleep, she let go, sighed sleepily and pushed herself up to sit beside him. "You're alive."

"I can't tell from the tone of your voice if you are pleased or not."

"I'm relieved. I keep hearing noises, and I think it's them, come back to rob us."

Roan winced again, but this time at his inability to have provided her with the slightest bit of security. "We're safe," he said. "Our bags are the only thing of value. They won't be back." Even if they did return, Roan had no doubt he could and would squeeze the life from them with his bare hands in spite of his battered body. He gave Prudence a sympathetic smile. "I know you will defend me most ardently," he said. "I like that about you, Prudence Cabot."

She clucked her tongue at him. "I was terrified," she said. "I thought they were going to kill you."

So had he, but Roan didn't like to think about that. It reminded him of a time he was in Canada, set upon by some men over a card game. He thought he would die that night, too, as the men had come seemingly from nowhere for him and Beck, brandishing sticks. It was a miracle that he and Beck had emerged from that encounter alive—and able to walk. They'd lost their horses, however, and had it not been for the kindness of a widow and her very lovely daughter, well…

Roan didn't want to think of that now. He was glad that he hadn't met his demise tonight. Very glad, indeed.

"You must be thirsty," Prudence said, and began to pick herself up.

"I'm all right," he said, and smiled reassuringly. "Americans are a hardy lot. I refuse to allow a few English brutes to beat the spirit out of me." Even if that was exactly what the Englishmen had done. "Why don't you sleep?" he suggested to her. "I'll keep the eye that's not swollen open."

Prudence smiled wearily. With the weak light from the embers, she looked even younger than he'd originally thought. How old was she? Twenty years? Younger? He got up, put wood on the fire and stirred the embers beneath it.

She rubbed her temples. Her hair, which in this new light looked even more spun of gold, had come completely out of its pins. When she noticed him looking at her she said, "I hope you can forgive me."

"Forgive you?"

"For this," she said. She drew her knees up under her gown and wrapped her arms around them, resting her chin on her knees. "If I had joined Dr. Linford as I was supposed to have done, you would have been on the public coach and never would have encountered those wretched men."

"What's done is done," he said, wincing as he moved his back against the tree once more, settling there. "No point in dwelling on it. We can only go forward from here."

She idly played with a stick beside her foot. "Admit it. You wish you'd never laid eyes on me."

"I will admit no such thing because it is not true," Roan said. "But satisfy my curiosity, will you? Why did you really avoid Linford? Were your sisters' actions really so awful?"

She groaned. "It's really too mortifying to confess."

"It can't be more mortifying than sleeping on a riverbank, can it?"

She smiled. "That is a very good point." She pushed locks of golden hair from her face and considered her stick a long moment. "I suppose it all began when my stepfather, the Earl of Beckington, contracted consumption," she said. "Augustine—he's my stepbrother—was to inherit all. He's very generous, but his fiancée did not fancy sharing the family fortune with four stepsisters who were not married and had no current prospects."

Roan winced again, but this time, it was in sympathy for the man who would have a wife and four unmarried sisters. He could not imagine the amount of money that would be spent on shoes alone.

"My mother was very little help to us, unfortunately. That was the same time she began to first exhibit the signs of madness."

"She's mad?" Roan asked, uncertain if Prudence meant it in the literal sense of the word.

"As a cuckoo bird," Prudence solemnly confirmed.

"We tried to hide it, for we all knew that once society discovered it, things would be said. Gentlemen would fear that madness might somehow run in our blood and be introduced into their children through any daughter of hers."

"Do you believe that?" he asked. He'd never really thought of it before now. But then again, he very rarely thought of marriage.

Prudence shook her head. "My mother's madness began with a carriage accident. There's no history of it otherwise, but it hardly matters. No one among the Quality would risk it. Added to that, we were without our stepfather to provide a proper dowry. Suddenly, everything looked quite impossible for us."

"So that's the scandal," Roan said. "Your mother's madness. That's why you said your sisters were married unconventionally. Someone not in keeping with your situation, is that it?"

"I wish that's all there was to it," Prudence said, sighing. "The scandal began with my older sisters, Honor and Grace. Once it became clear that the earl would die, and Augustine would marry Monica Hargrove, and our mother was mad, they had these perfectly ridiculous ideas for how to gain offers of marriage." Prudence sounded perturbed by this. "Their idea was to marry before anyone discovered our woes. They reasoned that if they hooked a rich husband, they'd be able to help my mother, as well as Mercy and me when we were cast out of society," she said with mock darkness.

Roan shrugged. "Sounds oddly reasonable."

"Perhaps in theory," Prudence agreed. "But in practice, it was scandalous. Honor proposed marriage quite publicly to a wealthy man of illegitimate birth, and

Grace attempted to trap a man into marriage and did so very successfully—only she trapped the *wrong* man."

Roan laughed.

Prudence did not. "All of this is well-known in London and the Quality, you know, and as a result of their actions, and my mother's madness, and our lack of dowry, Mercy and I are not considered a very good match. Mercy hardly cares—she is quite talented with her art, and she is determined to be an artist of note. She swears she will never marry. Lord Merryton paid a dear price to have her admitted into a prestigious school to study, and Mercy is beside herself with joy. She says she is perfectly content to travel the world and create beautiful art. She doesn't concern herself with society and advantageous marriages."

"Do you?" Roan asked.

Prudence's shoulders slumped. "I don't know. I suppose I do. It's been four years since Grace trapped the Earl of Merryton into marriage. No one has shown the slightest interest in me since that time, and I think I will die of tedium. And to make matters worse, I've resided at Blackwood Hall for the past two years, which is as remote a place as this," she said, gesturing around her. "I care for my mother. I am occasionally invited to this evening or that, but I have no society to speak of. I am only two and twenty and I am destined to be put on the shelf."

"That can't be true—"

"But it is," Prudence said. "You can't possibly understand my situation, I think, but that is why I put myself on that coach today. I wanted…" She paused and drew a deep breath. "I wanted to know what it feels to *live*. I've always been good and decent and I've followed all the rules, and it didn't matter. Honor and Grace are married, and they love their husbands and they have beautiful children. Mercy has set her sights on something else entirely. All I ever wanted was to marry and have a family of my own, and it appears I can't have that. Now all I want is to know what life feels like outside the walls of Blackwood. I want to know adventure. I want to feel excited about something. I want to know all those things I've lost since I've been shut away."

Roan didn't know how to assure her. He knew nothing of the way marriages were made in England, but he understood her. In New York, they'd had a time of it settling Aurora on one gentleman who met with their satisfaction of being worthy of her and their business interests, so he could see how something like this might affect a woman like Prudence. Even he was prepared to sacrifice for the sake of his family's prosperity and standing.

Prudence was watching him, her luminescent gaze seeking reassurance, he supposed. He wanted to say something to soothe her. "Life is... It is what you make it," he tried, the words sounding inadequate to him.

"Yes?" She leaned slightly forward, as if she feared she might miss a piece of valuable advice that might turn her life about.

How he wished he could give her that. "What I mean is that life doesn't come to you. You can't sit in some parlor and wait for it to appear at your door."

Prudence nodded as if to agree with what he said.

"No matter what your circumstance, it is up to *you* to create the life you want to live."

"Do you truly think so?"

"Of course I do." Roan lived by those words every

day. Yet he was keenly aware he would never offer such advice to Aurora. She was a year older than Prudence, and he would never give that girl as much as an inch, knowing that she'd take a mile. But here he sat, offering it to Prudence, essentially suggesting to her that what she'd done today was not only all right, but perhaps even justifiable given her circumstances.

Did Aurora have the same, unfulfilled desires as Prudence? Should he find her behavior justified? Roan was strangely uncertain.

Which made him a worse scoundrel than he'd realized. He knew as well as he knew the pain in his side that he advised Prudence Cabot to follow her desire because he liked her. He *liked* that she had boarded his coach because she'd found him appealing. He liked that she had been with him today, nestled tightly between his legs. He liked the way she'd fearlessly brandished a gun and shot that cretin, in spite of the fact she might have seen them both killed.

He had enjoyed this day of adventure with her. It had made him long for his own freedom of choice. Of course Roan had his freedom—he could do whatever he liked. But of late, he'd felt the weight of responsibility. Of needing to give his word to his father and John Pratt. To be fair, he hadn't promised Susannah anything at all other than to return soon…but all else was understood. It was assumed by everyone he would formally propose marriage to her when he returned and had settled Aurora.

Both he and Aurora were bound to marry for the sake of the family.

He looked at Prudence with her hazel eyes and golden hair and plush lips and said, "I think you should live as you want." It wasn't a lie—it was everything that made him who he was.

Prudence's response shocked him. Completely and utterly *shocked* him. Because the moment he uttered those words, Prudence half lunged, half fell across him, landing awkwardly against his chest, her lips finding his. Pain shot through him and he sucked in his breath, but Prudence was not deterred. She kissed him as ardently as he'd kissed her under the sycamore tree.

He hadn't meant she was to seek *this*. He put his hands on her arms and pushed her back, grimacing.

"Oh!" she exclaimed at the sight of him, and stroked his face, her fingers trailing hot across his skin, touching his bruised lip and swollen eye. "Did I hurt you? I meant to… I thought I'd—"

"I know what you thought," he said, and put his hand on her hip, pushing her to her side. "You thought to take advantage of a poor, disabled man." He moved her onto her back, rolling with her so that he was on his side. "Never underestimate a man's strength, no matter if he's been injured," he said. "And *never* doubt that every man is a scoundrel, no matter how he appears. Every last one of us is bursting with desire for women like you. Look at me now, Pru, look carefully, because this is how pure desire appears. I should leave you be. I shouldn't touch you, but I am bursting with desire."

He moved over her, kissing her, and when he did, Prudence made a kittenish sound that sluiced through him. Roan's pain began to slough away—he felt nothing but raw want rising up in him. His blood began to percolate, even as he scolded himself for it. He was the man he despised. He'd made promises, given his word…but he was weak. He was as weak as a toddler with a jar of candy when a woman as beautiful as Prudence lay beneath him. The devil in him urged him on, encouraged by her lusty response.

Prudence's arms went around his neck as she kissed him, her tongue twirling around his, her lips so soft beneath his. This was what he'd warned her of. "You want adventure, Prudence Cabot?" he rasped as he moved his mouth across her cheek to her ear, grunting a bit at the pain that sudden direction had caused him.

"Yes," she whispered. "Yes, Roan, I do."

She could not have said anything more arousing to him; Roan growled as he nuzzled her neck. Prudence made a noise in her throat that sounded a bit like the cooing of a dove, and it only made his blood run hotter. He slowly, painfully, moved his hands down her body, finding her breasts and ribs, her waist.

Prudence grabbed his head between her hands and kissed him, nibbling at his lip. "Ow," he muttered, and she quickly moved her feathery little kisses to his cheeks, his swollen eye. Roan dipped his hand into the bodice of her gown, his fingers closing around the warm flesh of her breast. He didn't want to stop, never wanted to stop caressing her buttery skin.

He trailed kisses down her neck to her chest, pressed his mouth against the swell of her breast and thought he'd never tasted flesh so sweet. She was divine, as soft and pleasurable as any woman. The night was swirling around them, darkness and milky light spilling across her skin, casting shadows that moved and captured him. He slowly inched down, following the trail of moonlight on her, until he found the hem of her gown. He pushed it up, his hand finding warm, soft flesh beneath.

Above him, Prudence was breathing hard, her chest

rising and falling with each full breath. Her hair was a wild tangle of leaves and curls. She was quite a mess, and yet he'd never been so aroused by the sight of a woman as he was by her on the ground under the tree.

He kissed the soft inside of her knee. He forgot his aches and pains, his mind having skipped ahead to thoughts of moving inside her.

Prudence sighed, long and soft and full of pleasure. The sound of her pleasure sent him barreling down some invisible slide, tumbling into a night that shattered around him. His hands moved on her body, one on her breast, which he'd somehow managed to free from her gown. Another hand skimmed her bare leg, sliding up, slipping in between them and into the slick folds of her sex. He heard his groan, heard the ache of want in it. He nipped at the flesh of her thigh now, while his hand caressed her. Her scent wrapped around his head, made his mouth water, made his body pulse with hunger for her flesh. He couldn't bear it; he managed to rise up, somehow balancing on his arms above her, nudging in between her legs. She looked up at him with a lusty smile.

"I warned you of scoundrels, didn't I?" he said gruffly.

"I don't recall," she said, and with the back of her hand, stroked his face.

Roan groaned and bent his head, taking her breast in his mouth, then moving down her body once more, pushing her gown up to her waist, his hands sliding under her hips. Prudence's knees came up on either side of him, and as he sank between them, and touched his mouth to her sex, she gasped, arching her back. She grabbed his hands, wrapping her fingers tightly around them as he plunged his tongue into her body like a starving man, then feathered her with little strokes, circling around, nipping and teasing her.

Prudence groaned with pleasure, the sound of it so primal and raw, that Roan worried he would die of the longing he'd never felt so deeply or intently as this. He was desperate to be inside of her, but just as desperate not to be the heathen who would ruin her on the banks of a brook. No matter how desperately he wanted to. No matter how desperately she wanted him to.

When Prudence cried out at the exquisite agony of his tongue, he closed his mouth around her, lightly nibbling her with his teeth, and then sliding his tongue across her again.

She sobbed with pleasure, lifting her hips to him, arching her back and her neck as she reached the pinnacle of her desire. Roan held her steady, determined that she would wring every last moment from this. Prudence whimpered once more, then came crashing back to earth. She threw her arm over her eyes and panted. "You really *are* a scoundrel," she said, and groped for him in the dark.

"You really are beautiful," he said. He gingerly made his way to her side, settling on his back.

Prudence rolled into him, her arm pillowing her head. "That was…that was *astonishing*," she said. Her smile of delight seemed to radiate the night. "I had no idea," she said, more to herself. She rested her head on his shoulder.

Roan tried to think of what he ought to say at a moment like this, at her awakening to the power of her sex over man. But as he could scarcely grasp how he felt about it, he couldn't think of any platitude or words of warning that seemed to fit the occasion. As it turned out, it hardly mattered—Prudence was at last asleep, confident in the circle of his arms. So confident, in fact, she snored lightly.

Unfortunately, Roan was very much awake now, his body aching in more ways than one. *What have I done?* He'd been lost in a moment—he could have impregnated her, for God's sake. He was the man he'd warned Aurora against. *Susannah*...

Ah, hell.

The sooner he saw Prudence to Himple, the better. Roan felt even more protective of her now, and much more desirous of her, too, feelings that were more fraught with danger for him personally than anything this country might show him. Thieves and highwaymen were lambs compared to the fear he held for his own desire. He was anxious to put Prudence on a coach, to get his hands on the little hoyden Aurora, and be gone from England before he did something he truly regretted.

Roan fumbled for his purse to see how much cash he had. He patted down his pockets.

There was no purse.

He eased Prudence onto her back and sat up, patting himself down with both hands. *No.* He moved on all fours, feeling around the ground where he'd fought those men, knowing it was a futile search. Those wretched men had taken it from him along with their bags.

He muttered a vile curse against Englishmen under his breath. He had to think. But what he thought of was his auburn-haired, brown-eyed hellion sister. No, it wasn't fair to blame her for the events of this day, and yet that was precisely with whom Roan was angry. Had

Aurora come home when she was supposed to, none of this would ever have happened.

But that was the way it was with Aurora and it had always been so. Aurora enjoyed the attentions of young men. Like the woman lying beside him now, she was uncommonly pleasing to the eye. She had a spirit and look that turned men into idiots, promising her whatever Aurora wanted to hear. Who had she met here? What had he promised her?

But Roan had believed that Aurora truly cared for Mr. Gunderson. Gunderson was a quiet and studious man, and may have seemed an odd choice for Aurora at first glance. But he adored her as men were wont to do and had all the other requisites required for a husband: he came from wealth, resided on a large Connecticut estate, he adored her and the marriage was advantageous.

He was only beginning to wonder if Aurora chafed under the idea of an "advantageous" marriage, too.

Roan glanced down at his charge. She wanted the same thing apparently that Aurora sought. It was the women of the day, he thought. Walking about New York and London in their little herds, wanting things like *adventure* and *fun*. He sighed, caressed Prudence's arm.

She stirred, made a sound of contentment.

Damn it, when she sighed like that, he wanted to give her as much adventure as she could abide. What was happening to him? What was he thinking?

Roan refused to figure that out, afraid of what he might discover. What he would force himself to think from this moment forward was that he had best get Miss Prudence Cabot to her friends as soon as possible. Before he did something as rash and imprudent as Aurora.

He refused to listen to the small voice telling him that was impossible, he'd already done it.

CHAPTER NINE

A CARESS ON Prudence's cheek felt distant, as if it had come from another world. It annoyed her, and she shrugged away from whatever it was. The jiggle of her shoulder made her think that perhaps she was still on the coach, still dreaming.

"Prudence."

Her name, whispered in that low, silky voice, and followed by the brush of whiskers across her chin, forced her to swim to awareness. She opened her eyes, blinking at the darkness. She was unable to grasp exactly where she was...until the sound of running water penetrated her thoughts. The brook.

Roan.

She opened her eyes, saw his face.

"You sleep like the dead," he said.

His eyes and lip were not as swollen and bruised as they'd seemed last night. Prudence smiled at the memory of them, on his coat, under the stars. How delicious, how very *shocking*—

"I have a surprise for you," he said softly. "I found our bags."

"Oh!" Prudence sat up. "Where?"

"On the road. They've been ransacked but there are still some things within."

Prudence pushed her hair from her face and knelt

next to her valise to look inside. The contents were topsy-turvy; she pulled out the few items that remained. A clean chemise, her stockings. But a lovely green silk gown was gone, and so were the silk embroidered shoes she'd refused to allow herself to don yesterday, as they were too fine to be ruined. Her lovely shoes! She dug deeper and discovered the hairbrush and comb with the ivory handles—a gift from Grace—was likewise missing, as well as her reticule.

Roan had tossed out a shirt, a waistcoat, some shaving implements. He scraped his hand along the bottom, as if searching for something. He suddenly kicked the bag with all his might.

"What is missing?"

"My banknotes," he said, and raked his fingers through his hair. "They stole all my money."

"*All* of it?" Prudence asked.

"They may as well have done. I am without a single coin until I reach the trunk I sent on to Himple."

"What do we do now?" she asked.

Roan reached for her hand and pulled her into his arms. "We persevere, Prudence Cabot. We go and find our trunks." He let her go and began to collect his things. "And if we discover that the entire countryside is filled with thieves and ne'er-do-wells, I will personally carry you on my back into London and fill a wardrobe with gowns and shoes."

Prudence smiled dubiously. "Would you really, Mr. Matheson, just for me?"

He grinned, put his hands on her shoulders and spun her around to button her up. "I would do it only for you. But if my trunk has also been stolen, I will have nothing but my indomitable spirit and a desperate need to reach the Bank of England to guide us." He kissed her.

Prudence sighed with contentment. The world Roan had introduced her to last night was one she had heretofore inadequately imagined. She thought again about the ecstasy in his hands and smiled at the cool blue sky and the tiny sliver of pink on the horizon. This adventure, as troublesome and disastrous as it would be for her personally in the end, had nonetheless made her feel reborn. She'd been unshackled from the rules and expectations of proper society. She was living, truly living, for the first time in her life. "I'm ravenous," she murmured.

He bent his head, nuzzled her neck, his arm going around her waist. "So am I."

Prudence blushed, the meaning behind his words clear to her in a way that would not have been apparent to her yesterday.

"Come, wash in the brook. We haven't far to go today."

She made her way to the brook and scrubbed her face with her fingers as best she could. She knotted her hair at the nape and let it hang down her back, but looked down at her gown. It was wrinkled and dirty and looked as if she'd slept in it. This would not do— she couldn't very well appear at the Bulworths' looking as though she'd been dragged behind a cart all the way from Blackwood Hall. She would have to find some place to bathe and repair herself as best she could.

They rode on, and brilliant, gold light began to overtake the pink of the morning on the horizon. The mist that had settled onto the fields over night began to lift. The attack of last night seemed almost like a dream.

It felt to Prudence as if the world's curtain was lifting for her. Never had she seen such verdant greens, such buttery yellows or taffy pinks. She wanted to emboss this morning on her soul, to never forget how she felt on the first dawn of her awakening from the ennui that had threatened to drown her.

"Isn't it beautiful?" Prudence asked.

"What?"

"The landscape. The countryside."

"It's nice," he agreed.

"Nice! It's lovely, Roan. I can't imagine America looks like this."

"It doesn't," he said. "American has a different sort of beauty. Rugged, so many parts of it untouched. Not in the city of New York, obviously," Roan said. "But if you were to ride north as I often do, you might go days without seeing another person."

"No villages?" Prudence asked. "No crofters, no sheep?"

"There are some settlements and fields and livestock on the main roads. But America is so much larger than this island. It would be impossible to inhabit it all. I can't describe how stunning is a landscape untouched by man."

Roan began to talk about America, its forests and valleys, the snowcapped mountains, the wide, sweeping rivers. It sounded enchanting to Prudence. She longed to see it, to ride through that vastness. She could imagine Roan in that setting, on a much younger horse, his bags and bedroll strapped to the horse's rump. She pictured him gathering wood and building a fire in the middle of a forest, then roasting a rabbit he'd snared. Prudence had no knowledge of how such things were done, but she guessed that a man as lusty and strong as Roan Matheson would handle them with ease.

He told her about New York City, too, and a more genteel image of Roan began to form in her mind. He mentioned the City Hotel, and the dancing assemblies held there. She pictured a gentleman dressed in flowing tails and a silky white waistcoat who was a fine dancer, surprisingly light on his feet as he circled around the ladies he partnered with. She could see his bright smile, the twinkle in his topaz eyes as he showered them with compliments. She saw the debutantes of New York gathering behind their fans, giggling and whispering about the fine figure he cut, their eyes darting to wherever he was in the assembly room.

He told her of the small house his family kept in town, on Broadway Street, very near the Park Theatre. His family, he said, were patrons of the arts and the theatre. But he was most animated when he described the family's country estate in the Hudson Valley. Prudence imagined him walking, perhaps with a dog or two trailing along, down a vast green lawn that led to the edge of the Hudson River. She could see him working to train the horses his family kept and bred, as he did not seem the sort to trust that to anyone else. When she listened to him, she imagined estates more lush than Longmeadow, the Beckington estate where she'd grown up, or Blackwood Hall.

Prudence began to dreamily imagine herself on the New York estate, walking across the landscape he described, fingers idly skimming across rhododendron blooms, or her skirts dragging against a dewy green lawn.

Roan spoke about his family's business again, the

plans they had, the work he did for them. It occurred to Prudence that what was missing from his speech was the mention of a society, a wife, plans for marriage. "You speak of your family's legacy, and yet you haven't mentioned marriage," she said.

Roan said nothing. His silence was enough to make her turn her head to look at him. "You will marry, won't you? Have your own sons?"

"Of course," he said tightly. But his demeanor was so strange that Prudence had a sudden and horrifying thought—he *was* married. "Oh dear God," she said, and turned around.

"What?"

"Are you…are you *married?*" she made herself ask, dazzled by her own stupidity.

"What? No! Of course I'm not. Do you think I would— Pru, for God's sake." He put his hand around her waist. "I hesitate not because I am married. But… in honesty, I have an understanding with someone. Not an understanding as much as an expectation. The truth is I hardly know her, and God knows I've not actually proposed anything to her. But a marriage to her is one that will benefit the Mathesons and her family."

Prudence felt as if she'd been punched in the gut. She found it difficult to catch her breath for a moment. "I see," she managed to say. Lord, she was naive!

"No, you don't see," he said. "It's an arrangement—"

"I had no right to ask," she said quickly, and closed her eyes, wishing she had never opened her mouth, wishing she could live on with her fantasy of what might have been. But she had opened her mouth, and now she felt sick. "What's her name?"

There was another hesitation at her back. At long last, he said, "Susannah."

Susannah. She was beautiful, Prudence thought. She was in America, waiting for him. She was the woman he'd wake up to, and she...

"Pru, I shouldn't have—"

"I asked for it," she said sharply, cutting him off before he ruined the memory of last night completely. "It's quite all right, Roan. It's not as if I thought you'd offer to..."

God, I am ridiculous.

Prudence didn't finish her thought. She didn't need to—he knew what she meant. She was wrong to feel she had any right to him at all. Last night had been about adventure. It had been about the experience of *living.* So why, then, did it suddenly feel so painful?

An uncomfortable silence swallowed them. Prudence stared into the distance and thought of America. Of apple trees and green hills.

She had no idea how long they rode in silence until Roan leaned down and said softly, "Look there." He pointed over her shoulder.

Prudence looked in the direction he indicated and saw the curls of smoke rising above the treetops.

"A village," he said. "That's a happy sight, isn't it?"

But a swirl of panic rose up in Prudence, rudely jerking her back to reality. "Oh no. No! I can't go into a village like *this*," she said, glancing down at her dirty gown, the tail of her hair. "I need a fresh gown, to put up my hair."

"As much as I would like to oblige you, I don't think there are any baths that can be drawn out here," Roan said. "And neither do I have a fresh gown for you."

"You must allow me this! My family—"

"All right, all right," he said, and tugged her back into his chest. "We'll take a detour and follow the brook until we find you a suitable place to freshen." He tugged at the reins of the horse and turned off the road, leading the nag down the trail beside the brook that had followed the road.

The brook turned west, and in the middle of a copse of trees, they found a small lake. It wasn't very large—perhaps only three acres in all—and lily pads had choked off half of it. But cool, clear water lapped onto a grassy bank. Prudence could see grass waving just below the surface, and a bit farther out, the grass gave way to sediment. "It's perfect," she said, and removed her shoes and stockings, then hiked up the hem of her gown and waded in, ankle deep. *"Oh."* She closed her eyes and delighted in the delicious feel of the grass tickling her feet, the cool water lapping around her ankles.

"Do you swim?"

Prudence glanced over her shoulder at Roan. He was standing on the bank, one foot propped on a rock, his arms folded, watching her. "Yes," she said. "Do you?"

His gaze slid down her body and he reached for his neckcloth with one hand, pulling the ends free of the knot. "Like a fish," he said. She watched him discard his coat and waistcoat, too, and pull his shirt free of his trousers. His gaze never left hers, the shine in his eyes making Prudence feel a little light-headed. His promise to another woman notwithstanding, her thoughts skirted across the memory of last night. They were almost to Himple. This extraordinary adventure would come to an end, and so would the most wonderfully intoxicating thing she'd ever known in her life. The damage to them both had been done. That's why Prudence hesitated only a moment before she reached behind her and undid the buttons of her gown. She pulled it over her head and tossed it onto the shore, and stood there in her chemise.

Roan's eyes darkened. His gaze traveled her body once more, but slowly, as if he was taking in every detail, committing it to memory.

She smiled and turned about, wading into the pond until her chemise floated about her waist. Her nipples jutted through the thin fabric, and Prudence spread her arms out to each side, so that her palms skimmed the water. She spread her toes, too, and let the mud squish between them.

This was a familiar feeling—it reminded her of her childhood. What a wonderful childhood it had been, too. She was so young when her father, a bishop in the Church of England, had died so unexpectedly. Her mother had remarried the Earl of Beckington, who was himself a widower, and the four Cabot sisters had trouped off to Longmeadow to be properly schooled in all the things an earl's daughter was required to know. Music and needlework, painting and archery, geography and history. But when they weren't at their lessons, they had acres and acres to explore. The sisters set out every summer day with their stepbrother, Augustine, in tow, who always followed them about like a puppy, warning them of all the dangers he imagined they would encounter.

One of their favorite summer pastimes was to spend the afternoon at the lake with their books. Augustine rarely came along—he was afraid of eels in the water, he said, although Prudence couldn't recall a time she'd seen an eel. Prudence could picture the four of them now, walking down to the lake in single file, Honor carrying the picnic basket her mother had insisted they take along, and Grace with their books wrapped in a strap and hung over her shoulder, like a schoolboy. At the lake's edge, they would strip down to their chemises and swim, diving beneath the surface, floating on their backs. When they'd tired of that, the four of them would lie on the grassy banks to dry, eating the cheese and bread from the basket, reading aloud from their books.

Oh, but she missed those days. Before they were out in society, before they'd entered the restrictive *haut ton*, before their every move was scrutinized, their words repeated across Mayfair salons. Standing in this lake with its lily pads, Prudence felt as if she were back at Longmeadow. As if she'd somehow stepped back in time, free to be the girl she'd been then.

She *could* be the girl she was then, at least today. Prudence abruptly dipped down, spread her arms across the water and kicked. She was swimming. *Swimming!*

She tucked beneath the surface and exploded into light again, laughing and sputtering at the small little shock the cold had given her. She swam out into the middle of the lake, expecting Roan to call her back, to warn her as Augustine would warn them. *Your chemise will drag you under the water, you fool!*

Roan didn't call her back. Roan let her swim.

Prudence rolled onto her back and floated a bit in the middle of the lake, blinking up at the clear blue sky above her head. Her hair fanned out around her like seaweed, and she idly moved her hands, coasting along, feeling the sun's warmth on her face, slowly moving her feet.

She turned her head and saw Roan still standing where she'd left him. She flipped around and swam slowly toward the shore. "Can you guess how long it's been since I've swum in a lake?"

He shook his head.

"Years," she said, astounded by it. "I'd forgotten how much I like it."

She dipped down again and swam toward him, until she could stand in waist-deep water. She gathered her hair over one shoulder and with both hands squeezed the water from it. "Come and join me!" she called up to him.

He shook his head.

Prudence laughed at him. "Do you fear me now?"

"I fear what you're doing," he said. "The risk is too great."

"Oh?" She ran her hands over her head. "It's my risk to take, isn't it?"

"It's also mine," he reminded her.

Prudence smiled. She stepped closer to him. "Roan… we will be in Himple within the hour. I will be sent off, and you'll go home, and…and won't you swim with me, only once?"

He smiled in that charmingly lopsided way he had. "You make this impossible, Pru. I'm a weak man." His eyes moved deliberately over her. It was a dangerous look that he wore, one that was clear in its desire, and it made Prudence's heart beat quicker. But she didn't move from where she stood. She brazenly let him look at her, standing still as his gaze lingered on her breasts, clearly visible through the wet cotton of her chemise. She couldn't believe all that had happened to her in the past twenty-four hours, how astoundingly different she felt. Yesterday at this time she'd been dreading the journey to Himple. And now? Now she was looking at a stranger with as much desire as he looked at her. She could feel it beating steadily in her heart, in her limbs, between her legs. She was alive. She was so alive.

Look at him. Roan was magnificent. There was no other word for a man built as powerfully as him. She recalled his mouth on her sex, how he'd held her so carefully and tenderly after he'd catapulted her to such carnal delights, his hand idly caressing her arm. She could see the heat in his eyes, even from a distance. Prudence had seen that look in men's eyes before, but she'd never really known what it was. And she'd never seen it so deeply rooted as it was in Roan.

She dived under the water, swimming below the surface, letting the water carry her a bit before coming up for air, and glanced back at Roan.

The last time she'd swum like this, she'd been so young and ignorant of the world and the way things went, of all the things that mattered, and would be expected, and would be frowned upon. But nothing like that mattered in this little pond with the lily pads. This adventure had whisked her away from all the trappings of her life.

Roan had moved to the very edge of the water, his gaze so intent it seemed to burn her everywhere it touched her. He wanted her, and she wanted him. Prudence wouldn't deny it—she wasn't going backward. She would never be a maiden debutante again.

He lifted one leg and pulled off his boot. Then the other, first removing his gun from it. Prudence watched him as he unbuttoned his trousers and removed every stitch of clothing from his magnificent body. Roan was starkly naked now, his member erect. He was all hard planes and rippling muscles, and he walked unabashedly into the pond, his legs churning the water as he trod toward her. He seemed heedless of the bruises on his body, heedless of the possibility of anyone discovering them. He seemed heedless of anything but her.

Prudence was enthralled. She was breathless and giddy, and desperately wanting all that he would do to her, would show her.

As he reached her, Prudence put her arms around his neck. Roan wrapped her legs around his waist and his arms around her back. They bobbed in the water like that. He supported her weight and kept his gaze on hers, as if he were trying to determine what to do with her. But Prudence could feel his cock against her, a sensation that electrified her.

"Well, Prudence?" he asked as his gaze slid to her mouth, his expression reminding her of a man who had not eaten all day and was seeing a morsel before him. "What have you to say for yourself? Now your adventure has become mine."

She smiled.

"I wouldn't smile like that were I you, a virginal debutante with no notion of how it stokes fire in a man," he said gruffly. "I don't dip my toes in risky waters. I dive in, even when I can't see the bottom."

A delightful little shiver ran up her spine. "Is there any other way to take a risk?"

Roan made a noise that sounded almost like a growl. "Risks have consequences, you little hellion. Are you prepared for the consequences?" he asked, trying to sound stern.

Prudence wished he would touch her like he had last

night, his hands on her breasts and between her legs. "Kiss me," she commanded him.

Roan frowned at her and pushed a strand of wet hair from her neck. "I'm very serious, Prudence. Are you prepared for the consequences of this? Of your adventure? Of this *swim*? If you're not, then by God, I beg you to tell me now, before I lose any control I might muster. Tell me now so I can take myself back to shore and away from the temptation of you. Say it now, this instant. Say, 'Go away, Roan.'"

What he asked was fair, but Prudence had known her answer before he'd ever removed his boots. "I am prepared for the consequences," she said. "Quite." She kissed his mouth.

With a groan, he closed his eyes and pressed his forehead to hers. "You were supposed to say no. You were supposed to slap me, push me away. I am astonishingly powerless when it comes to you." He slid his hand roughly over her head. "You intrigue me, Prudence. You're beautiful, you're clever. You are everything a man could want. But…" He winced. "I don't know what to do with you."

"You will see me to Himple," she said. "And then think of me fondly in the years to come." It hurt her to say it, but what choice was there?

Roan grimaced as if that were too painful for him, too.

"Neither of us is free," she said. "But at *this* moment, I am in a pond in the middle of nowhere, feeling things I've never felt before and may never feel again. I haven't asked you for any consideration, Roan, and I don't expect any. You asked me if I was prepared for the consequences, and I said yes. I am not a fool—I understand what that means."

"Ah, Prudence." He looked in her eyes, almost as if he was searching for something—a doubt, perhaps? A moment he might convince her otherwise? He would not find it—she was two and twenty. She might die a spinster, but she would not die an innocent one.

He must have understood it, because in the next breath, he was kissing her. He was cupping her jaw, his fingers splayed in her wet hair, and he was kissing her.

And Prudence was kissing him back, her hands on his bare chest, her fingers riding over the hard planes of it, then down to his waist and hips. She felt the same heat in her as she'd felt last night, a desire that flared quickly and burned brightly, licking at her, spreading as if it was fanned by a gale wind. Prudence wanted to touch every inch of him, from the soft lobes of his ears, to the muscles in his back, to the ripples in his abdomen, to his hips.

He pushed her chemise from her shoulders, down to her waist, then moved his mouth to her breasts. The sensation of his teeth and tongue on her was exquisite. She felt scorched and unquenchable as he moved his hands and mouth on her body. How would she ever return to being Prudence? How would she ever live knowing that this sort of desire existed in the world?

She took his earlobe in her mouth, teased it with her tongue. She nuzzled his neck as her fingers drifted across his nipples, arousing them to stiffness. He groaned with satisfaction, a sound that was astoundingly erotic to her ears.

With his hand, he found her sex, stroking her, dipping inside her. His touch and his desire for her pushed her beyond yearning. He was propelling her into an unbearable place of being, where she could expire with pleasure.

Roan suddenly straightened and lifted her up, sliding his hands under her hips and guiding her, so that his cock was pressed against her entrance. She was slick; she could feel her body responding and naturally opening to him. He kissed her as he slipped his fingers into that heat, his thumb stroking the core of her pleasure, making her gasp with delirious pleasure.

"I can't bear it another moment," he said through the grit of his teeth, and pressed against her. He kissed her tenderly as he began to work his way inside of her, pushing a little, withdrawing a little, and again. Prudence began to relax. She was slipping into a dreamlike state, amazed at how their bodies fit together, of how pleasurable it was in spite of the tightness, and the prick of pain as he pushed past her maidenhead. She let her head drift back as he pushed deeper, moving carefully at first, taking her deeper into the pool of desire and submerging her in the feel of his body, of this carnal act, of the swirl of emotions riding up in her. His strokes lengthened, and with one arm, he anchored her to him, watching her as he moved, as if it were vital that he see her.

With every stroke he reached deeper and faster. Prudence moaned, helpless as Roan began to stroke her in rhythm to his body moving inside her. Her body began to tighten around him, sweeping her away along its wave. With a whimper of pleasurable defeat, she dropped her head to his shoulder and shuddered with her release.

Her climax was met with his more powerful one—

with a strangled sob of ecstasy, he removed himself entirely from her, releasing into the lake as he gathered her up in his arms. He was gasping for air, his hold on her was tight, his kisses to her cheek and her neck soft.

Her legs slid from his waist. The water around them began to settle. He braced his palms on either side of her head and softly, carefully, kissed her forehead, the bridge of her nose, her mouth.

Prudence was sore. She was breathless. And she was intoxicated. She'd never imagined it like this, and she would be grateful to Roan Matheson for the rest of her life for having shown her this part of life. She would love him for this, and she would never regret the past twenty-four hours. Not for a single moment.

"Are you all right?"

She nodded and smiled at him. She wrapped one arm around his neck and kissed his cheek. "You've managed to astound me twice now, Mr. Matheson."

He smiled, too, but it was an uncertain one. He continued to hold her, bouncing around a bit in the lake, laughing at what the fish must think of them. He teased her, caressed her, his gaze wandering from her ear to her nose, to her neck and her shoulder, his smile tender.

After a while he said, "We should remove ourselves from this lovely lake before we are discovered."

Prudence nodded, but she would be perfectly happy to remain here. She pictured a cottage on this small lake. Roan would walk out every morning to fish, and she would cook biscuits or some such—Cook had shown her once; maybe she could remember it. At night, he would read to her while she knitted socks for him. And then they would retire to their little bedroom with the windows open to the stars, and he would do this to her, over and over again.

That was the dream she would carry with her for the rest of her days. She would not think of the truth when she indulged in her daydreaming, or the heartache she would feel when it came time for him to go, or the ache she would feel every time she thought of him. She would remember only these moments.

CHAPTER TEN

PRUDENCE MUTTERED UNDER her breath as she dug through her bag, searching for something that might improve the look of her gown. When at last she did emerge from the trees, she had put a wrap to good use, tying it around her bodice to hide the worst of the dirt. She had also put her hair up rather artfully with the few pins she had, but without benefit of help or a mirror, her coif was askew.

"Well?" she asked, casting her arms out and turning around. "What do you think?"

He thought that with her sparkling hazel eyes and sensual smile, she was beautiful. Perhaps even more beautiful than the day he'd first laid eyes on her. "I've never seen anyone lovelier."

Prudence laughed. She looked down to smooth the folds of her skirts.

Roan wisely omitted any commentary about her ruined gown or mention that her coif was hanging a little strangely. "Shall we carry on?"

He'd become uncharacteristically nervous as he'd waited for her to make herself presentable. He'd looked out over that small lake, realizing how exposed they'd been. What if someone had happened upon them? But he'd been so caught up in the moment, so bewitched by the water nymph swimming around in that thin cotton chemise, inviting him in, that he'd lost himself in the moment. The only trouble was that he had yet to find himself. He was becoming increasingly besotted with that golden-haired imp.

Roan was also keenly aware of how much time he'd wasted in his hunt for his sister. Every moment he wasn't in pursuit of Aurora was a moment he risked losing her. It was so unlike him—he'd always been a man of integrity and responsibility, the one to whom his family turned to solve problems. That Roan was still in Ashton Down. He didn't recognize this Roan. And yet, he didn't know how to go back.

He wasn't sure he even wanted to go back.

"All right, then, I'm ready," Prudence said.

She had her bag in one hand. She looked like a vagabond. If Roan didn't know her, he'd expect her to offer to read his palms. He tried to hide his smile at that thought.

"What?" she demanded.

"I'm just happy that you are, at long last, ready to continue on with our little journey. I have a sister to catch and a trunk to find if you haven't forgotten."

"Oh, I've not forgotten," she assured him. "I am as anxious to see my trunk as you are yours."

Roan settled her on the back of the horse and once again strapped their bags onto the old nag's rump. He walked alongside the horse, leading it back across the meadow and the wide swath the nag had mowed. The old girl would probably want a nap now.

He liked walking, even at the pace of a turtle. He needed the physical exercise to expel his frustrations with the thievery and his own bad behavior.

Prudence, however, seemed almost jovial, as if she

were very much enjoying one disaster after another. He supposed she was too privileged and too young to appreciate just how wretched their lot was, but he was desperately aware of it. If his trunk had gone missing and he was forced to go to London to the central bank— he had no idea how far they were from London—he might never find Aurora.

Prudence was talking, he realized, something to do with a garden party where an illustrious guest had fallen in a fountain and had needed rescue. His thoughts were racing, plotting and planning for what would come next if they reached Himple and found their things missing.

They passed through the trees over which they'd seen the curls of smoke. When they rounded the bend, Roan said, "Look ahead, Pru—we've reached Himple."

Prudence sat up.

Himple was a village, a *real* village, with a proper high street, a central green and houses tucked into narrow lanes that meandered away from the high street. There were people, too, scores of them out on that warm summer afternoon. Carters moving their wares, women carrying buckets of water away from a central well, children playing in the roads. Roan felt immeasurably relieved as they rode down the main road. He brought the horse to a halt before a building with the emblem of the Royal Post emblazoned proudly in the window. He whistled for a stable boy. The boy hurried to him and took the reins as Roan helped Prudence down, then unlashed their bags. "Stable her," he said to the boy. "Feed her well. She deserves it."

The boy touched his cap and tugged the horse's bridle to move her along.

Prudence was already at the door of the Royal Post

office, peering into the window. When Roan opened the door for her, she walked in and cried out with delight at the sight of her trunk against one wall. His was beside it. "Yours?" she asked Roan.

"Yes, thank God." He walked to the trunks and squatted down to have a look. Miraculously, the lock was intact.

A man with a wide, flat nose and garters around his sleeves wandered out of a back room. He was holding a monocle, which he polished as he eyed them. "Yes, please?"

"Mr. Roan Matheson," Roan said. "I've come to collect my trunk. The other one belongs to Miss Cabot."

The clerk continued to clean his monocle as he squinted at the trunks. He moved to a small counter, put the monocle to his eye and began to rifle through some papers. He picked one up and brought it close to his face. *"Ah."*

"Ah what?" Roan asked.

"The black trunk is marked for Roan Matheson," he said, and glanced up. "That you?"

Roan glanced at Prudence. "Yes, as I said."

The clerk looked again at the paper. "The second belongs to Miss Prudence Cabot." He looked up. "Is that you, miss?"

"It is."

"You're the lass the stagecoach lost when the wheel broke, are you?" His gaze flicked disapprovingly over Prudence. The color rose in her cheeks.

"And you're the gent who went after her," the man said to Roan.

What was it to this man? Roan responded with a dark look for the man.

The clerk did not seem to care that Roan looked at him in that way. He turned back to the paper and said, "The Cabot trunk will be picked up by Mr. Barton Bulworth's man at noon on the morrow." He removed his monocle then and looked at the two of them.

Roan could feel the tension radiating off Prudence. "Tomorrow?" she repeated, and looked at Roan uncertainly. He knew what she was thinking—what was she to do until the morrow?

"Aye," the clerk confirmed. "And you, sir? Where am I to have the trunk delivered?"

Roan stared at the man. "I'll take it with me. I intend to be on the four o'clock stage for West Lee."

"You want the southbound coach. It's come and gone, comes through promptly at one o'clock—"

"Ah...I think the gentleman means Weslay," Prudence quickly interjected. "It's his accent," she added, a bit softer, and avoided making eye contact with Roan.

"Ah!" the clerk said triumphantly, and smiled. "A Yankee, I'd wager. I've heard the accent is a wee bit coarse."

"Coarse?" Roan echoed.

"The northbound coach came through at three o'clock," the clerk said. "Right on time, too."

Roan gaped at him. This journey was nothing but one obstacle after the other. He felt as if he might come apart at the seams, just as a tent had come apart with a strong gust of wind at a wedding celebration he'd attended several years ago. "Three!" he said, his fury hardly contained. It was only twenty past.

The clerk casually braced his elbow on the counter and said easily, "The afternoon northbound stage comes by at three o'clock. Every day, three o'clock. Why, he's never more than a quarter hour late. Unless there's rain. If there's rain, he might be a bit delayed," the clerk said, settling in, warming to his explanation. "A good rain can slow the best drivers, you know, what with the roads in the condition they are. I remember the year it rained every day. Not a light rain mind you, but heavy rains. They lost a bridge up at Portrees, but the Royal Post, it still ran. Just ran late every day, sometimes as much as four or five hours. Sometimes as much as a *day*—"

"I beg your pardon, sir," Prudence said sweetly, stepping forward a bit, putting herself between Roan and the clerk. "We find ourselves in a bit of a dilemma. I should call on Mrs. Bulworth at once. Surely there is some method of transport to the Bulworth estate?"

"No," he said with a shake of his head. "Not this time of day. Had you come earlier, you might have talked the dry-goods man into taking you. I believe he was out that way. But you're too late. You can ride with the Bulworth man on the morrow. Not too many go in that direction from here. You came the long way to reach the Bulworth estate, didn't you? Them that goes to Bulworth come down from Epsey."

Prudence glanced helplessly at Roan.

"There is no other way we might continue our journey?" he asked. "No cab for hire, no portage?"

"Not through Himple, no sir. There's an inn down the lane here, the Fox and Sparrow," the man said, gesturing to his right. "It's a decent inn, if you ask me. One wing is for the gentlemen, the other for families." He looked at Prudence again. "Mrs. House is the innkeeper's wife. You might tell her you fell on hard times. She doesn't usually take in single women."

"Pardon?" Prudence said, her brows dipping into

a frown. "Why shouldn't Mrs. House accept single women?"

"When is the next coach?" Roan asked, cutting Prudence off and surreptitiously touching her hand to keep her from protesting.

"Ten o'clock on the morrow," the man said. "It will be on time, too, as it's a Royal Post. Never tardy, not the Royal Post, not unless there's rain. Otherwise, you could set your pocket watch by them, that's certain. Old Mr. Stainsbury, he sets the church clock—"

"Is there a porter around? Someone who can see our trunks to the inn?" Roan interrupted.

"Eh? Oh," the clerk said, clearly disappointed to be cut short. "I'll have the post boys bring them up. They'll expect a few coins for their trouble. They'll carry up a bath, too, if needed." He glanced again at Prudence.

She gasped. Her hand went to her hair, no doubt discovering that another tress had come down.

"The post boys, now *there's* a set of riders who won't tarry—"

"Thank you," Roan said quickly. He opened the door and held it open for Prudence. "Miss Cabot?"

Prudence swept out before him, mortified. "I think I might die of shame," she said when Roan stepped out behind her. She tried to tuck her hair back in.

"That would be a tragic ending to our outing," he said. He took off his hat and ran his hand over his head.

"What are we to do?" she asked.

"We'll take rooms at the inn." He smiled at her. "And we'll give the boys a crown to bring up the bath the clerk thinks you ought to have."

With a roll of her eyes, Prudence started marching in the direction of the inn.

As it happened, there were no rooms left for single men, a fact Roan happened to overhear when he stepped inside to let the rooms with a bit of money Prudence had pinned to her pocket. That settled it to Roan's satisfaction. He didn't want to be away from Prudence, not after all they'd been through. And yet, he'd felt terribly presumptive that he would share a bed with her, not with the truth of their lives tearing through the curtain they'd pulled around themselves. Roan had taken enough from her. But he wanted more. God, how he wanted more.

He was, therefore, almost elated to learn there were no single rooms left.

Mrs. House, a harried-looking woman with sharp cheekbones, informed him she had one room left when he stepped up to the bar. "It has a table, two chairs and a bed," she said. "Will that suit?" she asked as she filled two pints with ale.

"It will suit," Roan said. "But I will also require a bath."

Mrs. House was shaking her head before he finished speaking. "I've got no men to carry it up. Look around you, sir, they're all drunk."

"I've got men to carry it up. But I'll need water. And a roast chicken if you have it. Bread, olives—whatever you've got."

Mrs. House frowned as she pushed the tankards across the bar to a serving girl. "I've got one housemaid," she said. "I can't spare her—"

Roan didn't know how much money he slid across the bar to her, but it was apparently enough. She looked at him askance, then wiped her hands on her gown and picked up the note.

Roan smiled. "My wife has had a very trying day, madam. I would very much like to improve it for her."

"Your wife, is it?" she asked sarcastically.

"It's her father," Roan said. "He hasn't long. We're racing against time to reach him."

"Poor dear," Mrs. House said mockingly. "Take her up, then. And send your boys round to the back for the bath. I'll have it readied."

Roan fetched Prudence, and they followed the young men and their trunks up to the room. It was small, but it had a window that looked out over the green. After the past thirty-six hours, the room looked sumptuous to Roan. He promised the boys two crowns each upon delivering the tub.

"From where do you hail?" he asked the oldest boy when they returned with the tub.

"Midlothian, sir."

"Near here?"

The boy nodded.

"There is an old nag in the stables. She's not worth a farthing, but she's plodded a very long way and deserves to graze in peace." He handed the boy a five pound banknote. The boy's eyes widened. "Take her home, put her to pasture."

"A *horse*?" the oldest boy repeated with awe.

"Not a horse. A nag. Be good to her."

The boy looked excitedly at his companion. They were eager to claim their unexpected prize. Roan chuckled as he closed the door behind them. Those boys would curse him when they saw the old girl.

He turned from the door. Prudence was in her trunk, pulling gowns and frilly lacey garments from it. He was quick to open his trunk, too, to make doubly sure the banknotes he'd tucked away were still there. It was with a great amount of relief to find them there.

Prudence had laid out a variety of gowns on the bed—silks and brocades, satins and velvets, and was studying them critically when the housemaid brought their dinner and wine.

The smell of food drew her from her interest in her clothes, and she eagerly sat across the wooden table from Roan. They pulled meat from the roasted chicken, served on a cracked platter. "Do you think," he asked, pausing to lick his fingers after pulling apart the chicken, "that the food is really as good as it tastes?"

She giggled. "I know only that I have never tasted a chicken roasted to such perfection." She drank heartily from her wineglass, as if she'd wandered forty days and forty nights through the wilds of England's west country. When she'd had her fill of food and drink, she leaned back in her chair with one hand draped across her middle, looking like a sated cow. "That was *wonderful.*"

Roan laughed. It *was* wonderful. He'd had far better food in far better establishments than this old inn, but this was the meal he'd remember—Prudence's lips made shiny from the chicken, her eyes bright with happiness and the bit of sun coloring her cheeks. She was, to him, quite beautiful.

A knock at the door signaled the water for their bath. Over the next ten minutes, two girls hurried in and out with their buckets, pouring steam water into the copper bath until it was nearly full.

Roan gave them a banknote, too—he had nothing smaller—and their eyes bulged at their riches, just as the post boys.

"You'll have nothing left at this rate," Prudence said with a laugh.

Roan smiled. He locked the door behind the girls and turned back to Prudence. "Your majesty, your bath awaits," he said.

"I've never been so desperate for a proper bath," she said, and stood. She moved a chair around to rest beside the tub, then put some of the jars from her trunk on the seat. Then she removed her grimy clothes. She smiled saucily at him, like a lover. As if she'd never been the innocent debutante she'd been only a day or so before. She was bolder now. More mature. Roan liked that.

She was soon bare before him. Roan had always found the feminine form the greatest work of art, but Prudence took his breath away. She was curvy, soft and pliant, and the sight of her made him yearn to touch her.

She stepped into the tub and lowered herself into the water. Roan's pulse turned hot as she leaned her head back against the tub and closed her eyes. Her hair pooled in the water around her and over her breasts. "It's heaven," she murmured. "Thank you, Roan."

"Let me wash you hair," he suggested.

She opened one eye and smiled with surprised. "Will you?"

He picked up the ewer from the basin. "I will." He brought the wine bottle and their cups first, and set them on the floor. He moved her things from the chair and sat, then dipped the ewer into the water. Prudence sat up and leaned forward; he poured water over her hair to wet it, watching the water and her hair stream down her back.

"I think Mrs. Bulworth will be very appreciative that I arrive in clean dress and with my hair properly put up," she said with a wry smile. "She won't know how she owes you a debt for it."

Roan smiled and lathered her hair.

Prudence sighed and closed her eyes again, relaxing as he washed her hair. "I will miss you," she said softly. "Is that madness? I've known you a day and a half, and yet I know I will miss you more than breath."

Roan hesitated a moment before continuing in the work of washing her hair. He would miss her, too—just how much he would miss her amazed him. "I will miss you, too," he admitted.

He dipped the ewer and poured it over her hair to rinse it. She said nothing as he finished her hair and put down the ewer.

Prudence grabbed his hand. "Come in," she said.

He laughed. "That wash tub won't accommodate us both."

"It will," she said, and drew her knees up to her chest.

Roan very much doubted that they could fit in the tub, but he wasn't above trying. He quickly disrobed, aware that Prudence's eyes were on him, her gaze brazenly sliding over his body, drinking him in. More than one woman had seen him bare as he was now, but this was the first time that Roan could recall wanting a woman to find him as appealing as he found her. He stepped into the tub, braced his hands against the edges, and carefully lowered himself in. Water sloshed over the sides when he did, and Prudence laughed with delight. Roan was stuffed into that bath, but grateful for the wash.

She helped him, rubbing soap on his chest, on his neck and face. He helped her, too, lathering up her breasts, her abdomen. She laughed at him when he dipped his head to wet it, and she came up on her knees to return the favor of a hair wash. "Shall I shave you? I shaved the earl when he was no longer able."

"I'd like that," he said.

Prudence reached over the side of the tub and found the razor he'd taken out, the cream for his face. She smiled as she leaned forward and carefully scraped the two days' growth of beard from his face.

When they had cleaned themselves, Roan poured wine for them both. He liked this, sitting in a bath with Prudence. Her hair was slicked back, and her breasts rode just above the water line, her face softly golden in the light of the fire. Roan had never been so captivated, never so content.

They talked about family, and horses and dogs, of which they shared a love. He told her about a canal so many of them were trying to see built, from Lake Erie to New York City. "It will change commerce as we know it," Roan said.

Prudence told him what she would recall of her father, who had died when she was rather young, and of the person her mother had been before her madness. "She was so beautiful," she said wistfully. She told him about her mother's second marriage to the Earl of Beckington, who clearly had loved his many stepdaughters. She told him about London society, and the balls and garden parties and many soirees. She laughed ruefully. "Those days are behind me now, I'm afraid."

That sobered him. If ever a woman deserved to be toast of a ball, it was Prudence. He could picture her in an expensive ball gown, jewels glittering at her ears and throat, her smile illuminating those around her.

"What will you do?" he asked quietly. "After you've called on your friend?"

"Assuming Merryton hasn't sent an army after me?" Prudence asked, and splashed him. "I suppose I'll return to Blackwood Hall and wait."

"Wait," Roan repeated, not understanding. "For what?"

Prudence shrugged. "For an offer."

Roan must have showed his dismay at that, because she smiled and wiggled her toes against him. "Don't be glum, Roan. It's what debutantes do. What else is there for us, really?"

"But surely you are allowed an occupation."

Prudence laughed. "Such as governess or teacher? I wouldn't mind it—in fact, I should like it very much. I always fancied I'd have lots of children. I don't know what will become of me, but young ladies of certain standing are not meant to work. They are meant to marry well and arrange seating cards at supper parties." She smiled and flicked water against his chest again. "I envy Mercy in some ways. She found her escape from the tedium through art. I should have been as diligent in my endeavors."

Roan tried to smile, but he could see the hint of despair and apathy in her lovely eyes, and it made him slightly ill.

Prudence looked away. She sipped her wine and put it aside. She trailed her fingers over bathwater that was now tepid, if not cool. "Our adventure comes to an end on the morrow, doesn't it?"

"It doesn't have to end there," he said recklessly. Those hazel eyes could entice him to anything—to ignore his morals, his responsibilities. He knew it, but spoke his heart anyway. "Come north with me."

Prudence smiled and looked up. "And do what? Present myself as your cousin? To people who might actually be acquainted with my family? And if I do, *then* what? It would end the day after that, would it not?"

Roan wanted desperately to say what she wanted to hear—that he would stay in England, or that somehow, against all odds, they would find a way to continue their adventure, and that he would court her properly. That he would make that offer she was waiting for. Perhaps he wanted to say those things to himself. But it was impossible—he had a family, a life, a thriving business in America, and people who were depending on the promise he'd made to his father about Susannah Pratt. Moreover, he had to take Aurora home. Aurora had made promises, too, but more than that, his mother was frantic about her daughter. He had to return her to his mother, if nothing else. As much as he would have liked to, as desperately as he wanted to, Roan simply couldn't play swain to Prudence's debutante.

She misunderstood his silence. "You don't have to say anything," she said. "I knew from the beginning that no matter what happened, this would never be more than a lark. I will look back on these few days with great fondness and…and gratitude."

"Gratitude," he said bitterly, and closed his eyes. He felt awful—anxious and angry, at complete odds with himself. "A strange word, given that I have taken terrible advantage of you, Pru. I have taken something from you that can't be replaced."

"Roan!" She sat up and cupped his chin with her hand. "How can you say so? I *followed* you. I gave you

every indication. I wanted you so, Roan. I *wanted* you
to touch me. I wanted to feel—" She groaned. "I wanted
to feel all of it! I'm not a girl. I knew what I was doing."

Roan searched for the right words to say and found
none that could possibly describe the torment in him.
"Neither will I ever forget these days," he said, instantly
finding those words inadequate. He leaned up, too, took
her hand in his. "*Never*, Pru."

She smiled at him with such tenderness that he could
feel it swelling in his heart...but then her smile turned
impish. "My adventure is not yet over, is it?"

Roan smiled, too. "No. No, it is not." He rose up like
a beast from the tub, water dripping everywhere, and
picked her up. He stepped out of the tub and carried her
to the bed, laid her on her back and crawled over her.

She stroked his face, his wet hair. "Roan."

Roan's body and his heart reacted instantly to his
name whispered on her breath. Something had burst
in him, something tender and caring, something that
burrowed through to the dark, dank places of his soul
that had never been touched before.

Prudence sighed and exposed her fragrant neck to
him, inviting him. He kissed the point just behind her
earlobe and slipped his arms behind her back, crush-
ing her to him. "I want you," he said against her skin.
"I want you so, Prudence." He filled his hand with her
breast, kneading it, then moving down her body, still
moist from the bath.

Roan could feel her body pulse with his touch. He
could feel the race of her heart, the heat in her skin.
Her scent, her weight in his arms, her softness aroused
every fiber. He was ravenous for her.

He took her breast in his mouth and felt his pulse

leap at the sound of pleasure she made. The urge in him felt vital; he believed he'd never desired a woman as completely as he did this night, in this English inn. The need to be in her, to fill her with himself was overwhelming. He pressed his erection against her, moving, feeling her body next to his. He pushed an image of Susannah from his mind's eye, as well as the burgeoning question of whether he could ever feel anything even remotely close to this for her.

He slipped his hands in between Prudence's thighs, his fingers moving into the slit of her sex.

"Oh God," Prudence moaned.

It was almost unbearable to hold himself against her without entering her, but he wanted to prolong this as long as he might. He wanted to make the moment with her last forever in his mind, and he clenched his jaw as he moved down her body, determined to do the same for her. He kissed her belly, then moved down, his mouth brushing the spring of honey curls, inhaling her scent.

Prudence grabbed his head, twining her fingers in his hair. She was panting—or was that him? He was moving by instinct now, parting her legs and slipping his tongue into the damp lips of her sex. His heart was roaring as she bucked beneath him, and the sounds of her pleasure engorged him. But Roan held on and explored her thoroughly with his mouth in a manner he had never known another woman.

In a manner he would never know another woman. Not like this. This belonged to him and Prudence.

Prudence began to move against him, pressing him to move faster. When her release came, he could bear it no more; he rose up and braced himself above her.

Prudence gave him the smile of a woman greatly satisfied and, much to his surprise, took him in hand. The sensation of her fingers wrapped so securely around his cock was unbearable; he grit his teeth to keep from losing his control. He reached between them and covered her hand with his, showed her how to move her hand on him.

She watched him as her hand moved, her expression both curious and jubilant, as if she'd discovered gold. Roan clenched his jaw, wanting the pleasure she was giving him and fearful of a monstrous release.

When he could bear it no more, he grabbed her wrist, made her stop. Prudence smiled and, innocent that she was, he could see in her sultry gaze that she understood what power she held over him. It was a man's curse, he supposed, as he slipped his hand between her legs again, a finger sliding into her, to be so hopelessly bewitched by the feminine form. It was his own special curse to be hopelessly besotted by an English debutante.

He shifted in between her legs. "You drive me to madness," he said softly. "Utter madness. I can't imagine that I might have come to England and never found you."

"Don't forget me, Roan."

"Never, I promise you," he said, and entered her, pushing gently, settling inside of her. He gathered her up and rolled onto his back. Prudence gave a little gasp of delight and braced her hands against his chest. Roan lifted up and kissed her tenderly, catching her bottom lip between his teeth, as he continued the exquisite movement inside of her. He felt a bit in awe of the physical and emotional joining of a man and a woman, and marveled that he'd ever felt it so naturally, so completely.

He kept moving, and Prudence began to understand the rhythm. She began to move with him, leaning over him so that her damp hair brushed against him. He lost himself in her in that moment, utterly and completely.

Prudence collapsed onto his chest, her head on his shoulder, her hair on his face and across his eyes. "Is it always so…so passionate?" she asked breathlessly.

Roan brushed her hair from her face, then stroked her back. "It's never been so passionate for me."

She lifted her head; she was glowing—her smile, her eyes, all of her—shining up at him like a star fallen from heaven. Roan almost groaned aloud at his poorly poetic thoughts. Was he really thinking such things? God help him, he was.

Prudence kissed him, then rolled off him, onto her back beside him. She thread her fingers through his and they lay there, side by side, holding hands and staring up at a bare wooden ceiling.

Roan didn't want to let her hand go. It was strange to feel his heart wrap around his thoughts, but there was something about this woman that had sunk deep into him, the roots curling around and anchoring in him, deeper and heavier than anything he'd felt. It made him feel oddly vulnerable, too, as if she had opened a door in him he never knew was there and had let herself in. He wanted to slam it shut and lock her inside forever.

Roan was struggling to reconcile a growing infatuation with the deep attachment he felt for her now that he'd taken her virginity. He couldn't make sense of what he was feeling, of the many conflicting thoughts in his head. Of the desires that were beginning to rise up in him, desires he'd never felt in his life.

Prudence startled him by popping up and smiling

down at him. "Do you think that... Mightn't we do this all over again? It's not yet morning, is it?"

He cupped her face, studying her. "Where did you come from? What have I done in my life to find this treasure?"

She laughed and crawled on top of him.

"No," he said, grinning up at her. "It is not quite morning."

CHAPTER ELEVEN

MORNING DID COME, and much too fast for Prudence. She and Roan lay in each other's arms, exploring each other's bodies and making love into the morning hours. She'd slept fitfully and awoke when the sun began to spill in through the small window of their room. She groaned, wrinkling her nose. What was that *smell*?

Ah, yes. The chicken and wine.

She lifted Roan's arm from her belly and rolled over, into his chest. He lay on his side beside her, his eyes closed, his breathing deep. She kissed his chest twice and sat up.

He had opened one eye and was watching her. "You're insatiable," he said, and raked his fingers through her tangled hair.

"I think perhaps I am," she said, as the thought occurred to her.

She shifted and kissed his lips, then rolled over and swung her legs over the side of the bed. She had been initiated into a beautiful, lovely, tender private world these past two days and she was loath to leave it. But leave she must. Prudence felt remarkably clearheaded about it. She had to return to her life. Roan had to find his sister and return to his promises, and a family who needed him.

Clearheaded, perhaps, but it hurt her heart too much

to feel him in her again, and she stood up, afraid that he would touch her and her resolve would crumble. It felt as if the slightest breeze would crush her, and she'd end up begging him to stay, like a poor relation. Like a ward. Like someone with no hope.

Prudence pulled a linen sheet around her. She was quite sore, really, but it was a delicious soreness, something she savored. Every movement reminded her of the magic she'd discovered in his arms.

She moved to her trunk and picked up the dark green day gown with the brown trim.

She heard Roan behind her, rising from the bed. She heard water splashing at the basin, then his rummaging about for the things he needed. She busied herself at her trunk so that he would not see the tears that burned behind her eyes, a peculiar mix of both happiness and sick regret.

Was it possible to fall in love with someone so quickly? Was it possible to find someone so completely compatible by mere chance? How could she ever think of another man with the impression of Roan's hands on her body? How could she ever look at another pair of eyes and not see the golden topaz of his? How would she live the rest of her tedious life, knowing that her heart was somewhere on the other side of the ocean?

It would be her secret burden to bear, the thing she carried with her always. Prudence could picture herself at family dinners, her heart aching as everyone laughed around her. When matches were made, when babies were born, when Christmases were celebrated, and her sisters gathered their loved ones around them Prudence would think of Roan.

It was unfair, so terribly unfair. And yet, it was.

Roan dressed as Prudence occupied herself with putting on her dress and packing her things. She would not let Roan see her distress, she would not be a mewling debutante, pawing at her lover. She meant what she'd said—she knew exactly what she'd been about when she put herself on that stagecoach. She couldn't have imagined all that would happen, but she'd known what she was doing, and now she would live with the consequences. By God, she would watch him depart today with her head held high.

Prudence prepared herself to watch him leave, and in fact she preferred it that way, that he go first. She was certain she might hold her feelings at a good distance until his coach had gone down the road. But as her rotten luck would have it, the Bulworth man appeared at the inn before noon, over two hours early.

"I understood you'd not come for the trunk until noon," Roan said crossly, as if it were the poor man's fault he'd come early.

"I dunno, milord," the man said as he kneaded his hat in his hands. He looked to be eighteen or nineteen years of age. He had a scattering of whiskers on his chin and his nervousness erupted into splotches of red on his cheeks. "I just come when Mr. Bulworth tell me to."

"It's all right," Prudence, said, and put her hand on Roan's arm. He looked a bit different to her this morning, with his hair combed and his jaw clean-shaven. Even more virile, more imposing, a feat she would not have thought possible. But his eyes were different—the shine was gone from them. They looked almost brown to her now, and the tiny little lines of worry around them made him look a bit sad.

"Well," she said, trying to sound cheerful. "I guess

we must say our farewells, mustn't we?" She smiled at the Bulworth man. "That's my trunk just there," she said.

He nodded, donned his cap and picked up her trunk, managing to hoist it onto his shoulder.

Prudence gamely tried to smile at Roan, but she couldn't manage it. "I'd ask you to write, but it seems rather futile, and I think it will only distress me more—"

He suddenly grasped her hand. "You can still come with me to West Lee."

"Weslay," she muttered.

"Listen to me," he said. "We might say you are my cousin. Cousin Prudence and Aurora's companion, to see her home."

"Roan! The moment I uttered a word they will know I'm not an American. And it is quite possible that I will know someone there. Penfors is a viscount, you know. He may have been acquainted with my stepfather, or Merryton."

"But—"

"But," she said, grasping both of his hands in hers, "I must go, and so must you. Is there really any other option? As much as I would…as I would love to carry on with you, I've pushed every boundary. I'll be lucky to see the outside of Blackwood Hall as it is. And more than that, I don't know if I can bear it. The more I am with you, the more I want…*everything.* Do you understand me?"

Roan sighed. He squeezed her hands in his. "Yes, of course I understand you. You're right, Pru. Were it not for Aurora…" He shook his head and glanced down. "To come with me would be far too foolish…even for you." He glanced up and smiled ruefully. "When will you return to Blackwood Hall? I'll come to see you before we go—"

"No!" she exclaimed, and stole a look at the boy. "That's impossible."

"I must—"

"No," she said again. Her face was heating. "It will be worse if you come."

He looked stung, but Prudence couldn't bear it if he came to Blackwood Hall.

Roan gripped her hand tighter. "I'm not ready for you to go, Prudence. I may never be ready for it, but I can't—" He clenched his jaw and looked away.

His words were an arrow that pierced her heart. "Why couldn't you be English?" she moaned.

"Why couldn't you be American? We're star-crossed, Pru. There's no other damn way to look at it. Believe me, I've tried."

Prudence bit her lip to keep the sob lodged in her throat from escaping. "Well," she said. "I suppose I ought to…" She gestured to the wagon where the Bulworth man waited.

"Yes." Roan swallowed. He offered his arm, and then escorted Prudence to the wagon and helped her up onto the seat. Prudence leaned over and kissed his cheek. She hated that most of all—it was the sort of kiss she might have given Augustine, the polite, chaste, so-good-to-see-you-again kiss that society and propriety allowed, and it was maddening.

Roan stepped back, his hands clasped behind his back. "Godspeed, Miss Cabot."

"To you as well, Mr. Matheson."

"Shall we drive on, miss?" the driver asked her.

"Yes, go, please," she said, and lifted her hand as the wagon pulled away. As they began to bounce down the road, she twisted about on the bench.

Roan stood in the road, watching her. He stood there until she could no longer see him, or he her. And somewhere on that dusty road, between her and Roan, lay Prudence's heart.

"Rather warm, ain't it?" the young man asked congenially. "Not had any rain to speak of. So dry it's ruined the crops on Tatlinger's farm. I heard he might sell to Bulworth."

"Yes, awfully dry," Prudence said. The young man continued to talk, but his words were like the chatter of a bird to her—only noise, nonsensical sounds, because she was too mired in her own miserable thoughts to be polite.

"They bring the Ferguson boys up to help harvest. There are six of them. I say each of them can do the work of a draft horse hisself."

She'd done the right thing today. She always did the right thing, with the glaring exception of one afternoon in Ashton Down. There was no question that she would have to explain her absence, and she would think of something. But she would not mention a camp. Or a lake choked with lily pads. Or the luxury of a room and a bath and the exquisite connection to a man who was not her fiancé. A man who had been a stranger to her forty-eight hours ago. It was absurd to feel so bereft. She scarcely knew him!

She had done the right thing; she always did the right thing.

What if she carried his child? He'd been careful not to leave his seed in her, but last night…last night, the moment had overwhelmed them both. Prudence thought of her courses—she was due to have them in a week. And what would Prudence do for that week? Wait, that's what, because to do anything else, to go any further than she already had was to invite the worst sort of scandal. Perhaps even charges of a violation of morals or some such. Prudence had no idea what sort of charges of immorality and vile behavior could be brought against her, but she could picture herself standing before a magistrate. *Yes, my lord, I lay with a man out of wedlock...*

"Bobby Ferguson, I'd reckon he's the biggest of them. Stands a full head taller than his brothers and looks as wide as this wagon."

What was the boy saying now? Prudence turned away, her gaze skimming over yellow fields.

What honor did she have, really? What was there in honor, if it meant no life at all? And if that were so, why *couldn't* she go to Weslay? Why couldn't she wait the week with Roan? She didn't know Penfors personally and was certain they had never been properly introduced. He wouldn't know her at all.

Ah, yes, but if he had guests, there was a chance that Prudence would know someone. But would she, really? Who would come from London all the way to Howston Hall at this time of year? It was too hot, too dusty for such a long journey. She could almost hear Lady Chatham holding court in her salon. *If Penfors meant for us to come, he would have invited us in June. Not in August. The roads will be dusty and the journey too hot. He never meant for any of us to come.*

The other ladies would agree with Lady Chatham because they always agreed with her. It was quite pos-

sible that Roan would find Penfors and his family alone. And if they claimed not to be acquainted with Aurora, what then? Roan would be hopelessly lost. A stranger in their midst with no connections. Would they even allow him entrance?

"Seen him lift a rock the size of a sheep once. No help at all."

Prudence sat a little straighter as a thought occurred to her. How could she *not* go to Weslay? How could she leave the poor American man to navigate English society? It was reprehensible of her, really, to let him go alone, especially after he'd saved her.

"Very nearly dropped it on the poor farmer's feet. He didn't actually hit his feet, mind you, but the farmer howled like he had." The young man chuckled at the memory.

"Turn around," Prudence said, so softly at first that she scarcely heard herself.

"Pardon?"

"Turn around!" She twisted on the bench and looked back. The village had disappeared, as if the empty land-scape had swallowed it up. "Turn around, turn *around*!" she cried, and shoved both hands against his shoulder.

The young man looked at her as if she'd lost her mind.

"Turn around!" she shrieked.

Whether she frightened him or he finally understood that she meant it, he pulled the team up and laboriously shifted them about in two steps back, then two steps forward, until the team and the wagon had turned about. It seemed to Prudence to take hours.

"Mr. and Mrs. Bulworth, they're expecting me,"

he said, looking concerned. "They're expecting me to bring *you*, miss."

"You can tell them you waited and I didn't come."

"What, you mean tell them a lie?"

"What is your name?"

"Robert, miss," he said, wincing a little, as if he expected she would have him dismissed.

"Robert, listen to me. I have left something very important undone. Do you understand? I can't in good conscience do that, can I? And the only reason I am leaving the important thing undone is because Mrs. Bulworth is expecting me. You must tell her that. You can say it, can't you? That I left something undone and will come as soon as I can."

"I don't know, I don't know," he said fearfully. "Mr. Bulworth will box me if he thinks I've done something I ought not to have done."

"But that's just the thing, isn't it? You must help me right a terrible wrong. Drive faster! Can you not make them run faster?"

"We'll lather the horses!"

"But it may be too late! Please, *please* try and make them run faster."

"Hiya!" Robert roared, startling her, and slapped the reins against the horses' backs. They broke into a run so quickly that Prudence bounced high in her seat, she shrieked with surprise as she grabbed the handrail to steady her.

A quarter of an hour later, they barreled down High Street, and slid to a rough halt between the inn and the post house.

"Oh no," Prudence said. "No, no, no." It was too

late—the mailbags that had been set out this morning were gone.

"What do I do now, miss?" Robert asked.

But Prudence had already launched herself from the wagon's bench. She ran into the post house, startling the clerk inside. "Has the Royal Post coach come?" she asked him anxiously.

"Yes," he said, as if that were a ridiculous question. "She ain't never late, not unless there's rain. Left promptly at a quarter past."

Prudence gasped and pressed a hand to her chest. The pain to her heart was very real, bubbling through her like a streak of hot grease. "Which way?" she asked.

"Only way it'll go this time of day." The clerk pointed north.

Prudence whirled around and ran outside. She looked at Robert and his team of two horses. The Royal Post was pulled by a team of four. It was impossible that a team of two horses could catch a team of four fresh horses.

It really was too late, and Prudence felt her body sag with the weight of her loss.

CHAPTER TWELVE

ROAN FELT ILL.

Not physically ill—he would have welcomed something as mundane as that. Just...*ill*.

He'd taken one look into the interior of this coach, seen the young mother with her two children and a highborn gentleman who nodded congenially at him, and he'd shut the door without a word. He'd stalked to the back of the coach, where the coachmen had loaded his bags, and two sacks with the official seal of the Royal Post, and had climbed onto the back bench.

He was angry with himself for having allowed this... *affair* with Prudence. That's what it was—a dalliance. What else could it have been? He could tell himself that she was beautiful, and that he, being a man with urges more powerful than any force, had no hope of resisting the temptation of her. He told himself that like the dalliances before this, the sting of ending it would subside by the time the coach left Himple.

Roan could tell himself any number of things, but as that damn post coach positively meandered down the road, none of the things he told himself seemed to ease him. The only thing working in him was a fervent, regretful longing.

He was being irrational. Childish. Where was the man in him? Where was that mighty being capable of tamping down useless emotions? The one who could agree that a marriage to Susannah Pratt would benefit all concerned and easily convince himself that was reason enough to marry? That man was apparently lying in the road, trampled by his runaway emotions because Roan was truly and utterly heartsick.

They stopped in a hamlet to change horses. Roan glanced at the two men in worn brown coats and buckskins who rode up top with him. None of them looked very talkative, and for that Roan was grateful.

As the coach rolled away from the hamlet, the fresh team as plodding as the first, Roan closed his eyes, hoping to block the image of Prudence leaving, twisted around on the seat beside that boy to see him. But in his effort to block that image, another one, of the two of them last night, invaded his thoughts. Of Prudence's creamy flesh, of the soft curves of her body, of how fragrant she smelled and how silky her hair. *How she'd gazed at him. How it had felt to be inside her.*

A strong shiver ran down his spine.

The coach rocked unsteadily, and his mood grew blacker. He hoped they reached West Lee soon, for who could say what tree he might fell, what beast he might taunt if this ordeal didn't end. He stared off into the distance, watching fields turn to forest, then turned his attention to the ribbon of road they left in their wake as they jangled along. That was when he noticed a wagon coming at them. And at quite a clip, too.

The driver was bent low over the reins, and Roan couldn't make out if the driver meant to catch them or pass them. Whatever he meant to do, he was driving much too fast for that wagon.

The guard had noticed them too and pulled his gun

from his shoulder and readied it. "Highwaymen?" a passenger asked, but the guard said nothing.

Roan squinted at the wagon through the dust the post coach was kicking up. That was no highwayman. Highwaymen did not make daring mistakes in wagons, they made them on horseback. A movement to the driver's right caught his attention and Roan gasped. *That* was Prudence, and she was trying to stand!

"Slow the coach!" he shouted and surged to his feet. "Stop!"

"Sit down, sir!" the guard ordered him. "You'll fall and break your neck but good."

"Halt!" Roan shouted. "Halt, halt!"

"What call have we to stop?" one of the men demanded. "So that we might be robbed?"

"That wagon is for me!" Roan yelled. "It's for me!"

"Then let them be for you at the next stop," the man barked. "We don't all stop for it."

"Halt the goddamn coach!" Roan roared. The guard shouted at the driver, and the coach began to slow so quickly that Roan did indeed almost fall from it.

"Bloody hell," the man in buckskins swore at him as the wagon shuddered to such a violent halt behind the coach that it appeared as if it might come apart.

The two horses were lathered and breathing hard as if they had raced all the way from the Bulworth estate. Roan leaped to the ground as Prudence scrambled down from her seat. "What are you doing?" he exclaimed. "What utterly mad, foolish, imprudent thing are you doing?"

Prudence was beaming. She was breathing as if she'd run alongside the team of horses, but she was beaming.

"Weslay," she said as she tried to drag breath into her. "Maybe I ought to see you to Weslay."

Emotions Roan didn't recognize rushed through him, and he grabbed her up in a rough embrace.

"Maybe you ought," he muttered, and kissed her cheek. He put his arm around her and dragged her to the coach, yanked the door open and practically shoved her inside. "Make room, make room," he commanded, and to Prudence he added, "I'll get your things."

He stalked to the wagon and took her trunk himself, carrying it to the coach and lashing it on. He grabbed her smaller bag, too. "There you are," he said to the young driver, and handed him a banknote, the value of which he didn't even notice. Whatever it was, it was not enough, it could never be enough. Roan was elated, his heart rushing with the thrill of knowing she'd come back to him.

He carried Prudence's smaller bag to the coach's interior.

"What of the cost of her passage?" the driver called down.

Roan handed him a few coins and stuck his head in the door of the coach. He could see by the expressions of the other passengers that his bulk was not welcome inside, but he came nonetheless, fitting himself in beside her and taking her hand in his, held it tightly.

Prudence was speaking to the man she was pressed against, her speech animated, her breath still ragged. "…thought perhaps I should take the morning coach, but my father he…he is particularly unwell and I shouldn't like to go alone. So we raced ahead to catch the post coach and…and my cousin."

She was explaining herself, he took it, and he knew

a moment of consternation—she owed these people no explanation. But she beamed at Roan, clearly pleased with her story.

The man beside her, who was dressed in a coat of navy superfine, a brocade waistcoat and boots polished to a very high sheen, smiled as if particularly amused by her story. "My, all this way to travel with your cousin?"

Roan gave the man a look that conveyed fair warning.

"Yes, my cousin," Prudence said, nodding with great enthusiasm. Too much enthusiasm, really—no one was that excited to see a cousin.

The gentleman noticed it, too, Roan could see, and smiled again, his knowing gaze meeting Roan's over the top of her head.

Let him think what he wanted, Roan didn't care.

Prudence smiled up at Roan. "You're not cross with me, are you?" she asked gaily. He noticed her face and clothes bore a thin coat of dust from the road. But he saw only the color in her porcelain skin, the flash of happiness in her eyes. "It seemed the only possible solution."

"I am very happy you heeded my advice. But how—"

"I don't know!" she said with breathless enthusiasm, anticipating his question. "I thought we'd never reach you."

"We are fortunate that these post teams plod along, aren't we?" he said. He smiled, too, as if this were all a trifling thing, a silly thing for his young cousin to do. But he was acutely aware of the gentleman's study of him and Prudence, of the way the mother made her children look away from Prudence. And still, he didn't care, he didn't *care*. She was *here*, beside him, and he was astounded by how happy her race to catch him had made him. Imprudently so. Disturbingly, imprudently, ridiculously so.

Perhaps she understood him, for Prudence laughed lightly and her eyes shone at him. "I lost my bonnet," she said.

"You lost your bonnet!" he repeated absurdly, and chortled with joy, so loudly that he drew the attention of the others in the coach.

The coach rolled on, through forests of chestnuts and oaks, past fields dotted with sheep and cattle. The land began to roll, the fields giving way to big hills that taxed the teams. They changed horses every ten miles now instead of fifteen, and on one of those stops the gentleman from the coach sidled over to Roan. "Your cousin is quite comely."

Roan slowly turned his head and glared at him. "And?"

"She's English, isn't she? And you are…well, I don't know what you are, but judging by your accent I'd say you're an American."

"What of it?"

The man shrugged. "Nothing at all." He smiled at Roan and sauntered away.

The man made Roan uncomfortable. He worried for Prudence. Still, he reasoned once they reached West Lee, they'd never see the man again. In the meantime, Roan wouldn't allow the man's overt curiosity to dampen his happiness.

They continued on, passing over old stone bridges, rolling past a castle ruin and disappearing into the shadows beneath a canopy of trees. A few pine trees began to appear in the mix of foliage as they wended north. The sun was sinking into the western horizon. Roan longed to be off that coach and be with Prudence while he could. He thought he was on the verge of expiring with impatience when at last they crested a hill and one of the coachmen shouted "Weslay! Weslay's next!"

"Look there," Prudence said, and pointed out the coach window. In the distance, a large house sat majestically on a hill, built of graying limestone and anchored by two square towers on either end. The house was so large that it boasted enough chimneys to warm the entire Hudson Valley in winter.

"Howston Hall," said the gentleman next to Prudence. "It is the home of Viscount Penfors."

Roan was startled. *That* was the Penfors residence? That's where Aurora had gone? "It's enormous," he muttered.

"Sixteen guest rooms," the gentleman said, and at Roan's look, he added, "his lordship is a friend of mine. I am rather familiar with the property."

That was unwelcome news. Prudence must have realized, too, they'd not be rid of him, as Roan felt her stiffen beside him.

The coach veered right and rolled into the picturesque village with its whitewashed cottages, a pair of churches with tall spires and a lovely center green, upon which some elderly gentlemen were lawn bowling in the late afternoon. All the passengers disembarked here; the team was taken out of its traces, and several men appeared to remove the luggage and then pull the carriage to a brick carriage house at the end of the high street.

The woman who had ridden in the coach bustled her children across a crowded street and disappeared into a path between two buildings. The two men who'd ridden up top disappeared into the inn. But the English gentleman lingered.

Of course he did.

"I shall inquire if there is transport to the hall, shall I?" Prudence asked, shaking out her skirts as she spoke.

"To the hall?" the gentleman asked, overhearing her. "I beg your pardon, I thought you were hastening to your poor father's side."

Prudence blinked. "We are. We *will*. But we should pay our respects to his lordship while we are so near."

"Well, then! If you're among his lordship's guests for the weekend, there is no need for transport—I've already arranged a carriage." He smiled at Roan. "You and your cousin are welcome to join me."

"Oh no, we wouldn't think of imposing," Prudence said, and glanced at Roan from the corner of her eye. "We'll manage well enough."

"Impose! It's a carriage, Miss…?"

"Thank you, but we might linger in the village. It's lovely." She clasped her hands and turned partially away from the gentleman, pretending to admire the village.

But the gentleman was not going to be swayed. "This is not Mayfair," he said jovially. "There are not hacks on every street corner. You best seize your opportunity, and I am happy to be of service. That is…if you are certain you are not needed by your ailing father?" He smiled.

Roan didn't know about Mayfair, but he could see the flush in Prudence's neck and knew she did not want to get in a carriage with this man. He was also aware that the gentleman was probably correct—there were not many alternatives other than their feet. He stepped forward. "Her father is in good hands. We should like to pay a visit to his benefactor."

"Oh, his *benefactor*," the gentleman said, looking very amused now.

Roan wanted to plant his fist in the gentleman's face. "Is there something you'd like to say, sir?"

"Only that I would be happy to take you up to the hall."

Roan was uneasy with this turn of events. But he was also acutely aware that Aurora may be up on that hill now, preparing for supper. He swallowed his pride and misgivings—if Aurora was there, he had to reach her. "Who might we have the pleasure of thanking for this offer?"

"Lord Stanhope," the gentleman said cheerfully, and Roan was certain he heard a tiny mewl of despair from Prudence. "And you are...?"

"Matheson," Roan said.

Stanhope's gaze slid to Prudence.

"We'll just get our trunks," Roan said.

"I'll have the boy do it. If you'll just tell me the names on your trunks?"

"They're heavy," Roan parried. "Cousin, will you come? You can carry the valise." He put his hand on Prudence's elbow and quickly moved her away from Stanhope.

"Roan," she whispered frantically. "This is a *disaster*." She stole a glimpse of Stanhope over her shoulder. "I should never have come! I should have stayed on the wagon, I should have gone to Cassandra!"

"No, you shouldn't have, you should have done precisely what you did and come with me. I have never been so happy to see anyone as I was to see you. I don't know who he is, but, Pru, don't fret," he said as he examined the luggage on the sidewalk. "He's curious."

"He's Lord *Stanhope*!" Prudence frantically interrupted. "He's an *earl*, Roan."

"Royal?"

"What—*no*!" She grabbed Roan's arm. "I *know* him," she whispered hotly.

"Calm yourself, Pru. He'll see your distress and suspect any number of things."

She nodded, agreeing, and took a breath. "I know *of* him," she amended, a bit calmer. "I have never been formally introduced, but Honor has, and he is familiar with my family and belongs to the same club as Augustine. He will know my name, he will know what I've done and he will tell all of London!"

Roan looked to where Stanhope was chatting with a porter and gesturing in their direction. "You have nothing to worry about," Roan said. "You're my cousin, remember? Miss Cabot has—"

Prudence gasped and punched him on the arm.

"Ow," he said, surprised by the strength of her swing.

"Don't utter that name!"

"I only meant to remark that…*she* has stayed behind at Blackwood Hall—"

Prudence gasped and punched him again.

"I didn't say it!" Roan protested.

"You said Blackwood Hall," she hissed, her eyes darting to Stanhope. "All of London knows who resides at Blackwood Hall now."

"All right, I understand. I won't—"

"All of London will know it," she frantically said

again. "*All* of London, and you may trust I will be made the laughingstock of the *haut ton*. Why, *why* did I ever think I could be like my sisters?" she pleaded skyward. "I never even wanted to *be* like them, but look at me. I'm the worst of us all! Merryton and Augustine will have my—"

"Pardon." It was Stanhope again, having appeared at Roan's elbow, still smiling as if he and Roan and Prudence were enjoying a little secret.

Prudence pressed her lips tightly together and turned away from him, as if she were now trying to hide her face. "My boy will take your things. You need only point." He chuckled, as if he found it all very amusing, and walked away again.

"It is beyond hope," Prudence said weakly.

This woman standing beside him, looking so utterly dejected, had been the picture of calm and determination the past two days, happy to play the part of cousin or wife, happy to experience her adventure with him. She'd shot a man and kept her head, for God's sake. Roan didn't know what it was about this man that should change it, but he wanted to box his ears for having ruined it all. "Be still," he said soothingly, and put his hand to the small of her back as he pointed to the trunks for the boy. "We'll be rid of him soon enough."

"Oh, Roan," she said in a tone that sounded as if she pitied him. She smiled sadly. "*You* will. Not me."

Roan felt a roil of guilt and the weight of their folly slowly closing in on them.

As the trunks were loaded, Lord Stanhope gestured for them to board the carriage. He helped Prudence inside the coach. Roan followed and sat beside her and across from Stanhope, eyeing the man closely, debating what was to be done with him. Their lark had shifted from intensely pleasurable to troublesome. He'd been so happy to see Prudence, he hadn't thought through what was happening. He couldn't help agree with her—she should have stayed on the wagon. She should have gone on to her friend.

As the carriage rolled from town, Stanhope said to Prudence, "I beg your pardon, miss, but I've yet to have the pleasure of your acquaintance."

"Matheson," she said slowly, surprising Roan. "I am Miss Matheson."

One of Stanhope's brows rose curiously over the other. "*Matheson*. It is my great pleasure to make your acquaintance, Miss Matheson. Now you must tell me from where you hail. You look quite familiar to me, and I think perhaps we've met before? Almack's perhaps?"

"I'm sure we haven't, my lord," Prudence said quickly, shaking her head. "I am from the west country. How very kind of you to bring us along. This is a lovely carriage. The springs seem new. Are they new?" she asked, bouncing a bit on the seat.

The *springs*? Roan looked at Prudence.

"I hardly know," Stanhope said, his gaze steady on Prudence. "The carriage is hired."

"Where is your home, my lord?" Roan asked, drawing the man's attention to him.

"London," Stanhope said. "Near Grosvenor Square."

"Have you just come down from London? What's the news?" Roan asked, and continued to pepper Stanhope with questions so that he couldn't question Prudence. For her part, Prudence ignored them, fanning herself as if she were overly warm.

But when Roan began to question Stanhope about

London trade—to satisfy his own curiosity if nothing else—Stanhope waved a hand at him, his signet ring blinking in the waning light of the day. "I don't concern myself with trade, sir. So. You're cousins, are you?" he asked before Roan could begin to speak of the weather. "I would suppose, Mr. Matheson, that your father is your cousin's relation by..."

"Brothers," said Roan, at the very moment Prudence said, "My mother." The moment she did, she closed her eyes and pressed two fingers to the point just between her brows.

Stanhope laughed. "There seems to be some confusion."

"Not at all," Prudence said, recovering at once. "My mother is married to his father's brother." She smiled, and Roan sensed she was rather pleased with herself for having thought quickly.

Stanhope was clearly entertained by this ridiculous banter. The three of them were all very aware that the lies were piling up in the interior of that carriage, but only one of them was diverted by it. The question Roan wanted answered was what, exactly, Stanhope would do with the lies. For the moment, he looked as if he would like to have carried on, poking and prodding Prudence, but the carriage turned and Howston Hall came into view.

Roan was momentarily distracted from the dance of words with Stanhope because the house was even grander as they neared it. He couldn't begin to imagine how Aurora had gained an invitation here. Through what acquaintance? For what purpose?

The road went through the forest, so only the front of the house was visible, but even that small glimpse was enough to startle one into silence. It stood three stories high, all stone. Rows of sparkling windows on each floor looked over the forest. Ivy covered one of the two anchoring towers, and a trellis of roses had been trained to create an arch over the doorway.

The carriage turned onto the drive, circling around an enormous green, in the middle of which was a stone fountain, fashioned to look as if three fish were leaping over one another, their three mouths open and spouting water. Two peacocks strutted about the fountain, pecking at the grass.

The house was a beautiful, idyllic vista. Roan had never seen anything quite as grand as this, except perhaps in books, or in paintings that hung over mantels in New York, and he couldn't help be impressed with the size of it. The house where Roan's family resided, considered to be one of the grandest homes in the valley, and situated in a setting very similar to this, was only half as large.

The carriage rolled to a stop.

The pair of double doors that marked the entrance suddenly opened, and a butler and two footmen—Roan supposed this, given their livery—ran out onto the drive and stood at attention as the coachman came down from the bench up top and opened the carriage door.

Stanhope was the first to alight, and paused just outside, offering his hand to Prudence.

"My lord, you are welcome," the butler said. "Madam."

Roan stepped out of the carriage behind Prudence just as a very short and round gentleman came hurrying out of the house. He had florid cheeks and a wide nose, and looked to be in the vicinity of his sixth decade. Close on his heels was a woman who was a head taller than him, and nearly as round. She had the sort of soft, doughy face Roan's grandmother had sported in her dotage.

"My lord Stanhope! We thought you'd not come!" the man said happily.

"You'll be very glad you have, you know," the woman said, bubbling with enthusiasm. "You've missed all the excitement! Redmayne very nearly shot Lady Vanderbeck!"

"*Shot* her!" Stanhope exclaimed, and took the woman's hand, bowing over it.

"Silly woman means with the badminton cock, of course. We won't allow Redmayne to have a gun, not after last time, what?" the man said. "Oh! You've brought friends," he said, seeing Roan and Prudence. He cast his arms wide. "You are most welcome!"

Stanhope, Roan noticed, did not dispel the idea that they were friends, but merely looked at Roan as if he expected Roan to deny it. Roan wasn't about to do any such thing, not before he at least knew who this man was to his sister.

"How do you do," Roan began, but was interrupted by galloping horses and laughing riders who thundered onto the drive.

"Penfors, really!" cried one woman. She was dressed in a ruby riding habit with a matching hat placed jauntily to one side of her head. "You didn't tell us the road's been washed away!"

"Has it?" asked the short, portly gentleman, who was, apparently, Lord Penfors. "I wasn't aware. Were you aware, darling?" He turned toward the woman who'd come out with him.

"I've heard no reports of it!" she protested as if she were being accused. "Cyril?" she shouted, twirling about, marching toward the house. "Cyril! What is this news of the road being washed away?"

"Stanhope!" the woman in ruby called out. "You bounder, you." She leaped off her horse and ran for him. "I knew you'd come!"

Stanhope laughed. "I take great exception to being called a bounder, madam. I have not yet reached that lofty status," he said, and greeted her enthusiastic hug with one of his own.

"Oh, Penfors!" the woman said as she linked her arm through Stanhope's, "you must welcome Mr. Fitzhugh into our party." She gestured to a gentleman who was still seated on an enormous, fine, black stallion. "He has come from Scotland with a very big purse, as it seems he sold the castle after all."

"Yes, of course, you must join us, Mr. Fitzhugh. You are most welcome," Penfors said as the man hopped down and a groom ran out to fetch his horse. Fitzhugh bowed low and scraped his hat against the road, thanking Penfors before running to catch up with Stanhope and the woman in ruby, who were walking inside. The other riders moved on, laughing and chatting on their way to the stables.

That left Penfors, and Roan and Prudence standing awkwardly in the drive as servants bustled about them. "Oh, I do beg your pardon," Penfors said, tilting his head back to look up at Roan. "Have we been introduced, my lord?"

"Regrettably, no," Roan said. He saw Penfors's wife bustle out of the house and hurry toward them. "I offer my sincere apologies for arriving unannounced. I am Roan Matheson. And this is—"

But Penfors suddenly pivoted about before Roan could introduce his supposed cousin. "Cyril!" he shouted. "A room for Mr. and Mrs. Matheson! They are Stanhope's guests so it must be a *good* room, Cyril, not one in the west wing."

"Oh no!" Prudence cried. "You mustn't—"

"Nonsense, madam. Stanhope is our very good friend, and therefore, so are *you*." He looked at Roan. "I wouldn't think of putting you in the west wing. We save those rooms for the scoundrels who turn up uninvited." He laughed heartily.

"My lord!" his wife said, having arrived in their midst once more. "That is not true." She looked at Prudence. "We simply do not welcome scoundrels at Howston Hall."

"You can't say that we don't," Penfors said. "Did you look about the supper table last night?"

"I *can* say it and I just did. Now come with me, Mrs. Matheson," she said, holding out her hand to Prudence. "Is your maid coming?"

"I haven't—"

"Oh, that's quite all right. We've plenty of girls. I daresay we employ all of Weslay here, do we not, Penfors?"

"Yes, quite a lot of them. All right, then, Matheson, are you a good hand in cards?" Penfors asked as Lady Penfors began to drag a stricken Prudence along with her.

"I, ah…I neither win too often nor lose too often," Roan said.

Penfors roared with laughter at that, startling Roan.

"What a strange way you speak! That must be Eton. It's Eton training isn't it? I was a Cambridge man myself."

"My lord! Do stop talking and allow the poor man to his room!" his wife yelled. "They will quite obviously want to bathe before supper, and we haven't much time."

"No, we haven't, have we?" Penfors asked, peering at his pocket watch.

"Mind you keep your bride close, Matheson," she shouted over her shoulder. "Penfors is quite right, we've a house full of rakes and rogues!" She laughed gaily as she maneuvered Prudence in the door and disappeared into the house.

"If you will follow me, sir," the butler said, and walked briskly behind the footman who carried the trunks.

"You seem alarmed," Penfors said. "Do you shoot?"

Roan paused. "Scoundrels?"

Penfors laughed so hard, his eyes squeezed shut and tears leaked from the corners as he settled one hand on his belly to contain it. "What a delight, a delight! Did you hear him, Mother? He's very clever!" Penfors shouted, even though his wife had gone inside. He hastened toward the entrance, leaving Roan to bring up the rear.

CHAPTER THIRTEEN

THE GUEST ROOM they were rushed to was sumptuous, Prudence thought, with a high, feathered bed and tall, double windows with a magnificent view of the lake behind the house. The bed was surrounded by brocade hangings, the floor covered in thick carpets, and above the mantel, a masterfully rendered depiction of a fox hunt.

Prudence hardly noticed any of it—she frowned at Roan every time she passed him as she paced before the hearth, pausing only once at the window, her arms folded tightly, to watch two swans glide westward. It appeared as if they would glide right into the setting sun. That's what Prudence felt she'd done—she'd been so blinded by the bright light that was Roan, so enthralled, she'd glided right into a ball of fire.

She whirled away from the window and passed Roan again, this time halting before him, her hands on her hips.

He was seated, his boots propped on a footstool, a glass of brandy dangling from his fingers. He arched a brow.

"How can you sit there as we swim into the sun?" she demanded of him, gesturing to the window.

"Pardon?"

Prudence waved her hand at him—there was no time

to explain the volatile mix of emotions now, how the joy and hope and been swallowed whole by Stanhope. "Stanhope knows me, I'm certain of it. Do you realize what that means?"

"No," Roan said, and shook his head. "Pru, he doesn't *know* you. He has an idea of you, that's all."

"An idea of me! What do you mean?"

Roan sighed. He put his brandy aside and his feet on the floor, then leaned forward, bracing his arms against his knees. "How shall I say it? He has an idea of the sort of woman you are—"

Prudence gasped and whirled away from Roan.

"No, I didn't—" Roan's hands were suddenly on her waist, and he pulled her back against his chest. "I didn't say it to distress you. But what he knows is that something is amiss, and a man's thoughts naturally wander in that direction—"

"Naturally?"

"What I mean is," he said, squeezing her to him, nuzzling her neck, "that this is the most plausible explanation, given that he knows nothing of our circumstances. You said you've never met him. He doesn't know who you are. You must keep in mind that we'll be gone as soon as I find Aurora, and you won't see him again."

"How do you know that I won't?" Prudence shrugged Roan's hands from her and stepped away, turning around to face him. "Roan..." She paused, uncertain how to express herself. "This has been the most astonishing and wonderful thing to ever happen to me. I thought I could carry it with me. But when I saw him, I..." She groaned. "I've been such a bloody fool!"

"No, I won't abide that," Roan said, pointing at

her. He slipped his fingers under her chin, forcing her to look up at him. "You've been a vibrant, beautiful woman who has quenched her thirst for life. If you denounce our adventure for *that* popinjay, you will slay my poor heart." He cupped her face. "You won't slay me, will you, Prudence?"

Prudence couldn't resist a small smile. "No."

"Good girl," he said, taking her in his arms. "I'd hate to strangle a man before supper."

Prudence sighed and rested her head against his chest. "What do we do now?"

"What can we do? We're here. I must inquire after Aurora. So I suggest we take the bath Lady Penfors has graciously offered. We'll attend this insufferable supper and hopefully find Aurora there or at least hear some word of her, some idea of where she might have gone. And then, we take our leave of Howston Hall. As you said, in the end, no one will be the wiser."

"You don't understand, Roan! He is an *earl*, he moves in the same society as my family."

"Listen to me," Roan said sternly. "If you see Stanhope at some future date and he is rotten enough to question you, or suggest that you were here, you merely deny it. Prudence Cabot wasn't here tonight. Prudence *Matheson* was. It is the word of a chaste young debutante against a man, and from what you've told me, no one will believe that you, tucked away at Blackwood Hall as you are, will have somehow appeared here without escort or invitation. I can't believe it when I say it out loud."

"It does seem very simple when you say it," she said uncertainly.

"I think it is still as simple as it seemed to you in

Ashton Down when you put yourself on that stage-coach, Pru. We've come upon a bump in the road, but it's nothing we can't overcome. It's one night. Look at what we've done! And you think a man as namby-pamby as Stanhope will ruin us? *Impossible.* We are a formidable team, Miss Matheson."

She smiled ruefully. She wanted desperately to agree, and to believe Roan, and when she looked up into his topaz eyes, she could see that he desperately wanted to believe it, too. How she wished she would never return to her life. How she wished that she and Roan could keep looking for his sister, across England, across Europe, across the world, just the two of them surviving by their wits.

"Come here," he said soothingly, and drew her closer, kissing her softly. When he kissed her like this—so tenderly, so caring—Prudence could believe him. She could believe that this would be all right in the end.

A knock at the door separated them; Roan slipped away from her and allowed the footmen in with the bath, and the maids behind him with the water. "I shall leave you to your bath, Mrs. Matheson," he said, and picked up his brandy and wandered into the adjoining sitting room.

After a bath, and a bit of brandy herself, and a girl to help her put up her hair, Prudence did feel somewhat better. She was prepared for Stanhope's questions and was determined to make a game of it, staying a step or two ahead of him.

She dressed in a gold silk with delicate embroidery, and a pale green train embroidered with the gold of her gown. The girl who had come to help her dress threaded a green ribbon through Prudence's hair and put it up.

After the past two days, Prudence felt a bit like a princess. She donned an emerald necklace and matching earrings and her favorite satin shoes.

Roan was in the sitting room, standing at the window, his hands clasped at his back. He'd dressed in a formal coat with tails and dark trousers. "Roan?"

He turned around at the sound of her voice. A snowy-white neckcloth was tied just below his chin and stood out starkly from the black-and-gold-striped waistcoat he wore. He looked magnificent, as robust and handsome as a man had ever looked to Prudence. *A prince. An American prince.* Her heart swelled with adoration. Or was it love? Whatever she was feeling was deep and flowing.

Roan's gaze slowly moved over her, taking her in. "Dear God, how beautiful you are."

She blushed with pleasure and glanced down. "That is kind of you to say."

"You are as lovely a woman as I have ever seen in my life." He shook his head. "But you must hear that from many admirers. They must all tell you what a unique beauty you are."

Prudence laughed self-consciously. "No."

"I mean it," he said, and touched the back of his hand to her cheek, then brushed his knuckles against her décolletage. "You have astounded me every day, but tonight, you've taken my breath away." He leaned down, kissed her tenderly on the lips.

She smiled and stroked his jaw. "I adore you, do you know it?" She twined her hands around his neck and pulled his head down. "You're very handsome yourself. I suppose *you* hear that from all the little birds flitting about you in America, don't you?"

"Birds don't flit around me," he said, and kissed her as his hands slid down her ribs, to her hips. But he didn't linger, lifting his head with a sigh. "You're a temptress. I would like nothing better than to tear that gown from you now, seam by seam." He ran his thumb lightly across her lip. "How did it happen? How were you standing on that green in Ashton Down on the day, the hour, the moment, I should arrive?"

"I would ask the same of you."

"For the rest of my life, I will ask myself that question." He shook his head and kissed the top of her head. "All right, then, Prudence, chin up. Smile at them as you've smiled at me, and they will be charmed to their toes and eating out of our hands by midnight."

She slipped her hand into his. "I confess I prefer the little fire on the brook with only you and me and the nag."

Roan laughed. "Never let it be said that Roan Matheson doesn't know how to woo a lady."

IT WAS ONLY half-past seven, too early for supper, and yet there were at least two dozen souls in the salon if there was one, and all of them appeared to have been in the wine for hours.

Penfors greeted them at the door and insisted on taking them around, introducing them around as "Stanhope's guests." Stanhope, Prudence noticed, did not attempt to correct Penfors, but merely smiled at Prudence as if they'd conspired together in this.

She refused to acknowledge him, her skin tingling with the agony of her dread.

Roan's gaze scanned the crowd, searching for his sister. All the while, Lord Vanderbeck, a thin man lacking a firm chin, was quite taken with the idea that Roan would hail from New York, and caught him up in a torrent of questions. What was the commerce, how did the navy fare, had he ever been to Philadelphia. Roan answered politely and seemed at ease with the gentleman.

Vanderbeck was tedious, and Prudence found herself looking around, too, for a woman who might resemble Roan. She was so intent on her search that she was startled when Lady Penfors appeared at her elbow.

"You don't want to listen to *that* blowing wind," Lady Penfors said loudly, apparently uncaring if Vanderbeck heard her or not. "Come, there are others for you to meet."

Prudence was introduced to the young, ginger-haired Mr. Fitzhugh, who very openly admired her décolletage. Mr. and Mrs. Gastineau barely spared her a look. Mr. Redmayne and his companion, Mr. True, politely greeted her, and Mr. True pointed out his sister, the widow Barton. Prudence recognized the widow Barton as the woman in ruby who had so exuberantly leaped off her horse to greet Stanhope.

And then she saw Lord Stanhope a few feet away, his gaze locked on her. It seemed she would have his undivided attention once again. He started in her direction, but Lady Penfors barreled in between them.

"Stanhope, I wonder why you've not introduced Mrs. Barton to your friend."

Prudence avoided Stanhope's gaze. "How do you do?" she asked politely of the woman.

Mrs. Barton had lively brown eyes and a charmingly dimpled smile. "Oh my, *you're* quite a beauty, aren't you?" she said as she surveyed Prudence from the ribbon in her hair to the tips of her satin slippers.

"This is Mrs. Matheson," Lady Penfors practically bellowed.

"Ah…" Prudence could feel the rush of heat to her face. She frantically thought of how to correct Lady Penfors, but Mrs. Barton spoke first.

"What a *stunning* gown," she said approvingly. "It looks to be the work of Mrs. Dracott," she added, referring to the most sought-after modiste in London.

Prudence had never dreamed anyone would make note of her gown. As it happened, it *was* the work of Mrs. Dracott and Prudence was momentarily stunned into silence. Mrs. Dracott's clientele was very elite. To admit she wore a Dracott gown was tantamount to admitting she was more than what she'd let on.

Mrs. Barton laughed roundly at Prudence's momentary fluster. "I've stepped in it, haven't I? I've forgotten that Mrs. Dracott's gowns are above the reach of most. I've been *very* fortunate in that regard." She turned a little to her right and to her left to draw attention to her pale rose silk gown.

"It's beautiful," Prudence said, realizing she was meant to comment.

"Thank you," Mrs. Barton said with a wink. "I should like to paint *your* gown!" she said with a swirl of her fan above her head, and Prudence wasn't entirely certain if she meant to paint on her gown, or copy it onto a canvas. "Who has made it?"

"Who?" Prudence repeated, then cleared her throat as she desperately searched for an answer. "My, ah… my mother."

Stanhope chuckled, drawing Prudence's attention.

"Silly man!" Mrs. Barton said, and leaned against Stanhope. "What, do you think that only a modiste might put thread to fabric? Of *course* her mother fashioned her gown!"

"If you say so," Stanhope said, smiling at Prudence.

Prudence's heart began to sink to her toes. She had the very nauseating feeling that Stanhope was referring to *her* mother in particular, that he somehow knew it was impossible for her mother to sew anything—much less a gown as intricate as this.

"I can very well imagine that lovely train swimming about behind you as you dance," Mrs. Barton said. She suddenly gasped. "That's it! We must have a dance. Lady Penfors!" she shouted, forcing Prudence to lean back as she waved her fan across Prudence in the direction of Lady Penfors.

That was the worst idea—Prudence was certain she'd be made to stand up with Stanhope.

"A grand idea," Lady Penfors called back. "Yes, yes, we must, straightaway, after we dine. Cyril! Where are you, Cyril? Send down to the village for musicians at once!"

"Is it possible to find musicians at this late hour?" Prudence asked, trying to derail the plans for dancing.

"You can't object. It's been decided," Mrs. Barton trilled as the harried butler reached his mistress's side.

There was a lively conversation between Lady Penfors and Cyril after which Cyril scurried away, gesturing for a footman, and Lady Penfors began to clap her hands as if she were trying to gain the attention of a group of children. "Attention! Attention everyone! Supper is served. Find your partners, please, and prepare to promenade!"

As the guests began to find their partners, Roan made his way to Prudence's side. "You must promise to come at once and save me if Vanderbeck comes in my direction," he muttered. "Shoot to kill if you must."

"Did you find her?" Prudence whispered.

Roan shook his head. "I haven't seen her. I tried to ascertain if all the guests were down for the evening, but the question invited more talk from Vanderbeck."

There was no opportunity to say more—Mr. Fitzhugh sidled next to Prudence and remarked that they'd gone without rain for far too long now, and didn't she think the south lawn looked a bit brown?

In the dining room, Prudence was relieved to see that she and Roan were seated across from each other and at the opposite end of the long table from Stanhope. Not that it dampened his interest in her; Prudence could feel his gaze on her, making the hair on the back of her neck stand. Mrs. Gastineau sat to her right, and an elderly gentleman, Lord Mount, sat on her left. He was quite old and quite deaf, which Prudence thought might have something to do with the amount of hair growing in his ears.

No one around her seemed curious as to her presence. No one looked askance at her or Roan as if they suspected a deception. Roan was right—she had only to make the best of it, and it would be over soon. She began to relax as the meal was served. She glanced around at the people gathered. It was a strange collection of guests, and she was not acquainted with any of them, save Stanhope. Moreover, Howston Hall was so removed that she could now agree with Roan—the chances of her seeing any of these people again seemed very small.

The supper was actually quite pleasant. They dined on soup and pheasant, they drank wine, and the conversation centered around the planned shoot on the morrow. It was after the plates had been cleared and ices were being brought in that Roan found the opportunity to inquire of Penfors if his sister had come to Howston Hall. "She would have come within the last fortnight or so," he said.

"Miss Matheson!" Lord Penfors said loudly, startling Prudence and several others. She glanced around her and noticed that down the table, Stanhope was watching her. She looked away.

"Aurora Matheson," Roan said. "In her last letter she wrote that she was staying with friends who intended to travel here to call upon you."

"Me?" Penfors said, looking confused.

Roan looked slightly concerned. "She's young," he said. "She has auburn hair and brown eyes."

"Ah, yes, the American girl," Penfors said suddenly. "Such a delight she was. Very witty, that one, and quite good on the hunt."

"The hunt?" Roan repeated uncertainly, as if he suspected Penfors had the wrong Aurora.

"That's *it*!" Penfors suddenly declared, shoving his forefinger high in the air. "That's where I've heard your manner of speech! I thought it Eton, but no sir, you speak in the way that you do because you're a Yankee!"

Roan glanced at Prudence. "Yes," he said curtly.

"A *Yankee*," Mr. Gastineau said. "My grandfather was there, you know, in the colonies, in seventy-seven. Harsh winter. Lost two toes."

"The winters can be brutal," Roan agreed, and turning back to Penfors he asked, "I beg your pardon, my lord, do you mean to say that Aurora has come and gone from Howston Hall?"

"Oh my, yes, she's gone," Penfors said. "When was that, Mother?" he called, rapping loudly on the table to gain his wife's attention. He succeeded in gaining everyone's attention.

"Eh, what?" Lady Penfors responded irritably. "What do you bang on the table?"

"The American girl! When was she here?"

"Oh, the *American* girl! Cute as a button, wasn't she?" Lady Penfors said, suddenly smiling. "Quite good at the hunt."

Roan looked at Prudence with a look of pure confusion.

"Yes, yes, but when was she *here*?" Penfors asked, rapping the table again with his knuckles.

"Here?"

"Yes, here!" he shouted.

"Well, you needn't shout, Penfors, we all hear you very well indeed," Lady Penfors said crossly. "I can't recall when she was here, precisely. When the Villeroys were here. She returned to London with Mr. and Mrs. Villeroy, you will recall. Cyril! When were the Villeroys here?"

"They've been gone a fortnight, madam," the butler said.

"A fortnight!" Lady Penfors yelled down the table, as if no one had heard the butler but her.

"She's gone to London?" Roan repeated, his brow furrowing.

"She took a fancy to Albert, do you recall, Penfors?" Lady Penfors said, then giggled like a girl, pursing her lips naughtily.

"Albert who?" Roan asked.

"Al-*ber*, Al-*ber*," Penfors said, and to Roan, he

added, "she almost drove the poor young man to drink with all her insistence on calling him Albert."

"My sister?" Roan asked, confused.

"Lady Penfors!" his lordship exclaimed, clearly annoyed that Roan wasn't following his line of thought.

"What?" Lady Penfors called out.

"Never you mind, Mother, have your pudding. We've worked it all out. The American girl took a fancy to the Villeroy boy and returned to London with him and his family! Isn't that so?"

"Yes, that is so," Lady Penfors confirmed. "Albert!"

"Al-*ber*," Penfors shouted back at her.

"Christ Almighty," Roan muttered, and sat back, staring into space.

"There's no call for alarm, sir," Penfors said congenially. "The French aren't as randy as they once were. Rather sufferable now, aren't they? And the boy is no threat to your sister. I doubt he could lift a linen without a bit of perspiration."

Mrs. Gastineau laughed at that. "Albert Villeroy. He's a whiff of a boy, isn't he, with high cheekbones and fine, slender hands," she said to Roan.

"I don't care if he has hands like mutton chops," Roan said.

Penfors laughed and pointed at Roan. "Look here, Matheson's in a snit! Our American girl has gone off with the Villeroy boy, has she? Lovely girl your sister, Matheson. Lovely. Quite good at cards."

Roan looked as if he might come completely undone. Prudence pictured him unraveling, starting with his neckcloth, spinning off like a top. "Pardon, my lord," she asked quietly, "but would you happen to know where in London the Villeroys might have gone?"

"Well, of course I know! I've dined there often. Not in the fashionable part of Mayfair, mind you, but on Upper George Street. Do you know it?"

"Yes," Prudence said absently.

"There you are," Stanhope said, and looked at Roan. "Your cousin knows where the Villeroys are, Mr. Matheson. You might send her in after your sister with a shield and a sword."

"Cousin!" Lady Penfors echoed incredulously.

A silence fell over the table. Prudence felt the rush of heat to her face, the fluttering of her heart. This was the moment Stanhope would expose her lie and she would be humiliated before everyone gathered.

But Lord Penfors suddenly howled. "You devil you, Stanhope! She's much too young for Matheson, I grant you," he said, indicating Prudence, "but don't malign the good Mrs. Matheson with your jesting."

Stanhope graciously nodded his head. "I should rather cut out my own tongue than malign the good Mrs. Matheson," he said. "Forgive me, madam, I misunderstood. I thought you were cousins in addition to… your arrangement."

"Goodness, my lord, you should know better than anyone, shouldn't you? They are *your* friends," Lady Penfors said.

"Indeed they are, my lady," he said.

Prudence said nothing. She looked at Roan, whose jaw was as firmly set as the fist that rested next to his plate.

"Oh my, look at the time, Penfors!" Lady Penfors said. "Send for the port."

Thankfully, the supper ended there, and the ladies were instructed by their hostess to retire to the grand salon to oversee the preparations for dancing, while the gentlemen were similarly instructed to enjoy their port.

It was astonishing to see that the musicians had indeed come up from the village while the Penfors guests had dined, a ragtag group of four men who were busy tuning their instruments. By the time the gentlemen rejoined the ladies, Lady Penfors was eager to have the dance get underway, opening with standard country figures.

Roan had scarcely entered the room, his gaze seeking Prudence. He'd almost reached her when he was intercepted by Mrs. Barton, who appeared at his elbow, her smile sultry. "You must allow me to teach you a country dance, sir."

"I think—" Roan tried, but she wouldn't allow him to speak.

"You *must* humor me. I'm very keen to dance with a tall American stranger." She slipped her hand in between his elbow and body, then flagrantly squeezed into his side. "Do Americans dance, Mr. Matheson? Surely not as we do. I think you must like the reels there, don't you?" she asked, tugging him away.

He glanced helplessly over his shoulder at Prudence.

"Mrs. Matheson?"

Prudence whirled about at the sound of Stanhope's voice. He smiled charmingly at her, his eyes blue and shining. "It *is* Mrs., isn't it?"

Prudence lowered her gaze a moment to steel herself, then slowly lifted it. "What do you want, my lord?"

He laughed, delighted. His face softened with his smile and he looked boyishly handsome. "To dance! What did you think? I'll confess that I've been brought into Mrs. Barton's scheme. She inquired after your companion almost before she was off her horse, and I must warn you, she may not allow him to return to you. She can be very determined in that way. I'm to keep you in good company."

"Oh, is *that* what you are to do?" she asked skeptically.

"Of course," he said cheerfully. "It would look peculiar to all if you remain in this corner, frowning as darkly as you are. You don't want to draw undue attention to yourself…do you?"

Prudence understood him, all right.

"Line up, line up!" Lady Penfors shouted as if marshaling forces to attack enemy lines. "The dancing will commence!"

"Come then, cousin, there's no avoiding it," Stanhope said low. He smiled and offered his arm to her again.

With a sigh of frustration, Prudence put her hand on his arm and allowed him to lead her onto the dance floor.

As the first strains of music lifted, Prudence looked for Roan, and curtsied without thought to her partner. She was surprised to see Roan move effortlessly through the first steps; she'd assumed that the English dances would be too foreign to him. But he seemed well at ease. She herself was startled when Stanhope grabbed her hand and pulled her into the first steps.

"You'll have to look at me, I'm afraid."

Prudence looked at him.

"Not even a hint of a smile?" he asked, teasing her. "Perhaps you are still cross with me for the remark I made over supper," he said as he twirled her about before letting go. "But surely you can appreciate my confusion. At first, you were merely his cousin, desperate to reach an ailing father. And then you magically became his wife. It's all very curious."

Stanhope had pale blue eyes, Prudence noticed. A strong chin. He possessed good looks, and under any other circumstance, she would have welcomed his attention. But tonight she found his look and manner unctuous. He arched a brow, waiting for her response as they moved one step to their right and a couple passed down the line.

"You seem out of sorts," he said, still smiling, his gaze still intent on her.

There were so many lies now that Prudence couldn't think of what to say. She'd always been unfailingly honest, and these deceptions were taxing her. But there was one more lie she would tell, one more chance to save what remained of her tattered reputation. She said flatly, "You obviously know the truth."

He arched a brow. "The truth?"

"Don't pretend. The truth is we eloped," she announced. "Just as you suspected." She smiled, pleased at least that there was nothing he could say about that, no holes he could poke in her words.

"*Did* you?" he said, and took her hand again, twirling her about. "How daring! I'm sure you had a good reason."

Prudence colored at the insinuation behind that remark. "Of course."

"Is there a child growing in you?" he asked casually.

The question was so unexpected that Prudence almost choked on a gasp. *"No,"* she said with all due indignation, and sent up a silent prayer that there was no child in her.

Stanhope merely shrugged. "Isn't that why most people elope? Perhaps I am mistaken. Frankly, one never
hears of it, really. There are always rumors of it—this
girl eloped with that boy," he said casually. "Personally, I've never known any debutante to do anything un-
toward. Well, with the notable exception of the Cabot
sisters."

Prudence's heart stopped beating. She missed her
step, stumbling over his feet in her shock. But Stanhope
smoothly caught her and turned her about as if he had
expected her stumble. They both moved one step to the
right. She gaped at Stanhope—how could he know? She
looked frantically about for Roan, but he was twirling
a laughing Mrs. Barton around.

"Don't be alarmed," Stanhope said soothingly.

Don't be alarmed? She was panic-stricken! She felt
flush, could feel a bead of perspiration trickle down her
neck. *Good God, Prudence, don't faint.* What did he
want? Money? Would he extort money from her now
to keep his silence?

Stanhope clucked his tongue at her. "Judging by the
way you are gaping at me, I take it you are surprised
I've not been fooled by your ruse."

"You are mistaken—"

"Come now, Miss Cabot. Has no one ever com-
mented on the remarkable resemblance you bear to your
sister Grace? I had always heard the younger Cabot sisters were the true beauties, and now I see that is true."

Prudence swallowed down another swell of nausea.
"You are acquainted with Grace?"

"Yes, of course. I've also had the great pleasure of
making Mrs. Easton's acquaintance, as well," he said,
referring to Honor.

That was it, then—there was no denying it. Whatever happened now would be nothing compared to the joy she'd known with Roan. She'd been destined to be a spinster anyway, hadn't she?

Stanhope took her hand, twirled her around and let her go, sending her back to her line. They took another step toward the front of the line.

Prudence pressed a hand against her abdomen to soothe her roiling nerves. Rage was building in her, with Stanhope, with the world.

"For heaven's sake, don't faint, darling. That will make it far worse, won't it? You mustn't fret. You've managed a great deceit and I don't intend to reveal it."

Prudence didn't accept his reassurances. She hadn't grown up in the upper echelons of London society without learning how treacherous it was. "I don't intend to faint, my lord," she said coolly. "What do you want? Money? Because I will tell you now I have none."

"That accusation pains me," he said with a wince as they reached the top of the line. He held out his palm to her. She put her hand in his and he swept his arm around her back to lead her down the line. "I want nothing at all, Miss Cabot. I would never take cruel advantage of a woman."

Prudence didn't believe him. She knew nothing about him, but she didn't believe him, not for a moment.

Her heart was pounding, her body perspiring. She danced by rote, the steps as familiar to her as walking. How many times had she and her sisters practiced them? How many dances had she attended? She dipped and leaped and smiled when she should without thought, without anyone seeing the distress that was filling her to almost bursting. Her steps were light and carefree, but when they reached the end of the line, Prudence jerked her hand free of his. "Thank you, but I don't care to dance any longer."

He shrugged. "Enjoy your evening, *Mrs. Matheson*," he said, and with his hands clasped behind his back, he strolled away as if he was touring a garden and smelling roses.

Prudence looked around her, uncertain where to go, where to hide. Everywhere she turned she saw treacherous, knowing faces. It felt as if all the people gathered in this salon knew what she'd done.

When she felt a hand on her arm she jerked away, certain it was Stanhope again.

"Pru!"

She whirled around; Roan's expression was one of concern. "What's happened? What's wrong?

Calm yourself. Poise. She had to be poised. Unruffled. Serene. "I'm fine." She forced a smile. "I'm just... I'm tired. I want to go to bed."

"Penfors won't—"

"Give them my regrets, will you?" she asked quickly, before Roan could argue against it, and slipped away from him, walking briskly to the door of the salon. She didn't look back, but kept walking, smiling at the footman who held the door open. But once she stepped in the hall, Prudence ran, down the carpeted hall and up the grand staircase of Howston Hall like a thief. She ran to the suite, shut the door behind her and locked it. No, no, she couldn't lock it—Roan would come, he would think she'd locked him out. She unlocked it, then backed away from the door, staring at it, her chest rising and falling with anxiety, half expecting Stanhope to burst in.

No one came.

Prudence could see her future spreading before her. She didn't know where or when it would happen, the day Stanhope revealed her scandal. In a museum? At the opera? Would he do it with a whisper, or would he announce it at a ball? She could see it, could see the whispers begin, his smug smile as he watched heads turn, one by one, each person whispering in another's ear. She could hear the laughter, could see Merryton's dismay, Easton's anger. *Have you heard of Prudence Cabot? Yes, the quiet one! As it happens, she is the vilest of them all...*

"You brought this on yourself," she whispered. For so long she had resented Honor and Grace for what they'd done. It was because of them, she'd reasoned, that she had done what she had in Ashton Down only a few days ago, seeking any bit of adventure she could find.

But this had nothing to do with Honor and Grace. This was all *her* doing—the deceptions, the choices, her indifference to propriety, the desires that had propelled her. Her sisters hadn't created a bit of this for her—Prudence had done it all on her own. She knew when she forced the boy to turn the wagon about what it would mean for her. It went beyond the pale to travel with a man when she was not his wife, to dine at a lord's home pretending to be his wife, to share a room with him.

Prudence had believed herself superior to her sisters, but she was as human as they were, as propelled by desire as they had been.

She dropped to her knees on the carpet, her hands braced against her legs, dragging the air into her lungs that she could not seem to catch. With a moan of anguish, she fell onto her side and stared up at the papier-mâché medallions on the ceiling, the ropes and berries that had been fashioned in the corners. She was the *worst*.

She stretched her arm along the carpet and closed her eyes, thinking back on her life. She thought of the idyllic childhood at Longmeadow. The years spent in London, four girls, enthralled with society and the soirees and the supper parties. She saw herself at Black-wood Hall, wandering about the corridors for hours, looking for something to occupy her, feeling so empty. That terrible feeling that she was standing still.

The past few days with Roan had been the most exhilarating, the most exciting days of her life. She'd been buoyed by hope and promise. She'd been excited and engaged and she'd laughed and she was *breathing*—

The door suddenly opened and a rush of air swept across her face.

"Good God." Roan was suddenly beside her, helping her up, his hands caressing her face and her hair as if searching for an injury. "Tell me. It's Stanhope, isn't it?" he asked, his eyes narrowing, his expression turning to hot fury. "Did he do something? Did he touch you, did he—"

"No, no," she said, shaking her head. "He didn't touch me. He was a perfect gentleman. But he knows who I am," Prudence said. "He knows."

The color drained from Roan's face. He shook his head, refusing to believe it.

"He knows that I'm Prudence Cabot."

Roan sat back; his hands fell away from her face. "What did he say? What does he want?"

She laughed bitterly. "Nothing," she said with a

shrug. "That's what he said. He wanted nothing. He'd not reveal my secret." She laughed again, this time more in awe of her own stupidity. "I may be a fool, but I'm not naive—"

"Damn him," Roan said. He stood up, his hands on his waist. "*Damn* him."

"I have to go home," Prudence said sadly. "I must be there when word is out."

Roan looked worried. He took her hand to pull her up, then pressed his palm to her neck as his gaze moved over her face. "Where, to Blackwood Hall? I'll take you there if that's what you want, Pru. I'll explain."

Prudence shook her head. "To London, to my sister Honor. She'll know what to do." She swallowed down the bitter truth of what she must do. "She and Augustine must hear this from me."

Roan's gaze was fixed on her. Prudence could sense his struggle, wanting to make this right, but perfectly unable to do it. What could he possibly do? Give up everything in America and marry her? "Yes, of course," he said, his voice strained. "I'll go now and arrange for a carriage to take us in the morning."

"No," Prudence said, and gripped his hand. "Please don't go yet—"

"Only to arrange a carriage," he said, cupping her face tenderly. "I'll come back to you in moments."

"Not yet, Roan, please," she said, catching his hand. "Because when you walk out that door, even if only to arrange a carriage, it's the beginning of the end. I don't want it to be the end yet. Not yet. Please don't go. Not yet."

Roan's face fell. "Oh, love." He folded his arms around her and held her tightly, rocking with her a moment, his mouth in her hair. But then his hands began to move on her, slowly caressing her, and Prudence's blood began to flow with his touch. She could feel her skin heating, her heart running. She had to have these last few hours in his arms, and closed her eyes, surrendering to the moment, pushing all else from her mind.

She was consumed the moment he touched her. His lips, soft and warm, glided over her skin. His touch, intense but reverent, made her feel as if she were floating in a pool of desire. It spiraled down her body, flowed into her breasts and groin. She began to drift on that sea, his hands and mouth pushing her further and further from shore. Every touch sizzled and burned, every kiss tingled.

Prudence was aware of her gown falling away— first the train, then the buttons of her gown, his fingers deft and quick, and the slide of the fabric down her body. Next her chemise and undergarments drifted away. "How is it that you look even more beautiful with every passing moment?" he muttered, and Prudence's desire turned to liquid heat. She touched his shoulder, her fingers trailing down his chest to his waistcoat, which she unbuttoned. She undressed him as he slipped his palms under her breasts.

"I don't want it to end," she said, and pulled his shirt over his head. Roan growled with desire; Prudence rose up on her tiptoes to kiss his nose, his eyes, his cheeks as he worked on the rest of his clothing, tossing the articles aside.

When he'd removed it all, he picked her up and moved to the bed, laid her down and locked his gaze with hers as he moved over her. Prudence imagined she could see the same yearning in his eyes, the wish that this would never end. The same determination to have it all, here and now, because he might never have it again. He kissed the hollow of her throat, lingering there, and the curve of her neck, then traced a path from her neck to her breast. He took each breast in his mouth, lavished them with attention. Prudence let the desire roll over her in great, lapping waves, sinking deeper into the depths of the pleasure until she was suspended in it. She abandoned all maidenly anxiety at being unpracticed in the art of lovemaking and cast herself out, willing to go where he led her, no matter what.

Roan pressed against her. "How I want you," he said. "I think I could die of wanting you."

"Don't." She brushed his hair from his face.

Roan drew a rigid nipple into his mouth. His mouth was like fire, his fingers the torches he used to inflame her. He stroked her, his touch sinking deeper into her folds, boldly exploring and teasing her. He pressed his body into hers, filling her, and Prudence closed her eyes so that she'd feel it all, not miss a moment of it.

He didn't speak as he moved in her, his rhythm deliberate, tantalizing, his hands stroking her, teasing her. He slipped an arm under her hips and lifted her slightly, sliding in deeply. The sensation was so pleasantly raw that Prudence lost sight of herself and everything else but the feel of his body in hers, of his strength and tenderness and adoration. He slid in and out of her while his thumb began a gentle, swirling assault over and around the nub of her arousal. Prudence was panting, gripping at his skin under her fingers, tasting his skin on her lips.

She erupted almost without warning, groaning with ecstasy, her cry caught by Roan's kiss. He reached his climax behind her, coming at the end of one last powerful thrust and quick withdrawal, his seed warm on her abdomen. He was still panting as he slid his thumb across her cheek, and Prudence realized she had shed a tear of raw emotion in their coupling.

Roan pulled her into his chest and rolled with her onto his side. His breath was warm on her neck, his heartbeat steady and fast against her chest.

She didn't want it to ever end.

Roan soothed her, his hand running over her hair, playing with the ribbon that had come unwound along with her coif. "Come to America," he said, his voice rough with emotion.

"Pardon?"

"Marry me, Pru. Come to America."

Prudence braced her hand against his chest and rose up to look at him. He was earnest, his gaze full of raw emotion. "But you've promised—"

"I know," he said. "But I've not promised her. I hardly know her. It's my father I must convince."

"Roan, you can't."

"I can," he said. "I *will*." He roughly pushed her hair back from her face. "Prudence...I *love* you," he said. "I've tried to persuade myself that it's not possible, not like this, not so quickly. But I do. I can feel it, here," he said, tapping a fist to his chest. "I feel it in every moment, in every breath I am with you. There are obstacles, yes, but look what we've overcome in the past few days. Marry me and come to America. You said there is nothing for you here, that you will live behind walls. There is everything for you there."

"My family is here," she said. "My sisters, my nieces

and nephews. My *mother*. How can I leave them? How can we know that we won't be other people entirely?"

"What do you mean?" he asked, confused.

"I mean that this, with you, has been magical," she said, resting her hand over his heart. "It seems almost as if you appeared from air to grant all my wishes. You've shown me an adventure that has far exceeded anything I might have ever dreamed. But *married*? In a foreign land, with different customs, with a different family? We've neither of us any notion of what the other expects...do we?"

Roan looked startled. It pained Prudence to say so, but she was not so blinded by her adoration of him to think that the adventure they'd shared would carry on day after day into a new world and into a marriage. What if she discovered things about him that made her unhappy? What if his family couldn't accept her? How would she cope, so far removed from her own family?

Roan frowned as if trying to find a good response.

"Stay in England," she said suddenly, and grabbed his face between her hands. "Stay here, stay with me."

"No, Pru, I can't," he said. "How would I provide for you? I am the head of my family's business. They rely on me for our livelihood. I am involved in the building of the canal. There is too much at stake, not only for me, but for my entire family. And there is Aurora. I promised my mother I would bring her home."

"But...my family relies on me, too," Prudence said softly. She could feel tears in her eyes as they gazed at each other, the reality of their different worlds rushing in to fill the space around them.

Roan stroked her hair. "Think about it," he said. "Promise me you'll at least do that."

"Roan, I—"

"No," he said, and covered her mouth with his hand. "Don't answer until we've reached London. Just think on what I've said." He withdrew his hand from her mouth. "I'll give you the moon, I'll give you the sun. Whatever you want, Pru, is yours. I swear to you, we will still be us, just as we are now."

"Roan…"

"I believe what I say," he said, his gaze searching her face. "Don't give me an answer now. Consider it. Please." He looked as if he couldn't bear for her to say no.

But she couldn't say yes.

Prudence rolled onto her back and stared up at the canopy. Roan slipped his fingers in between hers, and they lay there, neither of them speaking.

Prudence was confused by her emotions. She was losing them in this vast world, in this man who had wrapped himself around her heart. He was floating away from her, floating back to America. *Oh God, how she would miss him*. It would be unbearable, truly unbearable.

Could she go with him? Could she leave all she'd ever known behind and walk so blindly into the unknown? The practical side of her, the side of her that ruled her head, that kept her within the bounds of propriety, made her a dutiful daughter and sister, said no. The practical side of her said that if she went to America with him, and wed him, the magic would fade away and the blunt realities of a marriage made in haste would overshadow the magic of this week.

The practical side of her said all of that, but her heart kept whispering *yes*.

CHAPTER FOURTEEN

EVERY TIME ROAN tried to close his eyes to sleep, he couldn't keep them closed. He kept opening them to assure himself that Prudence was still there beside him and hadn't disappeared into a dream quite yet.

It was remarkable to Roan that when he'd first seen Prudence in Ashton Down, he'd thought her beautiful in that way men have of thinking every female is beautiful. It was nothing more than an appreciation of curves and lips and remarkable eyes. When he'd realized that she'd not intended to come on the stagecoach before he'd arrived, he'd thought her amusingly and ironically imprudent. His opinion of her had been much like his opinion of Aurora—charming and foolish. And he'd believed he was indulging Prudence's desire for an adventure, much like he would indulge his sister when he was not so very cross with her.

Now he wasn't certain of anything, not one damn thing. He knew only that somehow, Prudence's adventure had become his adventure. *His!* A man who had spent his childhood in the wilds of New York, who traveled alone to the Canadian border, across vast wilderness to look after their business. To think that he would find such adventure in sedate, pastoral England was absurd, but he had. In fact, it had been one of the biggest, most stunning adventures of his life. And he was a changed man for it.

He feared he would be a wounded man for it when it was all said and done. Oh, but Roan had meant what he'd said to her tonight—come to America, be his wife. The thought had gurgled up, bursting through the surface of his thoughts so clearly and precisely that he'd known without a doubt it had come directly from his heart.

There was, obviously, the glaring problem of Susannah Pratt. That would be an unpleasant task, and one certain to ruffle feathers. But Roan didn't feel responsibility for Susannah. He didn't really *know* Susannah. Theirs was no love match—it was hardly even a civil match at this point. One day, she might even thank him. And if not, Roan didn't care. He was willing to risk her disdain, his father's displeasure, Mr. Pratt's anger, for love.

He, Roan Matheson, would risk all for love. The world had flipped on its head and turned everything upside down.

And yet, the euphoria of his feelings was tampered by the pressing worry of Aurora. Roan had expected to find her here, or, at the very least, be told she'd just left. Gone a fortnight? Was Aurora ruined? Had she done something as spectacularly foolhardy as Prudence?

At dawn, he dressed and closed up his trunk, then roused Prudence with a kiss. He went downstairs and sent a girl up to help her dress and asked for a carriage to be brought round to take them into the village. "What time is the coach to London?" he asked the butler, Cyril, who was looking a bit bleary-eyed that morning.

"Ten o'clock, sir. It will take you as far as Manchester. It's two full days' journey to Londontown."

Roan nodded and glanced at a mantel clock. Two days in a crowded stagecoach, two days of wanting her, two days of hoping she would agree to marry him. Roan was not very practiced with the true affairs of the heart, obviously, but he knew that Prudence had to come to her answer on her own. She was right—he was asking a lot of her.

The desire had to be hers as much as it was his. They had to share the determination to overcome the ocean between them or it would never work—not here, not there. Perhaps, Roan mused, he was asking a lot of himself, too. Prudence might be right.

He sighed and pushed the thought away. He didn't want to think about that now. He couldn't think about it now, not with his sister weighing so heavily on his mind.

The carriage was brought round and their trunks loaded. No one was on hand to see them off—at Roan's inquiry, Cyril said, "His lordship and his guests retired to their beds just before dawn. They have not roused themselves."

Roan suspected they wouldn't rouse themselves for several hours. What a lot they were, here at Howston Hall. It was almost like stepping into a strange dream. Roan didn't understand how men lived without purpose or occupation—he was as eager as Prudence to be gone from here.

Their trunks were brought out, Prudence trailing behind, looking a bit pale, Roan thought. She was wearing a pretty yellow traveling gown, and as he helped her into the interior of the carriage, he happened to catch sight of Stanhope. That man sauntered out onto the drive. "Leaving so soon, Mr. Matheson?" he asked pleasantly.

Roan closed the door of the carriage and stalked to where Stanhope waited. They stood eye to eye. "What in hell do you want?" he demanded softly.

Stanhope arched a brow as if Roan amused him, then looked past him, to the carriage. "Only to wish you Godspeed, sir. Perhaps I'll see you again in London."

Roan said nothing, but turned on his heel and strode back to the carriage.

Prudence had very little to say on the drive into the village. From there, the coach to Manchester was crowded, much more than any of the coaches they'd yet been on, and Roan had to ride up top while Prudence rode in the carriage crowded between the coach wall and a woman who carried a cat in a cage on her lap.

The weather turned quite warm and uncomfortably moist. It felt to Roan like his despair and worry were pressing down on him, embedding in his skin.

In Manchester, he secured a room for them at the public inn. But the long journey from Weslay had been so uncomfortably jarring, and the day so thick and warm, that they'd collapsed onto a lumpy bed and slept like the dead. They were up at dawn again the next morning, boarding a coach that, impossibly, was even more crowded than the one to Manchester.

After another interminable day of riding apart due to the crowding, of their private thoughts carrying them away from each other, Roan and Prudence arrived in London. It was half-past eight, and the sun was beginning to set. Roan worried about Prudence; she seemed to be swaying lightly on her feet, exhausted to the bone by her adventure.

"I'll find us a place for the night," he said, his hand on her waist to steady her.

"Oh no," she said, and put her hand on his arm. She smiled, but there was no heart in it. "I've lived half my life in London—people around Mayfair know me. It's best that we go to my sister."

Roan didn't like it, but he understood it. He rubbed his temples and realized that his head was pounding with a terrible ache. When had that come on him? "I'll take you there," he said. "Give me the direction and I will take you to your sister."

She looked down and fidgeted with the string of her reticule. "What will you do?"

He would find a place to drink away his grief. "I'll find a room somewhere."

The last slivers of pink were beginning to fade from the late-evening sky when they arrived at the house on Audley Street. The air was so thick now that it pressed against Roan's throat and chest. He looked up at the house Prudence directed them to. It was painted a sunny yellow, four stories tall with balconies on the top three floors. The windows facing the street—sixteen in all— stood as tall as Roan. Light was glowing invitingly through the windows.

The hackney driver had deposited them on the street along with their trunks. Prudence sat heavily on them and stared up at the house. "I don't know what to say," she said absently.

Roan sat beside her, put his arm around her waist and kissed her temple. "I'll tell them what has happened. Leave it to me."

"You're a dear," Prudence said with a smile. "Thank you…but somehow, I think that would make it all worse." She turned his head to her and kissed him, her lips lingering on his for one crystal moment.

"What will you tell them?"

She shrugged. "The truth, I expect." She smiled. "Most of it, that is."

Her eyes shone up at him, and Roan suddenly felt lost. "Pru," he said, his voice rough with the emotions that rushed through him, regret and hope in one unsettling mix. He stood up, pulling her with him, his arms around her, his face in her hair, her neck. He couldn't bear that the end could be near. He couldn't bear the thought of leaving England without her. He lifted his head, held hers between his hands. "It's only been a few days, but I can't imagine being without you."

"Neither can I," she said softly. "In truth, I can't imagine much of anything at present, only that I don't want to go on without you."

"Then don't," he said.

Prudence smiled ruefully and pulled his hand from her face and leaned back. "If only it were that simple. We must go in, Roan."

Roan was in no such hurry, but Prudence slipped away from him and walked to the door of the yellow house. She lifted the brass knocker and rapped three times. Several moments later, the door was suddenly pulled open and the light of a candle spilled out onto the street. Behind it, Roan could see the shadow of a man. He moved the candle so that he might peer out and squinted at Roan and Prudence. He was slender, with dark hair and darker eyes. He was handsome, Roan thought, and wondered if he was Mr. Easton.

The man looked first at Prudence, then at Roan, who stood behind her. One brow rose above the other. "Well," he said. "This ought to make for an interesting evening. Miss Prudence, do come in. Miss Prudence's companion, you are welcome." He stepped back and bowed.

"Thank you, Finnegan. May I introduce Mr. Matheson?" She glanced nervously over her shoulder at Roan. "This is Finnegan, Mr. Easton's butler."

"And valet," Finnegan said with a smile for Roan. "Do come in."

Prudence stepped inside. Roan reluctantly followed, removing his hat as he stepped inside the foyer.

The Finnegan fellow looked him up and down, which Roan thought was a bold thing for a butler to do, and said, "Mr. and Mrs. Easton will no doubt be overjoyed that you've not met yet with your demise, Miss Prudence."

"Are they at supper? Shall we wait?" she asked.

"They've finished their evening meal and have put their children to bed. They are now at repose in the green salon. Follow me." Finnegan's gaze flicked over Roan once more before he turned and walked up the stairs, holding the candle aloft to lead the way.

It was an immaculate home, Roan noticed. There were portraits hanging on the walls above the wainscoting, polished wooden handrails on the stairs. He couldn't see the carpets very well by the light of a single candle, but he could feel the thickness of them beneath his feet.

When they reached the first floor landing, Finnegan said, "May I say, Miss Prudence, I am very glad to see you have not been kidnapped by pirates and taken off to India, as Miss Mercy has put forth. And quite adamantly, I might add."

"She would very much like to have that tale to chew on, wouldn't she? But how do you know what she thinks, Finnegan? Have you seen her?" Prudence asked.

"Of course," he said. "The entire family has come to London to confab over your disappearance."

Prudence glanced uneasily over her shoulder at Roan.

Finnegan walked briskly ahead to a pair of polished mahogany doors. He threw one open without knocking.

"What the devil, Finnegan?" a male voice complained.

"If I may, sir, madam," Finnegan said, "someone has come whom I think you will very much want to see."

"I won't," the man within said. "I've had enough guests for one day. And I will thank you not to allow Lady Chatham into this house again. The woman is unconscionably long-winded."

"George," a woman's voice said, softly reproving.

Prudence looked at Roan and tried once again to muster a smile. She squared her shoulders and stepped into the room behind Finnegan. Roan heard the gasp of shock and the woman shrieked, *"Prudence!* Oh dear God, where have you been? We've been sick with worry!"

Roan followed her in; Prudence was already in the embrace of a woman who he assumed was her sister. A fire blazed cheerfully at the hearth. A basket of needlework had been turned upside down and there were papers scattered on the floor and at the feet of a large man who stood eye level with Roan, his gaze as hard as Roan's would have been, were he in the man's shoes.

"Who the bloody hell are *you*?" he demanded of Roan. "Prudence, for God's sake, where did you get off to? Don't you know how we've agonized? Explain yourself at once!"

"At least kiss her and welcome her back, George," the woman said. She had black hair, quite different from Prudence's gold. She was wiping tears of relief from her cheeks with the tips of her fingers below bright blue eyes.

The man, George Easton apparently, grabbed Prudence roughly and kissed her cheek, then held her another moment before setting her back and glaring down at her. "What have you to say for yourself?"

"I left a note in Ashton Down—"

"A note!" her sister said. "That you had gone off with an acquaintance! An acquaintance that no one else knew!" She suddenly gasped and gaped at Roan. "Is *he* the acquaintance?"

Roan meant to answer that question, but before he could utter the words, he was blindsided by a fist to his jaw. He staggered backward, stunned, and gingerly touched his fingers to the place the man had hit him.

"George, no!" Prudence shrieked, and threw herself in front of her brother-in-law. "It wasn't *his* doing—it was mine! I owe him a debt of gratitude—he helped me!"

George yanked on his waistcoat and glared at Roan.

Roan moved his jaw around to assure himself it wasn't broken, then glared back at Easton. He understood the man's anger, but he would not stand for that.

"Please...this is Mr. Roan Matheson," Prudence said with her hand on Roan's arm. "And these two," she said to Roan, "are quite obviously my sister Mrs. Honor

Easton, and my brother-in-law Mr. George Easton." She
had a withering look for the latter. "May we just…may
we sit?" she pleaded. "There is so much to tell you."

"Yes, of course," Mrs. Easton said. "Finnegan, some
brandy, please?"

"Whiskey for him," George said, flicking his wrist
at Roan. "Who are you, where did you come from?" he
challenged Roan as he gingerly worked his jaw.

"Will the answer rile you?" Roan asked.

Easton sighed. "No doubt it will. Look here, I apologize. I may have struck you prematurely. From where
did you come?"

"New York."

"Oh good *God*," Easton muttered as if that were the
dregs of hell.

"All right," Mrs. Easton said, eyeing Roan suspiciously. "You'd better tell us what happened, Pru. Augustine is quite beside himself. And Grace? Well, she is
hysterical! Dr. Linford sent word immediately that you
were not in Ashton Down where you were supposed to
be, and they've had a man looking for you ever since.
You can't imagine what we've feared. But this morning, the man told us that *you* forced the wagon to turn
about and take you back to Himple on the way to the
safety of Cassandra's house! Why?"

Prudence glanced at Roan. She cleared her throat.

"Mr. Matheson, please do sit," Mrs. Easton said to
him, and indicated a velvet-covered settee.

"If you wouldn't mind, I prefer to stand," Roan said.
He wanted to be on his feet if Easton charged him
again.

But Prudence sat. She practically fell onto the settee

as if collapsing under the weight of the week. "I don't know where to begin."

"You had best begin with the moment you left Blackwood Hall, for that's the last anyone has seen you," Easton said sternly.

That was where Prudence began, relating the sequence of events that had occurred since her disappearance, beginning with Roan being confused about Weslay.

"And I helped him buy passage on the next coach. And…and then? Then I followed him," she said with a sheepish shrug as she finished her tale.

"Followed him," Easton repeated carefully, as if he'd misunderstood.

"But *why*?" her sister cried. "Why would you do such a thing without a companion or a maid? That's so unlike you, Prudence. You're always very careful about such things. I can't imagine why—"

"Because I fancied him, Honor," Prudence said flatly. "Isn't it obvious? I fancied him! I was quite smitten, actually—" Roan couldn't help smiling at that "—and I thought that as I would live my life behind the walls of Blackwood Hall, without society, without an offer, why not take one opportunity to do something for me? I meant to get off the coach in Himple and carry on as planned and no one would be the wiser, but the wheel broke and Linford came, and I should have worn my boots!"

"Pardon?" Easton asked, then looked at his wife. "What is she talking about?"

Prudence took a breath and continued on to describe how the wheel of the stagecoach had broken and how fear of encountering Linford had compelled her to abandon the stagecoach once it was repaired. She told them how Roan had come after her, concerned for her safety, and about the purchase of the old nag, and how they'd slowly made their way, arriving at a public house that evening. But they'd found the company too rough, and they were right—they'd been followed and robbed, and Roan beaten.

"Oh my God," Mrs. Easton moaned.

"He saved me, Honor," Prudence said.

"I saved you? She shot him," Roan said to her sister.

"Oh," Mrs. Easton said, as if she were in pain, and sank into the cushions of the settee. "Did you…did you *kill* him?"

"No," Prudence said. "At least, I don't think I did."

"You should have," Easton said. "Shoot to kill, Pru."

"I agree," Roan said, and noticed that Easton was looking at him a little differently.

"Oh, Pru!" her sister said, taking Prudence's hand in hers, holding it tightly between her two hands. "What an ordeal you've suffered. You poor thing. Then what did you do?"

Prudence looked at Roan. "He'd made a fire, and I…I sat with him, holding the gun in case they came back."

"All *night*?" her sister whimpered.

"Yes. All night."

Easton turned then and leveled a dark look on Roan. Roan returned one just as dark.

"Shall I kill him now?" Easton asked. "Or is there more?"

"George!" Prudence and Honor said at the very same time.

"It's not his fault," Prudence said. "It's mine."

"It's not entirely yours, Pru," Roan said, his gaze on Easton. "But I won't apologize for any of it."

"Oh no?" Easton said, turning around to face Roan.

"George, darling," Mrs. Easton said, coming off the settee and hurrying to her husband. "Remember that *you* were not always very caring of propriety—"

"This is different!"

"It's not," she said, and touched his face. That seemed to calm him; he clenched his jaw and turned back to the fire.

"Wait, George, please. Hear all I have to say," Prudence begged him. "We reached Himple the next day," she continued, quickly resuming the story before Easton could react. She told them how she'd intended to carry on to Mrs. Bulworth, but had had a change of heart, and had gone after Roan's post coach. She offered no explanation for it, and at that point, Roan supposed none was needed.

But when Prudence told them about Howston Hall, Mrs. Easton gaped at her. "You went as *what*? His other sister? His daughter?"

"Daughter!" Roan said, taken aback. "I'm thirty years old, madam."

"What do you think, Honor?" Prudence said softly. "Not his sister or his ward. Not his mistress."

For the second time, Mrs. Easton came off the couch. "Oh no. *No.*" She pressed her hands against her abdomen. "Oh, Pru, you didn't, did you?"

"You see?" Easton said, gesturing at Roan. "I should have killed him the moment he walked into this room!"

Roan turned to face him. "If you would like to step outside, Mr. Easton, I'd be more than happy to respond to any questions you might have."

"Oh for heaven's sake," Mrs. Easton said. "Both of you, stop it at once!"

"It's even worse," Prudence admitted.

"Worse?" Easton bellowed, casting his arms wide. "How could it possibly be worse?"

"Lord Stanhope was there. Actually, he was on the post coach from Himple. And…and he knew who I was."

"How?" Honor asked. "Have you made his acquaintance?"

"No," Prudence said. "Or Lord Penfors for that matter. I thought I'd be safe, that no one could possibly know me. But Stanhope guessed who I was because of my resemblance to Grace."

"Well, of course he did," Easton said. "You look like twins."

"No, they don't!" Mrs. Easton protested, and waved her hand at her husband and turned back to Prudence. "What did he say?"

Prudence looked at Roan. "He said he would keep my secret…for now. But I know he won't. I think he means to extort money."

"I would imagine that's the least of what he intends to do," Easton muttered.

"Oh dear God," Mrs. Easton said, and sank down onto the settee in shock. "We can't let Merryton hear of this, do you understand? Can you imagine what he might do?"

"Maybe we should," Easton argued. "He'd certainly take care of it, wouldn't he? Well? Go on, Pru—then what happened?"

"My sister was not at Howston Hall," Roan said. "We came at once to London."

"She'd left a fortnight ago," Prudence explained. "In company of Mr. and Mrs. Villeroy, bound for London."

"The Villeroys?" Mrs. Easton said, and looked at her husband. "On Upper George Street? What were *they* doing with Penfors? The Villeroys keep to themselves. I rarely hear of them in society."

"They have a son," Roan said. "It is imperative that I find my sister. She is engaged to be married and must come home."

"And you?" Easton asked. "What do you intend to do after dragging our Prudence across the English countryside?"

"George, please," Prudence said wearily. "You're angry, I understand, but we won't apologize for it. I won't apologize any more than you and Honor did, or Grace and Merryton."

"I beg your pardon!" Mrs. Easton said, clearly appalled.

"Not once did I hear a word of apology for what you did," Prudence said.

"What has that to do with you?" Mrs. Easton demanded angrily.

"Everything, Honor. You made everything more difficult for me and Mercy. You know you did."

"Say no more, Prudence!" Mrs. Easton said, her voice shaking with fury.

Roan put his hand to Prudence's shoulder, but she shrugged him off. "But I don't blame you, Honor. I understand you now. I *understand* you," she said again. "Our heart leads us where it leads us and we can't resist it. I didn't understand that before."

"My situation was vastly different from yours,"

Mrs. Easton said angrily. "I had three younger sisters to think of."

"Your situation was no different than mine. You fell in love and you married him."

Mrs. Easton gasped at the implication of Prudence's words. She looked wildly at the three of them, her gaze settling on Prudence, "You can*not* marry him," she said, pointing at Roan.

"I can if that's what I choose," Prudence said firmly.

"What exactly are you implying?" Mrs. Easton said quickly. "Don't even think of it, Prudence! You are staying here, of course you are."

"I don't know what I intend to do, Honor," Prudence said hotly. "But I will not be shut away from life because of what you or Merryton or anyone else thinks! It is *my* life to live as I see fit."

Mrs. Easton gasped and whirled around to Roan. "How dare you put such ideas into her head!"

The force of Mrs. Easton's disdain and horror clenched like a vise around Roan's gut. He looked at Prudence. "She doesn't need me to tell her what to think," he said. "She has a fine mind of her own."

Prudence smiled gratefully, buoying him.

"What rubbish! You've preyed on an innocent woman—"

"Honor," Prudence said simply.

Mrs. Easton looked at her sister for a long moment, then whirled away, her fingertips pressed to her cheeks.

"Well, then, now we have quite a mess," Easton said angrily. "What are we to do?"

"My priority is to find my sister," Roan said.

"Yes, just go," Mrs. Easton said angrily.

"Darling," said Mr. Easton, his hand tangling with

his wife's. "It's too late to call on the Villeroys tonight. We'll go on the morrow."

"We?" Roan asked, eyeing him warily. He didn't trust this man—he wouldn't be the least bit surprised if Easton tried to have him thrown into a jail.

But Easton snorted. "I don't know how you do things in New York, but in London, you need an introduction before you go rapping on doors."

"Are you suggesting you will make that introduction for me?" Roan asked suspiciously.

"Yes, yes, I'll make it, of course I shall," Easton said impatiently. "That's the only way to send you on your way."

"Thank you," Roan said. "If you will excuse me, I will take my leave."

"What? Where are you going?" Mrs. Easton exclaimed.

"To find an inn."

"You'll stay here," she said firmly.

"Honor—"

"George, he will stay here," she said firmly. "He has brought Prudence to us. She might have been eaten by wolves or worse, and *he* brought her home. Of course he will stay here!"

"Do you think that perhaps given their…*association*," George said, enunciating the word, "that perhaps that is not a very good idea?"

Mrs. Easton snorted. "After what happened at Howston Hall? I think it is an improvement."

Easton couldn't argue with her, but Roan could feel the burn of Mrs. Easton's eyes on his back as he followed Finnegan to his room.

THE ROOM FINNEGAN showed him to was small but well-appointed with a comfortable bed and a window facing the street, which Finnegan pushed open. The night breeze lifted the drapery panels and the humid air brushed across Roan's skin.

God, what turmoil they'd created. And still, Roan didn't regret it, not any of it. He wasn't put off by the Eastons' anger. He understood it better than they knew. But Roan also knew from experience that anything worth having was worth fighting for. Prudence had mettle, and that made him love her more.

He stood at the window, closed his eyes and felt the night breeze on his face. He thought of Prudence, saw her smile, the shine of her hair, the glimmer of laughter in her eyes. He recalled that day in the pond, how she'd embraced her sensuality and had driven him to madness with desire.

He had never realized, never suspected, how fulfilling love was. But now that he knew it, he would not let go of it. He would not let go of Prudence, no matter how difficult it was. He had as much mettle as she. More.

Roan hadn't recognized just how tired he was until he laid his head on a softly scented pillow and on linens smelling of lavender. He put out the light and fell into a deep, dreamless sleep. When something caught his arm, it took a monumental effort to pull himself to the surface.

"Roan."

He opened his eyes. Prudence was there like a vision from his dream, in a sleeping gown, her golden hair falling around her shoulders. She put her fingers to his lips to silence him and crawled on top of him.

"Do you think this is wise? I don't think I can reach my gun," he whispered.

He could see her smile in the moonlit room. "I think we're safe—I heard George snoring."

"Mmm," he said, unconvinced. But his hands were on her hips and his cock was hardening. "Go back, Pru. They're angry with us and they will welcome any excuse to hang me."

"I'll go back," she whispered, and kissed his cheek, then his ear. "But not before I have the opportunity to thank you."

"For what?" he asked dreamily, closing his eyes as she moved to his neck.

"For giving me the adventure of my life. For showing me how to live."

Roan opened his eyes. He caught her head between his hands and made her look at him. "Don't thank me," he said gruffly. "A thank-you sounds final and a bit disparaging."

"I don't mean it to," she whispered. "I adore you, haven't I said so?"

Yes, she had said she adored him. But Roan was acutely aware that she'd not said she loved him. He was suddenly struck with fear that she didn't love him, that he'd invented it all, and in the light of morning, back in familiar surroundings, she'd see her emotions as foolishness.

"I want you to love me. I want you to marry me," he said.

She caressed his face.

"Pru, I—"

She silenced him with a kiss.

Roan gave in and slipped his hands under her gown,

slid them up over the warm, smooth skin of her thighs, then in between her legs. Prudence began to kiss him, sinking down onto his body.

This, Roan thought, was what he wanted in his life. This moment with a woman he loved was what made life worth living, wasn't it? He cursed the heavens for having allowed him to realize it with a woman who lived a world away from him. When he entered Prudence, and slid into the oblivion of sexual pleasure, he could think only that he loved her.

The next morning, Roan awoke to the sound of birds chirping beneath a gray sky. Prudence was gone. Like a wraith, like a fragment of a dream, she had slipped away from him.

He would remember that night in the days to come. He would remember how she looked, how soft her smile, how naked her eyes. He would remember how it had felt to have love reverberating in him.

But mostly, he would remember how he'd wanted her, wanted love, with all his heart.

CHAPTER FIFTEEN

PRUDENCE SLIPPED OUT of Roan's room sometime before
dawn and crawled into her bed, emotionally and physically spent. One week ago, she'd yearned for something
to fill her days, something that would make her feel
the corners of her soul. But tonight, she was feeling
things, so many conflicting things that her emotions
were a shambles. Every moment she was with Roan
was another breath lost to joy, another flutter of her
heart. Every moment away from him was a nervous
ache. Was this love? Was it love that burned so hot in
her chest? Would one journey across an ocean douse
the flame, or would it make the flame burn brighter?
Those questions tormented her.

Prudence rose later than usual, and when she arrived
at breakfast she found Honor and her oldest daughter,
Edith, at the table.

Augustine was in the breakfast room, standing at
the windows and peering out, his familiar, corpulent
shape swaying a little from side to side as if he were
humming a tune to himself.

"Good morning," she said sheepishly.

Augustine whirled around, his eyes wide. "Prudence
Martha Cabot!" he said loudly. "I should lock you away
in a tower."

"You can't lock Auntie Pru away!" little Edith cried

as Augustine barreled around the table, knocking into a chair in his haste to reach Prudence. He grabbed her up before she could speak and squeezed her tightly to him.

"Mamma, don't let him lock Auntie Pru away!" Edith sobbed.

"Uncle Augustine isn't locking anyone away, darling," Honor said. "He was teasing Auntie Pru."

"Well, of *course* I won't lock her away," Augustine said, and let go of Prudence. He turned about to the little girl and said, "But you mustn't *ever* run away as Auntie Pru has done. Do you promise me?"

"I promise," Edith said, and slid out of her seat, running around the table to throw her arms around Prudence's legs.

Prudence dipped down and swept her niece up in her arms, holding her tight. "I didn't run away, darling. I went on an adventure!"

"That's an appalling interpretation," Honor said, appearing next to Prudence. She ran her hand lovingly over her daughter's head. "Come along, Miss Edith, your nurse is waiting for you." Prudence reluctantly let Edith go. She watched as Honor led her from the dining room, wondering how she might never see Edith again. The thought twisted unpleasantly in her chest.

"Prudence, dearest," Augustine said anxiously when the pair had left the room. "What have you done?" He took Prudence's hands in his. "How we worried for you! You must have a care for your virtue."

She wanted to argue that she must care for her virtue, that it was her virtue to do with what she liked, but she said simply, "I'm sorry, Augustine."

Augustine looked very earnest as he squeezed her hands. "I thought we might put this all to bed before word gets round, but I think it too late! Lord Stanhope caught me at White's—"

"What?" Prudence gasped. "When? How?"

"When? Last night. He said he'd borrowed a horse from Howston Hall and had accompanied the estate's agent to London. He said he'd been pleasantly surprised to make your acquaintance there."

Tendrils of trepidation began to snake in around Prudence's gut. "What did he say?" she asked weakly. She could imagine it all, the ever-present, knowing smile on Stanhope's face. *I met Mrs. Matheson, my lord. I hadn't heard your sister had married!* Poor Augustine. He was a simple man and liked a simple life. She could imagine his shock, the way he'd bluster and fidget through such an encounter.

"He said he should like to come round this evening and speak to me privately, that's what," he said nervously. "And when I mentioned it to Honor, she confided in me that you had been there with *a gentleman*," he whispered, as if Prudence had been in the company of Satan himself.

"Oh God," Prudence moaned.

"Pru, darling, I won't ask about the gentleman, for I think I can't bear to *hear* it," Augustine said as Honor walked back into the dining room. "But I think it best if you hurry back to Blackwood Hall straightaway. Out of sight, out of mind, as they say."

"And what good will that do?" Prudence asked him, and walked away, to the windows. "It won't stop anyone from talking. Does it even matter if people talk? Haven't they said all there is to say about the Cabot sisters?"

"What? Of course it matters!" Augustine said, his voice rising. "Do you mean to dishonor us all?"

"Fine. Send me into hiding like a criminal," she snapped irritably.

"I don't think that's what Augustine means," Honor said evenly.

"Not at all," Augustine insisted. "I mean only that it is best for you to remain out of society for a time until this blows over," he said sternly. Having delivered his brotherly warning, he rose up on the tips of his toes and down again, then yanked at the bottom of his waistcoat, pulling it over his belly. "You must never give us a fright like that again, Pru," he said, wagging a chubby finger at her.

"No, of course not," Prudence said bitterly. "I shouldn't do anything but stay out of sight and speak when I am spoken to—don't worry, Augustine. You won't have me to fret over. Perhaps I will marry the mysterious gentleman and solve the problem for you."

She had never seen her stepbrother look as shocked as he did in that moment. His jaw dropped open. His eyes widened with alarm. His lips moved as if he wanted to speak but was incapable. And then he found his tongue. "I beg your pardon, you mean to do *what*? Who is this bounder?"

"He's not a bounder! He's an American!"

Augustine looked as if he couldn't draw his breath. "He's a *what*?" he shouted, the force of his voice very nearly lifting him off his feet.

"Prudence! Stop this!" Honor cried.

"I'm only telling him the truth, Honor."

"And with very little regard for his feelings," Honor

said hotly. "Augustine, darling, let me sort it all out, will you?"

"I can't believe what she's saying," Augustine said helplessly as Honor took him by the elbow and began to guide him toward the door.

"I'll sort it all out, dearest. You should go home to Monica now," Honor said, referring to Augustine's wife. "She'll be terribly anxious to hear what's become of Prudence."

Augustine looked with great bemusement at Prudence as if he were looking at an apparition. Prudence felt another painful twist inside of her. She loved Augustine. She hadn't meant to hurt him. "Augustine—"

"Yes, she will be most anxious," he said, nodding to himself as Honor showed him out.

Moments later, Honor returned with a dark glare for her sister. "Are you happy now?" she asked irritably as she fell into a chair. "Augustine is beside himself."

"What would you have me say, Honor? Would you have me deny it? Would you have me pretend I have no feelings about it, that I don't know what I want?"

"No," she said as if speaking to a child. "But you might have shown a bit of tact."

Honor was right. Prudence sat on a chair across from her sister. "I apologize," she said. "You're right, that was badly done."

Honor sniffed. She looked away from Prudence a moment. "Do you really want to *marry* him?" she asked, and turned a shrewd gaze to Prudence.

"I don't know," Prudence said with honest misery. "I feel things for him that I've never felt in my life," she said, pressing her palm to her heart. "I can't imagine I shall ever feel this way again. And then it feels a bit like an ague, and I think it will pass. But it doesn't pass, Honor. It only seems to grow."

"Oh dear," Honor said. She suddenly sat up. "Listen to me, Prudence. Grace and Mercy are coming this afternoon. Can't we at least discuss it as rational, clearheaded sisters before you do something foolish and swan off to America? Will you not at least show us the courtesy of discussing something that would affect us all?"

"My life, my choices, will affect us all?" Prudence asked, bristling.

"Of course they do. Just as you so adamantly pointed out last night that my choices have affected *you*, your choices affect us. Do you think any one of us want to lose a beloved sister to *America*?" she said as if she could hardly say the word. "Are we not at least as important to you as this…this stranger? You would say the same, Pru, and you would demand the same consideration as us."

Prudence gazed at her beautiful older sister. She'd adored Honor all her life, had looked up to her, had idolized her. She could see the faint smudges of worry under her eyes this morning and knew that she'd put them there. Honor was right, of course. Her sisters were her world. They were the corners of her heart. But Roan was there, too. As improbable as it seemed, he had taken up space in the center. "Yes," she said calmly. "Yes, of course, Honor. I would never intentionally hurt any of you. Never."

Honor smiled wearily. "I know, darling," she said, and reached for Prudence's knee, giving it a squeeze.

"Where have they gone?" Prudence asked meekly.

"I suppose you mean Matheson? He and George

have gone round to the Villeroys." Honor stood up and walked to the sideboard, clearly not in a mood to discuss it.

Prudence could picture Roan arriving at the house on Upper George Street, the relief and consolation washing over him when he laid eyes on his sister, now assured that she was well. She could see him gather her up and hold her as tight as he'd held Pru last night, but out of fear she would slip away again. She could see Roan grasp his sister's head in his hands and study her face for any change in her, any glimpse of the girl she'd been before she'd left America.

"What time did they go?"

"Nine o'clock," Honor said. "George said he expected they'd be back by the noon hour." Honor turned from the sideboard and put a plate of breakfast food before Prudence. "Here, eat something. Put some color in your face." She quit the room without another word.

Roan and George did not return by the noon hour.

At two in the afternoon, Prudence was pacing the foyer.

Honor came down with her children, Edith, Tristan and Wills, all of them dressed to go out. "Where are you going?" Prudence asked as Honor separated Tristan and Wills from each other in the course of their overly boisterous play.

"To call on Lady Chatham. If I don't bring them round, she'll come here, and George will be unhappy."

"But…what of George and Roan?" Prudence asked.

"Who is Roan?" Tristan demanded, wrinkling his nose.

"No one," Honor said, a bit too quickly for Prudence. To her sister, she said, "They've obviously been de-

layed. Why don't you read? I've left some needlework
upstairs if you want to busy your hands." She ushered
her three young children out before her. "Stop pacing,"
she said to Prudence as she went out behind them.

Honor was right; Prudence needed an occupation.
She went upstairs and sorted through Honor's basket of
needlework, but found nothing to suit her. The heavy,
oppressive air of the past two days finally gave way to
rain, and she listened to it hitting the windowpanes for
a while as she paced the drawing room with her hands
behind her back, pausing occasionally at the windows
to stare out at the steady fall of rain, thinking. Examining her options from every conceivable angle. Trying
to sort through her feelings for a man who had filled
her heart and her imagination and taught her what it
was to yearn.

Where could they be?

She'd resumed trying to embroider a linen nap-
kin when she heard someone at the door. Her heart
lurched—Prudence unthinkingly tossed down the linen
and rushed to the front windows to peer out. She could
see nothing through the rain but a brown hat. The person wearing the hat hidden from view beneath it.

Still, it had to be Roan—who else could it be? She
whirled around, tucked in a bit of hair and clasped her
hands together, waiting.

Several moments later, she heard the light footfall
of Finnegan and caught her breath. Finnegan entered
the room and silently held out a silver tray with a calling card to her. A calling card? Roan wouldn't come
in with a calling card. Prudence looked at him hesitantly and picked up the card. The moment she saw

the name she threw it back on the tray as if it were a hot coal. *Stanhope.*

So this was it, she thought desperately. How much money would he want? Should she send word he should come back when George was home? No, no…she was *not* a coward. She'd brought this on herself and she would answer for it. Prudence squared her shoulders and lifted her chin. "Is everyone out?"

"Yes, miss," Finnegan said.

She nodded. "Show him up, please."

Finnegan turned, prepared to fetch him.

"Finnegan!" she said quickly, before he could leave. He turned back to her.

"Leave the door open, and please…stay close, will you?"

"Just outside," he assured her. "Are you certain you want to receive him?"

Prudence laughed nervously. "Not at all. Unfortunately, I must. Bring him up, please."

Stanhope entered the room and paused just over the threshold. He smiled and inclined his head. "Miss Cabot. Thank you for seeing me."

"Good afternoon, my lord," she said coolly.

"May I say, it's lovely to see you home and refreshed." He smiled warmly.

He was wearing a dove-gray coat over black trousers and waistcoat, a pristine white shirt and neckcloth. His hair—gold, like hers—was combed and trimmed since she'd last seen him. Prudence resented the sight of him. "How may I help you?"

Stanhope cocked a brow and smiled with surprise. "You seem uncomfortable, Miss Cabot. Is my presence so hard for you to bear?"

Oh no, she would not allow him to bait her. "I have quite a lot to tend to, my lord."

His pale blue gaze swept over her, assessing her. "Very well, I shall come to the point." He gestured to the settee near the window. "Will you at least sit?"

Prudence didn't want to sit, she didn't want anything to do with him. But she dared not show him any fear or reluctance, either. She moved stiffly to the settee and sat, her hands folded on her lap.

Stanhope flipped his tails and sat beside her. He smiled kindly, as if he were a friend. They weren't friends, they were nothing to one another, only mere acquaintances, and uncomfortably vague ones at that. He meant to extort her, so what was the point of smiling? "Yes?" she prodded him, wishing he'd get on with it. Her palms were damp, her heart racing.

"No pleasantries? No remarks about the weather, no inquiries about my safe return from Weslay?"

Her heart skipped at the mention of Weslay. "Are pleasantries really necessary? I know why you're here."

He actually laughed at that. "Do you, indeed? I suspect not, Miss Cabot. I've come with a proposition for you."

A proposition! She could only imagine what it was. She shifted uncomfortably.

"It's not an indecent proposition, if that's the idea you have."

"I am happy to hear it," she said coolly. "What is your proposition?"

He sighed as if dealing with a temperamental child. "I had imagined a gentler moment, but I see I won't be granted one. So I'll speak plainly—I think we might help one another."

Help. What an odd thing to say. Prudence frowned doubtfully. "How?"

"You are very comely," he said, his gaze wandering over her. "Any gentleman in this town would be very lucky to have you as his wife."

A self-conscious heat began to rise in Prudence's cheeks. "You said it wasn't indecent—"

"Hear me out," Stanhope continued undaunted. "It is no secret that scandal and your mother's unfortunate madness have made you rather untouchable, is it? And I think it obvious to you that if anyone were to discover your recent foray into the English countryside, it would be impossible for any gentleman of note to offer for you."

Prudence's humiliation crawled up the nape of her neck. "I certainly can't fault you for refusing to flatter me, my lord. Did you come expressly to humiliate me?" she asked evenly. "If so, you've wasted your time. I am not easily humiliated, thanks to all the reasons you've so candidly listed."

"Humiliate!" he said, surprised. "Quite the opposite, Miss Cabot. I've come to offer for your hand."

That brought Prudence up short. All rational thought flew out of her head. She stared at him, confused as to what scheme he was perpetrating.

"Naturally, in doing so, I am prepared to overlook all of the reasons I've listed that make you an unsuitable match for anyone else. Frankly, I couldn't care less about them. I find you appealing in many ways. And, as it happens, my estate is entailed to such an extent that I am in need of a sizable dowry. I suspect yours will do."

Prudence suddenly couldn't breathe. She was indignant, but unsure why. The truth was that had it not been for Roan, she could imagine herself being strangely grateful to Stanhope. Of course she would have hoped for something a bit less transactional about this offer, but that was the way of her world. No matter how people dressed it, marriages were made for connections and financial and social gains. Sometimes great affection was tied to it. Sometimes, not.

Of all the things she had expected from Stanhope, an offer of marriage—to an *earl*, no less—was wildly beyond anything she might ever have imagined. And yet there was something so mercenary about it that Prudence couldn't help recoil from it. She didn't want a bloodless transaction. She suddenly realized how desperately she wanted love.

"You will not have heard a word against me, I suspect," he blithely continued as if he assumed she agreed with his reasoning. "You will be the Countess of Stanhope and all the attendant privileges that brings. I will cherish you as a husband ought, honor you, father your children and keep you in society as you are accustomed. Who's to say? We might even grow to genuine affection." He smiled.

Prudence couldn't believe it.

He cocked his head to one side and looked at her curiously. "I know this must come as a shock, but you can't disagree, can you?" he asked, his gaze falling to her lips. "Ours is as good a match as either of us might expect to make at this point, isn't it?"

"No," she said, her voice a bit breathless.

"No?"

"No, my lord, it's not. I won't accept your offer."

Stanhope frowned for the first time since she'd met him. "Why? What option do you have?"

"Surely that is obvious to you. I intend to marry Mr. Matheson," she said, and she meant it. She loved him. She loved him desperately, and she would risk everything to be with him rather than remain here and face men who had the same motives as Stanhope.

His eyes widened with surprise. And then narrowed as if he didn't understand. "Pardon?"

"I am marrying—"

"Yes, I heard you. Do you mean you'll leave your family behind? Or does the Yankee think to remain in England?"

"I will go there," Prudence said.

Stanhope rubbed his chin. He looked as if he were working something out in his head. "What does your family think of this?" he asked. "Beckington, Merryton, Easton. What do *they* say to it?"

Prudence didn't answer that question.

She didn't need to. Stanhope understood her. "I see. They either are unaware of what you intend or are unhappy with your choice."

"It doesn't matter what anyone thinks," Prudence said. "I love him."

"Ah, *love!*" Stanhope scoffed, sweeping his arm out as if he were on a stage. "A roll in the proverbial hay is not love, Miss Cabot! You are naive if you think so."

Prudence surged to her feet. "What is it to you?"

Stanhope gained his feet, too, and stood so close that Prudence was forced to tilt her head back. "You're being foolish. I have offered you a solution to your troubles."

"What you've offered me is a heartless transaction, my lord. Not an offer of marriage."

He nodded as he considered her. "Rethink your response, Miss Cabot," he said, his voice low and cool.

"Give my offer the courtesy of serious consideration. I'll call again in forty-eight hours."

Prudence bristled. "Come in forty-eight hours if you like, but I will still refuse you."

Stanhope shrugged and glanced down at the carpet. "Isn't your sister due to enter the Lisson Grove School of Art?" he asked idly, and slowly lifted his gaze.

Prudence froze. It felt as if her heart skipped several beats before it found its rhythm again. "How dare you. She has *nothing* to do with you or me," she said, her voice shaking with indignation.

He was not bothered by it. "You may not be aware that my grandfather endowed that school. One word from me, and that would end Miss Mercy Cabot's hopes of drawing bowls of fruit."

Prudence began to quake deep within herself. She thought of Mercy, of the way she'd spoken with great excitement for weeks about that school. She had her paints ready, her canvases. She had made a list of all the things she would take with her. She studied books of art and practiced her talent every day. "You wouldn't *dare*," she said breathlessly.

"It seems to me that it would be much easier for all concerned if you would see how advantageous my offer is," Stanhope suggested mildly. "You'd be a countess with two houses to see after. I'd have your dowry. Your sister would have her school." He shrugged as if it were as simple as that.

"If it's a dowry you want, my lord, then offer for someone else!"

"Ah, but I am not as heartless as you think. You are the one who inspires me, Miss Cabot. I find *you* appealing."

Her mind was whirling; she felt as if her heart was incapable of absorbing what was happening. "You're despicable," she said low. "Why would you punish Mercy? What purpose would that serve?"

"It's called vengeance, Miss Cabot. If you take this opportunity from me, I will take one from your family."

She gaped at him. "You're a beast."

He shook his head. "I'm practical." He touched her chin. "I want you to be practical, love. There were four and twenty at Howston Hall. Sooner or later, memories will be revived. Even if you have your way and sail for America, what will become of those you leave behind when tongues begin to wag? What will become of young Mercy Cabot, with no art school to occupy her?" The shine in his eyes had changed—he looked almost triumphant. "I'll see myself out," he said, and with a bow of his head, he walked out of the study.

Prudence stared blindly at the space he'd vacated, her mind racing, her heart beating as if she'd suffered a great fright. She couldn't move, she could scarcely think.

Finnegan appeared. He frowned at her and poured a tot of whiskey, which he put in her hand. "Are you all right?" he asked.

"No," Prudence muttered. She suddenly whirled around and rushed to the window. It was still raining. She watched Stanhope get on his horse.

Had he really just come here and offered her marriage?

"Is there something I can do for you?" Finnegan asked, his concern evident.

"No, thank you, Finnegan. I'll be fine. But I need to

lie down. Will you excuse me?" she asked, and hurried out, retreating to the privacy of her room.

If only Roan would come back! she thought desperately. He would know what to do. She needed someone to lean on, someone who could help her make sense of all that had happened, of what was the right thing to do.

But Roan didn't come. And as the afternoon wore on, it became increasingly apparent to Prudence what she had to do.

CHAPTER SIXTEEN

GRACE AND MERCY darted in from the rain just behind
Honor and her children, and as Honor sent her children
to their nursemaid, Grace and Mercy bustled Prudence
into the drawing room and fluttered and chattered
around her, demanding to know where she'd been and
what she'd done.

Mercy's blue eyes were bright with excitement. She
held a long, slender, highly polished wood box as she
demanded the minute details of Prudence's adventure
and then hung on to every word, laughing at inappropriate times, gasping in unison with Grace.

Neither of them seemed particularly surprised by
what Prudence told them, and she suspected that they'd
already heard the worst of it from Honor or Augustine.
When Prudence finished her story, Grace gave her a
fierce hug, then set her back. "Now that I've seen with
my own eyes that you are quite all right," she said, her
hazel eyes darkening, "I can ask you if you've lost your
bloody mind."

"Grace!" Mercy said.

"You cannot imagine the distress you have caused
me and my husband with your deception!" she continued. "Merryton has been nothing but generous with
you, Pru, and only asks that you think of your virtue

and the family name in return. How could you be so careless? How could you be so defiant?"

"How were *you* so defiant?" Prudence shot back.

Grace gasped, her eyes widening. "Don't you dare throw my mistakes in my face! I may have been wrong, but it was obviously divined. Merryton and I are quite happy now, aren't we? And besides, my situation is very different from yours. I was trying desperately to save us all."

"You and Honor both seem to think you have the exclusive right to bad behavior. Is my situation really so different?" Prudence asked calmly. "I want only to save myself." Grace could flog her for all Prudence cared—her heart was too heavy to muster much interest. "You and Honor are married. Mercy has her art school. I had a thirst for adventure."

"Look," Mercy said, and opened the box she was guarding so closely and held it up to Prudence. "Augustine gave them to me." Inside the velvet-lined box were four paintbrushes of varying sizes. The handles were inlaid with pearl. "I think they came at a very dear price. The bristles are sable, you know. Those are the best sort of brushes."

"Mercy, not now," Grace said wearily, but Mercy was single-minded and had been for weeks. Prudence looked at her younger sister as she pushed her spectacles up on her nose and admired her paintbrushes. Her face was glowing with pleasure, and Prudence imagined how devastated she would be if she were denied the opportunity to attend the Lisson Grove School.

"Did you know that over one hundred artists applied for six available chairs?" Mercy asked, looking up from her brushes. "Can you imagine, Prudence? It's the most prestigious art school in all of England, and I have one of the six chairs for new students!"

"Really, Mercy, now is not the time. Prudence has gone off and done something wretched and we really must address her," Grace said irritably.

Just then, Honor came into the room. "Address what?"

"I have asked Prudence to explain her behavior and she won't."

Prudence shrugged. "What would you like me to say, darling? That it was wrong of me? All right, it was wrong of me. But I don't care that it was."

"Pru!" Grace exclaimed with great frustration.

"I have apologized," Prudence reminded them all. "What more can I do? I can't turn back the clock." The good Lord knew how desperately she wanted to turn back the clock, to go back to that day at Ashton Down and never step on that stagecoach. If she hadn't, she would have spared herself the pain of a broken heart.

"Oh!" Grace said, throwing up her hands in surrender.

"Do you think," Mercy asked, peering at Prudence through her spectacles as if she were a specimen in a museum, "that you are feeling yourself? It really is unlike you to go off like that."

"No, Mercy, quite the contrary. I am at *last* myself. For the first time in four years, I am not defined by what Honor and Grace did, don't you see?"

Grace gasped as if she'd slapped her. Mercy said, simply, "Yes, I do. I understand completely."

Grace looked to Honor for help.

Honor shrugged. "She's right." But then she turned

to Prudence and said, "Well? Are you going to tell them?"

"Tell us what?" Grace said. "What else could she possibly tell us?"

All three pairs of eyes fixed on Prudence, waiting for her answer. She looked at their faces, at their hope mixed with a bit of trepidation of what she'd say. There was no one closer to her than these three. They'd been a troop since they were small, one for all and all for one. Her sisters were pieces of her, and she pieces of them; they understood each other completely.

A rush of heat swept through Prudence as she thought about life without them. Her gaze moved to Mercy, who was clutching her box of paintbrushes. Mercy had spent the entire summer wrapped in her plans for the art school. For her, everything depended on that one opportunity.

"Pru! You have us on tenterhooks! What will you tell us?" Mercy demanded.

"I've had an offer," Prudence said. Her voice sounded distant to her, as if it were coming from someone else.

Grace gasped. Mercy stared at her. "From who?" Grace exclaimed. "Not this…this *man* you've been cavorting with?"

"Yes," Prudence said. "From him. But I've had another."

"What?" Honor all but shouted. "What are you talking about? I left not three hours ago, and you've miraculously gained another offer in that time?"

Prudence nodded. "From Lord Stanhope."

A moment of stunned silence was followed by sheer pandemonium. Prudence's sisters were talking at once, questioning her, claiming disbelief and pressing her for details.

Prudence told them everything…everything except that he'd threatened to take Mercy's position at Lisson Grove. She knew what Mercy would do if she heard what Stanhope had threatened, because it was the same thing Prudence would do. Mercy would remove herself from the school and therefore remove the power of Stanhope's threat to force Prudence to his will. Either way, the girl standing before her, clutching her box of paintbrushes, would lose.

Mercy would not lose. These were Prudence's consequences to bear. If she'd never stepped foot on that stagecoach, Mercy would never have been threatened.

"I don't believe it!" Honor's voice was full of wonder. "What did you say?" she asked Prudence.

Prudence did not answer—they heard a commotion downstairs at the door at that moment, and Honor whirled about. "It's George!"

All four of them rushed from the room, flying down the stairs to the foyer.

George was there, all right, the ends of his dark hair dripping with rain. He handed a wet coat and hat to a footman and removed his dress coat. "It's a bloody deluge," he said apologetically.

Prudence ran past him, to the open door, peering out. *Where was Roan?* There was no one else outside, save the boy who was taking George's horse around to the mews. Her breath caught in her throat; she whirled around to George.

"We've been beside ourselves with worry, darling. Where have you been?" Honor asked, throwing her arms around her husband's neck as he tried to untie his neckcloth.

"I'm sorry to have worried you," he said, kissing her cheek.

"Where is Matheson?" Prudence asked.

"He'll be along within an hour or two, I expect." George succeeded in untying his neckcloth and the ends dangled down his waistcoat. "I see the virtues have gathered," he said, and kissed Grace and Mercy hello. "Where's Merryton?"

"He'll be along later," Grace said. "What happened?"

"Give me a warm whiskey and a fire and I'll tell you everything," he said. He seemed exhilarated as he slipped his arm around Honor's waist and winked at Prudence. "Shall we go up?"

"You can't keep us in suspense!" Mercy cried as Honor and George began to move up the stairs, Prudence quickly on their heels.

"Mercy, you won't believe the day we've had. What madness," George said cheerfully, and glanced over his shoulder to Prudence. "I can't believe I have cause to even utter these words, but, Pru, you are *not* the most willful young woman I've encountered this week."

"George Easton," Honor said as they entered the main salon. "Will you please tell us what has happened?" She went directly to the sideboard to pour him a whiskey.

"All right, all right," he said with a grin. "I'll tell you everything. Matheson and I went this morning to the Villeroys', as you know, and he wasted no time inquiring after his sister. Villeroy confirmed that indeed, Miss Aurora Matheson had been a guest in their house for several weeks, and that the entire family had only recently returned from a country house visit to Howston Hall."

"What were they doing at Howston Hall?" Honor asked curiously.

"Never mind that," Prudence said. "Thank God, you found her."

"Oh, we found her, all right," George said jovially. "Thank you, my love," he said to Honor as he accepted a whiskey from her. He took a good long sip before continuing.

"Naturally, Matheson assumed he'd found her," he continued. "He asked that she be made aware of his presence and called down to the salon at once. But the Villeroys gave each other a very curious look and neither of them responded straightaway."

"No?" Mercy asked as she sank down onto the settee.

"No," George said, and sipped from the glass. "In fact, it was very apparent to me that the Villeroys were intentionally talking circles around the central question of where, precisely, was Miss Matheson. Mrs. Villeroy said it was early yet, and her husband asked if the breakfast had been put away, perhaps they shouldn't have been so hasty, and they engaged in a bit of a quarrel over breakfast."

"I don't understand," Prudence said.

"Well, neither did Matheson," George said with a laugh. "I feared he would put a fist through the window as the Villeroys sorted out their breakfast."

Prudence gasped.

"Calm yourself, Pru, he didn't do that. But after several minutes of listening to the Villeroys bicker, he rather firmly insisted they bring down his sister. That is when Villeroy admitted that she had gone."

Prudence's heart seized. "Gone?"

"Yes, *gone*." George paused and looked at Honor, then the rest of them and smiled as if he had a secret. "Along with their son," he added in a low voice. He arched a brow and then drank more whiskey.

The Cabot sisters all gasped at the same moment.

"Villeroy explained that their son Albert had taken quite a liking to Miss Matheson. He'd offered for her hand, Miss Matheson had accepted. I'll tell you that Matheson had to turn and walk to the windows then, and I could see from the grip of his hands that he was working very hard to keep his wits about him. But Villeroy went on to say that he and has wife thought, and wisely so, that it was passing strange for a young woman from America, without benefit of family, or a firm fix on her dowry, to accept that proposal. They told their son he could not marry her."

"So she ran away!" Prudence cried.

"She *and* Albert ran away," George said. "To Gretna Green."

"Oh dear God," Honor said. "What a disaster."

"Matheson wasn't aware of Gretna Green or the significance of it, and it fell to me to explain to him that his sister was eloping with the Villeroy lad. He suffered a bit of apoplexy at first—he was quite unable to speak. But then Villeroy said that they'd been discovered missing only that morning. They'd also found a note their son had left for them, professing his undying love and devotion to Miss Matheson and telling him of their intention to wed."

"Oh! It's terribly exciting, isn't it?" Mercy asked from her perch on the edge of the settee cushion.

"Well," George said, his eyes shining with the scandal of his tale, "Roan Matheson wouldn't accept that. He said to me, 'Which way to Gretna Green?' I pointed him north. Then he asked if I might sell him a horse. I was about to tell him that I couldn't very well sell him a horse, but Villeroy stood up and said if Matheson intended to go after them, then so would he, and he had a horse Matheson could ride."

"So you all went to Gretna Green?" Honor asked, her disbelief evident.

"I couldn't very well let them go off, could I, a Frenchman and an American? Who knows what trouble they might have met? I thought it was my duty to see them safely through, so I sent a footman for my horse."

"But…" Honor looked confused. "You couldn't possibly have gone to Gretna Green and come back in a single day."

"No, indeed," George said, clearly enjoying himself. "Luck was on Matheson's side, I tell you. The rain has made the roads to the north nearly impassable, and the progress of the coach the young lovers had taken was slowed considerably. We caught up to them in Oxford." George suddenly laughed. "You've never seen such a look of surprise as was on the face of Matheson's sister when she saw her brother riding up alongside that coach. He was in quite a fury and I think if anyone had tried to stop him, he would have tossed them off the earth."

Prudence realized she had both hands pressed to her chest. "Oh my God," she said nervously. "I can't bear to know what happened then."

"I'll tell you. Villeroy took his son in hand, and Matheson his sister. They are all returning to London. Miss Matheson had quite a lot of things to be gathered from the coach and from the Villeroy house, apparently. I invited them to stay here, darling," he said to Honor. "Matheson intends to depart for Liverpool by week's end."

That was two days. It felt as if the room was moving beneath Prudence's feet. So many thoughts and emotions were spinning in her, relief for Roan, despair for them both. Her heart, cracking and shattering in her chest, her lungs, shriveling up, incapable of proper breathing.

"Finnegan!" George shouted, "Where are you, Finnegan?"

The butler appeared a moment later. "We'll have two guests for supper. They ought to be along by eight o'clock."

"Yes, sir," Finnegan said, and disappeared again.

An invigorated George Easton looked at the four Cabot sisters and tossed back his whiskey. "I believe I'll have another. I think I've earned it."

"I'll have one, too," Prudence said as Honor stood up to pour her husband another whiskey.

No one said a word about that.

CHAPTER SEVENTEEN

THE END OF the young lovers' flight to Gretna Green was a spectacular moment in Oxford. As many onlookers standing with mouths agape, Roan marched his sister to a coach bound in the opposite direction of Scotland and surrendered his horse to Mr. Villeroy so that he might lead his red-faced, verbally combative son home.

Aurora Matheson accompanied her brother without complaint.

The moment they were situated in the coach that would carry them back to London, Aurora turned her big brown eyes to Roan and said tearfully, "I'm *so* glad you came."

Roan had been prepared to blister her with words, to upbraid her up one side and down the other for her foolishness, her recklessness, but her pitiful look and earnest words effectively collapsed his roaring anger. He sighed, took her hand in his. "What in hevean were you thinking, Aurora? You had to have known we'd not approve. And what of Mr. Gunderson? I thought you held some esteem for him!"

"I did! I do!" she said. "I don't know why I said yes to Albert. I never truly believed he'd go through with it—he's rather meek, really. But he kissed me and said, 'let's go,' and I was lost, Roan. It was so romantic."

"Romantic," Roan scoffed. "You were going to marry a man because you found elopement romantic?"

She sighed. "It's inexplicable, I know. But I believed I loved him."

"You loved him?" he asked incredulously, forgetting, for a moment, that he had found love on a sunny afternoon in England. "Why didn't you come home with Aunt Mary and Uncle Robert? You knew Gunderson was waiting. Surely you weren't in love with Villeroy then!"

"No! I'm a fool, Roan," she said, morosely. "Albert Villeroy speaks with such a flourish. He convinced me that there was much yet to see and do in England, and that he'd be traveling with his parents, and they'd be calling on friends at great estates, and I lost my head! I wrote to Mr. Gunderson, did Aunt Mary tell you? I explained to him I'd sail home by the end of summer."

"But you didn't tell him why, Aurora, and he is a clever young man, as you know."

She sighed and looked down at her lap.

"I understand the desire to experience life before you marry," he said. "But the Villeroy fellow doesn't seem the type—"

"I know, I *know*," she said. "But he was so earnest in his esteem, and in the past few weeks, I began to believe that I really did love him," she said. "I don't expect you to understand it, but I know what I felt, and I felt love for him. And yet, when I saw you, I was overcome with…relief. I realized I wouldn't have to go through with it. I realized I could go home and I almost wept with joy."

Roan thought of Prudence and wondered…had she been overcome with relief when she'd seen her family? Had she made her impassioned plea for his sake, as Aurora had done in Oxford for Villeroy? No, no, he would know if Prudence's feelings were as frivolous as his sister's feelings. He would know if she'd felt relief at seeing her family.

Aurora sighed and rested her head against his shoulder. "I suppose I've ruined everything."

"With Gunderson?" he asked, and shifted her so that he could put his arm around her. "Probably so."

She sighed again. "Do you know the strangest thing? I miss him."

"You have a questionable way of demonstrating that."

"Oh, I know I've made a mess. I'm so ashamed."

"Then why did you do it?" he asked helplessly, unable to understand how her head worked.

She sniffed, wiped her gloved fingers beneath her eyes. "Don't scold me anymore. I know how awful I've been."

"Very," he agreed.

She whimpered. "At least I haven't ruined everything," she said petulantly.

"What do you mean?"

Aurora blinked up at him. "I mean that at least *your* engagement is still intact. You would never go back on your word, not like me. I'm awful, Roan! I realize now how irresponsible and unfeeling I've been. Father will never forgive me."

Roan gave her a pat on her shoulder. "He'll forgive you. He always does. Funny that he's never been so quick to forgive me."

"You! You've never done anything to displease him.

And besides, you're a man. Men can do whatever they please."

"That is not entirely true," he said. "I may have more freedom than you, but I still have a responsibility to our family." He was painfully aware that Aurora was right; he always honored his word. What was a man without his word, really?

But wasn't there some honor to following his heart, too? To keep his word now…well, the stakes felt too high. He could no more imagine himself with Susannah Pratt by his side for the rest of his life than he could imagine himself singing and dancing on a stage. It was impossible. Especially now, especially now that he knew what love was.

"Perhaps," Aurora said. "But at least when you marry Susannah Pratt, you may continue to do as you please. When I marry Sam Gunderson—*if* I marry Sam, I'll have to do as he wants."

Roan didn't say anything to that.

"Where are we going?" Aurora asked. "Do we sail tonight? I should like the chance to say goodbye to my friends."

"I am hardly inclined to allow a social swath through London after what you've done," he said gruffly. "Tonight, we will be the guests of Mr. and Mrs. Easton. We'll see about your farewells tomorrow."

"Easton," she repeated. "Who are they, friends of Auntie Mary?"

"Of mine," Roan said. He didn't say more than that, not trusting himself to speak about Prudence without a torrent of emotion spilling out. He wasn't ready to tell Aurora what had happened to him here. He needed to think how to broach it. Everything had happened so fast that he hadn't yet considered how, exactly, he would break the news to his family.

"Of yours?" She looked at him curiously. "How do you know anyone in London? Have you been here long?"

"A few days," he said.

Aurora cocked her head. "There is something you're not telling me, Roan."

He couldn't very well hide it, so Roan told Aurora about Prudence. About the coach, the trip across the English countryside. About falling in love.

Aurora took it all in without a word, listening intently. When he'd finished, she considered all he'd said for a very long while. "What of Miss Pratt?" she asked.

"I never proposed to her."

"But everyone expects—"

"I will tell her as soon as we arrive in New York."

Aurora pressed her lips together and nodded. "What will Father say?"

Roan gave her a squeeze of her shoulders. "I suspect he will be gravely unhappy with us both."

Aurora turned her head and looked out the window. She said nothing more about it.

MERRYTON AND HIS children joined the sisters before supper. Grace had obviously told her husband some of what had happened, because it seemed to Prudence that he could scarcely look at her.

"My lord?" she said.

He glanced at her briefly and said, "I am relieved you are safe, Pru. But I think it best if we speak of… this," he said, as if he couldn't think of a word to describe what she'd done, "at a more opportune time." He turned away from her and went to the sideboard.

Merryton had always been a man of few words, but Prudence could feel his displeasure radiating from him.

"He's here!" Mercy cried, bursting into the green salon.

"Mercy, you gave me a fright," Honor said. "Who is here?"

"The *American*," Mercy said, and hurried ahead of Prudence and Honor to have a look at the man who had prompted Prudence to take that fateful ride on the stagecoach.

Roan had removed his coat and hat by the time Prudence reached the top of the stairs. He looked up and smiled at her, his gaze warm. She could see the fatigue and relief in his face, and she smiled, too. But her heart was breaking.

It took Prudence a moment to notice his sister. She was handing her cloak to a footman. "Thank you," she said, her voice sweet, her accent flat like Roan's. She turned and looked up to where Honor, Mercy and Prudence, and now Grace, having decided against waiting patiently to meet them, had gathered at the top of the stairs.

Miss Aurora Matheson was quite pretty, with auburn hair and vivid brown eyes. She resembled Roan—they had the same nose, the same cheekbones. She looked both surprised and delighted as the four sisters made their way down the stairs, Prudence in front. When they reached the bottom of the stairs she sank into a curtsy. "Mrs. Easton, how do you do," she said to Prudence. "I beg your pardon for the terribly late intrusion."

"I beg your pardon, I'm not Mrs. Easton," Prudence

said, and held out her hand to Aurora. "I am Miss Prudence Cabot."

"May I present my sister, Miss Aurora Matheson," Roan said, his gaze on Prudence as he made the introductions.

When he was done, Honor poked Prudence in the back, prompting her to speak. "It's a pleasure to make your acquaintance, Miss Matheson," Prudence said. "I've…I've heard quite a lot about you."

Aurora smiled. "I hope it hasn't all been wretched! I beg you forgive us arriving so late and disheveled. I told my brother there is a lovely hotel right around the corner, but he insisted on coming here."

"He was right to insist," Honor said graciously.

"I would never dream of imposing," Aurora continued. "I hope you haven't heard *that* about me." She smiled, seemingly not the least intimidated by the unusual situation that had brought her here.

Honor exchanged a look with Prudence. "It's no imposition, Miss Matheson—"

"Oh, you must call me Aurora," she said brightly.

Honor paused. "You must be famished," she said, changing tracks. "Won't you come up and have some wine? Supper will be served in a half hour."

"Thank you. I am *very* hungry. I suppose you've heard about my escapades," she said, giving her brother another look. "We've scarcely had a bite all day."

Mercy giggled with surprise, her bright blue eyes moving between her sisters, looking for the sign that they were as surprised by Aurora Matheson's forthright manner as she was.

"Shall we go up?" Honor asked, and put her hand on Aurora's elbow and guided her to the stairs. Mercy was right behind them, fascinated with the American bird, and Grace behind her.

Prudence looked at Roan. He touched her hand, his fingers twining in hers for a moment before he lifted her hand to his arm to escort her up.

"Are you all right?" she asked softly.

"I'm fine. It's been a taxing day. You?"

"It's been a taxing day," she agreed.

"I want to talk to you," he said. "But I dare not leave Aurora alone with your family for as much as a minute." He smiled wearily and led her up.

He was right to be cautious. In the first quarter hour after their arrival, after the Mathesons were introduced to Easton and Merryton, Prudence scarcely said a word. Aurora was bent on apologizing for her appearance at their home without proper invitation, but seemed blithely unaware or uncaring of the trouble, of the situation she and her brother had caused in this foreign land. She somehow seamlessly turned the conversation around to acquaintances that she and Honor might have in common. It was remarkable, really, how easily this girl entered their home and was welcomed. She was strangely forthright, but bubbly, and quite easy to like. She had a zest about her that made one forget she had almost eloped with a Frenchman this morning.

Prudence wished she had a bit of that zest. "The roads were bad, were they?" she asked Roan quietly as Aurora continued to speak with great enthusiasm about a ball she had attended in the spring.

"They seemed much worse to me without my companion to natter on about them," he said, and smiled at her fondly.

Prudence blushed a little. "I would have liked to have gone, if only to see your face when you found her."

"Red with fury, I'm sure," he said. "It was all I could do not to throttle her then and there." He glanced across the room to his sister. Prudence could see the affection for her in his expression. "I pity the poor man who marries that girl."

When supper was served, Prudence marveled that Aurora could be so gay and relaxed. It was as if the Eastons had invited them for supper. It was as if they'd all long been friends, instead of the troubled truth between them all. Aurora even laughed when George made a remark about their chase to Oxford.

"It was more of a crawl, wasn't it? Quite tedious! I apologize for any inconvenience, Mr. Easton. I didn't mean to cause such a stir."

"You didn't mean…" Roan started, and sighed heavenward. "A *stir* is the least you have caused."

"Oh all right," Aurora said cheerfully. "I can see that you haven't forgiven me yet." She fixed her sparkling gaze on Prudence. "Miss Cabot, I understand you have seen the Howston Hall! Isn't it magnificent?"

"Yes," Prudence said uncertainly.

"I was quite enchanted by the swans and peacocks. What do you think, Roan, shouldn't we have swans and peacocks at home?"

Aurora continued on in that vein. She was excited and chatty and didn't seem the least bit upset that her elopement had been foiled. Prudence was devastated by what had happened to her. She was worried about who she'd hurt and inconvenienced by it. How could Aurora be so indifferent? She looked at her family, all of them staring at Aurora as if they were watching a rare creature. Merryton kept his hand in a fist, lightly tapping it against the table. George leaned back, in his chair, transfixed. And Mercy kept giggling as if she found Aurora quite entertaining.

Prudence kept stealing looks at Roan, and every time she turned her attention to him, she found him looking at her. His gaze was contemplative in a way Prudence had not seen from him before. She wondered if he was feeling the same uneasiness, if he felt the slight shift in the air. She wondered if he would be as easy as his sister when it was over and done. If, in a few days' time, he too would be laughing about his great adventure in England.

She turned her attention to Mercy, so carefree, so diverted by the unusual American creature, and thought of her box of brushes. It was all too much. Prudence forced herself to eat something so as not to draw attention to her despair, and then struggled to keep it down. She was grateful that Aurora was taking the center of attention, pulling it away from the darkness that was creeping in around her.

After dinner, Roan suggested that he and his sister retire. It was the proper thing to do, given the circumstance, but Aurora looked disappointed.

"Matheson, might I have a word before you retire?" George asked, and to Merryton, "My lord?"

"Certainly," Roan said, and strode out of the room with them, unafraid.

Prudence felt almost panic-stricken as she watched them go. She wondered what George meant to say. If there was anything to be said to Roan, she wanted to be the one to say it.

Finnegan came in to the dining room and said, "I've

taken the liberty of putting Miss Matheson's things in the blue room."

"I'll bring her up," Prudence said.

"Thank you," Aurora said. She smiled at Prudence, her gaze locking on her. "That would be lovely."

The bedroom at the end of the hall had china-blue walls and a snowy-white counterpane on the bed. Aurora flounced onto that counterpane and sighed up at the embroidered canopy. "It feels divine. The bed I had at the Villeroys' was so lumpy!"

Prudence leaned up against the vanity, watching her, wondering what Roan had told her about the two of them. "You must be exhausted."

"A bit," Aurora agreed. "I'm *dreading* the drive to Liverpool. The roads are so wretched, and I was bounced about all day today and I ache all over."

Prudence pretended to straighten things on the vanity and looked at Aurora in the reflection of the mirror. "May I ask...are you sad?"

"Sad?" Aurora pushed herself up to her elbows as she considered that. "A little, I think." She smiled ruefully. "Not as sad as Albert. He was so distraught when we were caught that I feared the poor dear would burst into sobs."

She was so flippant! It annoyed Prudence. "Didn't you love him?" she asked, perhaps a bit too sharply. She wanted to add that they'd been on their way to marry, presumably because they were in love, and to be thwarted at the last minute must have been heart-wrenching.

Aurora gave her a funny look and slowly pushed herself up, so that she was sitting on the edge of the bed. "It's funny, really—I truly thought I loved him.

Of course I did, or I would have never agreed to elope. But when I saw Roan on that horse, shouting at the driver to halt before he started the team away from the station, I was so...*relieved*. I can't describe it any other way. I was relieved. I felt as if I had been saved, almost from myself."

Prudence looked at Aurora skeptically. But the young woman nodded earnestly. "I know that must sound deplorable to you. In one moment I was running off to marry Albert, and in the next, I was glad to be rescued. I think I was infatuated," she said. "Infatuation feels very much like love, did you know? Have you ever been infatuated?"

Prudence felt a funny twist in her gut. Was it infatuation that burned in her and not love? How did one tell the difference? "Ah...I don't think so," she said uncertainly.

"Poor Albert. I don't think he was infatuated at all. I think he truly loved me. My father is right—we are too impetuous."

"We?" Prudence asked.

"Roan and I," Aurora said.

Roan, impetuous? Prudence wanted to ask in what way Roan was impetuous but was afraid to speak, afraid of betraying her feelings for him.

"Roan can be very passionate about his ideas," Aurora said.

Yes, Prudence could agree that he was.

"Do you know it was he who first spoke to me about my fiancé, Mr. Gunderson? Well...he *was* my fiancé. Roan says he is very displeased with me now," she said, as if it weren't the least bit odd to speak of another fiancé on a day like this. "Roan was the one who convinced me that a marriage to him would be quite advantageous for the entire family. And how important it was that we think of marriage in those terms." She smiled. "I understood him, of course. And I suppose I was made agreeable by the fact that I've always esteemed Mr. Gunderson."

"That's…that is the way marriages are made here, too," Prudence said, thinking of Stanhope. "For connection. For fortune. I suppose for affection, too."

"Affection is what I feel for Mr. Gunderson," Aurora said. "I feel wretched that I've hurt him and I hope he'll forgive me. I rather think that's what Roan feels for Susannah Pratt," she added thoughtfully. "Affection. Not love, at least not yet, but certainly affection." She smiled at Prudence. "Very well put, Miss Cabot."

Not love, but affection… Those words struck Prudence like a knife to her back.

"What is it, have I said something wrong?" Aurora asked.

"No, no, I just…" Prudence shook her head.

Aurora stood up and walked to the vanity where Prudence was standing. She stood beside her and picked up a hand mirror set in porcelain and pretended to study it. "I feel quite awful about everything, you know. Now that I've ruined Mr. Gunderson's regard for me, I suppose it's doubly important that Roan honor his commitment to Mr. Pratt and marry Susannah. Not that I have any doubt that he *will*," she said, and smiled sweetly at Prudence. "My brother is unfailingly a man of his word. If Roan says he will do something, he will do it."

She put down the mirror and turned to face Prudence. "And as I said, he has such affection for her.

He's cross with me, you know. He didn't want to leave her, and now he wants to hurry back."

Prudence gaped at her. Did she know that Roan had asked her to marry him? Was that why she spoke so freely about Roan's intentions?

Aurora's smile deepened. "Life is so much easier without unnecessary complications, don't you agree?"

Prudence understood her. She couldn't speak. Her thoughts were rushing over themselves, but one thing was crystal clear: Aurora Matheson was telling her not to complicate Roan's commitment.

"Oh, but I am *exhausted*!" Aurora said airily.

"Yes, of course," Prudence said. "I'll leave you now." She walked out of the room and moved blindly down the hall, reeling at the message Aurora had just delivered. Roan was committed. His family expected it. No matter what he wanted, Aurora had made it quite clear that he was expected to honor his word. She desperately wanted to speak to him, and crept downstairs. The door to George's study was closed, and a thin shaft of light was coming out from beneath it. She could hear the low voices of men behind the door.

Prudence climbed back upstairs, passing the drawing room, where she could hear her sisters talking. She carried on to her room, each step heavier than the last. It felt a monumental effort to even drag herself onto the bed, where she lay on her side, staring out the window, her thoughts whirling around Stanhope, Mercy and Roan, the man who had awakened her to the world. Her heart felt as if it were shattering.

The rain had ended and the clouds were breaking. The moon was peeking out between them. A lonely moon, gray and sickly.

CHAPTER EIGHTEEN

IT WAS HALF past twelve when Roan made his way up to his room by the light of a single candle. He moved with deliberation, trying to swallow down his angry indignation for the "compromise" George Easton had offered him.

They thought him a bloody bounder, a scoundrel, which Roan supposed he deserved.

Easton was in shipping, he'd said, and had been eager to explore bringing the American cotton market to England. He had suggested to Roan that they could partner together, with Roan acting as his agent in America...in exchange for leaving Prudence in England.

"You can understand, surely, our concern," Easton had said as Merryton looked on, as easily if they were talking about a horse. "Not five days ago, our Prudence was on her way to visit a friend who had given birth to her first child. Today, she is contemplating sailing to America to marry a man she scarcely knows."

It was all Roan could do not to put his hands around Easton's throat for thinking he could buy him. Instead, Roan calmly explained that he had not lured his sister-in-law into a nefarious trap and suggested that George Easton put his cock in a goat.

That comment caused Lord Merryton to turn to the sideboard and pour three whiskeys.

"Calm yourself, Matheson. You can't fault me, can you? You've just retrieved your sister from a similar situation," Easton said.

"I am not Villeroy," Roan said sharply. "Do you think I've made this offer like a young pup? That I don't understand how sudden it is? I love Prudence. I have spent days in her company, at least as much time as I might have spent courting her under your watchful eye, sir. Granted, things have happened far too quickly, and in a manner that we both find surprising and unexpected. But that doesn't change the fact that I have come to love her. I would suggest the same thing happened to you," he said to Easton. "And to you," he said to Merryton.

Easton and Merryton exchanged a look. Merryton handed the whiskeys around. The man hardly spoke at all, but he said to Roan as he lifted his glass to him, "Think carefully, my friend. With great change comes great responsibility."

Great responsibility. As if Roan didn't know that.

He opened the door to his room and stepped inside, jumping a little when he saw Prudence standing there. He had expected to see her tonight, but he'd thought she'd come later, slipping into his bed in the middle of the night as she had before. But Prudence was still dressed in her evening clothes, her hair still up. An emerald solitaire glittered at her throat. He noticed the pale cheeks, the dark smudges under her eyes, the look of utter exhaustion, but he ignored it and put aside the candle, made two great strides to reach her, grab her up and kiss her as if he'd been missing her for days instead of hours.

When he would look back on that night, Roan could acknowledge that he knew the moment he saw her standing in his room that he felt something different, a significant shift between them. Nonetheless, he kissed her passionately, one hand cupping her face, one hand sliding down her hip, pushing her into his body. But Prudence put her hands against his chest and pushed him back.

"What is it?" he asked breathlessly, his body aroused and pressing for more, his heart telling him to ease back.

"Roan—"

"What?" he asked, and ran his hand down her face. "Are you all right? You look almost ill, Pru. God, are you…have you conceived?"

"What? No, no," she said, shaking her head.

"Are you sure—"

"Yes, I'm *sure*—"

"Then what is wrong?"

"I have something to tell you."

Roan dropped his hands and stepped back. His heart began to race.

She drew a deep breath. "Lord Stanhope called on me today."

Roan was stunned. All he could think was that he'd never wanted to actually kill a man in his life until that moment. "For extortion? Come, let's go to your brothers-in-law now. I just left them in the study—"

"To offer marriage," she said quietly.

It felt as if the air was sucked from the room. *Mar-*

riage? Prudence touched his face, but Roan drew back.
"I don't understand," he said gruffly.

"It's very simple. He needs my dowry because the
entail on his estate is too great."

"The what?" Roan asked, shaking his head.

"The entail," she said again. "It's something great
estates do—they leave everything to future generations
so that their immediate heirs can't sell off the properties. It often leaves very little money for the current
heirs. Stanhope said it was a practical solution for us
both, as no one else would offer for me, and he needed
what would come with my hand."

"No one—but *I* have offered for you, Prudence!" he
said sharply. "Did you tell him that?"

"Yes, of course I did," she said, and tried to touch
him again, but Roan turned away from her.

His heart was beating out of his chest. He could feel
something vital collapsing in him. "And?"

"He thinks I am foolish to turn down his offer and
leave England, and I…maybe I am."

He felt the ugly slash of her words through the center of his chest, and still he didn't believe it. He glanced
up; Prudence's eyes were glistening with unshed tears.
"What are you saying, Prudence?" he asked low, and
reached for her hand, taking it in his. "What the hell
are you saying?"

She made a sound as if she were choking. "Maybe
we've been too hasty," she said, her voice was shaking.
She seemed nervous. *Too* nervous.

"Is that your idea?" he asked, pulling her closer. "Or
did Stanhope say something else to you?"

Prudence opened her mouth as if she wanted to
speak, but shook her head. "It makes sense, Roan.

M-my family is here. My *life* is here. I can't leave it all behind because I had a passionate affair over the course of one week. One week, Roan! You can't really expect me to give up everything for one week. Maybe what we've felt is infatuation. Maybe we were caught up in the adventure and imagined something more."

Roan's heart detonated, collapsing with the rest of his insides. He felt almost ill. "I love you, Prudence Cabot," he reminded her. "God help me, I don't know how it happened but I love you. I thought you loved me. Why are you deciding now that one week is not worthy of your consideration? Why are you telling me that some other man has offered marriage and you find it more agreeable?"

"It's not! I never said that it was!" she cried.

"Are you afraid? Is that it?" he asked, roughly caressing her face. "I grant you America is very far away, but I won't keep you from your family. I'll bring you to England as often as you like." Even as he spoke the words, he knew that he couldn't promise her such a thing.

And it hardly mattered. Prudence was already shaking her head. "It's not that simple."

"It was that simple last night. It was that simple when you lay in that bed with me. There is something you're not telling me," he insisted.

"No. I've told you everything. I realize how practical Stanhope's offer—"

"Damn you," Roan said brusquely before she could try and convince him she should accept the offer. His collapse transformed into fury, swelling up in him. He suddenly grabbed her arm and yanked her into him, catching her by the nape of her neck. "How can you do this, Pru?"

"I don't want to do it," she said tearfully. "You have to believe me, Roan. It's not what I want to do. It's what I have to do."

His feelings darkened and he let her go. "I don't deserve this."

"I know," she said, and a single tear began to slide from the corner of her eye.

"You're careless. You're selfish. You have taken something from me that I will never have back. And worse, you've made me an accomplice in taking something from you that you will never have back. Does your Stanhope know that?"

She bit her lip and glanced down.

"You've put us both at great risk and now you will toss it away as if it meant nothing. I didn't come here looking for anything but my sister, but *you* put yourself on that coach. I fell in love with you, Prudence. I asked you to marry me and damn you, you gave me every reason to hope!"

She caught a sob in her throat. "I'm so sorry," she said. "From the bottom of my heart."

He set her back, away from him. "I should have known. I was caught up in the moment, I was captivated. But I should have known you would never leave here."

"That's not true—"

"Good night," Roan said, and opened the door.

"Roan—"

"Good *night*," he said again.

He didn't actually see her go out. His fury and his

disappointment turned into a sharp pain that stabbed at him. He was the biggest goddamn fool in the world.

WHEN MORNING CAME, Roan methodically went through his toilette, then gathered his things. He and Aurora would be leaving today, taking rooms in a hotel until tomorrow, when he could arrange passage to Liverpool. He went downstairs and found Mrs. Easton, Mercy and Aurora still at breakfast. He did not look for and he did not see Prudence.

Roan greeted them as politely as he could and declined Finnegan's offer of a plate; he had no appetite. Aurora, however, had a hearty one. It never ceased to amaze him that she could bounce back so quickly and completely from her follies. How he yearned for that ability today. He stood anxiously, wanting to get on with things.

A footman stepped into the room and bowed. "The carriage has been brought round, Miss Matheson."

"Thank you!" Aurora said cheerfully, ignoring Roan's look of shock. She said to him, "I should like to say goodbye to my friends. Mrs. Easton very kindly made the carriage available."

"What? *No*," Roan said sternly. "We are moving to a hotel this afternoon and leaving for Liverpool tomorrow. You will not be traipsing alone around London."

"Tomorrow!" Mrs. Easton said.

"I won't be traipsing at all," Aurora said. "Mercy is coming with me."

"Please don't deny me the opportunity to gad about, Mr. Matheson," Mercy said. "I'll be entering the Lisson Grove School of Art soon, and I won't have the luxury of time to call on friends." She stood up and gathered her gloves. "Good day, Honor! Good day, Mr. Matheson!"

Aurora stood up and kissed Roan lightly on the cheek. "I'll be back by two, I promise." She and Mercy flitted out of the room like a pair of kittens.

The room was silent when they'd gone; Roan looked at Mrs. Easton.

She was watching him closely. "Tomorrow?" she repeated.

"Yes."

"Prudence didn't tell me," she said carefully.

"She doesn't know. She won't be accompanying me, Mrs. Easton, so you may rest easy. If you will excuse me, I have quite a lot to do before we take our leave on the morrow." He bowed his head and went out before she could question him.

Roan didn't know how to leave England, quite honestly. How did one quit something like this? He felt completely vacant inside, as if he was leaving something large and important and vital behind and carrying a shell back to America. It annoyed him—Roan had never thought himself this man. He'd thought himself above common emotions and wants. Not that he hadn't wondered what it would be like to truly love a woman, but now he knew, and he didn't care for it. To love a woman was to become a mere ghost of a man.

He walked out of the dining room, eager to leave the house on Audley Street. As he walked to the foyer, however, he saw Prudence standing in the door of Easton's study. She had changed her gown, but she looked even worse than she had last night. He paused, looking at her, willing her to say something, to take it all back.

"Please don't hate me," she said. "I never meant to hurt you."

God, she sounded like Aurora now. "I don't hate you, Pru. I could never hate you," he said softly. "I love you. But I won't lie to spare your feelings. I won't pretend I'm not disappointed."

"So am I," she said.

They stood gazing at each other. It was madness. What was left to be said? He couldn't bear standing about, hoping by some miracle that things would change. He walked on and prayed that he would not be haunted by the vision of her standing in that door, or worse, of Stanhope and Prudence in a marital bed, that man's mouth on her breast, his cock inside of her.

He spent the morning and early afternoon arranging for a suite at a nearby hotel and passage to Liverpool the next morning. He sent a messenger to Liverpool to book passage to America. He occupied himself in every way he could until there was nothing left to be done but leave.

He returned to Audley Street in a hackney and had it packed with their things. He was as ready as he could possibly make himself to leave Prudence, and announced their departure.

Mr. and Mrs. Easton, their children, and Mercy all came to see them off. So did Prudence, of course, standing off to one side. Roan could hardly look at her—it was as if she were on a funeral march.

Easton jovially clapped his shoulder. He'd done a complete turnabout with Roan since his arrival. Apparently, he'd seen something in Roan that he liked. "I hope you'll at least think about what I've suggested," he said, referring to the cotton trade. "I could have my agent draw up some figures and send them over if you like." He extended his hand for Roan to shake.

"Thank you for your hospitality," Roan said, shaking his hand. He said nothing about the trade. He couldn't care less about the trade.

Mrs. Easton, holding her youngest son, smiled sympathetically. She put her hand on his arm and said, "I wish you Godspeed, Mr. Matheson. Bon voyage, Miss Matheson."

"I do hope the weather is good," Aurora said lightly. "It's such a *long* voyage."

"Forty days if we're lucky," Roan remarked absently.

As Finnegan helped Aurora into the hackney, Roan turned to Prudence. The others moved on to the coach to give them a bit of privacy, and peered inside, listening to Mercy and Aurora promise to write each other.

Prudence gamely tried to smile.

"Pru," he sighed. "Words fail me."

Her bottom lip was beginning to tremble and she bit down on it. "I beg your forgiveness," she said in a rush. "You have shown me the best days of my life and I will always be grateful. *Always*."

"Ah, Pru," he said sadly. "I don't want your bloody gratitude." He reached into his coat pocket and removed a folded piece of vellum. It contained more words, words he had labored over until the sun had come up and, still, they were woefully inadequate. But these bungled words were the only thing he had to give her. He lifted Prudence's hand, put the letter in it and closed her fingers around it. "I love you. I will always love you. Remember that."

Roan was aware of the Eastons, and of Aurora, who was now hanging out the window. Of Finngean and the coachman and people walking on the street. "Good-bye." He didn't care that everyone was watching. He suddenly grabbed Prudence up. He kissed her fully and without regard for anything but her, kissed her cheek, her neck, and then forced himself to let go. He turned away from her, put his back to her for fear he would do it again, and put himself in that coach, then pounded on the ceiling to signal he was ready.

The coach rolled away from the curb.

"Are you all right?" Aurora asked, staring at him in wonder.

He wasn't the least bit all right. His breath was constricted, his heart pounding. Roan ignored his sister. The coach turned the corner, and Roan glanced out the window.

Prudence hadn't moved at all. She was still standing there, clutching his letter.

Aurora saw her, too. "Don't be sad, Roan," she said, and put her hand on his knee. "There are many gentlemen in London. With her fine looks and gentle disposition, they'll be queuing at her door, won't they? And you! You'll be married to Susannah Pratt, just as you planned."

Roan turned his head and looked out the other window, clenching his jaw to keep from bellowing in pain.

CHAPTER NINETEEN

PRUDENCE WATCHED ROAN'S coach until she could no longer see it. She might have stood all day had Honor not come out and put her arm around her shoulder, forcing her inside. "Come have some tea," Honor suggested.

"No, thank you. I want to rest now. I slept so poorly last night." Prudence went up to her room where her grief turned poisonous. She vomited into the chamber pot.

Then she wept.

Much later, Honor tried to soothe her, but Prudence curled into a ball on her bed and insisted she keep the door shut and the drapes drawn. "For God's sake, Honor, let me be," Prudence begged her.

"I only want to help," Honor said.

"You can't help me," Prudence said angrily. "No one can help me. Just leave me *be.*" How could she possibly convey the depth of her grief? The seething disappointment of having felt so deeply for a man who was, very literally, as far removed from her as was possible? This wasn't infatuation at all—this was pure heartbreak.

It wasn't until late that afternoon that Prudence found the courage to read Roan's letter. He wrote in long, bold strokes.

Dearest Prudence,
It is three o'clock in the morning, and there is very

little left of the candle. As I've lain in bed, feeling the space beside me cold and empty, I composed a brilliant letter to you in my mind, one that I believe adequately conveyed my feelings for you. But when I rose to put pen to paper, all the elegance of my thoughts was lost. I am utterly incapable of describing the depth and breadth of my feelings. Is it love? I think it is, but I am no scholar when it comes to the heart. I know only that I adore you. I want to slay dragons and lay them at your feet. I want to conquer nations and make you their queen. My life has never lacked for anything, but from this day forward, it will always lack for you.

She read his letter over and over again, intermittently weeping and then staring off in the distance and seeing nothing.

Prudence somehow managed to rouse herself the next day, determined not to drown in her grief. She dressed and allowed Honor to drag her on a call to Augustine and Monica.

"Prudence, darling!" Augustine said, greeting her with a hug. "I've been made most happy—Lord Stanhope has called to speak to me about a *match*!" Augustine seemed oblivious to her distress, elated that the problem of what to do with Prudence had been solved.

"Will you accept his offer?" Monica asked, peering curiously at Prudence.

Prudence merely shrugged. "Why not? I suppose one man is as good as the next."

Augustine laughed loudly at that, and Prudence stared out the window.

That's all she could manage for a few days, staring out windows.

Merryton and Grace planned to leave London at week's end—Merryton could never bear to be in London long. Mercy busied herself collecting all the things she supposed she would need at Lisson Grove. Linens and soaps, ribbons and stockings. Life moved placidly along, everyone returning to their lives, moving with the tide of time. Everyone but Prudence.

Her life stood still.

Stanhope came round twice for Prudence, but Honor told him she'd come down with an ague, refusing to allow him to see her.

"I can't put him off forever," she said, pacing nervously before Prudence, who was sprawled on the chaise in her room. "What do you mean to do?"

"I told you. I will marry him," Prudence said.

Honor came to a halt and stared at Prudence. "Prudence—"

"Honor, please," Prudence said, throwing up her hand. "I don't want to discuss it."

Honor pressed her lips together and went out, leaving Prudence to stare at the tree branch that danced on a breeze outside her window. She wondered idly how many hours she'd stared at the branch this week, imagining Roan and Aurora on a ship bound for America. She could see him on the quay, overseeing the handling of luggage, glancing back over his shoulder at England. She could see him on the ship, standing at the helm, staring out over rough waters and thinking of Prudence.

Grace came one afternoon, probably at Honor's behest. Grace began in earnest to try and cheer Prudence, but Prudence was aware she needed more than cheering. She tried to rally, to rouse herself from the doldrums, but it felt as if her disconsolation had invaded her blood. She knew her sisters were losing their patience with her. So was she! This was not how she wanted to live, God no. And yet, she felt powerless to alter her thoughts.

She loved Roan Matheson. The world had not miraculously slid back to the familiar as she'd assumed. The glow of him had not dimmed. She just felt his loss more sharply as time marched on.

A day before Merryton and Grace were to return to Blackwood Hall, Stanhope came round a third time to call on Prudence. When Finnegan told her he'd come, and that there was no one to intercept him, Prudence sighed, pushed her undressed hair over her shoulder, and walked to the drawing room in her bare feet to receive him.

He looked surprised by her appearance when he entered the room. "Good afternoon," he said, taking in her dress and the hair that hung loosely down her back. "I heard the American had left. Now I see it is true."

Prudence's gaze was unwavering. She was numb to Stanhope now, and waited for him to say whatever he'd come to say.

"Have you thought about my offer?" he asked.

"Of course."

"And?"

"And, I haven't a choice, have I? I accept."

His smile seemed almost sympathetic. "I realize it is difficult for you now, but I think you'll come round to it."

"No," Prudence said calmly. "I will never come

round to it, my lord. And that I never shall will be your cross to bear."

He smiled indulgently, as if she were showing him a fit of temper. "I'm not unfeeling," he said, moving closer to her. "I will give you time to grieve your lover."

"How very kind of you."

He reached for her hand. With his gaze on hers, he lifted it to his lips and kissed it softly. Then he leaned down and kissed her cheek, his lips lingering, warm and soft against her skin. Prudence shuddered with despair.

"I will be good to you, Prudence," he said softly, his nose in her hair. "You will have all that you want. I will make you as happy as a wife can be made."

Prudence laughed ruefully. "You won't. You *can't*."

"You may be surprised."

"I don't love you. I will *never* love you."

Stanhope's smile faded and he eased back. "Fortunately for us both, love is not necessary for a match such as ours, is it?" He moved away from her. "I've called on Beckington. This afternoon I will call on Merryton to discuss the terms." He started for the door, but paused there and glanced back. "I saw Mercy outside. She seems quite happy about her opportunity to attend Lisson Grove. I am happy for her."

"Yes," Prudence said serenely. "She is a very lucky girl." With that, she turned her back to Stanhope.

She heard Stanhope leave. The windows were open to a fresh breeze and the sounds of people and animals moving about on the street drifted up to her, but seemed to move away from her at the same time. It seemed only minutes later that she heard a knock on a door, heard voices but thought it had perhaps been on the house next door.

Moments later, Honor appeared in the drawing room with Grace. "Prudence!" Honor said, hurrying to her. "Finnegan said Stanhope was here?"

"Yes."

Honor looked at Grace. "And?"

"And, I accepted," Prudence said dispassionately.

"Oh *no*," Grace whispered, sinking down onto a chair. "My God, Pru...what are you doing? What of love?"

Prudence laughed bitterly at that and brushed Honor's hand from her arm. "What of it? Many matches are made for less than love."

"You're not serious," Honor said.

"I am quite serious. Why shouldn't I accept it?" Prudence asked coldly. "It's likely the only offer I will ever receive, and at least Stanhope knows the truth about me. What would you have me do? Mope about and mourn for a love that is an ocean away? Wander about Blackwood Hall, or your house, or Beckington House and wait for another offer to come? I must do *something* with my life. I can't stand still! Do you know how hard it is to stand still?" she demanded shrilly.

"But you don't love him!" Grace cried.

"Stop being so melodramatic," Prudence said dismissively. "You didn't love Merryton when you wed, and you love him now. Mamma married the earl and she grew to love him very much."

"But Mamma first married Pappa because she loved him so," Honor said. "She married for love. She married the earl out of necessity."

Prudence shrugged and picked up a garment to fold. "I will marry an earl out of necessity. It seems rather the same thing to me. This is a solution, and a far better one than I ever hoped for only a fortnight ago."

"But it's not what you *want*," Honor insisted.

Prudence shook her head. She could hear the children upstairs, laughing and singing, and the sound of it, so innocent, so pure, made her ache. She would never have that. Never. Not because of the scandals that marked her family, not because of her mother's madness. Because now she couldn't imagine sharing that sort of happiness with anyone but Roan Matheson.

"I can't bear it," Grace said suddenly, standing. "Come, Honor."

"Come where?"

"Just come," Grace commanded. "She won't listen to us." She grabbed Honor's hand and pulled her from the room.

Prudence sank down onto the settee. She tried to picture her wedding to Stanhope. Only their families, she supposed. She didn't care where, or even when. She then tried to imagine the consummation of it. She pictured Stanhope in his night shirt, trying to fit himself into a body that didn't want him. It made her ill.

"Prudence."

Startled, Prudence leaped up from her seat. Lord Merryton was standing just inside—she hadn't heard him come in. He was impeccably dressed as he always was, his black neckcloth against a white lawn shirt making his hair seem even darker. "My lord," she said, and brushed the back of her hand against her cheek in a futile attempt to brush the flush of her thoughts from her skin.

Merryton clasped his hands tightly at his back, his jaw set as he moved deeper into the room. He kept his distance from her—he never stood close, as if he needed space between them—and considered Prudence for a long moment. "I shall come to the point. I was very angry with you for running off as you did."

"I know. I'm sorry, my—"

He held up a hand to indicate she should not speak. "I was angry. But I understood. I've always understood it. But now, my wife has come to me and she is very upset. She says you have agreed to marry Stanhope. Is this true?"

Prudence nodded. "He means to call on you to discuss the terms."

Merryton waved his hand as if that was a trifling matter. "Do you love him?"

"Pardon? *No*," she said to that preposterous notion. With Merryton, it was best to answer simply and honestly. He didn't care for a lot of nattering.

"Do you love the American?" he asked, moving deeper into the room.

Prudence swallowed. Her true feelings were so apparent now that she couldn't deny them to her herself or anyone else. "With everything."

His gaze narrowed slightly. "Forgive me, but I must ask—how can you be so certain? Are you sure it's not girl's infatuation?"

"I just know it. I *feel* it," she said, tapping her chest above her heart. "It's unlike anything I've ever felt before, as if there is something here, just under the bone. It's as if I know him in a way I couldn't possibly know him."

Merryton said nothing.

"It's a wretched feeling, to be honest. Utterly wretched. To know love like this exists but that I can't have it be-

cause he lives on the other side of the ocean is excruciating. It feels as if I can't breathe at all, and yet I'm
breathing." She suddenly realized what she was saying,
and blushed. "How foolish you must think me!"

"Quite the contrary," he said. "I think you have
nicely described the feeling of love. I don't know your
particular circumstance with the American, but I do
know this—I was prepared to marry a woman I didn't
love before your sister concocted her scheme. And I
can say to you now that my life would have been a sad
shadow of what it has become if I had done that. Love
has brightened my life beyond my wildest imagina-
tions."

Prudence blinked with surprise. It was highly unusual of Merryton to speak so candidly.

"If you love Matheson, you should marry *him*, Pru.
Not Stanhope."

"He's already gone. They've sailed! I can't very well
sail alone in search of him and land on a foreign shore
without introduction."

Merryton looked almost amused. "You are worried
about impropriety now?"

Prudence blanched. "No. But I…I've never been at
sea," she said uncertainly. "How could I go alone?"

"Easton's new ship is taking its maiden voyage to
New York in a fortnight. You could be on that ship, I
suspect, closely guarded by the captain."

Prudence stared at him, her mind rushing around
what he suggested. "But it's too late, my lord! What if
he has offered marriage, or gone to Canada, or…any-
thing might have happened."

"If that's true, if by some miracle he has managed to
marry himself in such a short time, or has gone away,

or has been kicked in the head by a goat, George's ship is returning to England. You will come back on that ship if necessary."

This conversation was confusing her. Merryton, of all people, demanded strict propriety in all things. How could he possibly suggest this to her? "What about all of you?" Prudence cried, sweeping her hand toward him. "What about my sisters and my nieces and nephews, and for God's sake, my mother? I can't leave you all!"

"We would all miss you terribly," he agreed. "But you must face the truth, Pru. Grace and I have our family and Honor and George have theirs. Mercy will be entering Lisson Grove in a fortnight. As for your poor lady mother, you know as well as I do that she doesn't know us anymore. She's been gone for a long time now, hasn't she? Hannah is devoted to her and she will take good care of her."

Prudence choked back a strangled sob.

"I never knew your mother, but I have children of my own. And I suspect, if she were with us today, she would want you to know love and true happiness just as she knew it. She wouldn't want you to agree to a match because you think it is your only hope. I certainly don't want that for you. I want only happiness for you."

Prudence didn't dare believe it was possible. Her blood began to rush with even the suggestion of it. "I can't."

Merryton remained silent, waiting for her to explain why.

"Stanhope said…he said that if I didn't agree to a match, he would see to it that Mercy's acceptance at Lisson Grove was revoked."

Merryton's expression darkened. "Pardon?"

"He said his family endowed the art school and with one word from him, he would bring her hopes to an end. And that if I agreed to marry him, he would leave her be."

Merryton stared at her for a long moment. He kept one hand behind his back, tapped his fingers with the other. At last he said, "Why didn't you tell us this before?"

Prudence blinked. "I didn't want to alarm anyone," she said. "I didn't want Mercy to hear of it—"

"I think that you should not fret over it, Pru," he said firmly. "I will take care of it."

"But how—"

"Leave that to me. But if *that* is the reason you have accepted Stanhope's offer and let the American go, I suggest you rethink your decision." He turned toward the door as if he meant to leave.

Prudence suddenly darted across the room and caught his arm. Startled, Merryton turned back to her. She threw her arms around his neck and kissed his cheek. "Thank you, my lord. Thank you so much."

He stiffened with the physical contact and carefully put her back. "You're welcome, love." He went out.

Prudence stared at the place he'd been standing, her mind whirling, her heart beating so quickly it pained her.

CHAPTER TWENTY

New York
Two months later

MR. GUNDERSON WAS not waiting patiently for Aurora's return, and even had he been so inclined, he lost all patience with her when she thought it prudent to explain to him that the reason she'd been delayed was because she'd very nearly married a Frenchman.

To say that Mr. Gunderson's hackles rose was an understatement. He was livid. Not that it mattered, really because in the time Roan had gone to fetch his sister and bring her home, Mr. Gunderson and Miss Pratt had begun an unlikely courtship, born of common ground, and now, they were to be married.

Which meant that Matheson Lumber had been ejected from the triumvirate Roan's father had carefully constructed. "I ought to send you to your aunt in Boston," he'd angrily shouted at Aurora.

Roan thought it was perhaps the first time he'd heard his father raise his voice to Aurora.

Naturally, Aurora apologized to her family for it. If there was one thing on which they could all depend, it was that Aurora *always* apologized for whatever she'd done.

"Why did you tell him you meant to elope?" Beck

had demanded of her. "He was already cross with you. Now he despises you and all of us!"

"Well, I didn't think I should lie," Aurora had argued. "I wanted to explain that it was only a moment of infatuation, but now that I am home I realize how foolish I was and I very much wish to repair it. He didn't give me the chance."

It was far too late for Aurora, but Roan had gone to Susannah to offer his apology to her and her father. It was Susannah, however, who had apologized to Roan. "I'm sorry," she'd said, peering up at him with her small eyes. "But I never thought you really held much esteem for me."

He'd looked at the dark-haired woman. She was short and squat, and her brow set in a permanent frown of worry. He thought of Prudence, of her sparkling eyes, her irrepressible smile.

"I, ah…I can't say that I knew you well at all, to be perfectly frank," he'd admitted.

Susannah had nothing to say to that. She had merely nodded. Roan wondered if that meant she agreed with him. Or did she merely understand him? Prudence never had any reluctance to speak her mind. God, how he missed her.

"Please forgive me, Susannah," Roan had said.

She'd nodded and had shown him out, her thoughts kept to herself.

Roan reported to his brother and sister what Susannah had said that afternoon when they went riding. Aurora took great exception. "Of all the things to say! Of *course* you held her in some esteem! Now it makes me cross that I ever defended her to Miss Cabot."

That brought Roan's head up. "What?"

"Hmm?" Aurora asked. Roan caught the bridle of her horse and reined them both to a stop. "Roan! What are you doing?"

"What did you say, Aurora? On what occasion did you defend Susannah Pratt to Prudence?"

Aurora blinked guiltily. "I thought I was doing the right thing!" she said quickly. "I'd made such a mess of things, and I didn't want us both to have gone back on our word—"

"What are you talking about?" he roared.

"Roan," Beck said sternly, but Roan would not let go of Aurora's bridle.

"Just…just that on the night we arrived, I might have explained to Miss Cabot that you were committed and held Miss Pratt in high regard—"

"A lie!" Roan said.

"Well, how was I to know?" Aurora stammered. "I thought surely you must hold her in *some* regard as you'd agreed to propose to her. I was thinking of our family, and I thought Miss Cabot needed a bit of a nudge to let you go."

Roan could only stare at his sister. Had she always been so impossible? Had she always done what she pleased without regard for anyone else? He let go of her bridle and spurred his horse on, needing to be away from her. He heard Aurora shout at him, but he paid her no heed.

He didn't know if he was angrier with Aurora or Prudence. Aurora for having said anything at all; Prudence for having failed to ask him if it were true. But then again, Roan had been angry with the world of late. He'd had almost two months to think of what had happened in England and the pain of having left Prudence had not abated in the least. There was not a day that passed she wasn't in his thoughts, not a moment he didn't regret not having fought harder for her. He had accepted her dismissal when he should have proposed marriage to her in earnest.

Aurora's regrets were public. His were not. To anyone around him, Roan appeared as he always had—confident and busy. But he was empty, depleted of spirit. He imagined Prudence married now. He imagined her in another man's bed, which was particularly torturous to him. He imagined that she had moved past her week of adventure, and could smile again.

Roan couldn't. He was hopelessly mired in his loss.

There was more talk of sending Aurora to Boston, but Aurora appealed to their father. "Susannah Pratt and Sam Gunderson are marrying next week. We've all been invited. I can't miss it, Papa. If I miss it, everyone will think it's because I have hard feelings. Don't you want his father to know there are no hard feelings?"

"Aurora is staying here," the senior Matheson announced at supper one night. "If she doesn't attend, everyone will think it's because she has hard feelings. I would not want his father to believe that is true, not if we are to repair our relationships there and have any hope of renewing our agreements."

Aurora smiled a bit smugly at her brothers. Roan and Beck rolled their eyes. It had been so all their lives and they knew better than to fight it.

The illustrious wedding would be celebrated at the City Hotel in New York, the only place large enough to accommodate all the guests. This was a society affair, and all of New York wanted to attend. Roan preferred what he considered a typical wedding: a small family affair in a parlor. Something that could be quickly done and from which he might quickly leave so that he didn't have to think of Prudence.

He tried desperately not to think of her. He tried to put the past behind him, but it felt impossible. He saw her everywhere, under every bonnet, walking down every street. Every woman in New York whose hair was the slightest shade of gold was, for the space of a breath, Prudence.

The day before the wedding Roan joined his parents at the family's town house on Broadway Street in the city. Roan wouldn't be in town long—he intended to leave for meetings about the canal as soon as the wedding was over. He would ride north, alone, with bedding and a shotgun and perhaps one of the family dogs to accompany him. That was where Roan intended to work out his bad humor. He'd never been a maudlin man and he didn't care to be one now. Fortunately, he'd be gone for weeks. He would not see bonnets or blond hair. He would forget. He would make himself forget.

When he arrived that afternoon at the family town house, Martin, the butler, held out a tray and informed Roan that a Mr. Lansing had come to call.

"Who is Lansing?" Roan asked, racking his brain as he picked up a letter from the tray.

"He is the captain of a sailing vessel, sir. He said a Mr. George Easton had sent him."

Just the name of Easton gave Roan a queer feeling. "Thank you, Martin." He went into the library and ripped open the seal of the letter, hoping and praying for any word of Prudence. Something. *Anything.*

The letter was nothing more than an introduction of Captain Lansing from Easton and an expressed hope that they might discuss the cotton trade. Enclosed were some figures Easton had mentioned about the sort of profits they could expect.

Roan tucked the letter away and thought of Prudence's eyes. Would it have been so very difficult to include a note from her? A message? At the very least, a postscript? *Miss Cabot sends her regards. Miss Cabot took her wedding vows on this date. Lady Stanhope is taking a bridal tour with her husband...*

There was not even a mention of her name.

The next morning, the wedding of Susannah Pratt and Sam Gunderson was held in a chapel, and the wedding luncheon served in the City Hotel. People gathered outside the windows of the hotel to catch a glimpse of the bride and to see the finery of New York's wealthiest. Roan stood to one side dressed in his best dark suit and silk waistcoat, wishing the damn luncheon would come to an end so he might go back to proper moping.

He noticed Aurora in the Gundersons' company, standing close. He even thought he detected a hint of a smile on the old man's face. He shook his head—his sister was remarkable in her ability to charm.

"A toast!" Mr. Pratt said jovially, having imbibed more than his fair share of champagne. "Roan Matheson, you should make it," said a jovial Mr. Pratt. "After all, you are responsible for our daughter's happiness."

The guests roared with laughter, all of them having heard the gossip, apparently.

Roan stifled a groan and stepped up to Susannah's side. He had to admit, in her wedding finery and with the glow of happiness on her face, she was much more becoming than she'd ever appeared to him before. She had artfully arranged her dark hair, and in her fine dress, she made a small, happy bride. Roan put his arm around her waist, dipped down to kiss her cheek and, with their backs to the window, he lifted a flute of champagne and toasted her union with Gunderson, wishing them many happy years. When the toast was done, the meal was served to fifty assembled guests.

Roan imagined the cost of feeding them all to be something that would make him uncomfortable. If this were *his* wedding, he imagined Prudence and him taking their luncheon alone, in a room in this hotel, with no one present but a girl to fill their tub with bathwater.

"You look glum."

Roan had been so lost in his rumination he hadn't even noticed Aurora. She cocked her head to one side and peered up at him. "What's wrong?"

"I'm bored."

"Really?" She sounded skeptical. "I thought it a lovely wedding. Miss Pratt was surprisingly lovely."

Roan smiled.

"How strange that you would be bored by it."

"How strange that you would be diverted by it."

"Oh, it's all water under the bridge now," she said with a flick of her wrist. "At least I had the opportunity to express to Mr. Gunderson how ardently I held him in my esteem, and how very sorry I was for having bruised his feelings. He said I was incorrigible, but he'd always known that about me."

"I suspect all of New York knows that about you."

Aurora laughed. "I'm really very happy for them, aren't you? They seem to genuinely admire each other. Oh! Speaking of admiration, I saw the most remarkable thing."

"What?" Roan drawled, uncaring.

"I saw a girl who looked so much like Miss Cabot that they might have been twins! Imagine, a woman who looks like her here in New York. She was unusually pretty, wasn't she? At least I thought she was."

It was as if everyone suddenly stopped moving, as if everything inside Roan had gone very still. "Where?" he managed.

"Outside, on the sidewalk," Aurora said, and pointed to the window.

Roan whirled about. There were dozens of people milling about, looking in the windows of the hotel.

"Goodness, it wasn't her, Roan," Aurora said, looking slightly alarmed. "It just looked like her. I didn't mean to alarm you."

Roan dropped his empty flute where he stood and strode for the door, pushing past several guests, upsetting one woman who cried out at him. He ran out of the hotel, jogged down the steps to the street and looked around him. Right, left, across the street. There were so many faces, so many people gathered to see the society wedding at the City Hotel.

No, she couldn't possibly be here. Aurora was right—it was just someone who looked like her. Surely there would have been some mention of her in the letter if she were here.

Now he felt foolish.

Dispirited, Roan turned to go back into the hotel. And when he did, he saw a glimpse of golden hair beneath a bonnet. The woman was walking down the street away from the hotel. It was another of the many Prudences Roan seemed to notice every day, but he shouted "Prudence!" nonetheless and began to push past people to reach her.

"Prudence!" he said again, catching up to her. He touched her arm.

The woman whirled around. "I beg your pardon!"

It wasn't Prudence, of course it wasn't! It would *never* be Prudence. When would he accept that simple truth? All the life went out of him and Roan decided in that moment that enough was enough. From that moment forward, he would not think of her. He would not mope. He would get on with his life once and for all. "I beg your pardon, I thought you were someone else," he said apologetically.

The woman walked on and Roan turned back. And when he did, his heart stopped beating.

Prudence was standing behind him on the walk, her hazel eyes wide with surprise. Roan couldn't speak—he couldn't even be sure she was real.

"I…I am so *sorry*," she said, and put her hand to her breast.

He didn't understand. "Pru?"

"I shouldn't have come," she said quickly. "I didn't realize what he meant when he said the City Hotel—"

"Is it really you?" Roan asked stupidly, still trying to make sense of it, to understand where she'd come from.

"It's my fault, Roan. Again!" she said with a nervous laugh. "But I won't keep you. I know that you are…occupied," she said, making a nervous whirling motion with her hand. "On my honor, I never would have come had I known. I just thought perhaps you were… I mean, I *hoped*, I hoped that you still felt…" She blinked. And then she bowed her head as she tried to gather herself.

She *was* real. His love, his heart's desire, was standing before him on a crowded sidewalk in New York. Roan took a cautious step forward. People were passing left and right, some slowing to have a good look at them. "I can't believe it's you," he said. "How...*when* did you come? Are you alone? Did someone come with you?" he asked, looking around them now.

"I am such a *fool*," she said sorrowfully.

"Fool," he repeated, not understanding.

"Don't try and spare my feelings. I don't deserve it. I saw you in the window, Roan. I know. I *saw* you."

"Saw me what?" he asked, confused, looking over her shoulder to the hotel.

"I saw you and your bride!" she blurted.

"*What?* No! No, no, Pru, that was... Oh my God, no, I didn't marry Susannah Pratt! Sam Gunderson did. I only made a toast." He mimicked the toast, one arm around an invisible Susannah, the other with his arm lifted in the air.

Prudence blinked.

"You thought I married? How could I, after England? How could I possibly?"

"You didn't? I thought— Aurora said—"

"Never listen to a thing Aurora says," he said, taking a step forward. "Good God, take *nothing* she says to heart. Even I have been reminded of it in the worst way these past few weeks. No, Pru, I am the same man I was when I left England. I feel the same way. No, that's not entirely true, I am far worse. I yearn for you every day."

A small smile began to form on her face. "Do you mind that I came?"

"You must be joking," he said, moving to stand before her. "I've thought of nothing but you, Prudence Cabot. Only you. I relive our moments together, I kick myself for having left without you, I wish for the days to pass quickly so I won't torture myself with memories, and I think of you, married. Where is he? Did Stanhope come with you?"

"No!" she cried, horrified. "Oh dear. There is so much to tell you." She reached for his hand. "Roan... I've thought of nothing else but you, either."

That lurch in his chest was his heart, the beat of it renewing with a vigor that left him a bit breathless. "Come," he said, linking her hand in the crook of his arm. "There is a tavern nearby—"

"But what of the wedding?"

Roan smiled. "I won't be missed."

In the tavern, he bought them two tankards of ale. Prudence hardly touched hers as she told him all that had happened in the past several weeks, including the details of Stanhope's offer and the threat he'd made to Mercy.

"Why didn't you tell me?" he demanded.

"I thought there was nothing you could do," she said. "I thought there was nothing anyone could do." She went on to tell him that she'd been so distraught when he'd left, she could hardly summon enough to care about anything else. She removed the letter he'd written her from her reticule and showed it to him. It was worn, obviously read many times. "This was all I had to keep me," she said. "In the end, it was Lord Merryton who convinced me to come for you."

"Merryton!" he said, disbelieving.

Prudence told him that Merryton had coaxed the truth from her and had made her see that she could reach for her desire.

"Thank God you did. What happened to Stanhope?" he asked.

Prudence shrugged. "I don't know, exactly. Grace

said he had a sizable gambling debt Merryton threatened to have called in. Of course Stanhope has no means to pay it. They reached some arrangement."

"And Mercy?"

Prudence's face brightened. "When I left for America, she was on her way to Italy with her class. She is very happy. She has dreams of seeing and painting the world."

Prudence told Roan how George Easton had put her on his ship in its maiden voyage to America, and how they had sailed through one violent storm that had put them off a few days. "I left three weeks after you did, but it took me a week longer to reach New York, I think. I was desperate to reach you before you married. George's agent found your house and gave me the direction. I was to send a note, but I couldn't bear it. I couldn't wait to see you, so I went myself. Your butler told me you were at the City Hotel—I think he was a bit shocked that I was calling like I was—and he failed to mention you were at a wedding."

"You can't imagine the sleepless nights," Roan said. He told her how he'd only recently learned that Aurora had tried to put her off. And how they'd returned to New York to find not only had the partnership their marriages would have sealed been disbanded, but their prospective mates had united in the long wait and had decided to marry. "It's just as well. No matter that I left you behind, I couldn't marry Susannah, not after what we'd shared. If nothing else, I realized that I can't marry merely for the sake of it. I can't devote my life to a woman I don't love."

"Oh, Roan," she said, and reached for his hand. "I must be living inside of a dream, because I can't believe I am sitting across from you now. I'm sorry. Please know how sorry I am for disappointing you—"

"Never mind that," Roan said. "Just tell me this—Do you love me?"

Her smile broadened. "I love you. I love you more than I've ever loved another being. I should have said it, I should never have let you leave without saying so. Do you still love me?"

"Utterly and completely," he said emphatically. "Where are you staying?"

Her smile deepened. "The captain secured rooms for me at the Harsinger Hotel. It's close to here—"

"I know exactly where it is," he said, coming to his feet. He took her hand and pulled her up.

Prudence laughed and allowed him to lead her out of the tavern.

The clerk at the hotel eyed them disdainfully, but he could tell from the cut of Roan's clothing that he had means, and with a banknote in his hand turned a blind eye as they scurried up the stairs to her room.

Prudence tossed aside her bonnet as Roan pushed the spencer from her shoulders. Their mouths and hands were on each other as they fell together onto the bed. "My heart was broken," Roan said as he ravaged her bosom. "I thought it would never mend and by God, I didn't care if it did. Now you are here, Pru. I can't believe it, you're here, and I feel whole again."

"I've been so wretchedly unhappy since you left," she said through ragged breaths as she dragged her fingers through his hair. "It was the most painful thing I've ever endured."

"I can't imagine anything less than spending my life with you. Marry me, Pru. You're here. Marry me."

"Yes," she said. *"Yes."*

Roan slid into her body and closed his eyes. The heaviness that had existed in him lifted, and he felt a sense of euphoria filling him up. He couldn't believe she was there, in his arms, warm and fragrant and... and he was going to marry her. He would spend every day for the rest of his life making their marriage an adventure for her.

She caught his face between her hands as he moved in her and said, "I love you. I will always love you." And then she smiled at him with the devilish gleam in her eye he'd seen the first day of their acquaintance, and Roan felt as if he were walking on clouds. Big puffy white clouds of love.

Good Lord, he was besotted.

EPILOGUE

THINGS HAPPENED VERY quickly after that long afternoon spent in bed at the Harsinger Hotel. A proper wedding was first and foremost on Roan's mind, and with the help of his father, he arranged it quickly. Prudence thought it was rather amusing that there wasn't any time for the Mathesons to get acquainted with the idea that their son had married an English girl out of the blue, because Roan set off with her north on horseback almost as soon as their vows were said.

Prudence loved every moment of it. She took Aurora's advice and wore trousers and rode astride. She felt strong and confident in them, and it helped that Roan seemed taken by her in the trousers, too. He said she looked like a tiny lumberjack.

Prudence also loved that every night, they would sleep in the same bedding, their horses tethered close by, and the pair of dogs that had come along curled at their feet. It reminded her of the first night they'd lain together under the stars, but wildly better. "This is the best adventure I've ever had!" Prudence declared with great exuberance one day.

Roan arched a brow at her.

"I beg your pardon. The *second* best adventure," she'd said, then smothered him with kisses.

When they returned to New York a month later,

they were met with some astounding news. Apparently, Mr. Gunderson's younger brother, Ben, had discovered a liking for Aurora's auburn-haired beauty at his brother's wedding and had fallen head over heels in love. Aurora and Ben Gunderson married on New Year's Eve, exactly six weeks after Roan and Prudence married. Roan and Prudence agreed that it was a very good thing Aurora married when she did, as her first child appeared "quite early" seven and a half months later.

Roan and Prudence were delighted to welcome their son a few months after that.

Drake Matheson, a big, healthy boy, was the apple of his father's eye. Prudence adored that child beyond measure. But she desperately wanted her sisters to meet him. The baby was too young to make the voyage, however, so Roan and George brought the Cabots en masse to America to greet the newest addition to their family.

Roan and George had indeed forged a new arrangement, wherein Roan and Beck acted as cotton brokers, sending off ship hulls full of American cotton to England on George's ships. George had two ships now, and the arrangement had proved a lucrative one for both families. But for the Mathesons in particular, the cotton trade, in addition to the lumber trade, had made them quite well-to-do. Roan and Prudence were building a house very near his parents for the large family they hoped to have.

Honor and George, and Grace, and Augustine and Monica arrived in New York to meet the newest addition to their family. Their party was missing Merryton, who had stayed behind with the youngest of their collective broods. "He's quite unable to make a voyage such as this," Grace said, one of the few mentions she ever made of her husband's peculiarities.

Neither was Mercy with them, obviously. She was still in Italy. "I think she will live there always," Honor said.

"Do you?" Prudence said, surprised.

"I think she has a *lover*," Grace said slyly, and giggled.

That night at dinner, Grace related that Mercy had written several letters home and was fully engaged in her life there. She had one more year in her schooling, and had recently sold a painting for a small sum. Mercy was thrilled that something she'd painted would be displayed in an Italian home.

"I can't believe it!" Prudence said proudly.

George looked around at the three oldest Cabot women. "No one can ever say the Cabot girls don't strive for what they want," he said with a laugh.

Unfortunately, the arrival of the Cabot sisters brought sad news to Prudence, too. Her mother had died over the winter. "A frightful ague," Honor said. "It was as if she had no desire to fight it."

The news filled Prudence with grief. But there was also some relief in her mother's death. Prudence had gone to see her mother before she'd sailed to America, and her mother had gazed at her with vacant eyes. Lady Beckington's spirit had long been gone out of her, and as the weeks and months had passed, she'd grown feeble and weak, her head and her heart nothing but the fragile shell of the woman she had once been. In the end, Honor said, she didn't even recognize Hannah.

Merryton had graciously kept the loyal Hannah on to help with the children.

Honor brought Prudence news of Stanhope, too, which she had confided one day when she and Prudence were walking. Prudence never knew exactly what Merryton said to him to make him cry off, but Stanhope had done so without equivocation. "I've heard his situation is quite dire," Honor had confided in Prudence. "They say the entail of his title is so great that *he* owes the *estate* each year."

"How dreadful," Prudence had said. "And how thankful I am that I didn't accept his offer."

"Perhaps he ought to find an occupation, other than offering for rich debutantes," Roan said crossly when Prudence told him later as they lay in bed.

That made Prudence giggle.

"What?" Roan asked.

"English lords don't *have* occupations. That's rather the point."

"You see, *that's* what's wrong with all the royalty over there," Roan said, casting his arm in the general direction of England.

The Cabots saw all of New York during their stay and proclaimed it smaller than they'd imagined it, but quite charming in that way colonies had of being rustically charming.

When it came time for them to return to England, Prudence cried buckets of tears, as did her sisters, while Roan and George stood by awkwardly, trying to soothe them all, but failing miserably. Augustine and Monica saw the prolonged goodbyes as an opportunity to tour the Matheson gardens once more.

That night, Roan and Prudence dined alone at the Matheson home on Broadway Street. With Drake in his crib, his governess asleep beside him, Roan and

Prudence had a quiet dinner. When the meal had been cleared, and the servants retired for the night, Roan reached across the table and stroked Prudence's face. "Are you all right?"

Prudence missed her family, but she had never been more certain of herself. She was precisely where God wanted her. To think that once she'd feared the marriage would ruin her adventure! It had only enriched it. She smiled at her husband with all the love she held for him in her heart.

"I know how much you miss them."

"Terribly," she agreed, appalled that she should tear up again.

"Any regrets?" he asked.

"Regrets?" Prudence stood up from the table and walked around to where Roan was sitting. She hiked her skirts and straddled his lap. "No regrets. Not once, Roan Matheson, and never will I have them. I am where I am meant to be."

He chuckled with delight as she moved on his lap. "Mrs. Matheson, I think you're a tart."

She wrapped her arms around his neck. "I learned it from you, you scoundrel."

"I tried to warn you about scoundrels but, naturally, you wouldn't listen," he said, his hand finding her waist, his body hardening.

Prudence thought of that moment in Ashton Down when she'd decided to follow this scoundrel. She would always wonder how a girl like her, who had always done what she was supposed to do, could so utterly abandon everything she was in a single moment. It was as if she'd been standing still for so long that the moment she moved, it all moved very fast.

She kissed the corner of his mouth, her tongue flicking across his lips. "I think I would feel much better with a bath. Will you wash my hair?"

Roan grinned and nipped at her bottom lip. "Will you let me in the tub with you?"

She kissed his mouth and slid her hand down his chest, to his cock. "Will you allow me to put my feet wherever I like?"

He cupped her breast with one hand, grabbed the tail of hair she'd let down with his other and pulled her closer. "Will you allow me to put my mouth wherever *I* like?"

"I will insist on it, Mr. Matheson."

"You *are* a tart. God, how I love you."

How she loved him. "Show me, you old scoundrel."

Roan did as she asked—he showed her just how deeply he loved her that night.

A month later, Prudence confirmed she was expecting her second child.

* * * * *

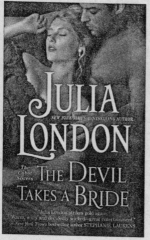

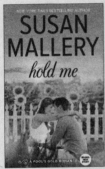

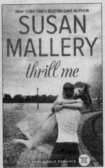

From #1 *New York Times* bestselling author

NORA ROBERTS

come two remarkable tales of the
O'Hurley dynasty—of dazzling talent
and sizzling passion

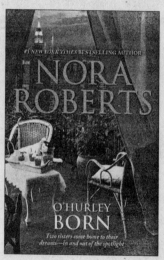

Two sisters come home to their
dreams—in and out of the spotlight

Pick up your copy today!